HIS WORDS WERE LACED WITH UNSPOKEN WARMTH, an affection that—in his human form, at least—he showed only to me. Still holding my chin, he rubbed his cheek once against mine and then tousled my hair, actions I both hated and loved since they simultaneously marked me as a child and as his.

"Be home by dusk, Bryn," he told me, before taking his leave. "Trouble's afoot."

I harrumphed. I was a human who had been quite literally raised by wolves. In my world, trouble was *always* afoot.

ALSO BY JENNIFER LYNN BARNES

Trial by Fire: A Raised by Wolves Novel

OTHER EGMONT USA BOOKS YOU MAY ENJOY

The Dark Divine
by Bree Despain

The Lost Saint: A Dark Divine Novel
by Bree Despain

Shadow Hills
by Anastasia Hopcus

Siren
by Tricia Rayburn

Undercurrent: A Siren Novel
by Tricia Rayburn

Raised by Wolves

Jennifer Lynn Barnes

EGMONT
USA
NEW YORK

EGMONT

We bring stories to life

First published by Egmont USA, 2010
This paperback edition published by Egmont USA, 2011
443 Park Avenue South, Suite 806
New York, NY 10016

1 3 5 7 9 8 6 4 2

www.egmontusa.com
www.jenniferlynnbarnes.com

THE LIBRARY OF CONGRESS HAS CATALOGED
THE HARDCOVER EDITION AS FOLLOWS:
Barnes, Jennifer (Jennifer Lynn)
Raised by wolves / Jennifer Lynn Barnes.
p. cm.
Summary: A girl raised by werewolves must face the horrors of her past to uncover
the dark secrets that the pack has worked so hard to hide.
ISBN 978-1-60684-059-7 (hardcover) — ISBN 978-1-60684-181-5 (eBook)
[1. Werewolves—Fiction.] I. Title.
PZ7.B26225Rai 2010
[Fic]—dc22
2009041157

Paperback ISBN 978-1-60684-211-9

Printed in the United States of America

CPSIA tracking label information:
Random House Production • 1745 Broadway • New York, NY 10019

For my family, close and extended—
the best pack a girl could ask for.

In Loving Memory of
Annie Mae Barnes,
An incredible woman
I never got the chance to know.

Raised by Wolves

CHAPTER ONE

"Bronwyn Alessia St. Vincent Clare!"

Four names, five words, one pissed-off werewolf. The math in this particular equation never came out in my favor.

"Callum," I said, feigning surprise at his sudden appearance in my workshop. "To what do I owe the pleasure?"

His eyes narrowed slightly. On a human, the same motion would have conveyed sharp irritation, but on Callum's face, the expression was mild, until and unless you looked for the power behind the gaze and caught a glint of the wolf staring back.

Growing up the way I did, you learn a few things, so I knew the dangers involved in standing my ground and the ones that came with letting it go. My right hip twinged just above the band of my low-rise jeans, and my fingers played along the edges of the scar that lived there. The Mark tied me to Callum and the rest of the pack, and it served as an ever-present reminder that they were bound to protect me as one of their own. It also drove me into a hierarchy I'd never subscribed to.

That and the whisper of the rest of the pack at the gates of my mind—closed for business, thank you very much—spurred me into choosing the lesser of two evils in my interaction with the aforementioned pissed-off werewolf.

Calmly, I brought my eyes to Callum's. The power coming off him made it an effort, even for me. After a few precious seconds of meeting his gaze, I flicked my eyes to the side. Protocol would have had me looking down, but I was about as far from submissive as you could get. I also wasn't a Were, and Callum wasn't *my* alpha, so despite the constant pull of the pack at my psyche, there was nothing in *Emily Post's Guide to Werewolf Etiquette* to say that I absolutely had to submit.

Callum responded to my subtle, pointed defiance with a roll of his amber-colored eyes, but he had the good grace to abstain from pressing me into the wall or down to my knees the way he might have if not for that pesky humanity of mine. Instead, he brought one suntanned hand up to his jaw and ran it roughly over the five o'clock shadow on his chin in a way that made me think he was mentally counting to ten. The action—and the frustration that drove it—reminded me that even if he wasn't my alpha, Callum *was* my legal guardian, the executor of my estate, and the closest thing I had to a brother, uncle, or mentor, all rolled into one. Despite my best efforts as a small child to convince Callum that he was not (and I quote) *the boss of me*, he technically was. As alpha, he took pack business seriously, and had I not had four names of my own to choose from, I could have easily gone by "P.B."—Pack Business of the first and highest order.

The Mark on my hip wasn't just for show.

"Bryn." Callum's voice, even-toned with not even a hint of a growl, brought me back to the present. I was somewhat relieved that the situation had been downgraded in his mind from meriting all four names to just one. Better still that he stuck with Bryn, which I vastly preferred to *Bronwyn.*

"Bryn." Slightly sharper this time, but mostly exasperated, Callum's voice forced me to focus.

"Sorry," I said. "Mind bunnies."

Callum nodded curtly and waited for me to address the reason for his presence in my workshop. This was supposed to be my sanctuary, a tiny slice of pack territory that belonged to only me, myself, and I. It wasn't much more than a stand-alone garage turned second-rate art studio, but I didn't much appreciate the invasion, or the way Callum kept his eyes on mine, confident that I'd eventually tell him exactly what he wanted to know. Experience told me that he was probably right. Callum could outwait anyone, and though he was only a few inches taller than me, and the muscles in his granite jaw were relaxed, the power behind his eyes was always palpable in his stare.

"I really don't know why you're here," I told him, selecting my words carefully. Most Weres could smell a lie, and Callum, the alpha of alphas in our corner of the world, would have known immediately if I'd offered up an excuse that wasn't technically true. Luckily for me, I *didn't* know precisely what it was that I'd done to merit a visit from our pack's leader. There were any number of possibilities, none of which I wanted to openly admit to on the off chance that there was something I'd done that he hadn't found out about yet.

"You have no idea why I might want to talk to you?" Callum asked, his voice never losing its calm, cool tone.

That was a trickier question to answer without crossing the border from half-truths into lies, but I'd had years of practice. This I could handle. "I really don't have an idea why you'd want to talk to me."

Technically, I didn't have *an* idea; I had several.

Callum measured my response. I wasn't stupid enough to believe that he bought what he was hearing (and smelling), but I knew him well enough to hope that he might not want to play this game all afternoon. He was the one who'd taught me to play it in the first place, but at the moment, he really didn't seem to be in the mood for a "surviving pack life" tutorial on obfuscation.

With a much-aggrieved sigh, Callum opted out of forcing me to speak, and instead, he itemized my transgressions for me. "Motorcycle. Algebra. Curfew." Callum never used four words where one would do—unless, of course, he was calling me by my full name, a trick that he must have picked up from watching television, since he'd been born in a time and place where middle names weren't standard fare. The rest of our pack took their cue from him. Of all of us, I was the only one with a middle name, let alone two...

"Bryn."

"Right," I said, valiantly fighting the mind bunnies, which had a vicious tendency to multiply at inconvenient times. "I let a boy from town give me a ride on his motorcycle, my algebra teacher's a sadistic imbecile, and I'm a bad, bad girl who doesn't believe in curfews. Can I go now?"

For a split second, I thought I'd pushed him too far. I imagined his wolf instincts overtaking his human ones, changing Callum into something harder and primal. Unless he actually Shifted, he'd keep his human appearance, but I knew better than anyone that smooth skin, sandy hair, and slightly upturned lips meant nothing. Wolves in sheepskin had nothing on werewolves masquerading as men; shape-shifters were dangerous when their beasts were loose on the inside but contained on the surface. As wolves, they were hunters. In human form, they could be deadly.

Come out, come out, wherever you are, little one. No sense hiding from the Big Bad Wolf. I'll always find you in the end. . . .

I clamped down on the flicker of anxiety, snuffing it out. I was well acquainted with the dangers associated with strolling down that path on memory lane. I also knew from years and years of experience that Callum never lost control; his wolf would never harm a human. In any form, Callum would have died before hurting me. Instead, he took my sass and responded to it just as he always had—with a warning look and the air of someone who was trying very, very hard not to laugh.

Slightly abashed because I'd maligned him with misplaced anxiety (*not* fear), I took Callum's silent chastisement and didn't push back at him.

"Motorcycle." Callum issued the word as a statement rather than a question, but I felt compelled to answer anyway. That's the way it was with Callum—once you stopped pushing back, once you submitted, you'd find yourself acting in line with his will. He would have had the same effect on any other human, whether they knew what he was or not. The Mark on my flesh, and the bond between us, let me recognize the compulsion for what it was, but I didn't fight it.

"A kid from school offered me a ride on his motorcycle," I said, by way of explanation. "I took it." I chose not to mention the fact that I'd nearly died of shock at the invitation. The kids in town didn't mix with those of us who lived in the woods, and I wasn't generally the kind of girl who drew attention from the male of the species. Any species. "There is a slight chance that the guy in question didn't want me driving aforementioned 'cycle, but I might have ended up with the keys anyway. I guess I'm faster than he is."

"I didn't train you to move so that you could steal motorcycles," Callum said sternly.

No, I wanted to say, *you trained me so that I could run away from fights I couldn't win—the kind where my opponents had fur and claws and very few weaknesses.*

Out loud, I opted for, "I gave the bike back. And Jeff barely even minded." I did, however, doubt that Jeff would be inviting me to homecoming anytime soon.

"Are you interested in this boy?" Callum asked, his brow furrowing. Despite the fact that he did a good impression of an overprotective big brother, I'd lived under his rule long enough to realize that his concern wasn't just for me or my heart.

"I have no interest in provoking interspecies aggression," I said, using the politically correct phrase for incidents involving young, stupid werewolves and young, stupid human males. "And, believe me, if I did, it wouldn't be for a guy who wouldn't let me drive."

I spent enough time resisting testosterone-driven dominance maneuvers in my day-to-day life. The last thing I needed was a human boyfriend who wanted me to play the simpering miss.

Callum stiffened slightly at the idea of my dating anyone, even in the abstract. Werewolves tend to be very protective of their females, and even though I wasn't anyone's actual daughter or sister or—God forbid—mate, Callum had ceremonially dug his claws into me when I was four years old. While that had no effect whatsoever on my humanity, by Pack

Law, it made me his. As a result, Callum's wolves owed me their protection, and as far as they were concerned, that made me theirs, too. If werewolves had been into using "property of" stickers, I would have been mummified in them.

I just loved the idea of being owned.

"I don't like the idea of you on a motorcycle, Bryn. You could get hurt."

I didn't dignify that particular concern with a response.

"I'm asking you not to do such a thing again, Bryn," Callum said, choosing his words carefully, making it clear that this was not an order but a request. Lot of good that did me—Callum's "requests" didn't leave much room for noncompliance. If I refused to give him my word, there was a good chance that he would turn the request into an order, and as the leader of our pack and one of the highest-ranked dominant wolves on the continent, Callum's orders were very close to law. Disobeying an official edict from the alpha meant incurring the wrath of the entire pack—some of whom refrained from sending me to my just rewards only because Callum had likewise forbidden them from killing me.

Framing my orders as requests let Callum keep the pack out of it, and that left him free to deal with me on his own terms, which was sometimes a good thing and sometimes not.

"Bryn?"

"Your request has been noted," I said, my lips twisting

inadvertently into an easy grin. "I don't anticipate there being any motorcycles in my future."

I was pushing him again, but I couldn't help it. You didn't get to be alpha of the largest pack in North America by winning popularity contests, and Callum was so dominant that the day I stopped pushing back would be the day that I was a member of his pack first and myself second.

To Callum's credit and my relief, he didn't push for a firmer promise—probably because there were still two major items left on his Bryn Agenda.

"Your algebra grade is lower than it could be. Education is important, and I'd not have you slacking off, sadistic teacher or no." His voice took on that odd, old-fashioned lilt he sometimes adopted, a mere remnant of the accent he'd had before coming to this country.

"Right. Algebra." With the spring semester a month under way, I was getting a solid B-plus, but it could have easily been an A, and Callum had all kinds of lofty ideas about the importance of my living up to my potential. It was impressively modern of him, considering that he predated Women's Lib by a couple of centuries—at least.

"Did you tell Ali on me?" I asked. When the pack had adopted me, Callum had Marked a second human as well. Alison Clare had come to Ark Valley in search of her sister, who'd left their human family behind when she'd married into the pack. No one had counted on twenty-one-year-old Ali tracking her sister to Ark Valley and unraveling secrets best kept in the woods. Any other alpha would have killed Ali the moment she saw her brother-in-law Shift. Callum had given her a choice.

And then once she'd chosen, he'd given her me.

At present, Ali was thirty-two, 100 percent human, recently married to one of the pack's males, and my foster mother. Adopted mother. Whatever. Putting a label on Ali's role in my life was somewhat difficult. I used her last name and had lived in her house for almost as long as I could remember. Despite the fact that she'd been practically a kid herself when Callum had initiated her into our world, Ali was the one who'd hugged and scolded and raised me from a pup (figuratively speaking, of course). Callum was my guardian on paper, but it was Ali who fed and clothed me, Ali who'd set up this studio so that I could have a place that was purely mine, away from the constant pull of the pack, and Ali who would ground me quicker than Callum could say my full name if she thought for a single second that I deserved it.

"Ali has her own concerns at the moment," Callum said, and I saw the faint ghost of worry on his otherwise unreadable face. Ali was eight months pregnant with her first child. Werewolf births were notoriously difficult, and many human women didn't survive.

Ali's sister hadn't.

I was not willing to consider the possibility that the same thing might happen to Ali. Ali was strong. She'd make it, and the baby would, too, and then he'd outlive her by, oh, say a thousand years.

Darn werewolves and their ridiculously long life spans.

"Was that it?" I asked Callum, hoping he'd get the message loud and clear that I wasn't going to spend a second worrying about Ali, who would be just fine-fine-fine.

"You on a schedule here, Bryn?"

I gave an exasperated huff. "No." I hoped he'd smell the half-lie for what it was. Just before he'd interrupted me, I'd been working on a new piece, and I was anxious to get back to it. Found art was all about the process, and His Royal Highness, the Werewolf King (and Grand Poobah of Pains in the Butt) was seriously disrupting mine.

"You broke curfew last night," Callum said sharply. The first two complaints had been mere warm-ups for this one. His features tightened, his brows drawing together in a *V*.

"If my curfew wasn't at dusk, I wouldn't have to break it." I felt as strongly about this issue as Callum did. Nighttime came depressingly early in winter, and I had no intention of being home each day by five.

"There is unease in the pack, Bronwyn. I would have you safe from it."

I was *Bronwyn* again, a surefire sign that he was dangerously close to issuing either an edict or a threat. Possibly both.

"If I cannot trust you to be home before nightfall, I will be forced to take further measures to ensure your safety." Callum's words were unquestionably set in stone, and the hardness of his tone told me that he meant business. In my experience, Callum's definition of "further measures" was disturbingly broad and ranged from taking me over his knee (when I was eight) to posting a guard outside my bedroom window. Right now, I wasn't at all worried about the former, which I'd long outgrown. The latter, however…

"Until I can be assured of your cooperation in this matter, I've assigned a team to keep an eye on you."

I scowled at Callum. "You have *got* to be kidding me." There was nothing in the world worse than werewolf body-guards.

"Bryn, m'dear, you know I never kid." Callum's brown eyes sparkled with just a hint of lupine mischief, which told me that (a) he was, in fact, serious about the guards, and (b) my moral outrage amused him, because in his mind, I'd knowingly brought this on myself.

"You suck," I grumbled.

He put two fingers under my chin and held my face so that my eyes met his. "And you are the most disobedient child I've ever had the displeasure of meeting." His words were laced with unspoken warmth, an affection that—in his human form, at least—he showed only to me. Still holding my chin, he rubbed his cheek once against mine and then tousled my hair, actions I both hated and loved since they simultaneously marked me as a child and as his.

"Be home by dusk, Bryn," he told me, before taking his leave. "Trouble's afoot."

I harrumphed. I was a human who had been quite literally raised by wolves. In my world, trouble was *always* afoot.

CHAPTER TWO

A<small>FTER</small> C<small>ALLUM</small> <small>LEFT ME ALONE IN THE STUDIO,</small> I <small>SET</small> about pretending he'd never been there at all. This was my space, and if growing up in the pack had taught me anything, it was the importance of marking your territory. Since I had no compulsion whatsoever toward scent-marking, the best I could manage was refusing to acknowledge the fact that my sanctuary had been violated at all. Turning my discerning gaze to my work in progress, I evaluated the day's efforts thus far. At present, the sculpture resembled nothing so much as a papier-mâché fire hydrant. I'd meant for it to be an oak tree, but *c'est la vie*. I was more concerned with my materials than the outcome per se. Chess-club flyers, notes passed in class, failed tests, and midterm papers—this was my medium. I was always happiest elbow-deep in things that other people had thrown away.

"Dusk in ten minutes, Bryn."

The words were issued from directly behind my left shoulder, and the only thing that kept me from making a sound somewhere in the "eep!" family was years of experience with frustratingly stealthy werewolves. Despite my own training and the bond I shared with the rest of the pack, if Weres wanted to sneak up on me, they could. Even in human form, werewolves were stronger, faster, and more capable of masking their presence than us non-supernatural types. The most I could do was attempt to hide my surprise when they caught me off guard. Today, I was certainly getting plenty of practice at that. First Callum, and now this.

I whirled on the intruder. "I don't care when dusk is," I said. As my best friend, Devon was morally obligated to listen to me whine, and if he was going to keep me from working on "The Tree (or possibly Fire Hydrant) of Knowledge," I was going to take full advantage of that obligation. "Nobody else has a five p.m. curfew."

Devon didn't bother to expend energy by disputing my words or acknowledging my whine in any way. He just leaned back against the door of my garage-turned-studio and waited for my ranting to subside.

"Besides," I continued, hoping to engender some level of sympathy, "Callum's put me on surveillance. I'm sure my babysitter will be showing up any minute to escort me home, whether I like it or not."

Fact of life: pretty much everyone I knew was stronger, faster, and less disturbed by the idea of throwing a girl over his shoulder and hauling her to a given destination than anyone had a right to be.

A slightly more satisfying fact of life: I didn't have to make it easy for them. I'd doubtlessly lose any fight I started, but it was the principle of the matter. That, and annoying werewolves was a good way to dispel pent-up frustration—if and only if they were bound to keep you safe and couldn't raise claw or canine against you.

Teeth ripping into flesh. Skin tearing like Velcro.

Glancing out the window in a show of calm, I wondered why my "escort" wasn't here already. Like Devon had said, it was almost dark, and Callum's wolves were nothing if not punctual. It was at that exact moment that I noticed the faint grin on Devon's face.

"*You're* my escort?"

Devon shrugged. "The Big Guy tells you to do something, you do it, even if it means babysitting a bratty little human girl who calls playing with glue *art*."

I reached over and smacked him.

Devon just smiled back at me. He was my best friend. My partner in crime. He was most certainly not my keeper. I was going to kill Callum for this. He knew that in my current frame of mind, I would have fought anyone else, but I couldn't fight with Devon, and Devon couldn't disobey Callum.

Insert four-letter word here.

"Have I mentioned that I really hate werewolves?"

"A time or two, I believe," Devon said. For no reason other than the fact that he could, he adopted a ridiculously affected

British accent. "Come along now, luv. Be a dear and walk with your old pal Devon, yeah?"

My best friend, the drama geek. If I didn't go with him now, there was a high probability that he'd keep switching accents until I caved. A werewolf channeling the Swedish Chef was not a pretty thing—and I had absolutely no desire to see it again.

"Fine." I sighed melodramatically. Two could play Dev's game, and if he was going to put his drama chops to use, I had every right to channel my inner diva. "If we must, we must, yeah?"

My own British accent was, in a word, horrid.

To his credit, Devon didn't wince. Instead, he adopted an austere look. "Indeed." He managed to maintain his serious expression for about two seconds before the two of us started cracking up. He linked his arm through mine and gently steered me out the door. We locked up and then headed down the trail toward town.

"Do you have any idea what's got Callum's panties in a twist?" I asked as we walked.

"It's a miracle he let you live past childhood, darling. I can't imagine anyone else talking about our esteemed leader's underpants."

Although his words were entirely true, I couldn't help but notice that they weren't an answer. "Don't evade the question, Dev. Callum said he'd put an entire team on me. I'm guessing that means more than just you and that you got the short straw tonight because—"

"Because Callum knew you'd be defenseless against my ample charms?" Devon suggested winningly. Of our generation in the pack, Dev was the largest, the strongest, and the most likely to turn alpha himself one day, but being Devon, he preferred to think his true power lay in other domains.

I rolled my eyes. "Because Callum knows we're friends," I corrected. Werewolves had heightened senses, and a person would have had to be deaf, dumb, blind, and just plain stupid to miss out on the connection that Devon and I shared. There were only a few other juvenile wolves in our pack, and with Devon's sense of flare (he was, I was certain, the world's only metrosexual werewolf), he'd never really fit in among the other pups. Then Callum had brought me home, Marked me, and given me to Ali. Most of the pack had ignored the tiny, shell-shocked human, but Devon claimed he'd loved me from the moment he'd seen me, shivering in Callum's arms, blood-spattered and wild-eyed. The two of us quickly became inseparable. It was to Devon that I'd said my first words once I started talking again, and with Devon that I'd mastered the fine art of mischief. He was *Devon*.

And now, Callum had placed me in his charge.

"I hate this," I said.

"I'm sure you do, Bronwyn Alessia St. Vincent Clare, but I'd not have you endangering yourself on my watch."

It took me a second to realize that Devon was channeling Callum. The impression was a hilariously good one, and it reminded me that even when he obeyed orders, Devon was not just another member of the pack.

"Your stubbornness is also your folly," Devon continued. He even had Callum's facial expressions—or lack thereof—down pat.

"Fine. You win. I'm laughing. Happy now?"

Devon grinned, Callum's quirks instantaneously melting off his heart-shaped face. "I'm ecstatic."

"The point is—" I tried to bite back my giggles, but that stubbornness/folly line was so spot-on that I was having trouble recovering. "The point, Devon I-wish-you-had-a-middle-name Macalister, is that if Callum's got an entire team watching me—including your fine wolfy self—then there's something going on. I want to know what it is."

"Leave it alone, Bryn." Devon's voice was soft and uncharacteristically serious. He knew something, he knew that I knew that he knew something, and he still wasn't telling. Ten-to-one odds, that meant that (a) Callum had forbidden him from telling me, and (b) Devon agreed that it was in my best interest not to know.

"Devon!"

"Bronwyn."

I really needed to come up with a better retort than "you suck."

The two of us walked in silence for a bit, until the trail veered off to the right. Ark Valley was about 90 percent woods, and the forest was protected by the town by-laws—not surprising given that the town was one of a dozen or so in a five-state area founded by Callum's pack, way back when. Every couple of decades, the pack moved, rotating through our territory just when the older wolves' agelessness began pushing the line from "incredible genetics" to "unnatural." We'd been in Ark Valley for as long as I could remember, and the towns-people hadn't gotten suspicious yet—at least about the aging thing.

"Your castle awaits," Devon said, gesturing to Ali's house.

"Not going to walk me to the door?" I asked, pretending to be shocked at his lack of gallantry.

"Of course I am. Many would think that a bonny lass such as yerself wouldst be able to stay out of trouble for a distance of fifteen feet, but I know better."

"Did you just use the words *yerself* and *wouldst* in the same sentence? You can't be a pirate and a courtier at the same time, Dev. It just isn't done."

In a gesture below the dignity of the average werewolf, he stuck his tongue out at me. Still, he walked me all the way to the front door, depositing me on the porch and waiting for me to open the door and walk across the threshold. I dug out my keys, unlocked the steel door, and stepped inside, just as dusk fell.

"Good boy, Devon," I taunted. "You got me home before dark. If you can sit, shake, and roll over, too, I'm sure Callum will give you a doggie treat."

"Forget Callum and his so-called panties," Devon said, finally taking his tongue back into his mouth so that he could speak. "It's a miracle that *I* let you live past childhood."

I snorted. On any other girl, it would have been a perfectly normal, if indelicate, sound to make. On me, it sounded more animalistic. More wolfish, even though I wasn't a Were. Hazard of being raised by a pack. For the most part, with a little effort and a lot of resolve, I could keep them out of my head, but they still snuck their way into my mannerisms. I'd never be one of them the way Devon was one of them. I'd never Shift to another form, and I'd never have a wolf sharing my body and stalking through the corners of my mind. But I'd never be like other girls, either.

I shook my head to clear it of thoughts—another gesture that wasn't as human as I was—and I realized when I zoned back in that Devon had already taken his leave. He'd made it to the trail and a good ways down it in a matter of seconds, not bothering to mask his inhuman speed. Nobody but Weres came as far into the forest as Ali's house. Nobody but Ali and me.

"Close the door and hang up your jacket," Ali called the orders to me from the kitchen. She had an uncanny sense for knowing what was happening in her house even if she couldn't see it. Before she'd bellowed, I'd been microseconds away from dumping my coat on the floor.

I followed her orders to a T and then walked into the kitchen, following the sound of Ali's voice and the scent of cooking food. I had a good nose—a matter of necessity in the pack, human or not—but I couldn't quite parse what I was smelling into its component parts. "Marinara sauce," I mused out loud. "Peanut butter. Onions. And..."

"Oreos," Ali declared, popping one into her mouth. "You want?" she asked after she'd gulped hers down.

I took the proffered Oreo and surveyed the rest of the kitchen. "Cravings?" I asked.

Ali shrugged hopelessly.

"Where's the steak?"

It didn't matter what Ali was craving, there was always meat involved. The baby had turned her into a carnivore, and Ali, who couldn't stomach even the sight of a rare steak eight months ago, ate them daily now. Such was the price of a Were pregnancy. That, and the fact that instead of kicking, like normal babies, Ali's son Shifted forms. A couple of months ago, I'd joked about selling tickets to watch her stomach during the full moon. Now, with the baby's birth closer all the time, it really wasn't funny anymore.

"I'm going to be fine," Ali said, reaching up to rub my shoulder with one hand.

"You always do that. It's like you can read my mind." I meant it as a complaint, but it came out nostalgic, like part of me was preparing to look back fondly on that habit when she was gone.

"I'm going to be fine," Ali said again. "You know me, Bryn. Have I ever backed down from a fight?"

Never. Before Callum had thrust me into her care, she hadn't even been a part of the pack. She'd only just found out that werewolves were real and that more often than not, they took human women as their mates. For an orphaned kid she'd never even met, Ali had abandoned her own life and risen to the challenge. She'd taken Callum's Mark and mastered it, insulating herself—and me—from most of what it entailed. There wasn't a Were within a hundred-mile radius that she hadn't stood up to on my behalf, Callum included. I thought that was why he'd given me to her, instead of to one of the other Weres. He'd made her Pack so that she could take care of me, knowing that she'd be unaffected by dominance hierarchies, knowing that she wouldn't put up with someone giving me crap just because they were dominant enough to think that they could.

"You're going to be fine," I said, repeating Ali's words. I believed it. I really did. I just forgot that I did sometimes. I'd seen too many women die in childbirth. Female werewolves were extremely rare, and human bodies weren't meant to carry werewolf pups.

"Where's Casey?" I asked, changing the topic of conversation and hoping that my thoughts would follow suit. "It's not like him to miss a meal." Ali's husband was an eater. And for the past eight months, he'd been quite the hoverer as well. Food plus Ali meant that he should be here, and even though I hadn't quite gotten used to the fact that it wasn't just me and Ali anymore—or the idea that when I slept, there was an adult Were sleeping down the hall—Casey's absence struck me as fundamentally strange.

"Casey's eating out tonight," Ali said. "Here, taste this."

I was so caught up in trying to figure out why Casey was "eating out" and what Ali wasn't telling me that I almost took the bite she offered me. At the last second, I came to my senses and realized that whatever concoction Ali's cravings had led her to create, I really, truly didn't want any part of it.

"Your loss," she said, spooning the goop, which definitely contained both the peanut butter and the marinara sauce I'd smelled, into her mouth. She followed it with an Oreo.

"I'm going to throw up," I said, gagging—and not just for show.

"It's all part of my master plan," Ali replied. "Cravings are just the pregnant woman's excuse for making everyone around her as nauseated as she is."

"You're evil, Ali."

She smiled and serenely took another bite. "I know."

I took refuge in the refrigerator and nosed around until I found something edible. Popping the container into the microwave, I turned my attention back to Ali, who was very good at distracting me—just not quite good enough.

"Your husband's not home for dinner, even though he hasn't gone more than ten feet away from you since you hit seven months. Callum decided to start enforcing my curfew and assigned an entire team to keep an eye on me. You're making pregnancy jokes to distract me from asking questions." I ticked the observations off on my fingers as I spoke out loud. "Something's going on."

"If I asked you to please, as a personal favor to me, stay out of it, would you?" Ali asked.

I busied myself by checking on my microwavable mac and cheese and didn't reply.

"Didn't think so," Ali sighed. "What if I told you that I was tired and cranky and very pregnant, and that I needed you to do this for me, because I can't take the extra stress right now?"

Now that was a low blow, and Ali knew it. I didn't want to be worried about her, and she didn't want me worrying about her. "You're going to be fine," I said, trying to respond the way I would have if I really wasn't concerned at all. "And telling me to stay away just makes me want to know more. It's obviously pack business, and there must be some danger involved, otherwise Callum wouldn't be pulling his 'trouble's afoot' routine. But it can't be too dangerous, because Casey's involved, and Callum would never risk him this close to your due date."

Ali didn't say a word. I tried to read her face, but she had an ability matched only by Callum's to hide her emotions completely.

"Do you really need me to leave this alone?" I asked softly. I couldn't risk hurting her, even if we both wanted to pretend that there was nothing—and could be nothing—wrong.

"Yeah, Bryn, I think I do."

"Fine," I said. "I'll leave it alone—for now. But I'm not going to like it, and once that kid is born, and you're fine, I'm getting a tattoo, piercing my belly button, and eloping to Mexico with someone you've never met."

She laughed and then stuck another Oreo in my mouth. As I was chewing, she tweaked my hair. "Bryn, Callum's got you under surveillance. You wouldn't make it a foot into a tattoo shop before someone yanked you back out."

"You never know," I replied. "Tonight, my guard was Devon, and I happen to know for a fact that he thinks tasteful body art is quite the thing."

Ali responded to my retort with one of her own, and we went back and forth for so long that it didn't occur to me until much later that she had assumed that my security team would still be in place by the time the baby was born. And that really made me wonder, because our pack had a tendency to take care of trouble very quickly. Threats were eliminated the instant they were identified. Callum ran a tight ship, and I couldn't imagine what kind of pack business would necessitate my being inside by dusk every night for a month or more.

Despite my promise to Ali, I couldn't stop thinking about it, and by the end of the week, I'd come to the realization that the weirdest part of all of this wasn't that something had everyone on edge. It was the fact that nobody would tell me what *it* was. The pack didn't just want me safe. They wanted to keep me in the dark.

And ever since the night the Big Bad Wolf had come knocking at my parents' door, I hadn't been overly fond of the dark. Not metaphorically. Not actually. I liked seeing what was laid out in front me. And if Callum and Ali and Devon thought they could keep me blindfolded indefinitely, they were wrong.

CHAPTER THREE

Two weeks to the day after Callum told me to stop slacking in algebra, I got a C-minus on a quiz. It seemed like a good counterstrike at the time. After our little encounter in my workshop, the almighty alpha had pretty much disappeared, but true to his word, bodyguards materialized every day like clockwork to escort me home by dusk, willing or not. My promise to Ali meant that I couldn't do more than keep an ear to the ground to figure out why, and everywhere I turned, there were unspoken whispers, the kind that pulled at my pack-bond and made my hipbone itch, just below the Mark.

"Callum's going to kill you, you know," Devon said as I tucked the quiz into my backpack with a quick, vicious grin. Technically, it wasn't *found* material, but I thought it would make a rather fetching rosebush all the same.

"I'd like to see him try." I'd given up on the idea that Devon might crack and give me some hint about what it was that had every wolf in a hundred-mile radius teetering on edge, gnashing their teeth, and closing rank around their females like we'd spontaneously combust the moment they left us to our own devices. "In case you haven't gotten the memo, I'm not so easy to kill."

Devon didn't flinch, but the fact that he didn't counter my words with a pithy quote from the Bard and/or *Dirty Dancing* told me that my words had sent his mind down the same paths that I tried my best to avoid. His pupils didn't dilate. His jaw didn't clench, but I felt a hum of energy like the striking of a tuning fork in the air between us.

It didn't take a genius to infer that Devon's inner wolf disliked the idea of anyone trying to hurt me. Plain old Dev didn't seem too fond of the possibility, either, and I knew from previous experience that neither boy nor beast particularly cared for being reminded that if things had gone differently the night Callum had brought me home, I might not have lived long enough to be a thorn in anyone's paw.

Blood. Blood-blood-blood-blood—

I stopped myself from thinking about it and helped Devon to do the same by jabbing his left side with my index finger. If we'd been alone, I might have butted him gently with my head, but this was high school, and the good people of Ark Valley had enough reasons to think that those of us who lived in the woods were just a little bit off.

"Ten-to-one odds Callum has either Sora or Lance on Bryn-duty tonight," I said, changing the subject with an unspoken apology for bringing up the previous one at all. "You Macalisters seem to be Team Bryn favorites at the moment."

Devon's lips settled into an easy, practiced smirk, and the nearly imperceptible tension in his neck and shoulder muscles receded. "If there's any justice in this world, watching you should convince them how lucky they've been to be blessed with a son such as myself."

"He says with patented Smirk Number Three."

Devon shook his head and made a sound somwhere in the neighborhood of *tsk-tsk*. "You're getting rusty, Bronwyn. That was clearly Smirk Number Two: sardonic with a side of wit."

I breathed an internal sigh of relief that Devon was fully himself again. All Weres felt the tug between their human sides and their wolves, but Dev fought it more than most. He danced to his own drummer and dared the world to tell him that a purebred Were should have better things to worry about than what he was wearing. All things considered, Devon was almost as much of a rarity as I was. The only difference was, his particular oddity—being the son of a female werewolf rather than that of a male Were's human mate—gave him the advantage over other werewolves, while mine meant that I'd always be the slow one. The weak one. The one who needed protection from pack secrets that came out after dark.

"Hey, Bronwyn?"

Until those words broke the surface of my mind, I'd been

deep enough in my thoughts that I hadn't been paying attention to the finely honed senses that would have otherwise warned me of an outsider's approach. Was I slipping, or what? It was one thing to let a werewolf get a drop on you, but a normal teenage boy? That was just embarrassing.

"Yes?" I hadn't expected to see Jeff (of motorcycle fame) in anything resembling a social setting for at least a semester. He'd been avoiding me since the moment I'd hopped off his bike, and like a chameleon, I'd faded into the background, keeping my distance from his human friends the way I had before my little joyride. As I turned to face him, I caught a whiff of a second scent—Juicy Fruit and plastic—and realized that he wasn't alone.

There was a girl with him, and she was smiling.

Two of my classmates, approaching me of their own free will? I glanced at Devon and raised an eyebrow, but his gaze was fastened on Human 1 and Human 2. They didn't even seem to realize they were being watched, and they certainly didn't feel me stiffen as Devon took a step closer to me.

Gently, I put a hand on Devon's chest and pushed him back. I'd told Callum I had no interest in provoking interspecies aggression, and I'd meant it. Previous grand-theft-auto attempts aside, my instinct to keep my head down and not draw attention to the pack was almost as well defined as the three parallel scars under the band of my jeans.

"You dropped this." Jeff held out a pen that I'd been using

to take notes (or rather, pointedly *not* take notes) before the bell rang. But as I reached for it, he twirled it twice and tucked it into the jean pocket of the girl standing next to him. "I think I'll keep it as payment due for that little klepto moment of yours with my bike."

The girl standing next to him had a name, and I knew it, but I didn't bother thinking it. She was a typical Ark Valley girl, a little too quiet, a little too sweet, with metaphorical claws lurking just under the surface.

"Jeff!" the girl said. "You're horrible. I'm sorry, Bronwyn."

But she didn't take the pen out of her pocket. Instead, she wrapped an arm around Jeff. I wasn't exactly an expert on human-courting behavior, but I sensed the ceremony of the moment. He'd given her my pen. She'd giggled. In another few seconds, they'd both walk away and never give me a second look.

Compared to the werewolf version of courting—he bites her, she bites him, his connection to the pack spills over onto her for all eternity—the whole thing seemed artificial and insignificant.

And yet, for a fraction of a second, I froze.

Sorry, Bronwyn.

I was human. They were human. Whatever games they were playing should have been my games, but my talents currently tended more toward flushing out an alpha who swept into my life just long enough to issue orders and disappear for weeks on end, busy with pack business more important than little old me.

Sorry, Bronwyn.

Devon put an arm around me and curled his lips into an expression I recognized as Smirk Number One: sarcastic with a touch of I-couldn't-care-less. "Why, Bryn," he said with a hint of Scarlett O'Hara in his voice, "I do believe he's given her your pen."

Devon's words freed up my mouth, which—true to form— spoke without consulting my brain. "Well, get Freud on the phone. He'll have a field day with this one."

That should have been the end of it, but unfortunately, algebra was my last class of the day, and that meant that Devon wasn't the only wolf in the near vicinity. Ark Valley was small, the combined middle/high school was even smaller, and even though I wasn't close to any of the other juveniles in our pack, when it came to confrontations with the outside world, we were family.

Or as they would have phrased it, I was *theirs*.

There were only three of them, and one was a seventh grader, but werewolves mature quickly. By age twelve, they look like teenagers, and by the time they're in high school, they could pass for twenty. Somewhere around fifteen or sixteen, their growth slows down, and most don't ever age past about thirty, no matter how many centuries they see.

Moral of the story? My age-mates were all physically

advanced for their age, and Jeff had reason to be looking nervous.

They didn't descend, not right away, and they didn't say a word. My pack-mates just circled us, with long, ambling strides, their eyes flickering from me to Jeff and back again.

Out of habit, I shut them out. Bond or no bond, nobody got into my head but me, and the last thing I wanted was to feel the low, dangerous vibration of a growl beneath the surface of someone else's skin.

To Jeff, they must just have looked like an odd assortment of strangely intense ruffians whose backwoods roots showed in every crevice of their faces. To me, they looked like Trouble, capital *T*.

I brushed my hand lightly against Devon's arm, and he nodded.

"Thank you for that extremely Freudian performance, Jeff. Sir, madam, we bid you good day." Dev boomed out the words in his best Sean Connery accent, but all the while, he kept his eyes on the others, staring them down, warning them not to come closer. There was a single moment in which I thought the others might disregard the warning and close in, but a few seconds later, the tension broke. Callum's wolves had ultimate control over their animal instincts, and they knew as well as I did that altercations with the outside world wouldn't be met with smiles and pats on the back from the pack's alpha.

Unaware of just how much of a reprieve they'd gotten, Jeff and his little lady scurried away, and I was left with four teenage werewolves—none of whom liked the idea of my walking home by myself.

General rule of thumb: except for Devon, the rest of our age-mates usually gave me a fairly wide berth. One seemingly mild glance from Callum was all it took to warn them away from thinking I was future mate material, and unless werewolves were on the lookout for a breeding partner, most of them didn't have any use for humans. There were at most a dozen of us human-types living in the woods at any given time, and besides me, every single one was mated to one of the pack's males. There were more human females, lots of them, buried in unmarked graves: the ones who hadn't survived taking on a bond with the pack during the mating process, the ones who'd died in childbirth, the ones who'd lived to a ripe old age while their werewolf mates stayed young.

No, thank you.

If Callum hadn't scared off any and all of my would-be suitors, I would have done the job myself.

"You three can go now," I said, trying to put a hint of Callum—understated authority and uncompromising power—in my voice.

Not one of them moved.

Since I obviously wasn't good at commanding their fear and respect, I tried to appeal to their rationality. "I'm fine. I'm safe. The outside threat just went *poof*." Unfortunately, this seemed to be falling on completely deaf ears. Jeff was gone, and if anyone had a claim to me, it was Devon, but our age-mates just stood there, flanking my position like the threat hadn't abated.

If I'd opened up my bond, I might have been able to figure out why, but I also would have been devoured whole by the power that flowed through the entire pack. I was connected to each of them through Callum's Mark, but just living with the pack had me treading water for every breath of independence I managed to take.

All of which meant that I had to rely on more subtle methods of finding out the things that I needed to know.

"Jeff's gone, and you're all acting like the threat is still here," I said. "Would I be correct in guessing that means that there is an outside threat? And would this be the same outside threat that has Callum insisting I be inside every day by dark?"

Devon groaned. The other three just exchanged looks. I'd promised Ali I wouldn't push things, and that was the only reason I wasn't out scouring our territory for the threat, slipping out my bedroom window at night to get a good look at whatever it was that came out with the moon—besides the obvious, of course. Weres could Shift anyplace, anytime, but it was harder for them to stay human at nighttime, especially during that time of the month.

But because I was Pack, I was safe. Even when they Shifted. Even when the moon was full.

Or so I'd been told, over and over again, for as long as I could remember.

"The threat isn't internal." As the words left my mouth, I transitioned from trying to convince myself to treating the entire situation as a giant logic puzzle. "And it's probably not a human." That much went without saying; no mere human could put an entire werewolf pack on high alert. "Whatever is putting the growl in your growlers isn't a foreign wolf, either, because it wouldn't take the lot of you more than an hour to send him back to his own alpha, tail between his legs. Unless, of course, he was a lone wolf, in which case Callum would take care of it himself."

Weres were pack animals, and nine times out of ten, loners were loners for a reason. Without psychic bonds to others of their kind, werewolves had a tendency to go Rabid. Give in to the desire to hunt. Hunt more than rabbits or deer. Given my history, it made perfect sense that the pack wouldn't want me to know if a wolf on our lands was on the verge of madness, but if that was the case, the whole thing would have been over and done with in seconds.

Werewolves policed their own, and a wolf that hunted humans was as good as dead.

"No, it has to be something bigger than that," I mused. "Something that you all see as a threat but that Callum won't let you eliminate. Something that makes you want to protect me, even though I don't need your protection."

All four of them bristled at that one—even Dev. He just got over it quicker.

"Gentlemen, I think I've got this from here," he said, and with a wave of one manicured hand and a glint of steel in his eyes, he sent our age-mates on their way before I could trick them into revealing anything I didn't already know.

"You did that on purpose," I told him.

Devon, his posture and body language still leaking dominance, snorted. "Darn tootin'. If you poke enough angry bears with sticks, someday you're going to get burned, sweetheart."

I was tempted to mock him for mixing his metaphors, but I didn't. In normal circumstances, Devon would have been on my side, hunting up answers and pushing the limits of my promise to Ali. The fact that he wasn't just made me want to know more.

"Ah, right on time," Devon said.

I realized that Callum was standing between us. He had a way of appearing out of nowhere, silent and deadly, and the carefully neutral expression on his face made me reconsider the wisdom of baiting him in the first place.

"I take it you're here about algebra?" I asked him. Callum had a pesky habit of knowing what I was going to do before I did it, and there wasn't a thing that went down in his territory that escaped his notice.

"A moment, please, Devon?" Callum asked, his tone perfectly pleasant. Devon nodded, his eyes cast downward as he stepped aside. The alpha's effect on his wolves was immediate and overpowering.

Bless my human immunity.

"Bryn."

That wasn't what I expected him to say. I expected him to yell-without-yelling. To narrow his eyes at me. To grab my chin in his hand and force me to meet his most uncompromising gaze.

He didn't. Instead, all he said was my name. My stomach twisted sharply. Something was wrong.

"Ali?"

"She's fine now. There were some complications. She's on bed rest."

The pack had its own doctor, a werewolf who'd been trained in the 1800s but did his best to keep up with modern medicine of both the human and veterinary varieties. In the past two centuries, he'd overseen more than his fair share of births, and it stood to reason that he knew what he was talking about. Besides, it wasn't like Ali could go to a normal hospital, not when her baby was anything but.

Blood. Blood-blood-blood-blood—

I tried not to think about the bad thing. I tried not to think about women, just like Ali, who hadn't survived. I tried not to picture myself hiding under the sink, terrified and alone, knowing there wasn't a single thing I could do to stop death when it came knocking on my door.

Callum brushed my hair out of my face, forcing my mind to the present. "She'll be fine, Bryn." He paused, and my Mark hummed in a way that made me wonder if his stomach was twisting, too. "I promise you, Ali will be fine."

Werewolves didn't make promises lightly. Callum, as alpha, was bound by his word. I really wanted to believe him, but there was no way he could know for sure. Even Callum wasn't psychic.

His lips curved upward, ever so slightly—half warning, half smile. "I also promise, little Bronwyn, that for the next three weeks until the baby is born, you won't so much as sneeze out of turn. You'll go to school. You'll go home. You can make as many paper fire hydrants as you want, but you'll stop pushing it."

I had a feeling that what he really meant was that I'd stop pushing *him*. Stop asking questions. Stop thinking about the scent of danger in the air, the indescribable buzzing that told me that something in our pack was off.

"Ali will be fine, and you'll be on your best behavior." The tone in Callum's voice sounded more like prophecy than an order, and I pushed down the urge to challenge him. Part of me wanted to, but the other part couldn't stop thinking about Ali.

You'll be on your best behavior, and Ali will be fine.

I inverted the order of Callum's words and silently made Fate a deal. I would do whatever Callum said, would do whatever *anyone* said, and in return, karma, the universe, *whatever* would see to it that Ali made it through alive.

Fair was fair. A bargain was a bargain—and at this point, all there was left to do was wait.

CHAPTER FOUR

"She's okay. She's okay. She's got to be okay." I turned on my heels and started walking back down the hallway, continuing my litany. "She's got to be okay, right, Lance?"

Devon's father—all 6'6" of him—was my current bodyguard and the least talkative werewolf I knew, so it wasn't exactly a shocker when he didn't respond. Only this time, I wasn't sure whether it was because he wasn't exactly social in his human form, or because he didn't know what to say. Bryn babysitting duty encompassed many things, but it usually didn't involve me teetering on the edge of hysteria and reaching out to the closest Slab of Werewolf to pull me back.

"Ali's going to be fine." I addressed my words to Lance's mammoth chest, unwilling to look him in the eye. "She's strong. She's never backed down from a fight." Speaking hurt my throat, which tightened as I tried to breathe. "Not everyone dies," I said more softly. "She's going to be okay, right, Lance?"

"Right," Lance said, suddenly discovering his voice. I glanced up at him, and his strong, Nordic features shuddered as he attempted something that resembled a smile the way that a great white shark resembles a goldfish.

That, more than anything, freaked me out. Ali was less than twelve feet away, behind closed doors with the pack's doctor, an hour into a labor that was more likely to kill her than not. My entire body was shaking, and no matter what I said, the ghosts dancing in the corners of my mind whispered that everyone *did* die. Maybe not in labor, but when it came to me and mothers, dying was the status quo.

And now, Lance was actually speaking to me and *smiling*, something he hadn't done in the entire course of my childhood, let alone the month he'd been part of my security team.

This could not possibly be a good sign. If he'd thought I was worrying over nothing, he wouldn't have said a word.

"I'm going to throw up," I said, turning again, this time to run for the bathroom. I slammed the door behind me and lunged for the toilet, but nothing happened. I was so scared, I couldn't even throw up. I had to get out of here. I couldn't just wait in our house, listening to Ali scream but barred from being in there with her. I couldn't pace up and down the halls, stopping only when someone came to tell me that it was over, one way or another.

If Lance was talking to me, that meant that he was far enough off his game that he might not catch me in the act of leaving. Ali let out another bone-crunching cry of pain, and I closed my eyes, willing myself not to hear her screams. Forcing myself to pay attention only to the goal of escaping, I crept toward the window, letting the inhuman noises ripping their way out of Ali's battered throat cover the sound of my steps. I lowered my body out the window and climbed down the side of the house. If I hadn't been in such good shape, thanks to the daily workout regime I'd been put through every morning since I was six, I probably couldn't have managed to make it to the ground without breaking both my legs, but between my training and my desperation to get away, it was a snap.

I hit the ground running and didn't stop. As a matter of reflex, I covered my tracks, running in patterns designed to make tracking me difficult. There were several streams in the woods, as well as the disturbingly named Dead Man's Creek, and I made a point of crossing all of them. Whenever I saw a second pair of tracks, I ran along them, and I loosed my emergency bag of cayenne pepper (which I kept on my person at all times) in an area where I knew any self-respecting tracker would take a great big whiff.

If that didn't throw Lance off, nothing would. Everyone else would be too concerned with Ali to worry about me.

I'd been instinctively covering my tracks for several minutes before I realized where I was going and why. For the past few weeks, I'd been the poster girl for good behavior. I'd kept up my end of the bargain with fate, and now it was the universe's turn to pay up. The way I saw it, I'd promised Ali I'd leave the pack's secret alone until the baby was born and she was in the clear. Now, Ali was in labor, and I needed a distraction.

Close enough.

As part of my poster-child act, I hadn't let myself actively think about the origin of the pack's unrest, and I hadn't formulated a master plan, but on a subconscious level, I think I'd always known where to go to find the answers. There weren't foreign wolves on our land. A human hadn't discovered our secret. There was a threat. An outside threat that couldn't be dispelled with tooth and claw. Whatever the answer to this puzzle was, my best chance of finding it was about a mile away, deep in the heart of the woods, sitting directly on top of the highest point of elevation in the valley.

Callum's house.

And for once, he wouldn't be there, and he wouldn't know that I had been until after I left. Then he'd kill me, but given the circumstances, I wasn't entirely sure that I would care.

I knew the way there by heart, even though I rarely found myself on Callum's doorstep. He preferred to come to me in my studio or at Ali's house. Callum's home was reserved for pack business. We all met there, twice a year: the wolves and their wives and Ali and me. It was a different sort of meeting than the pack's ceremonial runnings, where the Weres shed their human skin and let their wolves come out to play.

Those meetings I avoided like the plague, but the ones that took place at Callum's house required my attendance. There was always an artifice of bureaucracy to them, like anyone in a room full of Weres could forget, even for a second, that our lives weren't democratic in the least. My inclusion—and Ali's, before she'd married Casey—marked me as unique in the werewolf world. Humans, unless claimed and Marked as a wolf's mate, were never invited to Callum's house. They were never initiated into the pack. They certainly weren't adopted using a ceremony meant for pups whose mothers had died in childbirth.

They weren't Marked by an alpha at the ripe old age of four.

Long story short, the way to Callum's place, the inner sanctum of our werewolf community, wasn't the kind of thing a girl just forgot, and I made it there in record time. Not being a complete idiot, I paused as I got close, standing absolutely still and listening for several minutes. My hearing was good for a human, my senses as developed as they could be given my species, and I put every ounce of that to use, trying to determine whether or not anyone was guarding Callum's house. I doubted he would have anticipated my coming here, but if there were answers to be found inside, I might not be the only reason to guard them.

I closed my eyes. Concentrating on one sense at a time helped my accuracy. There was definitely someone inside, probably in the living room. And there, I thought, another one in the kitchen. There was no telling about the basement or the second floor. I opened my eyes, edged closer and closer until I was very near the house, and looked. And then, of course, I was promptly caught, because as quiet as I was, and as sneaky as I was, the people inside were werewolves, and any attempt at pitting my stealth against their stealth had roughly the same chance of success I would have enjoyed in challenging them to a wrestling match.

My first clue that things had gone awry was the person in the living room turning to look directly at me, her face tightening into a pointed glare. My second was the fact that the person I'd heard in the kitchen was now outside and stalking toward me, beefy fists clenched.

My third clue was a very, very audible growl.

"What are you doing here?" Marcus spat, grabbing me by the shoulder and turning me to face him in a way that hurt but wouldn't leave a bruise. He'd learned the hard way not to leave any marks, and he'd never learn more than that. I was Callum's, more connected to him than his most loyal soldiers, and for as long as I lived, Marcus would hate me for that. Any injury—physical or mental—that he thought he could get away with inflicting on me, he would.

It hadn't taken very long on my end for the feeling to become mutual.

"I asked what you were doing here, girl."

From Marcus, *girl* was an insult, and a large part of the reason that he hated me as much as he did. If the alpha had adopted anyone, chosen to teach anyone, that person should have been a werewolf, and he should have been male.

"C-C-C-Callum," I said, forcing myself to stutter as a means of stalling for the time necessary to think up a truth that wouldn't incriminate me.

"Callum?" Marcus said. "Is he hurt?"

As much as I hated Marcus, I couldn't deny his loyalty. He would have died for Callum.

"Bryn, is Callum hurt?"

I could count on one hand the number of times Marcus had called me by any of my given names, let alone my preferred one. I remembered then how awful I'd looked in the bathroom mirror back at home. Each of Ali's screams had carved itself onto my face: my eyes were bloodshot, my lips torn from biting down, and the shadows under my eyes extended down past my cheekbones. Every muscle in my body was tuned to anguish. And Marcus, who hated Ali nearly as much as he hated me, probably couldn't fathom the fact that I could be this worried about her. The only person Marcus cared enough to worry about was Callum, and he was taking my current state—and probably the fact that I was here and Callum and my team of guards hadn't stopped me—as a sign that something was seriously wrong.

A better person would not have taken advantage of this

fact. It was cruel, it was wrong, and it was stupid, but hey, it wasn't like Marcus could possibly despise me more, and knowing that he'd be happy if Ali died rid me of any guilt I might have otherwise felt for playing him.

"It's bad," I said, letting the tears that I'd kept myself from shedding all day come. Marcus, smelling the truth in my words, didn't notice that I hadn't specified *what* was bad. "Might not make it."

"Callum?" Marcus breathed. He gripped me with both arms, his fingers biting into my skin so hard that I could feel my flesh bruising. It occurred to me that I couldn't make Callum's condition sound too dire, because Callum was the only thing keeping me safe from Marcus, even now. "What's wrong with you? Talk! Is Callum hurt?"

"Callum's hurt," I said, thinking of how much I was hurting and how Callum loved Ali the way I did. "He's really hurt, Marcus."

"Where?"

"Our house," I said. And just like that, Marcus was gone, a blur of greasy hair and short, compact ferociousness tearing through the woods, convinced that he was on his way to save Callum.

I should have felt bad, but I didn't. I felt nothing—not even a hint of trepidation that Callum wasn't the only one who was going to kill me when what I'd been up to today became common knowledge.

One down, I mused silently, afraid that the wolf inside would hear me if I spoke out loud, *one to go.*

Since my cover had been truly blown already, I walked up to Callum's front door and let myself into the house. I made it exactly three steps into the foyer before a voice stopped me.

"*How* is Callum hurt, Bryn?"

Of course the werewolf inside had heard my conversation with Marcus, and of course it was someone smart enough to ask the right questions.

"What do you mean how?" I returned.

Sora's wide-set eyes narrowed, emphasizing the angles of her face. Clearly, she was not amused. "You know exactly what I mean, and you have three seconds to provide me with the truth, the whole truth, and nothing but the truth before you really, really regret it."

As a threat, it was less than precise, but the step she took toward me as she issued those words sold it completely. Female werewolves were incredibly rare. Our pack had two, and most didn't even have that, but somehow, over the past two hundred years, Sora had managed to rise above the males' instincts to protect their females at all costs. In the years I'd been with the pack, she'd been one of Callum's strongest, smartest, and most trusted soldiers.

She was also Devon's mother, which meant that she knew me all too well.

"Two seconds."

Well, shoot. "Callum isn't physically hurt," I said. "He's hurting because Ali's hurting. And if Marcus assumed otherwise, it's totally not my—"

Sora cursed, her dainty lips twisting sideways into a full-on snarl. She grabbed my arm and none-too-gently dragged me to the kitchen, where she quickly and methodically bound my wrists and my ankles and then tied me to the handles on the refrigerator and freezer doors. If I hadn't spent enough time at her house growing up to personally acquaint her with my affinity for picking locks, she probably would have just locked me in one of the spare bedrooms, but Sora had learned the hard way not to underestimate my resourcefulness.

I tested the resistance of her knots, and she snarled again, causing me to go very, very still.

"You are nearly too stupid to live, you foolish, reckless child." She didn't sound like Devon's mother. She sounded like Callum's right-hand man. "And you don't even realize what you've done."

"Marcus will be angry with me," I said, trying to prove that I wasn't completely ignorant of the inevitable consequences of my actions.

"He'll be furious—and not just with you," Sora said, checking her knots and making sure that I wasn't going anywhere. "He'll be angry with himself, and with you, and with Ali, because you're her responsibility."

Callum had Marked me, but as far as the pack was concerned, I was Ali's daughter. If Marcus hadn't hated Ali for her own sake, he would have hated her for mine.

"He'll be furious with Ali, and he'll be in her house. While she's giving birth. She's in enough danger as it is. She doesn't need Marcus adding to it."

My mouth went instantly dry. "Callum would...Callum would never let Marcus hurt her."

"The odds are against her, Bryn. Do you really think having a homicidal werewolf in her house is going to help? He may not strike out at Ali directly, but his being there will hurt her, I promise you that."

What had I done?

"I didn't—" I cut off, swallowed, and tried again. "I swear I didn't..."

I wasn't sure how to fill in the blank. I didn't know? I didn't think? I didn't mean to?

"I know," Sora said, sounding more like the woman I knew. "I'll go after him. I'm faster, but he has a head start. You'll be here when I get back." And then, like Marcus, she was gone, and I was alone, tied to a kitchen appliance in Callum's house, dully agonizing over the fact that I'd just sent a raging werewolf Ali's way. What if Marcus distracted the doctor? What if the stress was more than Ali's broken body could take?

I'd promised to be good. I'd lied. I'd broken my end of the

bargain, and Fate was angry. I didn't want anybody else to die because of me.

Homicidal werewolf. Sora's words rang in my ears, and my brain provided the accompanying visual.

Homicidal werewolf. Mommy. Blood-blood-blood-blood-blood.

Logically, I knew that I'd had nothing to do with my parents' death—that it wasn't my fault that I'd survived the attack and they hadn't—but the thoughts in my head had stopped making sense, the words dissolving into nonsense, images crumbling into nothing. As time ticked on, I forced myself to stand ramrod straight, because I desperately wanted to slump and refused to allow myself even that small relief.

I don't know how long I stood there. My muscles started aching, and words returned to me, and I just kept telling myself, over and over again, that if everything was okay, I'd never do something stupid again.

And then I heard the noise.

Screaming.

Words.

"Is somebody up there? Please! Please, help me. Can you hear me? Can anybody hear me?"

Somebody was in Callum's basement, and that somebody needed help. I knew I shouldn't respond, knew that anyone in Callum's basement was there for a reason. The yelling degenerated from words into sounds, and that was what made up my mind, because the wordless howling struck a chord with me.

Whoever was down there sounded like I felt. It didn't matter who it was or what he'd done. I had to help him, because it wasn't like I could do a thing for myself. Or for Ali.

I swung my bound ankles upward and twisted to angle my feet toward Callum's kitchen drawers—and in particular, his knife drawer. I pressed my heel against the drawer knob and pulled. A well-placed kick sent the contents of the drawer flying, and I eyed the largest of the knives. Straining against the ties that held me in place, I managed to slide the knife closer. I caught the handle between my heels, and stretched my hands down to meet them.

Success.

As I began cutting through the restraints, the sound of inhuman screams echoing in my mind, I tried not to think about the fact that my vow to abstain from stupidity had lasted for all of forty-five seconds.

CHAPTER FIVE

I HALF-EXPECTED SORA AND MARCUS TO RETURN before I managed to get myself untied, but either she hadn't caught up to him in time and there was major damage control to do, or she'd successfully intercepted him on the way to Ali's but had been forced to throw down in order to keep him from coming back here and tearing out my jugular. Either way, it didn't look like the cavalry was going to be stopping me from my endless pursuit of stupidity anytime soon.

Rubbing my wrists, which had gone numb under the duct tape, I took a baby step away from the refrigerator and the remains of my common sense. Callum's basement had always been off-limits to me, and I wasn't dumb enough to believe the restriction was in place because that was where he hid my Christmas presents.

Whoever, or whatever, was in the basement was probably dangerous. And based on the fact that Sora had felt it necessary to tie me up before she left, there was a very good chance that the danger in question was the very thing that had Callum assigning wolves to shadow my every move.

I paused when I reached the door.

I shouldn't be doing this.

I tested the doorknob, fully expecting it to be locked. It wasn't.

I really shouldn't be doing this.

I listened for a sound, anything to spur me onward or send me running, but heard nothing.

I have to do this.

Even if I ran as fast as I could, there was no way that I could get to Ali in time to offset any damage I might have done. My presence there would just make things worse for everyone, but twenty feet below me, there was someone in the basement. Someone who'd asked for my help.

Someone just like me.

I cracked open the door. Halfway through the job, I got tired of even pretending caution and threw it open the rest of the way. The basement was dimly lit, but my eyes adjusted quickly and I realized before the door even hit the wall and bounced back toward me what exactly it was that Callum kept in his basement.

Cages. Lots and lots of cages. I recognized steel when I saw it, and reinforced titanium—metals that wouldn't hurt a Were but couldn't be easily snapped, either. The doors on Ali's house were made of similar materials—added protection in case a wolf chanced to violate the mandate that made all humans off-limits as prey.

I walked down the basement stairs without even realizing I was moving, and my hand reached out completely of its own volition to touch the thick, tubular bars. The cages themselves were big—easily big enough to hold a hefty Were in either wolf or human form, with room for him to move and pace. The metal was cold under my hand, and something about it horrified me. I hated that Callum had given me a curfew. I couldn't imagine a larger loss of freedom—not like this.

"You came."

The voice took me by surprise, which just goes to show how out of it I was, since the whole reason I'd ventured into the forbidden basement was because I'd heard someone yelling.

I forced myself not to show that I'd been caught off guard, and responded without turning around. "I came."

Twin instincts battled inside of me—one told me that I had to act as if I wasn't concerned about my safety, because nothing whetted a Were's appetite like human fear, but the other told me that turning your back on a wolf was never a good idea. After a few seconds had passed, I casually twisted, leaning my back against the cage I'd been touching, my eyes searching out the person I'd come down here to see.

A boy, about my age. Dark hair, light eyes, a few inches taller than me and built along lean, muscular lines. He wasn't wearing a shirt, and something about the way he lay in his cage looked completely natural—and feral beyond anything I'd seen in a very long time. The expression on his face, in contrast, was entirely human.

"I wasn't even sure there was anyone up there," he said, his eyes on mine. "I felt Marcus and Sora leave, but then I smelled you, and I heard . . . I heard things."

I took a step forward, drawn toward him, this boy in the cage.

"You smell good," he said. "Like meat."

I immediately stopped moving forward. He sniffed the air again.

"Like Pack," he said, tilting his head to the side, trying to understand how I could be human but smell more predator than prey.

"I am Pack," I said. *And you're not,* I added silently. "I'm Bryn."

I expected him to recognize my name. Most Weres did—even those visiting from other territories. Even those in the grips of madness. It wasn't often that a human child was adopted into a pack, let alone by the alpha himself, and the circumstances around my adoption made me even more of a minor celebrity among this boy's kind.

"I'm Chase," he said.

"Kind of an ironic name for a werewolf." The observation slipped easily off my tongue. The boy didn't blink. In fact, I was beginning to doubt that he'd blinked once since I'd come into the room. "Werewolves do a lot of chasing," I explained. "And your name is Chase. Hee."

Some people laugh in the face of danger. Some people run. In my lifetime, I'd done both, but this time, with Chase's eyes on me, his posture more wolf than man, the best I could manage was a good old-fashioned babble.

"You're not a Were." There was a humming quality to Chase's voice, a slight vibration that could have been a growl, but wasn't. "You're not a Were, but you're Pack."

"I'm human," I said, "but I'm Callum's." I didn't lay things out for him further. In most situations, Callum's name alone was enough to protect me. Even though there were steel bars in between Chase and me, I couldn't dismiss the sense that his wolf was close enough to the surface that I might need to be protected. It was odd, really, because despite the fact that it was his pain that had brought me down here, Chase seemed calm now— not agitated in a way that would have his wolf taking control of the human.

"Do you know where Callum is?" Chase asked, latching on to the fact that I'd spoken a familiar name. "He was supposed to let me out. He was supposed to be back by nightfall."

"The sun hasn't set yet," I said. "It's still early. And Callum's not here, because he's taking care of pack business." No need to specify what that business was.

"It always feels like night to me," Chase said, his voice oddly reflective considering the fact that his eyes were beginning to change, the pupils dilating and changing color. "Callum says that will pass. He says I've come a long way in just a month, that it takes most people in my situation years to shut out the night, to resist the call to run and hunt during the day."

"And what exactly is your 'situation'?" I asked Chase, drawn to him even though I could feel his Change coming on, and everything I'd ever been taught told me that now was the time to get out of Dodge.

"My situation?" Chase asked, arching his back in a spasmodic motion that didn't match his casual tone at all. "I got bit."

Those three words turned my feet to lead. I couldn't move, couldn't walk back up the basement stairs. All I could do was watch as his muscles leapt to life, the tension running up his body like a stadium full of fans doing the wave, each contraction triggering another, until I wasn't staring at a boy.

I was staring at midnight-black wolf that easily weighed two hundred pounds. He had a few markings on his chest and paws, and his eyes flashed back and forth between pale blue and a dangerous yellow.

I shouldn't be here.

Chase didn't seem like a monster, but in this form, he could easily kill me without even meaning to. He'd said it himself: I smelled like Pack, but I also smelled like meat. Now that he'd Shifted, it was anyone's guess as to which would matter more.

He's in a cage, I reminded myself, but the words meant

nothing to me, because I just couldn't stop staring into his wild eyes and playing the last words he'd said before he Shifted, over and over again.

I got bit.

I got bit.

I got bit.

It was impossible. Werewolves were born that way. The condition was passed down from father to son, and very, very occasionally, daughter. Books and movies would have had me believe that any little scratch or bite could turn someone into a werewolf, but thousands of years of werewolf history said they were wrong. Unless it took place in the presence of the pack alpha and he forged a bond between biter and bitee, a nibble from a werewolf didn't do jack. And even with Marks like mine and the wives', the Mark didn't turn the recipient into a werewolf. I was living proof of that.

I got bit.

It would take much more than a "bite" to turn someone from a human into a Were. It would take an all-out slaughter, and no one could survive an attack like that. No one. For that matter, there were very few werewolves far enough gone to provoke their alpha's wrath by attacking a human and risking exposure in the first place. And yet...

I got bit.

In his cage, Chase stared at me, his eyes pulsing. A growl burst out of his throat, and he threw himself at me, slamming his wolf body into the side of the cage. I backpedaled toward the stairs and clambered up them.

I shouldn't have gone down there.

Still, I couldn't deny that I'd gotten what I'd been wanting: knowledge. I stepped over the threshold and shut the basement door behind me. My heart pounded as I bolted the door from the outside, my mind caught up in processing Chase's words—what they meant for him, and what they meant for me.

I got bit.

It was a miracle he hadn't died. He should have died.

Teeth tearing into flesh and back out of it. Blood splattering. Again and again, vicious, relentless, thorough. Blood-blood-blood-blood-blood—

"Oh, Bryn."

And then Callum was there with me in the present, his arms held wide, and I fell into them, caught up in bits and pieces of memories that wouldn't leave me alone now that Chase's words had opened the floodgates.

"You just couldn't stay away." There was no reproach in Callum's voice. That would come later, I was sure. For now, he just held me, whispering to me in the old language, little comforts that I understood without knowing the meanings of the words.

"How'd you know?" I asked. How did he know that I was here? That I needed him? How had he always known? How had he known that day, when he'd been the one to pull me out from my hiding place as Sora and the rest of Callum's men took down the rabid wolf who'd killed my family?

"Lance told me you'd gone, and I had a hunch."

Hearing Lance's name reminded me why I'd come here in search of answers in the first place. I'd needed to get away. "Ali?" I asked, the question coming out as a croak.

Blood-blood-blood-blood-blood . . .

I couldn't do this again. I couldn't lose Ali, too.

"She's sleeping, but doing well. And I imagine she'll be wanting to have a word or two with you when she wakes up, Bronwyn Alessia."

Jaws closing around Daddy's throat . . .

Callum forced me to look at his steady eyes and hear his words. "Ali's fine, Bryn. I swore to you that she was going to be fine, and she is."

"And the baby?" I asked, my stomach clenching with relief and with a deeper fear that wouldn't let go until I saw Ali for myself.

"The *babies*," Callum said, relishing the word, "are healthy. I believe they've expressed an interest in meeting their sister."

Twins? Ali was fine, and she'd had twins? It was almost enough to banish the blood-red haze that I could feel coloring every thought in my head. Almost, but not quite, because somewhere in my mind, I could still hear those three little words.

I got bit.

And each time I heard them, it killed me a little. But more than that, it also made me wonder, because there wasn't a wolf in Callum's pack who would attack a teenage boy. There wasn't a wolf in any of the North American packs who would have done such a thing, and I knew what that meant. I knew what it meant better than anyone.

Somewhere in our territory, there was a Rabid.

CHAPTER SIX

"THERE ARE BAD PEOPLE IN THE WORLD: MURDERERS and psychopaths and telemarketers who won't take no for an answer." I kept my voice soft as I spoke and—for the benefit of my audience—made a real effort at ditching my protective layer of sarcasm. "Sometimes, bad people do really evil things, and good people get hurt. Even kids."

My listeners hung on to my every word with round, wide eyes.

"Humans call their monsters sociopaths. We call ours Rabids."

Baby #1 (also known as Kaitlin or Katie or, if she was in a mood, Kate) signified her acceptance of my older sisterly wisdom by blowing a spit bubble of mammoth proportions. Baby #2 made what appeared to be a real effort at putting his left foot in his mouth. Reflexively, I reached my hand out and tickled his sole before catching his foot in my hand.

Alex (also known as Alexander, Little Guy, Big Guy, and Spot) wrinkled his baby brow.

"Got your foot," I told him loftily. Alex wriggled. Clearly, he was unsure what to make of this development.

"Messing with the minds of the next generation again, Bryn? For shame!" Devon's voice took me off guard. The twins, on the other hand, didn't seem at all surprised to see him. Even at the ripe old age of six weeks, their senses were better than mine. I would have sworn that they knew it, too, based on their little baby smirks.

"It's not like I have much else to do," I said. "Grounded, remember?" Winter had given way to early spring, and I was *still* under house arrest for my "antics" the day the twins were born.

Devon sat down next to me and started playing with Kaitlin's feet.

"I seem to recall this grounding that you speak of," he said. "Remind me again—is this the grounding that kept you from going with me to see the delightfully horrendous film adaptation of my seventh-favorite Broadway musical, or the grounding that came about because you almost got yourself killed? And didn't bother to bring me along? Hmmmmm?"

Devon loved playing the martyr almost as much as he adored cheesy movie musicals, and my being housebound was almost as bad for him as it was for me. Our age-mates in the pack (or "the Philistines," as Dev sometimes referred to them) couldn't quite grasp the appeal inherent in most of the things that Devon enjoyed.

"How many times do I have to say I'm sorry?" I huffed, finally releasing my hold on Alex's captive foot. I smiled at the way he joyfully flailed like there was no tomorrow once it was free.

"How many more times do you have to apologize?" Devon asked, pretending to ponder the question deeply. "At least thrice more, I should think," he said, slipping into a distinctively rhythmic pattern of speech that made me think that a reenactment of his seventh-favorite musical might just be forthcoming (again). Instead, though, he turned his gaze to Kaitlin and without even looking at me, he said, "You could have been killed, Bryn."

The way he was looking at Katie and the words he'd said reminded me that even though Devon was Dev, he was still a Were. He still had an innate desire to protect what he loved and to guard his females with his life. Without another word, he gently moved his hand up to Kaitlin's head and gently stroked her downy-soft hair. Katie blew another spit bubble, completely unaffected by the nearly rapturous awe on Devon's face. She was already used to getting that reaction from Weres, and when she was Katie and not the more tempestuous Kate, she reveled in it.

Just you wait, I told her silently. *It's all fun and games until they ground you until you're thirty.*

At this rate, Katie's teen years were going to be a million times worse than mine, which was a scary thought in and of itself. No one but Callum and Ali had ever cherished me as much as the entire pack seemed to relish doting on Ali's babies. Live twin births were rare in any pack, and Katie was only the second female born in Callum's territory in the past hundred years. Something about the chemistry involved in werewolf conception made it impossible for girl embryos to survive the first trimester, unless they were half of a set of twins and had a brother to mask their presence in the womb. I was a little vague on the medical details, but from day one, it had been clear that the twins were special—and that Kaitlin had a very, very long road ahead of her.

Which is why it was my duty as her older sister to ease the way, and that meant disabusing my pack of the notion that girls (in this case, me) needed protection. Unfortunately, Devon was the closest thing I had to an ally, and even he would have throttled me if he knew that I was working on a plan to see Chase.

Chase.

Just thinking his name knocked the breath out of me, yanking me back to that night in Callum's basement, as I'd watched Chase Shift, anchored in place by those three little words.

I got bit.

A grounding of epic proportions had not changed the fact that I had to see him again. On one level, I knew that it was a bad idea, knew that he was "unpredictable" and "not yet in control of his wolf" and that I would "find myself in a most unpleasant situation" if I "came within two miles of him." I even recognized that Chase had all of the instincts and none of the discipline of a full-grown Were, and I'd lived in this world long enough to realize what that could mean. Callum had impressed upon me again and again that Chase was a danger to me—and that I could be just as dangerous to him.

He survived an attack that would have killed a full-grown man, Bryn, Callum had said, his face absolutely serious, his jaw set, but he isn't out of the woods yet. If we can't teach him control, or if he were to hurt a human before he learns, the Senate would have him put down.

The Senate. As in the combined force of each and every pack alpha on the North American continent. When they met, the Senate tried for democracy, but I knew that when Callum said *they* would put Chase down, what he really meant was that Callum wouldn't use his power to stop them. He might even be the one to snap Chase's neck himself. Callum had few weak points, but I was one of them. Senate or no Senate, he'd kill Chase if Chase hurt me.

That was the only reason I'd managed to stay away this long. Up to this point, I hadn't even tried to break my house arrest, because the idea of something happening to Chase made me want to vomit up my internal organs.

He was, without exaggeration, the only person who could possibly understand what it meant to survive what I'd survived before my adoption into the pack. He was the only chance I might have to fill in the gaps in my memory of what had happened that night before Callum and his guard had saved me from the fate the rest of my family had met. I needed Chase, and I wanted to be near him, and some part of me couldn't shake the feeling that it was mutual, and that I would be the one to save him from himself.

Nobody knew what it was like to be torn between what it meant to be human and what it meant to be Pack better than me.

A high-pitched yip tore me away from my thoughts. Katie, ever the adventurous twin, had taken my mental absence as an excuse to Change, and now, instead of watching two babies, I had in my charge one human infant (to all appearances at least) and one rambunctious, wiggling-all-over, feet-too-big-for-her-body, whining-to-be-let-out-of-her-crib pup.

"I take it nap time ended just before my fortuitous arrival?" Devon asked.

Deciding not to mention that nap time had been briefly followed by story time, I nodded. Even in just a few weeks' time, Dev and I had started picking up on the differences between the twins: their idiosyncrasies, temperaments, and internal schedules. For example, without fail, when the twins woke up from their afternoon naps (or soon thereafter), Alex almost always needed to be changed, and Kaitlin, in contrast, needed to be Changed. She already loved her wolf form and would have spent all day as a puppy if Ali would let her.

Personally, I didn't blame her. In human form, the twins were far more advanced than most newborns, but as wolves, they were already more like toddlers than babies. Once she Changed, Kaitlin could walk (or run) on all fours and stick her damp little puppy nose into everything.

From her crib, Katie yipped again, clearly impatient. Little sis wanted what she wanted when she wanted it.

"Good girl," I crooned, scooping her up and setting her on the ground.

"Aren't you supposed to be encouraging her to stay in human form?" Devon asked me. For once, his accent and the set of his impeccably groomed eyebrows were completely his own.

"*Moi?*" I said innocently. "And how am I supposed to do that, hmmmm?" I threw Devon's own pet noise right back at him. "I seem to recall something about my being completely human and unable to control the forms of subordinate wolves."

Trying to force my will on Katie would have gone against everything I fought for on a day-to-day basis—not to mention the fact that opening up my pack-bond enough to force something on either of the babies would have left me vulnerable to having someone else's will forced on me. That was a can of worms that I wouldn't open unless and until I had to.

Kaitlin, blissed out in puppy form, sniffed at my shoes and then sneezed.

"And also," I added, "I like her better this way."

Katie nosed at the carpet and then gave it a good chew.

When it proved recalcitrant enough that she couldn't pull it up, she growled.

"Who's a fierce little girl?" I asked her. "Who's going to kick butt and take names and help her big sister get into all kinds of trouble someday?"

Devon snorted. "Sometimes, I think the term *bad influence* was invented specifically with you in mind."

Considering that he knew nothing of my deep-seated need to fight my way to Chase again, that was probably an understatement. Rather than say something that might give away my thoughts, I opted instead for a surefire distraction.

"Not it," I said.

Dev cocked one eyebrow at me, a trick that it had taken him years to absolutely perfect.

I gestured toward Alex, wrinkling my nose ever-so-slightly. "Not it." My nose wasn't anywhere near as sensitive as anyone else's in this room, but even I could sense something rotten in the state of Denmark.

Unlike me, Devon had an animal's tolerance of what I referred to as "diaper commodities." In addition to having superstrength, accelerated healing, awesome senses, and an extended life span, werewolves, I had recently discovered, were also pretty much immune to the horrors of poop.

Devon picked Alex up and sauntered over to the changing table. Alex made some vaguely unhappy sounds, but Devon banished them by singing what seemed to be a punk-rock version of "The Itsy Bitsy Spider." Halfway through, he segued disturbingly smoothly into a number from *Rent*.

The music soothed me as much as it did the baby, and I turned my attention back to Kaitlin, who now appeared to be very conscientiously stalking my shoelaces. I smiled half a smile at her puppy antics, wondering what it would be like to be able to join her, to shed my human skin and the confines that went with it and just live in the moment as a wolf. What would I look like with four legs and fur—would I be light-colored like Katie, or a darker timber, like Dev?

I wondered if I'd be velvety black with ice-blue eyes, like Chase.

And then, I was there again, in that moment, watching his muscles tense and pull and send electric pulses through my body as he Changed. With equally little warning, I was elsewhere and another set of blue eyes glistened yellow as a large, gray wolf with a white star on his forehead leapt for the throat of a human man whose features had long been replaced by Callum's in my memory.

Come out, come out, wherever you are, little one. No sense hiding from the Big Bad Wolf. I'll always find you in the end. . . .

A hand on my shoulder made me jump.

You've got to stop doing this to yourself, Callum told me with his eyes, but out loud, he didn't say anything to me at all—he just squeezed my shoulder once and turned his attention to Kaitlin.

"Ach, Katie-girl, what are we going to do with you?" His brown eyes soft and his mouth set with mock sternness, Callum scooped puppy-Kaitlin up in his arms. She lapped at his face and he bit back an indulgent smile. "If your mama sees you like this, she'll not be pleased," Callum said, before puffing out a breath that had my little sister sniffing like crazy.

Even without being a Were, I knew what Callum would smell like to her: safe and strong and home. He was the alpha, and in our world, that made him as close and important to Kaitlin as her own parents. As important as I hoped that I would be to her someday.

Eventually, Katie tired of the confines of Callum's loving hold, and she began to whine and wiggle, angling for the floor.

"I know exactly how you feel," I said under my breath.

Callum didn't bat an eye at my complaint. "You," he said to Katie, "need to change back to human form, and you"—he fixed his gaze on me—"my dearest, darling, and not-quite-grown little girl, need to trust that I have and have always had your best interest at heart."

My future mini-me and I were equally incapable of resisting Callum's orders. If Callum said to Change, Katie had to Change, whether she wanted to or not. For me, Callum had a different kind of pull. Years of shielding myself psychically from my bond with the pack may have dulled Callum's supernatural influence over me, but he still had a human one, and I couldn't deny the truth in his words. Callum didn't want to see me hurt, and he had no qualms about acting to ensure my safety. He cared for me.

Callum reached out and ran a hand over my hair, the same way Devon had stroked Katie's. Meanwhile, the little princess settled into her baby body enough to thrash her little baby arms, and she let out a shriek worthy of an opera-singing banshee. I had to give it to her, the kid knew how to scream with the best of them. I could almost hear the howl behind her unhappy cries.

Kaitlin—or Kate now, clearly—did not like being caged, not by orders she had to follow or by limbs that wouldn't do what they were told and skin that stubbornly refused to feel even the least bit like fur.

"Her Royal Highness is displeased," I told Callum, translating Baby Kate's wails into words.

He shifted her in his arms and crooned and patted her bottom, speaking to her in a mix of languages I didn't know and couldn't understand beyond the fact that once upon a time, he'd probably said the same thing to me. Kate resisted being consoled, but soon the wails died to whimpers and the whimpers to the occasional sniff. Expertly, Callum got her into a fresh set of clothing, since Shifting had destroyed her Baby Gap bodysuit and booties. Already, the twins were wearing clothes made for much older infants, and Katie, with her penchant for spending time in an animal form that aged much more quickly than she did, was growing even faster than Alex.

I'd never realized how fast Weres grew when they were this

small. We'd only had one or two live births since I'd been with the pack, and I'd never been up close and personal with those. I knew that Devon had always looked at least a couple of years older than I did, even though we were the same age, but the older we'd gotten, the more natural that difference had seemed. A six-week-old infant who looked like a six-month-old was much more bizarre than an almost-sixteen-year-old who could have passed for twenty. At this rate, Ali's babies wouldn't stay babies for long.

For some reason, that thought made me look at Callum again, and I wondered if he realized that inside, I was changing even quicker than the twins were on the surface. I think he knew, the way he always did. The heavy sadness of his eyes as he looked back at me glowed with something akin to premonition. In Callum's gaze, I saw the reflection of my own sudden self-awareness that I was barreling toward adulthood, and that the next words out of my mouth would be my first running leap in that direction.

A leap that even five minutes before, I would have fought tooth and nail against taking.

"I need to register a request for permissions," I said, using the officially sanctioned language for approaching the alpha as one of his pack. This time, I needed to do things right. Callum, his expression completely masked, set Katie back down in her crib and nodded to Devon, who left the room.

My stomach flip-flopped with the fear that he would say

no, but I made myself stand tall as he followed protocol to a T. "Your request has been registered. Define the terms of the permissions you seek."

I was suddenly very aware of the fact that I was in the room with Callum the alpha, not Callum who scolded me about algebra. My heart started beating faster and my mind went again and again to the beast inside him and from there to the things that a wolf as strong as Callum could do, if you tempted his ire and he were so inclined.

"I need to see Chase," I said, my voice quiet but firm. "I request permissions to have a supervised visit with him." About then, I started losing my rather tenuous grip on the control I was aiming for. "I'll do whatever you want, I'll follow every rule you set down, but I need to see him."

Callum looked at me and into me, his eyes steely and sharp. His poker face wavered for a split second when I voluntarily promised to follow the rules—a completely unprecedented event that would, in all likelihood, never happen again.

After roughly two and a half eternities, Callum finally nodded. "I'll grant your request, with conditions to be set down by the next full moon."

I hated the idea of waiting even a second longer than I had to, but I wasn't about to argue or look a gift wolf in the mouth.

"Thank you," I said, bowing my head, the way I'd seen other Weres do in the past. Callum stepped forward and pulled me into a hug, running his hand over my hair again, the same way he had when I was four and looking for solace after skinning my knees. At that moment, part of me didn't want to see Chase, because I didn't want to remember anything outside of the here and now, where I was safe and loved and part of something bigger than myself.

But another part of me knew that wasn't an option, not for me, because there were bad people in the world who did bad things, even to kids, and I wasn't the type who could stand by and pretend that there weren't.

If there was a Rabid in our territory, I needed to know.

CHAPTER SEVEN

THE NEXT FULL MOON WAS A SUNDAY IN MID-APRIL.
Even though it felt like I'd been waiting forever, when the big
day finally arrived, a thin cord of dread looped itself around
my neck like a hangman's noose. Growing up, I used to fake
the stomach flu on the day before a full moon. I'd retch and
moan and concoct secret mixtures of just the right texture
to throw into the toilet in order to make it sound as if I was
blowing chunky chunks. Ali was never fooled, but sometimes
she'd let me stay home from school anyway. I always thought
that it bothered her, too—watching them lose bits and pieces
of their human façades as the day wore on. I'd seen Weres
Shift hundreds of times, but it was different when the moon
was full. Even in their human forms, they exuded unnatural
energy, adrenaline and hormones battling inside their body to
determine whether they'd turn into a lover or a fighter. They
oscillated from one end of the spectrum to the other, snapping
and snuggling and just generally driving any humans in the
near vicinity crazy with the unpredictable bipolarity of it all.

For them, moonlust was a natural high.

For me, it was a hum. A high-pitched, disturbing hum of power, and the creepy, crawly feeling of someone watching me from the shadows. In fact, Callum had probably decided to make me wait until the full moon to hear the conditions of my visit with Chase because he'd hoped that I'd withdraw the request rather than venture directly into the belly of the beast on my least favorite day of the month.

But even with the noose tightening moment by moment and my stomach flipping itself inside out, I wasn't backing down. There would be no fake chunk-blowing today.

"Can I make you something for breakfast?" Ali pulled a kitchen chair away from the table, her subtle way of telling me that I would be eating breakfast whether I wanted to or not. I considered arguing, because my stomach was knotted up enough that the idea of jamming food down into it seemed ill-advised, but the expression on her face told me that she'd probably been up late with the twins, and that she'd waste no time putting the fear of God (and sleep-deprived mothers) into me if I balked.

"Cereal?" I asked.

Two minutes later, like magic, a bowl of cereal appeared in front of me on the table, and Ali took a seat, her eagle eyes watching as I swirled my spoon around in the bowl before taking a bite.

"Callum said you asked for permissions," Ali said, her casual tone belied by the fact that she'd known for weeks and hadn't mentioned it until now. "To see the new boy. Chase."

I shrugged and took another bite of cereal, my stomach clenching in protest.

"You've never played by their rules before," Ali continued on, leaning over and snagging a marshmallow out of my bowl and popping it into her mouth. "You don't ask permissions, you don't acknowledge dominance, and by the time you were in kindergarten, you'd clamped down on your end of the bond so hard that I thought you'd break it."

She made another grab for my cereal, and I pushed the bowl toward her. "Knock yourself out," I said. "I'm not hungry."

Ali pushed the bowl back my way and tilted her head toward mine. "Eat."

I ate. She watched, and finally, I realized that she was waiting for me to say something.

"I don't know what you want me to say."

"I want to understand why it is that the girl who has never met a rule she hasn't broken would voluntarily agree to give the *local patriarch* the power to set her limits in absolute stone."

"Patriarch? Puh-*lease*. It's Callum."

"Your words, not mine. And you're dodging the question."

The thing about asking permissions was that it required Callum to interact with me officially. I'd taken away his option of phrasing orders as requests, and I'd appealed to him as part of the pack, not as me. It had been a huge gamble, because if he'd turned down my permissions, and I'd gone to see Chase anyway, I'd have broken Pack Law and opened myself up to Pack Justice.

But Callum hadn't turned me down. He'd accepted my request, and whatever conditions he laid down today, I'd abide by them.

"I needed to see Chase, and this was the only way." I turned my head away from Ali but snuck a peek back at her out of the corner of my eye. "I couldn't have gotten anywhere near Callum's house on my own, not after last time. At least this way, I'll get to see him."

The visit would be supervised, and it would happen on Callum's terms, whatever those were, but by the time it was over, I'd have answers. Or possibly more questions.

I'd have *something*, and that was infinitely more than what I had now.

"Why this boy, Bryn? Why do you need to see someone who would just as soon eat your calf as look you in the eye? What could he possibly have to offer?"

Whoa. Ali was sounding suspiciously anti-Chase. Ali wasn't anti-anybody. I said as much out loud, and she shrugged.

"Casey doesn't trust him."

"Casey doesn't trust anyone," I replied. "He's paranoid like that. I mean, come on, he's a werewolf who installed a nanny cam in his kids' room." I pointed my spoon at Ali for emphasis. *"A nanny cam."*

Like anyone would hurt Kaitlin or Alex. The worst Casey had to worry about was me telling them things they wouldn't understand until they'd been verbal for at least a couple of years, and I knew (a) where the nanny cam was, and (b) how to disable it. Fatherhood had turned Ali's husband into a sub-urban soccer mom.

"Forget about Casey and promise me you'll be careful, Bryn. Callum isn't Callum when he's the alpha, and there isn't a single one of them that isn't dangerous."

This was our family she was talking about. Callum. Devon. Casey, Sora, and Lance. My age-mates. The twins.

"I'll be careful."

From the look Ali gave me, it was almost like she didn't believe me. How insulting.

"I can be careful," I said, somewhat disgruntled.

"Bryn, when you were six years old, you tried to bungee jump off a jungle gym by connecting the straps of your overalls to the bars with your shoelaces. Caution has never been your strong suit."

"And yet, I always seem to come out of it without a scratch." I smiled winningly. Ali gave me a look.

"You're a survivor," she allowed grudgingly. "And you've been lucky. That doesn't mean you have to press your luck."

I answered Ali's pointed stare with one of my own. "You worry too much."

"I'm your mother. It's my job."

From upstairs, a noise somewhere between an ambulance siren and a banshee's howl announced that at least one of the twins was awake for the day. For a few seconds, Ali remained seated, looking at me, and then she sighed. "Promise me you won't do anything stupid," she said as she stood up and took my empty cereal bowl over to the sink.

"I promise I won't do anything stupid," I said. "I know what I'm doing." Kind of. "I have to do this, Ali. And I'm trying really hard to do it right."

Ali nodded and, as she walked back by me to head upstairs, pressed a single kiss to my part. "You do what you have to do, Bryn. Just come home in one piece."

Those words were less than comforting, and for the briefest of instants, I considered giving up. Withdrawing my request. Falling prey to Ali's and Callum's best-laid plans to convince me that this wasn't the path down which I wanted to tread.

And then I cursed under my breath, stood up, and thanked my lucky stars that Ali didn't have super-hearing. The twins, on the other hand, had probably heard my epithet but wouldn't know what it meant or the fact that I wasn't allowed to say it. And hopefully, they wouldn't say it themselves, because it would make a poor entry in their baby books under "baby's first word."

"I'm going out, Ali. I'll be home...," I started to say that I'd be home soon, but in reality, I had no idea when I'd be home, because I had no idea what Callum would ask of me in return for the permission to see Chase. It could take all day, all night, all week…

And whatever it was, whatever he asked me for, I knew I'd say yes.

I met Callum halfway between Ali's house and his, in an area of the forest where the trees thinned out and the ground leveled off in a semicircle. Tonight, the Crescent would be filled, our pack's numbers spilling into the forest proper. Callum's house was where the pack conducted its human business. Here, they were wolves, and I avoided this patch of land the same way I eschewed dominance scuffles, disapproving lectures, and werewolves like Marcus who would rather see me dead than claimed by their alpha.

"Bryn." Callum greeted me with a single word and a slight smile. And then, without warning, he attacked. In a blur of motion, he was upon me, his leg snaking out to kick mine out from underneath me. Stunned, I moved entirely on instinct, twisting to angle my shoulder to the ground.

If you're going to fall, it's generally a good idea to control the way you do it. Using my own momentum, I rolled out of the fall, and instead of sprawling out on the forest floor, I bounced to my feet, my hands in loose fists, pulled tight to my chest. Automatically, I scanned the surrounding area for weapons. Holes into which I could trick my enemy into falling. Rocks that I might be able to crack a skull with. Sticks wide enough that I could channel Buffy and do the stake-through-the-heart routine, which was guaranteed to irritate a Were, but might also slow them down enough for me to get to higher ground.

Safer ground.

All of this happened in a fraction of a second—a half moment, or not even that. If I'd been thinking rationally, I would have realized that werewolf or not, official business or not, this was Callum, and I might have guessed that he was attacking me for a reason. I might have noticed that though he was going full speed, he'd pulled back to quarter strength, or less.

But I didn't.

When a human fights a Were, she doesn't have the luxury of thinking things through. You're stuck in slow motion against an enemy who moves so quickly that your eyes can barely follow the movement. You don't have time to think. You don't even have time to react. You have to anticipate. You have to be ready. You have to react to the things your opponent hasn't done yet, but will.

And you have to be lucky.

You've been very lucky, Bryn. That doesn't mean you have to press your luck.

Ali might have seen things differently, but at the moment,

I would have sworn that I wasn't pressing anything. It was pressing me.

Callum feinted left, but I was already moving the other direction and backward, and when his hand reached out to knock me to the ground, I'd already jumped. His blow threw me off center, but I managed to catch the limb I'd been aiming for anyway, and swung myself—slightly lopsided—up to stand on the branch.

As fast and strong and darn-near-invincible as they seem, werewolves aren't much for climbing trees. Their bones are denser than humans, and they don't have preternatural balance to go along with their stealth. Callum wasn't quite six feet tall, but he was muscular, male, and much heavier than I was, and there was no way this tree would support his weight.

For that matter, I had no guarantees that it would support mine for much longer, but beggars really couldn't be choosers. And mid-morning snacks can't afford to be finicky about the methods with which they attempt to avoid being eaten.

"You're getting faster," Callum said, "but you need to be more aware of your surroundings." And with those words, he shot into another blur of motion, running up onto a nearby stone and catapulting himself off it.

Incoming werewolf, zeroing in on me like a missile. Not a good thing. Not a good thing at—

"*Ooomph.*" Callum tackled me off my perch. I braced myself for contact with the ground, but at the last second, he twisted, putting his body in between mine and the ground, cushioning my fall.

Thankful for the reprieve, I nonetheless elbowed him in the gut, somersaulted forward and out of his grasp, and threw a rock at his head before I even realized I'd armed myself.

He caught the rock and smiled. "Good girl."

The tension melted off his body, and his posture changed utterly, a signal meant to tell me that this portion of our little meet and greet was over.

"Forgive me if I'm skeptical," I said, and like magic, I had more rocks in each of my hands.

"The only way I wouldn't forgive you is if you weren't," he said, and moving with a speed that fell more into the realm of impressively human than typically Were, he managed to disarm me completely, and he chucked me under the chin.

"You're a strong, smart girl, Bryn, but it's not enough. You've been slacking on your training."

If by "slacking," he meant "up at dawn every day for my entire life going through katas and self-defense moves and running like I'm prepping for a triathalon."

"If you want to see the boy, you'll have to do better."

And there it was: the first condition. I wondered if Callum's attack had been a test, if there was anything I could have done that might have convinced him that I was ready to see Chase now, or if he was just using my unusual willingness to comply with his wishes as an excuse to achieve a cog in some master plan. If the next condition involved me acing algebra, I was going to be very suspicious.

"I'll do whatever I need to do." I gave Callum a look that I hoped conveyed "you know I mean it," with shades of "don't toy with me."

"You'll see Chase once you've convinced me that you can defend yourself from him should things get out of hand. Until then, I'll expect you to double your normal training regimen, and I want you sparring with partners of my choice on a regular basis."

The idea of fighting someone who wasn't Callum didn't sit well with me. I would have been lying if I said that I'd never fought anyone else—I had, on occasion, handed touchy, grabby humans their butts on a variety of platters, but I was too smart to go around fighting Weres.

Besides Callum, there were only a few that I'd tangled with physically, even as practice, and I tried not to think about what it would be like fighting someone who I trusted less than Callum.

"Consider it done," I said out loud. "What else?"

We weren't exactly using the formal language of permissions and conditions, but we were both on edge—Callum because sparring under the influence of moonlust was no walk in the park, and me because being sparred with by a werewolf under the influence of moonlust sent a cold chill down the length of my spine.

Come out, come out, wherever you are. . . .

"In addition to increasing your training regimen, I have four conditions for the permissions you seek." Callum transitioned to alpha-speak, and I could feel the formality of it building a barrier between us.

"I'm prepared to hear your conditions, Alpha."

My words, every bit as formal as his, solidified the wall that held us apart, and if this hadn't been so important to me, that would have forced me to crumble. Losing Callum, even for a second, was worse than any condition he could possibly lay down.

Or at least, that's what I thought at the time.

"Once I deem you ready for your visitation or visitations—the number and times of which will be set in accordance with me—I'll select three members of the pack to accompany you and serve as chaperones."

Chaperones. . .or bodyguards? It was so like Callum to insist that I kill myself preparing for defensive maneuvers that he had no intention of ever allowing me to make.

"You will not see Chase with fewer than three members of the pack present, and during the course of your visitation, you will yield to their dominance on all matters."

Dominance. I hated the word. I hated everything it represented, and in that moment, I hated Callum for forcing it on me. The idea of letting three random Weres tell me what to do, of submitting to them in all things without an argument, made me consider blowing real chunky chunks right there on the spot.

"You're selecting the members of the pack to whom I have to submit," I said, restating his words as my own.

Callum didn't reply to the question in my voice, or say anything to assuage my reluctance. Instead, he just stood there, looking at me from the other side of that invisible wall.

"I agree to this condition, Alpha," I said, forcing the words out of my mouth.

"My next condition . . . ," Callum started to say, and then he looked at me, for real. "You're not going to like this one, Bryn-girl."

Uh-oh. Being Bryn-girl was a magnitude worse than being Bronwyn. When I was Bronwyn, I was in trouble, but I was only Bryn-girl when Callum was cushioning an otherwise deadly blow. The last time he'd called me that, someone in the pack had accidentally eaten an injured rabbit I'd nursed back to health.

I waited for Callum to elaborate, refusing to let him know the effect his words had on me.

"For the duration of the permissions," Callum said—and I took that to mean from the moment I started in on the extra training until my last visit with Chase was complete—"you'll acknowledge the pack. The bond," he clarified.

My adoption into the pack—though Callum had taken steps to make it legal in the human world—was more than just words on a sheet of paper. I smelled like Pack. I lived like Pack.

And, if I had let myself, I would have *felt* like Pack. I would have been bonded to them the way they were bonded to each other—supernaturally, psychically, instinctually.

I cursed. Callum waited.

He thought I'd back out. He couldn't imagine that seeing Chase meant enough to me that I'd give up being myself—and only myself—for any amount of time. But what Callum didn't understand was that I wasn't interested in seeing Chase the boy, or even Chase the werewolf. I needed to see Chase the hunted. And I needed that because without it, I was already incomplete.

I needed my memories back. I needed to know what it was like for Chase, so I could know what it had it been like for me, and I needed to know if there was a Rabid in our territory, because if there was, the only way I'd ever really be myself again was to know that he was dead and that he'd paid for doing to Chase what someone had done to my entire family.

Chase had survived. My parents hadn't.

"I agree to this condition, Alpha."

Callum visibly winced. If this had been any other power struggle between us, I might have felt victorious.

"Fine." Callum hadn't expected things to go this far. Or maybe he had, but he'd hoped very much that they wouldn't.

"My penultimate condition is that, in service of making this interaction official, you accept my conditions in front of the pack, at our moonlight congregation tonight—"

"I accept—"

"I haven't finished yet, Bryn. You have to stay for the Shift. You have to run with the pack."

Humans didn't run with the pack.

"You do realize that request is made of crazy, right?" I couldn't help shedding the formal dialogue for this one. Weres maintained their faculties when they Shifted. Most of the time.

"I'll have the pack in control, Bryn, but you can't see the boy if you're afraid of him. I've been working with him nearly every day, and his control is progressing rapidly, but he's too young to deal with the smell of your fear. You'll run with the pack tonight, and you'll continue to do so until the bond is strong enough that there's no room for your fear."

I'd heard of psychiatrists treating phobias by making people do things like put their hands into a pit of snakes, but this was just ridiculous.

"The bond protects you, Bryn. Once you open it, none of the others will see you as human. You're Pack and you'll run as Pack." He smiled, his lips quirking upward just the tiniest bit. "I think you'll like it, once you get past wanting to kill me for it."

"What's the final condition?" I wasn't agreeing to this one until I knew what he'd force on me next. For all I knew, he'd demand I cut off my foot, because if I couldn't maintain my composure as one-legged human among four-footed Weres, I couldn't possibly talk to one juvenile werewolf locked in a steel cage.

Callum said, "I'll tell you the final condition tonight."

I growled at him, taking some satisfaction out of the way the inhuman snarl felt working its way from my throat to my lips.

"Most pack members wouldn't have gotten forewarning on any of the conditions," Callum said, and then he reached out and tucked a strand of hair behind my ear. That simple motion was enough to completely pulverize the barrier between us.

"You're doing this to me on purpose," I said. "You're trying to torture me because you're still mad that I managed to ditch my bodyguards, break into your house, and uncover your secret basement boy."

"I'm doing this," he corrected, "because you're mine."

His.

Werewolves. They're all about possession. Sometimes, I thought that parents—even human ones—were the exact same way. Your behavior reflects upon *them*. They want the best for you, because you're *theirs*. Things that are okay for other people's kids are out of the question for you, and no matter how old you grow, or how far you run, you can't change where you came from.

"You're doing this because you suck."

Callum smiled charmingly, looking more like a boy than a thousand-year-old Were. "So I've been told, Bryn. So I've been told."

CHAPTER EIGHT

By nightfall, there were more Weres at the Crescent than there were students at my high school—an effect of living in a small town at the heart of a major werewolf territory. I knew every person there by name, though some had driven in from out of town, a commute they made, like clockwork, once every twenty-nine days. Callum's territory extended from Kansas up to Montana and though the majority of Weres were drawn to be close to their alpha, a few of Callum's wolves maintained peripheral status, living at the edges of our territory, away from Ark Valley and the rest of the pack. Of the peripherals, only two were missing from the Crescent, and their monthly absence persisted only so long as Callum allowed it.

Personally, I wished Alpha Dearest had required their presence tonight. Next to Devon, I had only one friend in our pack. Her name was Lake, she was my age, and she and her dad had spent summers in Ark Valley when the two of us were younger. Lake was one of our pack's only female werewolves and the most outspoken person I'd ever met. I couldn't help wishing that she and her dad had driven in from the edge of our territory for tonight's meeting. Purebred werewolf or not, Dev wasn't quite enough to counterbalance the members of our furry family who didn't exactly have warm, fuzzy feelings for the human girl standing in our midst.

"There's no shame in turning tail and getting the Helen Hunt out of here," Devon told me. "In fact, I would quite recommend it."

Devon being Devon should have calmed my nerves, but I couldn't manage so much as a smile. From the other side of the crowd, Callum began making his way toward me, and I could feel the sand slipping through the hourglass, each grain a punch to my stomach and a reminder that my time was running out.

Without a word, Callum placed his hand on the back of my neck, and though it was meant as a calming gesture, physical contact with the alpha had the hairs on my arms doing the wave, one after another.

To a normal girl, the energy in this place would have felt like an excess of adrenaline—something similar to the air in a locker room before a big game, or a math class in the moments leading up to an exam. But I knew better. This wasn't adrenaline. This was preternatural. It was ungodly.

It was pure, undiluted animalistic energy, and the moment I opened the bond to the pack and joined their group mindset, it wouldn't be an alien feeling on my skin, static in my arm hairs.

It would be inside of me, and I would be as lost to it as they were.

Callum's grip on the back of my neck tightened just a bit, and I wondered if my face had given my thoughts away so clearly. In another few minutes, they'd be clear enough to everyone, not in words, but in *feel*, as the bond let my emotions bleed onto them and into theirs.

Soon, Callum and I were standing at the center of the Crescent, Weres all around us. Sora, Casey, and Lance were the closest to me, with Marcus near the back, probably at Callum's orders. I couldn't take my eyes off him.

"Hello, brothers."

If Sora objected to the fact that Callum's greeting wasn't gender neutral, she didn't show it. I, for one, was feeling a little disenfranchised—not to mention outnumbered. There were easily a hundred of us in this clearing, and sleek, self-possessed Sora and I were the only females.

I was the only human.

One werewolf was dangerous. An entire pack was an immovable force, an unbeatable army.

I was outnumbered, unarmed, weak, and screwed. In that order.

"Hello." The pack murmured the word back to Callum in unison, but I could barely parse the syllables into their meaning. There was a sort of melody to them, an inhuman, musical tone that made it sound more like a hum of energy than any kind of salutation.

"One in our number has requested our counsel," Callum said. "Bronwyn, daughter of Ali, our ears are yours."

Though he followed protocol to a T, his words were unlike any that this circle had heard before. First there was the fact that I was a daughter, and the fact that my familial allegiance was given by my mother's name, and then there was the fact that everyone here knew that Ali hadn't given birth to me, that I was an orphan.

That I hadn't always been one of them.

The familiar sound of a spit bubble popping had me looking over my left shoulder, toward Callum's guard, and sure enough, I noticed that Casey wasn't the only member of my household here. The twins were present and accounted for: two babies among scores of men, a burly Were who I recognized as one of Casey's coworkers gently cradling one in each arm.

Well, at least I wasn't completely on my own. Though after a moment's reflection, I wasn't sure if that was a comfort or not. My allies in this circle consisted of a fashion-conscious teenage boy who believed in the holy power of the movie musical and two infants wearing shirts with little yellow and blue duckies on them.

An army, we were not.

Bryn. I felt a brush at the edge of my subconscious—not a word, but a gentle reminder—pushing against my hard-won psychic shields.

Right. Their ears were mine. I was supposed to be talking.

"I, Bronwyn, daughter of Ali, request the pack's permission to speak with Chase, the Survivor."

Since Chase didn't have familial ties, the title seemed apt, and I thought I saw a fleck of understanding in Callum's gaze, something that told me that he might have understood more than I'd given him credit for about my fascination with a boy who could kill me as easily as tell me the truth.

"As alpha of the Stone River Pack, I speak on behalf of my brothers in saying that I grant you these permissions, under the conditions as follow."

I was prepared to hear this part, and I found myself strangely grateful that I was Callum's and that he'd broken protocol enough to give me forewarning. I gave the requisite answers as he told me again about the way I would be expected to submit to those who accompanied me on my meetings, open my bond to the pack until this business was concluded, and run with them tonight.

And then Callum told me the last requirement. "In exchange for this favor, you will excuse yourself from any meetings involving the North American Senate for the next five months."

This was. . .unexpected. All of Callum's other conditions

involved me becoming more a part of the pack, and being a good little pack daughter, but this one pushed me away. The Senate didn't convene on a regular basis, and frankly, I had no desire to be there when they did. My bond with Callum connected me to his pack, and it made me smell like Stone River—and Callum—to other Weres, but I wasn't connected to any of the other alphas on the Senate. I didn't feel safe around them, and the artifice of bureaucracy surrounding the Senate did nothing to conceal the amount of testosterone pushing each of the alphas to test his dominance against the others. The eight of them had a gentlemen's agreement not to challenge each other, but I didn't relish being in a room with men nearly as strong as Callum who weren't bound by his word to keep me safe.

"I agree to this condition, Alpha," I said.

Was that relief on Callum's face? My stomach twisted sharply as his features settled back into an unreadable mask, and I had a single second to wonder if he knew something that I didn't.

Callum knew better than to leave me wondering long. His voice boomed out around me, calm and cool, saturated with power caged, and my thoughts stilled until all I saw was Callum, and all I heard were his words.

"Our conditions have been set and agreed to. The agreement is sealed." Callum took a step toward me and dug his fingernails slightly into my bare shoulder blade—not enough to draw blood, because this time, the motion was for show and carried symbolic but not literal power. In response, I bowed my head and then reached forward, my nails digging into his flesh, putting my seal on the agreement.

Bryn.

There it was again, the push at the outside of my psyche, and I realized that this time, the reminder was less about prodding me to pay attention and more of a gentle push against my defenses.

The defenses that I'd just agreed to let down.

I bit my bottom lip and nodded, and as I closed my eyes and walked myself backward through everything I'd done over the years to close myself off from them, to protect myself, to become my own person, a sob got caught in my throat. Callum might as well have ordered me to take off my clothes and let these men watch the strip show. I would be humiliated, laid bare, and vulnerable. Naked in every way that mattered.

Bryn. The echo was calming this time, but closer—under my skin instead of on top of it—and I shuddered, but pushed forward.

I took the things that were most *me*, the secrets I guarded most dearly, the dreams I'd see die before I revealed them, and I folded them into a tiny ball, tucking them away in my heart, in a place that went deeper than words or fears or emotions. I pictured that ball—a tiny sphere of light—and I promised myself that it would still be intact when I came back to retrieve it, that I'd still be me when all was said and done. If Callum saw what I was doing, his amber eyes gave no hint of that knowledge, and I heard his voice in my head again.

Bryn.

Giving in to its hypnotic call, I went back in the maze of my mind as far as I could remember, to the last time I'd stood before this Crescent, four years old and following Callum's edict to look at him, only at him, as he Marked me as his own. Ali had stood beside me then, all of twenty-one, and I wondered if she'd felt the way that I felt now. If she'd let them violate her for my sake.

And then I raised my eyes to Callum's, just as I had then, and I told him, with every part of myself, that I was his. That I was Pack. And that, for the first time since I'd learned to close myself off from the overwhelming will of the pack, I was really theirs, too.

Communal awareness came at me from all sides, like a wave knocking me off my feet and down into the undertow. My first instinct was to fight it, to run, to slam my mental walls back up ten times stronger than they'd been before, but they pulled at me, my pack-mates—their minds, thoughts, feelings, and emotions. Their togetherness. Their *wolves*. And even though I didn't have another creature inside of me to respond to theirs, my body seemed completely unaware of this fact. I needed to be with them. Closer to them. Among them.

I needed to be Pack.

On some level, I knew that this was the hardest thing, the worst thing about letting them in—I had no guarantee that I'd ever be able to get rid of them, because I had no guarantee that I would ever want to. The life I'd been living was no less than sensory deprivation.

Callum's hand was on my neck again, and I leaned into it.

Safety. Warmth. Alpha, my pack-sense told me.

Callum. Here. Mine. And then, one by one, the others came forward, placing a hand on me, touching me softly. It should have been creepy. I should have been giving lectures about my bubble and the fact that I despised having anyone stand inside it, but I wasn't.

Instead, all I could think was that for the first time in for-ever, Callum wasn't the only person who felt safe. He wasn't the only one I could trust to protect me, to save me, to let me be me, even when it caused him no small amount of strife.

This was my family. Even the ones I didn't like, even the ones who'd wanted me dead for as long as they'd known me—they were mine the same way Katie and Alex were. We were part of each other, and even if there was no love between us, there was something.

Pack.

I felt the change before I saw it—electrifying on my skin's surface, but world-changing inside of it. I could feel myself changing—not into a wolf but into the person I was in the pack. A daughter. A sister. A force of nature.

Their strength flowed through me. I couldn't force my human limbs to harness the power of their wolves, but I felt it, and for the first time in forever, it didn't scare me.

Callum arched his back, and with that single motion, his human form melted away, the transition from man to wolf as seamless as water going from a cup to a puddle on the floor. His fur was gray and tawny-tipped, and he stretched once, pushing his front paws into the ground and raising his tail, before straightening to his full height.

As a man, Callum was built more like a cowboy than a linebacker, threatening only if you knew how much power lay under his skin, but in animal form, his weight rearranged itself into something that took your breath away. No one, under any circumstances, would have mistaken Callum for a natural wolf. He was enormous, and with a wolfy smile on his face, he looked directly at me.

"*Arrrooooooooooo!*"

That sound—which I classified as halfway in between a howl and a Justin Timberlake solo—had me whirling around. Devon! He was larger than a normal Were, nearly Callum's size and not even full-grown. There was a Herculean grace to his movements, a lightness to his four-legged step.

My Devon.

He jumped up and knocked me gently over, and a second later, the two of us were rolling around on the ground, the way we had when we were still really little. He took care with his claws and teeth, and I dug my fingers into his belly, tickling and scratching, and when he buried his nose in my hair and *woofed* slightly, breathing in and out next to my ear, I smiled.

And then Kaitlin was there, barreling toward me at full speed. She dodged through the older wolves, and they carefully stepped aside, each and every gaze on her, their heads tilting to the sides with wolfish reverence.

Kaitlin dove headfirst into our wrestling match, and I wrapped my arms around her, lifting her puppy body up into the air and then bringing her down and rubbing my nose into her fur. She lapped at my face, and her tail beat viciously back and forth, so fast that her entire body was vibrating.

Girl! She seemed to say. *Sister! Pack! Bryn!*

The combination of these things seemed to be more than she could bear, and I let her prance up and down my body, until she lost her balance and rolled head-over-tail to the ground. The other wolves went deadly still beside me, but Katie bounced straight back up and with a dignified yip, brought Alexander down upon me as well. Struggling to keep up with his sister, he bounded over and immediately latched his teeth onto my pants leg and started tugging.

Katie was a wrestler, but Alex—I knew instinctively—wanted to run.

I wanted to run.

But I couldn't. Not yet. *Alpha. Alpha. Alpha,* my pack-sense was telling me, and in unison, Katie, Alex, Dev, and I turned to

Callum, who threw back his head and howled, a long, joyous noise that the others echoed.

That *I* echoed in my high, clear human voice.

And then we ran. Furry bodies all around me, bumping into me, weaving in and out of my legs, and I just jumped over them. I cried out to them. I sang and screamed and tried to outrun them, and even though I stood about as good a chance as one of the babies, they let me. Gray and gold and brown and white and black and every shade in between: the pack was a blur of colors, and even though I couldn't help but pick up on their awareness of my pale, patchy, furless skin, it didn't matter. Not to me and not to them.

Any one of them—save perhaps for the twins—could have killed me in a heartbeat. They could have broken my bones, snapped my neck, opened my jugular. They could have eaten me, destroyed me, torn apart my remains.

But they didn't. And the call of my connection to them was so strong that I didn't even think about the other wolves I'd seen in my lifetime: men Shifting into monsters, jaws snapping at human throats.

Instead, I thought of the wind in my face and the smell and taste of the forest, the feel of it under my brothers' paws.

The pack was safe.

The pack was together.

The pack was *mine*.

CHAPTER NINE

THE NEXT DAY, I WOKE UP AN HOUR BEFORE MY alarm went off with a cramp in my calf, leaves in my hair, and a strange substance that I desperately hoped was dirt under my fingernails. It took me a moment to remember, and then the night before came back to me like a dream. I'd felt powerful. Invincible. Safe.

And totally and completely unlike myself.

It was scary how easy it was to get lost to the pack-mentality. How right it felt to belong, despite the fact that belonging wasn't something I'd ever needed before. At school, I didn't really mind the way the other girls turned up their noses at me. I'd never really bothered much more with the fact that most of the pack tended to view me as Other, too. Unless they sensed an outside threat, I was Callum's pet and Devon's friend, not one of them, and that was fine.

But last night, I'd been something different. And even now, lying in my bed in Ali's house, I could feel them—each and every member of the pack: Devon curled at the bottom of his bed; Marcus prowling through his house with clenched fists and fist-shaped holes in his walls; Katie and Alex still asleep. Casey was...

Casey was in bed with Ali. And that was where I drew the line. Because, *eww.*

This whole pack-bond thing was kind of out of control. Especially if I followed the logic of my current situation to completion, because that told me that as much as I was in their heads, they were in mine.

Stupid werewolves.

Still in bed, Bryn?

Callum's voice was in my head, not surprising given the fact that he'd practically been there before I'd opened up to the others.

Are you reading my mind? I asked him point-blank, ignoring his question and the fact that I was probably due to start training any minute.

Your thoughts are your own, m'dear. Your emotions, physical movements, location, and instincts are another matter.

My *instinct* was to tell him that he blew. Trusting that he'd pick up on that little psychic tidbit, I rolled out of bed and stumbled to my closet, unsteady and wobbly on my feet. I felt like I'd run a marathon. Through a vat of cement. With weights on my legs.

The night before, I'd been too drunk on power to listen to

any objections my body might have had about the pace I'd kept. Today, however, each and every complaint was registering loud and clear.

We'll start with a morning run, I think. You've a bit of time before the school day starts.

I was sure that it wasn't just my imagination. There was some self-satisfied amusement in Callum's mind-voice. Didn't he realize it was Monday morning and that being up at this hour was almost certainly a crime against God and man? I wasn't sure if I'd be able to project my thoughts back to him in words—for all I knew, that might be an alpha-only skill, but I thought I'd give it a try.

Sadist.

His response came to me in colors and feelings, rather than words, but I got the message clear enough. He was laughing at me. Chuckling, in a fond kind of way.

I pushed at him—not to close off the bond but to shove him out of my head, or as far to the corners of it as he would go. He stayed for a moment, his presence taking over so much of my mind that I couldn't move. After making his point, he retreated.

Stupid werewolves and their stupid dominance maneuvers. It was bad enough dealing with them every day when it came to external conflict. The last thing I needed was people marking territory *inside* my head.

Without even thinking about it, I sent Callum an image of

a dog hiking his leg at a fire hydrant. And then one of a rebel flag from the Revolutionary War.

Callum didn't respond in my head, but I knew he'd gotten the message, because he met me at the front door, and the first thing he said, with a single arch of his eyebrow, was, "Don't tread on you?"

"More like 'don't metaphorically pee on my brainwaves,' but it's the same sentiment, really."

"Vulgarity does not become you, Bryn."

"Are you going to lecture, or are we going to run?"

He sighed, and I didn't need a bond with the pack to see that he was thinking that I had always, always been a difficult child. And then, just in case that point wasn't clear, he verbalized it. "You have always, always been a difficult child."

I smiled sweetly. "I try."

He jerked his head to the side and I nodded, and together, the two of us took off jogging. We followed the path for about a half mile, and then Callum veered off into the woods and jacked up his pace. I worked to keep up with him, even once we'd finished a five-mile loop and he started us back through again.

"Not bad for an old man," I told him, even though I was winded and knew he could continue on like this indefinitely.

"Brat," he returned, his tone completely conversational.

It had been a long time since the two of us had spent time

like this: one on one, without him swooping in to lecture me about something or make some grand declaration about my life and future in his territory. When I was really little, we'd done this a lot more. He'd taught me to fight. Every day, we went running, and when I'd wipe out at the end, he'd carried me on his back. And then I got older, and the times like this one had been fewer and further between. He'd taken a step back. Left me to Ali. Spent most of his time on pack business that I had no part in.

I didn't want to admit that it hurt that I'd had to open up the bond to bring that Callum back to me. Was this even real? If he spent time with me because we were more connected now, or because of the conditions he'd set down, did it mean anything? Or was I just another chore, the alpha doing his duty by the pack, bratty little human girl and all?

"I can finish this up on my own," I told him. "I've been doing my own training for years."

"And you've been slacking. You only push yourself so far, Bryn."

I got a feeling that he wasn't talking just about physical training. With the semester more than halfway done, I still had a B-plus in algebra when it wouldn't have taken much effort on my part to get an A. I was close to Devon but didn't bother with any of my other age-mates. If the "Tree of Life" wanted to look like a fire hydrant, I was willing to revisit the issue.

"If you start talking about college and life choices, I'm out of here," I promised him. "And if you have something else to do and somewhere else to be, don't let me keep you from it."

I got a vibe from him then—a twinge in my pack-sense that felt like being pricked with a lukewarm needle.

"I'm here and you'll deal with me, Bronwyn."

I took his words as an indication that a warm pinprick meant that he was feeling rather testy.

"Fine," I said.

"Fine."

As Calllum and I fell into silence, the voices at the edge of my mind—whirring, whispering ghosts of a something—made themselves heard more clearly. The constant barrage of emotions, filtered through the bond and blurred like words shouted from the bottom of a swimming pool, exhausted me as much as the paces that Herr Callum was jollily putting me through.

Focus, I told myself. *Focus on the here and the now. Focus on why you're doing this.*

I focused on Chase.

It was funny. I'd only seen him once, and I couldn't even picture his human face with any kind of certainty, but his wolf form and his voice were as clear in my memory as they would have been if I'd seen and heard them the second before.

I got bit.

I got bit.

I got bit.

That was why I was doing this. I needed to know what had happened to Chase, and I needed to know what was being done about it.

I opened my mouth to ask Callum point-blank if there was a Rabid in his territory—where Chase had been attacked and who they thought had attacked him, but just as I was about to let loose with the inquisition, a third set of tracks joined ours.

Lance.

Through the bond, he felt solid and heavy, and there was the faintest whiff of vanilla and cedar in his scent.

"Hey, Lance," I said.

Lance, of course, said nothing.

"Sorry about ditching you a couple of months ago," I said, intent on getting a response out of him.

Nothing. *Nada.* He just kept pace with me and Callum, without ever saying a word. The air between us felt almost as empty, but there was just a hint of something. It was either disapproval or amusement. Or possibly both.

Look at Lance, with actual emotions, I thought. And then it occurred to me that there was some chance he could hear me.

Can Lance hear my thoughts? I asked Callum silently.

He can feel them, same as I can, but fainter. Unless you want him to hear you. Most pups have trouble speaking mind-to-mind in human form, but you seem to be rather proficient. I attribute it to your stubborn nature.

"And stubbornness is my folly," I said out loud, snickering at my own joke, which Callum and Lance clearly did not get.

After a small eternity, in which I made a few more comments that made equally little sense to my companions and in which Callum chided me on my form not once, not twice, but three times—*you're slipping, Bronwyn Alessia. Stay on the balls of your feet*—Lance, Callum, and I came to a halt at the Crescent.

I bent over, hands on my knees, breathing hard. Maybe I was out of shape. Or maybe twelve miles was an inhuman (not to mention *inhumane*) distance to force someone to run. Either way, I wasn't in the best shape for a fight. Not that Callum or Lance paid much attention to my obvious pain.

"Now," Callum said, and Lance came at me, a wall of muscle and bulk. He wasn't as graceful as Callum, but he was lighter on his feet than a man his size had any right to be, and unlike me, he hadn't just abused both of his lungs in the cruelest of fashions.

Rather than move in the direction of his blow, diffusing its effectiveness, I followed my instincts and dropped to the ground entirely, his ham-shaped first missing me by a hair-breadth.

In a fight, gravity can either be your best friend or your worst enemy. With the odds stacked against me, I had to play nice with the elements. Unfortunately, dropping to the ground put me in a sensitive position, and as Lance bent toward me—probably dead set on picking me up and throwing me like a discus—my weight wasn't balanced enough across my body to give me any kind of flexibility in how to respond. From my crouched position, I could only go forward. And going forward meant going into Lance, which was something like driving a pickup into a steel wall.

So instead, I went through Lance. More specifically, I dove in between his legs. It would have been a beautiful move, too, but at the last second, I felt his feet snap together, snaring mine and leaving me entirely vulnerable.

"Bryn, to your feet. Lance, again."

At Callum's commands, Lance released me, and without a moment's pause, he came for me again, exactly the same as he had the first time. The predictability of his move gave me a fraction longer to think about my response, but thinking at all was a mistake, and he caught me in the shoulder.

Use the bond, Callum told me. *Feel his movements before they get there. Don't think. Just do.*

"Again," he said out loud.

This time, I managed to dodge Lance's fist, and when he brought his other leg back around mine, I jumped and then caught the fist he sent flying toward my face, intent on turning the momentum against him. Which would have worked beautifully if I'd been a Were. But I wasn't, and instead, the effort of stopping his fist put some major pain on my palm.

Don't let the bond convince you that you're one of us, Bryn. You're human, no matter how like a Were you feel.

"Again."

Time after time, Lance threw blows at me, and I dodged them, playing to my strengths. I was fast, I was light, and I wasn't afraid of playing dirty. I was small and flexible and—as Lance muttered at one point—completely insane. The bond let me predict his movements, but it did little for letting him track mine, because even *I* didn't know what I was going to do next.

"Again."

I was really beginning to hate that word. At this rate, I wouldn't even get to shower before my first class. Impatient, I decided not to wait for Lance to come to me this time. I broke the first rule of Fighting with Werewolves 101. I attacked. And then, my common sense came back to me, and in the microsecond it took Lance to recover from an unexpected blow to a very sensitive region, I turned tail and ran, and I was up a tree before he managed to get ahold of me again.

"Good," Callum said. I wonder if he noticed that I'd picked a taller tree this time. No way was Lance getting me off this branch with a well-aimed tackle. I waited for Callum to instruct us to begin again, but the word never came, and Lance looked up at me and smiled—or came as close to smiling as he ever did.

Then he nodded to Callum—a solemn half bow—and ran back off into the forest.

Callum looked up at me. "You'd best be getting to school. We'll run again tonight," he said. "And tomorrow, you'll fight Sora."

"When can I see Chase?" I asked.

"When you're ready."

"When will I be ready?"

"That remains to be seen."

"Do the words *straight answer* mean nothing to you?"

"Enough," Callum said, in his "This is the Final Word" voice of authority. I half-expected the bond between us to shake with the alpha-ness of it all, but it didn't. It was almost as if this tone—which I associated with Callum putting his foot down in the most intractable way possible—had nothing to do with Callum being the leader of our pack, and everything to do with him being Callum and me being me.

"There was nothing in my permissions about not asking questions," I told him, feeling rather secure in my perch.

"And there was nothing in your request about ending your grounding," Callum countered.

I narrowed my eyes. "That's Ali's decision, not yours."

Callum didn't reply, and it occurred to me that the expression on Ali's face when she'd reamed me out about my illegal adventure into Callum's basement had looked disturbingly similar to the look on the alpha's face now.

Okay, so maybe it had been a joint decision. And maybe

the conditions of my permissions weren't the only card that Callum had in his deck to hold over my head.

"Breakfast?" I asked, half as a peace offering and half to see if he'd take me up on the offer, or if he'd have other, more pressing pack business to deal with. "I could swing time for a Pop Tart if I skip out on my shower."

A human probably would have found the notion disgusting, but Callum wasn't human, and Weres didn't much care about sweat. "You'd have more time to shower if you could knock yourself down from that seven-minute mile." Callum's lips turned up in a subtle, lupine smile and then he inclined his head slightly, accepting my invitation for breakfast. I let myself wonder, just for a second, if he was here for more than just training me. If I wasn't the only one who remembered how much time the two of us had spent together when I was little.

"Are you coming, or do you intend to spend the entire day in a tree?"

The corners of his lips quirked upward, and I answered his question and his amusement by diving out of the tree, straight into his body, taking us both down to the ground.

Bit.

Bit.

I got bit.

I reminded myself that this was what my training was about. It wasn't about Callum and me. It wasn't about the pack—there, still, in the corners of my mind. It was about

Chase. Chase and the Rabid, questions and answers. That was what mattered.

"You're getting slow," I told Callum.

He threw me back to my feet and was on his own an instant later, but his words belied the ease of that motion. "And you, little one, are getting big."

CHAPTER TEN

————◦————

THEY SAY NOT TO BRING A KNIFE TO A GUNFIGHT. Extend the logic, and it's probably not much of a stretch to say that you shouldn't be relying on basic self-defense and martial-arts moves in an altercation with a werewolf. You should be bringing knives. And guns. And as much silver as you can physically carry.

Not all of the Weres I knew were allergic to silver—Devon wasn't—but the old myths about silver bullets weren't completely off base, either. Bullets had the potential to cause major problems, because accelerated healing increased the likelihood of a werewolf healing around a bullet, and having a piece of metal firmly embedded in one's innards had a way of leading to malfunctions. Beyond that, a good 80 to 90 percent of Weres *were* allergic to silver, the same way that most humans had a bad reaction to poison ivy. At best, it caused a rash and discomfort. At worst, if the silver got into their bloodstream, it could kill them. In any case, unless you were fighting a silver-immune wolf, like Devon, it ended up evening the playing field a little. They could kill you in an instant; you might, if you got lucky, be able to inflict some damage on them.

So I wasn't overly surprised when, after weeks of sparring with a good dozen members of the pack, Callum changed up my training regime and gave me claws of my own. He'd taught me to throw knives around the same time I was learning to tie my shoes, so that was nothing new. My aim left a little to be desired—I could only hit a bull's-eye about eight times in ten—but there was a decent amount of heat behind my throws, and if I could put enough distance between me and an opponent to make a long-range attack feasible, I stood a fighting chance of doing some damage—especially if the knife I was throwing happened to be made of silver.

Of course, werewolf communities didn't exactly look kindly on humans who carried silver weapons, and Callum had made it clear from the time I hit my first bull's-eye that unless I had very good reason to suspect that my life was in imminent danger, that particular alloy and any damage I might inflict with it were off-limits. Pack Law forbade werewolves from attacking humans, but humans who wielded silver weapons— or even carried them—were in a category of their own. The Senate was just as likely to put down a human intent on hunting Weres as vice versa.

So the fact that Callum had me practicing with knives and had actually mentioned the word *gun* in my presence was not altogether unexpected, but it was mildly disturbing nonetheless, because for the first time, I got the sense that he really did think that my life was in danger, or that it might be in the future.

Which, of course, made me wonder if there was something about Chase I didn't know.

"All right, Devon. I want you to put Bryn in a choke hold."

Those weren't words I was particularly fond of hearing, but as Devon complied, Callum's instructions to me proved even less welcome. "Bryn, I want you to break his hold and go in with the knife. You want to exact maximum damage in the short-term—disable him, but don't inflict permanent injury."

There wasn't much I could do with a knife—silver or not—to permanently damage Dev, but still, there were two kinds of people in the world: people who liked making their best friends bleed and people who did not. I fell into the latter classification.

"It's okay. Hurt me you will not, young Bronwyn."

"You do a terrible Yoda, Dev."

Even though the exchange between us was light and familiar, our bond to each other—and the rest of the pack—told me that neither one of us was comfortable with this. If the two of us had been inseparable before I'd opened my bond, there were times when I felt like we were practically the same person now. All of Callum's wolves lurked in the recesses of my brain, their eyes tracking my movements wherever I went. But even as our age-mates pulled closer to me for the first time in memory,

Devon stood as a barrier between us—a Slab of Werewolf, every bit as intimidating and significantly less silent than his dad.

Devon didn't want to hurt me. His wolf gnashed its teeth at the very idea, and for a split second, my pack-sense surged, and it was almost like Devon's beast was talking to me. Or something inside of me.

Females, it seemed to be saying, were supposed to be *protected*. Pups were to be *cherished*. The girl was *his*, and he did *not* want to be laying hands on her. He did *not* want to fight her.

Yeah, well, I'm not so hot at the idea of fighting you, either, I thought in Devon's direction. His head flicked forward, and I wondered how clearly my words had come through. It was weird. I'd been talking to his wolf instincts, not his conscious mind, but both parts seemed to understand me just fine.

"Well, children?" Callum prodded.

Devon slumped slightly, in a show of submission, and then followed Callum's directives to a T. He put one arm around my neck, and though he couldn't have been using even a measure of full strength, his grip was like steel. Since I'd spent the better half of the past week being drilled on effective escape maneuvers, my body responded immediately, twisting my legs to the side and using the firmness of Devon's grip to hold up my body as my right leg scissored up to kick him in the side of the face. His other arm went to grab my leg, but the movement gave me a window during which to butt my head into his elbow and flip out of his grasp.

Like lightning, I had a knife in each hand, and as Devon came at me—a blur of popped collars and freshly ironed designer jeans—I settled my arms into an *X* over my chest, with every intention of thrusting them outward in a *V*, slicing through his clothes and into his flesh.

But even the best-laid plans go astray.

Logically, I knew that Devon would heal—within an hour, if not minutes. Instinct was telling me to fight him, tooth and nail, claw and blade, with whatever it took to survive. But both logic and instinct lost out, as I caught sight of the label on Dev's shirt.

He should have been moving fast enough that my measly human eyes couldn't make out the brand.

He wasn't.

So I dropped my knives and with the heel of my right hand smacked him on the forehead.

Callum was not pleased. "Bryn!"

"What? He was going half speed, if that, and you want me to *knife* him?"

"I want you to be able to defend yourself."

"Against *Devon*?"

The question hung in the air in all of its ridiculousness. I didn't need to defend myself against Devon. Or Sora. Or Lance. Or anyone else Callum had set me up against. I wasn't even certain that I needed to be able to defend myself against *Chase*. He was just a boy. A new wolf. A Were who didn't quite have control of his animal instincts. One who was working every day with Callum to tame them.

He wasn't Attila the Freaking Werewolf Hun.

Callum's forehead wrinkled—a sure sign of frustration—and he turned his attention to Devon. "Do you want her to live?"

"Yes, sir."

"Then hit her. Hard. Go after her full speed. Don't hold back, because she needs to know not to."

Devon nodded.

"That's an order. Start again, both of you."

My skin hummed and throbbed at the tone in Callum's voice, and it echoed through each and every part of me. I shuddered, and then it was gone, but I could still feel the remnants of the order through Devon via the bond.

Females were to be *protected*, but the alpha was to be *obeyed*.

Quite a quandary for Dev, who didn't have the luxury of my humanity and my ability—bond or no bond—to make my own decisions even when Callum tried to force his will upon me.

Lips twitching spasmodically, Devon put me back in the hold, and I did the only thing I could think of to alleviate his guilt and put him in fighting mode for real. "Armani is for mama's boys, and a movie doesn't count as a real film if nothing gets blown up."

You're going down, Bronwyn. Them's fighting words.

I was distracted for half a second by the sound of Devon's voice in my mind, but as his grip tightened around my neck and the desire to breathe became paramount, something snapped inside of me.

Fight.

Fight.

Fight.

The burst of adrenaline came out of nowhere. It felt cold and calculated, but on some level I realized that my frenzied movements would have appeared feral to anyone observing them from outside of my body. I escaped Devon's grasp, back-pedaled, and before I had a knife in my left hand, my right was launching one directly at my attacker's heart.

Dev moved quickly, kicking the blade out of the way, and then he was on top of me again. I twisted my left hand, driving the knife toward muscles in his chest and shoulders. He batted me off with an inhuman growl, and I fell to the ground. He pounced, overpowering me, bringing his teeth to my neck. I rolled back, pulling my feet tight to my chest and using them to push against his torso, but he didn't move.

Trapped.

Blood.

Fight.

SURVIVE.

The world around me seemed to slow down with the strength of that command. The word—*survive*—pumped through my blood, burning me from the inside out like air held too long in lungs stretched past capacity. I saw nothing but a blood-red haze, granular and all-encompassing. One second, Devon was on top of me, and the next, I'd managed to dig my own teeth into his neck, which caused him to rear up, which let me stretch out far enough to grab my discarded knife, which—before I even knew what was happening—had gone straight for tendons I shouldn't have even been able to reach.

The details were lost to the tightening in my chest, the narrowing of my field of vision. All I knew was that I had to *fight*.

Bryn, stop. Callum's voice—the alpha voice—irritated me, and I shook it off, intent on escaping, but then it came again, louder. And insistent. And, strangely enough, more Callum than alpha. *Bronwyn, CEASE.*

And so I did. I stopped. The haze receded. And it wasn't until I froze in motion that I realized how quickly I'd come to cutting my best friend's Achilles heel.

Dumbfounded, I went absolutely still, and Devon, his eyes dilated and beginning to yellow, shook his head, clearing his mind and pushing his beast down. Of the two of us, Dev recovered first, and—after rubbing his red-rimmed eyes—he leaned forward, blew a single puff of air at my face, and then mimicked my earlier action and smacked me in the forehead.

"Armani," he said testily, "is for *gentlemen*."

I wanted to grin, but with the knife still in my hand, I

couldn't quite do it. Devon wasn't human. No matter what I'd done, his injuries would have healed faster than the bruise I'd given myself falling out of bed that morning. What scared me wasn't what I'd almost done. It was the fact that I hadn't even realized I was doing it.

What was wrong with me? What *was* I?

"Did the bond change me?" The words were out of my mouth before the question had fully formulated in my brain. "What you did to me when you Marked me, what I did to myself when I let the pack in…did that…am I…?"

"You're human, Bryn. The bond connects you to us—it changes the way you think and the way the pack thinks about you, but it doesn't have any physical effects."

"What do you mean it changes the way I think?" I asked. "I just went all Tarzan wild-child there. Don't tell me that's normal."

Don't tell me that's human.

"Bryn, Ali is bonded to the pack, once through Casey and once through me. Have you ever seen her go all 'Tarzan wild-child' on someone?"

Ali could wrangle kiddos with the best of them, but she wasn't strong physically. She wasn't a fighter—physically. And somehow, I couldn't imagine her facing off in a death match against any Were and coming out of it on top.

Then again, my bond with the pack was open. Ali's was closed.

I narrowed my eyes at Callum. "You swear you didn't change me?"

He nodded. "You, my dear, are exactly what you've always been."

I nodded back, but there was something in his eyes—faraway pupils oscillating in size—that made me wonder exactly what he meant by that statement.

But then Callum shook his head, like an animal trying to shake off a fly, and as his eyes settled, he said the word I'd grown to hate over all others. "Again."

Training. School. Training. Sleep. Wash, rinse, repeat.

Morning after morning, night after night, that was the way things went. With Devon, I fought using silver. With the others, steel. I went home with bruises. They went home bleeding. And somehow, each time I fought one of them, I felt closer to the pack. The bond that connected us was growing, and even though these training sessions were nothing like the way natural wolves play-fight as pups, the physical proximity and the intensity of it magnified my feeling that I belonged to and with the pack, the nagging sensation that I *was* one of them.

For the first time in my life, I felt like a two-legged, furless, wolf-less werewolf. As if being fifteen didn't give me enough identity issues, Callum's conditions were turning me into a giant ball of contradictions.

The bond told me that I was Pack; my physical limitations told me that I wasn't a Were. I liked fighting. I liked the rush. I liked my knives. But at the same time, the old lessons had been too firmly ingrained to allow me to forget that I shouldn't want to fight them, that it should terrify me, that my first and only prerogative when engaging a werewolf should be to create an opening and run. Hide. Climb something. Find protection.

Callum had spent my entire childhood teaching me that I wasn't a Were, that my life was always in danger, that I would always, always be at a disadvantage, but now that he had his wolves jumping me at every turn, I felt safer and more protected than I ever had.

Clearly, I was insane.

Bizarrely, I was also happy. Ali, on the other hand, was not. She refused to look at me when I came back from training sessions. Until I'd bathed and bandaged myself, I was invisible—unless I tracked dirt onto her clean kitchen floors. She adamantly refused to ask me about the conditions Callum had laid upon me the night of the full moon, and I didn't volunteer any of information.

Instead, the two of us got locked into a series of snappish fights about other things. She mandated that I spend more time at my studio, kept an irritatingly close watch on my grades as finals closed in, and outrageously threatened to ground me (again) if Devon and I didn't spend at least one night a week kicking back and watching TV shows on DVD. The more I threw myself into my training, the more she forced my hand in day-to-day life. The two of us engaged in an epic screaming fight one Friday when she somehow got Callum to rearrange my sparring schedule so that she and I could drive to the city and shop after school.

She just wouldn't let me be. Every step I took that brought me closer to the pack was countered with a move designed to pull me back. I never wanted this, Ali insisted on reminding me. There was more to life than fighting. I used to like doing other things. Did I want to miss out on life because Callum had decided to play God?

Personally, I wasn't sure what her problem was. I was fine. I was happy. And pack or not, I was still me. Did she want me to pretend to be normal? Who was she kidding?

I'd never been a normal girl.

And then, one Saturday morning, I came down to breakfast, and it all came to a head when she flat-out told me that I wasn't going to training.

Straw met camel's back. Breaking commenced.

"You have *no right* to tell me—"

"You do not want to finish that sentence, missy. You want to sit down, close your mouth, and eat."

"How am I supposed to eat with my mouth closed?"

"Bryn, that's *enough*."

Even Alex and Katie would have had the good sense to respond to the vein throbbing in Ali's forehead, but sense was not a quality with which I had been overly endowed, and I was sick of her telling me what I could and could not do. Sick of her trying to make me something I didn't want to be anymore.

"I'm going to training."

She raised a single eyebrow, and my heart stopped beating. Throbbing forehead veins, raised eyebrows . . . I was treading on dangerous territory here. Physically, Ali wasn't anywhere near the caliber of opponent I'd gotten used to facing off against on a regular basis. But she was *Ali*.

So I tried to be reasonable. "I have to go, Ali. I don't have a choice."

And neither, I hoped my words communicated, *do you.*

"There's always a choice, Bryn—even if you've already made it. And if you want to unmake it, if there's ever a moment when you're not sure that you want this anymore, or when it gets to be too much . . ."

"There's not."

She put her face right next to mine. "But if there is, you tell me. You tell me, and I will fix this."

Pack business didn't work that way, but it would have taken a braver soul than I to tell Ali that.

"I don't want to take it back. And I really do have to—"

She didn't let me finish. "You have to eat, you have to make your bed, and you have to run a brush through that hair of yours before you leave this house, but at the moment, that's all you have to do."

"That's not the way permissions work, Ali."

Her eyes narrowed, and my pack-sense backed my common sense in telling me to roll belly-up and let her have her way on this one.

"You're not the first person in the world to deal with the pack, Bryn. I know how permissions work."

The things she didn't say hung in the air between us: what she'd asked for, what she'd been forced to give. Whether she'd bargained on her own behalf, or—more likely—if she'd sacrificed bits and pieces of her autonomy over time to buy me mine. The questions were on the tip of my tongue, but Ali preempted my words by slapping some eggs on the plate in front of me.

"I know what you have to do to survive here, Bryn. I've been doing it for both of us for a very long time, but for the record, when I said that you didn't have to go to training today, I wasn't trying to start a fight with you." She sat down in the chair next to me and stared at my eggs, refusing to meet my eyes. Her voice went very soft. "Callum called. He's joining us right after breakfast, and then the two of you are going back to his place."

"Just the two of us?" I asked, trying not to tip my hand and let her see the flicker of hope building inside me.

"Casey will be going as well," Ali said. "Sora and Lance might be there, too."

Three wolves.

Three babysitters.

Three bodyguards.

"I'm going to see him?"

The tone in my voice left no question as to who the "him" in question was.

"Yes, baby. You are."

Ali hadn't called me baby in so long. All of a sudden, I felt like the world's most ungrateful brat for fighting with her.

"I'm going to see him."

The words weren't the apology I'd been aiming for, but Ali seemed to understand. "Yeah."

It felt like I'd be working toward this for so long that somewhere along the way, I'd forgotten that there was an end goal. Now that it was here and real, I couldn't believe it. Not at all.

"You're going to see him. You'll ask him what you need to ask him. You'll do what you need to do. And then, this will all be over. No more permissions. No more conditions. Just us."

No more fights.

No more bond.

No more running with the pack when the moon was full.

I'd be me again. The me Ali wanted me to be. I thought of the ball I'd visualized before I'd let down my shields that night at the Crescent and given myself over to the pack-mentality. The things I'd wanted and been before.

Were they still there, safe where I'd left them? Could I go back? Did I want to?

"Go on," Ali told me. "Get dressed. Make your bed. And for heaven's sakes, Bryn, brush your hair. You're starting to look like a cavegirl."

"Bryn want kill dinosaur," I said, pantomiming what I thought passed for a decent dinosaur-killing motion.

For the first time in weeks, Ali laughed. "Go on. And if you're very good, Ali show Bryn big heaping secret. *Fiiiiiirrrre.* Make tasty warm dinosaur meat."

I snorted. "Dork."

"Right back at ya, kiddo."

The exchange felt so normal. So human. So far from whatever it was that I was becoming, day by day. Now that I was going to see Chase, an insane part of me wanted him to see this Bryn—the one who laughed with Ali, not the one who Callum had molded into a paragon of self-defense.

"I'm going to see him," I said, testing out the sound of the words, wondering which me Chase would meet. "Today."

CHAPTER ELEVEN

"CASEY, IF THERE'S A HAIR ON HER HEAD OUT OF place when you get back, you're sleeping on the couch for the rest of your life." Ali kissed her husband as she said those words, but he didn't take her any less seriously for it. She moved to turn her threats on Callum, but he shook his head at her.

"Have I ever returned her to you in worse shape than I took her?" he asked.

Ali opened her mouth to answer, and my sarcasm barometer sensed an oncoming change in pressure, but Callum just gave Ali the eyebrow arch that she'd given me.

"Alison."

Apparently, I wasn't the only one who got the full-first-name treatment. "You've never brought her back irreparably harmed," Ali admitted grudgingly. "This better not be a first."

The other Weres in the room, including Casey, narrowed their eyes at her, their backs stiffening. My pack-sense told me that they didn't like the challenge to our alpha's authority.

It was unnatural. Ungodly. Impertinent. When Ali married Casey, she should have adopted his status in the pack, but she'd lived among them for too long without a place in the hierarchy to settle into one now, and her challenge rankled. At the very least, Casey should have known what he was getting into with Ali; she'd never made even the least effort to hide her lack of respect for pack tradition.

"Ali—" Casey started to say something, but the look on her face stopped him cold, and a wave of calm—originating from Callum—went through the room.

"I'll take care of her, Alison," Callum said, dispelling Ali's worries even as he calmed the wolves.

I always do.

Ali nodded, and then without another word, she walked out of the room. Callum turned his attention to me. "From the moment we leave this house, I'm invoking the second condition of your permissions. Sora, Casey, and Lance are dominant. You are not. Whatever they say, you do it. Whatever they tell you, you comply. There is no room for argument, no room for discussion, and there will be no leniency for disobedience. You're Pack and you'll act like it. Am I clear?"

In retrospect, it was a really good thing Ali had left when she did. And probably also not a coincidence that Callum had waited for her to leave before laying down the law, because I saw in his eyes that he wasn't guaranteeing my safety, not in all things. Chase wouldn't lay fang, claw, or hand on me, but

I knew what happened to subordinate wolves who challenged dominance.

It wasn't pretty.

"You're clear, Alpha."

Callum nodded, and we left, the five of us. I took a page from Lance's book and didn't say a word, and the others followed suit. Understanding passed between us, though—silent words and thoughts and feelings. The rumblings of their wolves; the butterflies in my stomach. I fingered the knives strapped to my side, seeking comfort in the familiar.

I don't know what I expected when we got to Callum's house, but it wasn't to see Chase sitting on Callum's couch, playing Grand Theft Auto, his fingers moving the controller with frightening accuracy, even when he turned away from the screen and looked directly at me.

"Hi, Bryn."

He was a far cry from the boy I remembered, caged in the basement, shadows in his eyes. But when I looked at him, really looked at him, I could almost see them. Almost, but not quite.

He just looked so *normal*.

Then again, so did I.

"I'll leave you to it," Callum said. "You have an hour."

I realized with a start that Callum was leaving. To give us privacy? Or as much privacy as anyone with three lupine nannies could have?

No. There must have been another reason for it. Callum didn't do anything without a reason, but I decided that I could debate his motivations and intentions later. Right now, I had an hour.

"Ummm . . . can I sit down?" I wasn't sure who I was addressing the question to—the other wolves, or Chase. The latter nodded and brought his legs down off the couch. I started to move forward, but a deep rumbling from Lance's lips held me back.

Apparently, this was the kind of thing that a submissive needed permission for.

I paused, and the three guards exchanged a look. "Chase, move to the chair. Bryn, stay on the couch. You're not to touch each other." Sora spoke each word with an emphasis that made me think that she was considering the way she verbalized the orders very, very carefully.

I ingested them, internalized them, and let my pack-sense get a grip on them. *Obey. Obey. Obey.* I had to obey.

Moving swiftly and with what I hoped passed for some amount of grace, I took up the spot Sora had indicated, and Chase slid over to the chair. His movements were so smooth that they were nearly liquid. He didn't move. He flowed. Chase may have made progress in learning to control what he was, but he still wasn't able to hide it. I didn't think anyone could look at him and not know that there was something different. That he was *more*.

"So…ummmm…how's it been?" I asked.

I cursed Ali for snapping me back into myself enough that the words didn't come automatically, that my first instinct was entirely human: to make small talk. I wanted answers. I wanted to push at his bond with the pack, to explore it, to get inside his head and absorb everything he knew, but I didn't.

I pushed down the desire and absorbed what my instincts were telling me instead. At some point, Callum had made Chase Pack. He was Stone River the way Lance was Stone River, the way I was, but until we were here, in the same room with each other, I'd never felt him. I hadn't realized Callum had brought him into the pack at all.

"I can't complain." Chase's voice was completely dry as he answered my question. "There's food. There's a television. We run through the forest at night. I have superhuman strength and don't particularly miss the foster-care system."

"You were in foster care?"

Focus, I told myself. *Ask the important questions.* But the human in me insisted that these *were* the important questions. That I'd been right all along to feel that Chase and I were the same.

"From the time I was eight. Dad took off. Mom died when I was little."

"My parents did, too. They died, I mean."

"You don't need to talk about that, sweetheart," Casey said, and for a split second, the fact that he'd used an endearment masked his words enough that I didn't realize that he meant them as an order. "Leave that subject alone. You don't want to get upset," he explained.

Part of me wanted to point out that in the time that Casey and Ali had been married, he'd pretty much steered clear of playing Daddy. Now was an awfully convenient time for him to suddenly become concerned with my mental well-being. Especially considering the fact that I had to obey.

Fine. I wouldn't talk about my dead parents. About how I didn't remember them. But if Casey thought that he was going to keep me from asking hard questions, he was wrong.

"What were you like, before?"

Okay, so that wasn't exactly a hard question, but I needed to know.

"Different," Chase said. "Quiet. Hard. Angry."

"And now you're...?"

"Angry, quiet, and hard?" he suggested with a quirk of his mouth that drew my eyes to a small crescent-shaped scar at one corner of his lips.

"Angry, quiet, and hard," I repeated, a smile tugging at the edges of my own. "Because that's so different."

"Everything is." He paused. "That night, when you came for me—"

"Yeah?"

"I'm sorry I, you know..."

"Wanted to eat me?" I suggested.

He nodded, and even that relatively benign motion was filled with eerie grace. I stared at his face, captured for a moment by the way the power of his wolf seemed to emanate from his skin. If I hadn't known better, I would have sworn that he was glowing, but luminescence wasn't a part of the werewolf package.

"You confused me," Chase said. "You're…"

"Different?" I suggested.

He nodded.

"It's kind of ironic." I tried to sound offhand. "You were raised by humans and now you're a Were, and I was raised by Weres, but I'm human."

"You're Bryn," he said, and the way he said my name made me think that in the past couple of months, he'd been indoctrinated into werewolf culture enough to know who and what I was. Little Orphan Annie. Oliver Twist. Bryn.

We were iconic, really.

"I want you to tell me what happened to you," I said, half sure that the others would step in, that they'd stop us from talking about anything I really needed to hear.

"It's really not that long of a story. I was working late, got off my shift, walked home in the dark, and this guy cornered me. One second he was a man, and the next, he wasn't. I kind of lost it and grabbed a pipe, I tried to beat that thing off me, but…"

"Didn't go so well?" I ventured to guess.

He nodded. "I got bit."

This time, the words didn't have the same effect on me. Maybe that was the point behind all of Callum's training. He'd been systematically working the fear out of me. He'd said it was so I wouldn't be scared of Chase, but I was starting to wonder if it was because there was a part of me that had been scared for way too long.

"Most people who get bitten die," I said, willing Chase to look at my face and read in it the meaning that I couldn't say out loud. "When Rabids attack, humans die. They don't change. They just..."

Die, I finished silently.

Our eyes met, and every muscle in my body tensed, ever so slightly.

Like your parents?

I didn't move. Didn't bat an eye. Didn't give any visual cue to the fact that Chase's voice was in my head. I also didn't respond to his question.

They told you not to talk about your parents, he said silently, *but technically, we're not talking.*

He understood. Thank God, he understood. Out loud, I said something else. "How did he bite you?"

"Throat first. Then stomach. It's hard to remember. Everything went dark after that. I think I managed to throw him off, but he kept coming back. First my arms, then my legs—"

"Enough," Sora said, cutting Chase off.

He stopped speaking, and the air around us seemed to shift, weighed down by the power of Sora's command. I looked from Sora to Chase and back again, and that was when I realized— he had to listen to them, too.

Obey. Obey. The pack was to be *obeyed*.

"I hear you like art," Chase said, probably under orders to make small talk instead of talking about being systematically disemboweled.

I nodded. "I used to."

I thought of my exchange with Ali that morning, of the bit of myself I'd hidden far away, and for a split second, it began to crack, and with it came the intensity with which I'd wanted to ask these questions, the incredible, undeniable need to see him.

"What did you like to do, when you were…human?" That wasn't the question I wanted to be asking, but I could practically feel my pack-bond as a leash around my neck, choking me, pulling me back from asking the things I really wanted to know.

You can fight this, a tiny voice whispered in the back of my head. Not Chase's. Mine.

Fight.

Fight.

Trapped.

Fight.

But I didn't. I slowed my breathing and pushed back the panicked haze that threatened to descend on my body the moment I realized just how tight my metaphorical leash really was. A low whimper caught in the back of my throat, and I waited for Chase's answer. For more than small talk. For whatever Callum—through his henchmen—would actually allow me to hear.

"Before the attack, I liked cars, Yeats, and having a lock on my bedroom door." Chase paused, and behind his wry, self-deprecating grin, I saw an echo of the whine still caught in my throat.

Out.

Out.

Out.

We wanted *out.*

Chase's eyes pulsed amber, and without a word, Lance walked over and put a firm hand on each of his shoulders. Forced him off the chair and to his knees.

A high-pitched sound escaped my throat, and Sora laid a hand lightly on my shoulder. She didn't push. She didn't force a confrontation, but as I leaned forward, her grip tightened, pulling me gently back.

"Look at me." Lance growled the words, and on the floor, Chase responded. His body jerked once, twice, three times against Lance's hold, and the smell of burning hair and men's cologne filled the air. The smell wasn't Chase. It wasn't Stone River. It was something different, something foreign, and it was here.

One second I was sitting and the next, Sora had shoved me at Casey. "Get her out of here!"

But since the order hadn't been directed to me, I didn't have to obey, and Casey's main concern seemed to be staring at Chase—staring and staring and daring him to come closer.

Pack. Not Pack. Pack. Not Pack. Pack.

The hair on the back of my neck stood straight up. I'd never seen anything like it before. Callum had made Chase a part of the Stone River Pack, but every wolf in the room was reacting like he was a stranger.

A foreign wolf on our lands.

A threat.

Mine, I thought.

A moment ago, I'd been talking to Chase.

He'd been in my head.

Even now, I could feel each spasm of his body in the corresponding muscles in mine.

"Chase. Look at me." This time, Lance's voice was low and soothing, but I felt the command behind the words, felt shades of Callum—*alpha*—in Lance's tone.

Look at him, I begged Chase silently, sure it would help, but uncertain why. *Look at Lance.*

He did, and slowly, the scent of foreign wolf receded, until the only thing in this room was us.

Me, Chase, Casey, Sora, and Lance.

Pack.

"What just happened here?" I recovered my voice before the others found theirs. If I'd been paying attention, I might have noticed just how close to the edge Callum's guards were.

How close they'd come to Shifting themselves.

"He's in my head." Chase's voice was soft. Too soft. Any other girl wouldn't have been able to make out the form of his words.

"Callum. The wolf. Both of them."

It wasn't Callum's wolf that had flooded the room with a foreign scent, and it wasn't Callum who'd put the haunted expression—empty and clear—in Chase's eyes.

It was the Rabid.

If a Mark connected you to a werewolf, what did a full-blown attack do? There wouldn't have been a ceremony, but…

"When the Rabid attacked you, did you feel it?" As far as stupid questions went, this one ranked pretty high, and I struggled to make myself clearer. "Did you feel it here?" I closed my fist and touched it gently to my chest. Casey still had a hold on my shoulder; otherwise, I might have moved and gone to Chase, who was still kneeling on the floor, to place my hand over his heart.

"I felt it everywhere," Chase said, his simple words cutting into me like a knife to the stomach. "Sometimes, I still do."

"I think that's enough for today," Sora said, and beside me, I felt Casey stiffen, his head dropping even as his spine snapped back. Sora had told him to get me out of there. He hadn't.

Dominance lash-backs. They were enough to give a girl fits.

"Bryn, outside. Now." Sora's words took on the hollow tone of an order issued at half strength, and I got the sense that the kid mitts were more for Chase's benefit than for mine. On the floor, Lance still had his hands on Chase's arms, but instead of holding him down, he appeared to be holding the younger wolf up. Just looking at him, I felt Chase's exhaustion, felt his muscles liquefy as the battle in his head subsided.

"I'm sorry." I hadn't planned on apologizing, but as Sora's words compelled me toward the door, the apology came out of my mouth anyway. Chase had been in control. He'd been Callum's. And something I'd said had ruined that.

"No sorry." Chase's voice was liquid, too, just like his muscles, fluid and flowing, one word running into the next as he closed his eyes. "Never sorry."

I was almost to the door by then, and the urge to go back, to go to him, was overpowering.

Obey. Obey. Obey.

If I wanted to see Chase again, I had to obey now, and Sora had told me to leave. Slowly, I brought my hand up to the doorknob.

Bryn? Chase's voice was a whisper in my mind, and the sensation sent a single chill up my spine.

Yes?

You asked what I liked, before. He paused, and the silence tickled my mind, the chill in my spine climbing its way to the hairs on the back of my neck. *Before, I loved cars, Yeats, having a bedroom that locked from the inside, and you.*

His words exploded in my brain, and if Casey hadn't had a hold on me, I would have stumbled.

You didn't even know me then. The part of me that still thought like a human would have rolled my human eyes at Chase's declaration that he'd known me long before we'd ever met, but my pack-sense wouldn't let me. Because deep down, Chase was Pack. He and I were the same, and there were situations in which you couldn't expect a wolf—Were or otherwise—to understand the concept of time.

Glancing back over my shoulder, I opened the door and stepped outside, directly into Callum. I wasn't sure when he'd gone out, or how much he'd been listening, only that he was waiting for me. Callum closed his arms around me, pulled me tight to his body, and held me the way Lance had held Chase—like I needed his support to stay vertical. Until I fell into his grasp, I hadn't realized just how close I'd followed Chase to the edge of something dangerous and scary.

I loved cars, Yeats, having a bedroom that locked from the inside, and you.

How willing I was, already, to go back.

"You did a good job," Callum told me.

Alpha, my pack-sense said in return.

Callum, I thought. But there was a part of my mind that was thinking something else. Thinking about someone else.

Chase.

"You're all right. You're safe. You'll see him again." Callum's voice was gruff, but to me, his words sounded like a lullaby, and my legs shook, threatening to turn to jelly beneath me.

Chase wasn't in control. Not fully. Not yet. And the man who'd done this to him, the monster who'd changed him, was still lurking in the recesses of his mind, the same way that each and every member of our pack was in the corners of mine.

"You're all right. You're safe. You'll see him again."

Alpha. Callum. Guardian. Pack.

The unspoken words all told me the exact same thing— Chase would be okay. Callum wouldn't give up the fight, wouldn't let the Rabid take one of ours. Alpha meant safety. Callum was safe—and so long as I kept up my end of the agreement, followed his orders, didn't run back to Chase and close the space between us, so was I.

CHAPTER TWELVE

FOR WEEKS AFTERWARD, THOUGHTS OF CHASE dogged my every step. It didn't matter what I was doing—running with Callum, sparring with Sora or Lance—Chase was always there, his blue eyes flecked with the incomprehensible. I saw him lying in the cage, the way he had that first night. I saw him on his knees, held down by Lance's stone-hard fists. I saw him the way he must have looked walking home from work on the day the Rabid systematically tore him to shreds.

He'd been human once.

He should have died.

And each time I imagined him, thought about seeing him again, I was reminded of the fact that I should have died, too. Jagged, uneven bits of that long-ago night worked their way into my consciousness, and like the pieces of a puzzle, I assembled them.

Someone had knocked on my parents' door. I'd run to answer, but hadn't. I'd stepped back. Mommy had rushed past me.

I'd stepped back again.

Blood. Splattering.

There were still pieces missing. I couldn't remember what my father had looked like. I couldn't remember the length of my mother's white dress. All I could remember was the man who'd turned into a gray wolf, the white star on his forehead, the blood.

Running.

Hiding.

Air hot in my throat. Burning my lungs. Panic.

I remembered pressing back farther and farther in the cabinet under the sink. I remembered the Bad Man's words.

Quiet. I remembered being so quiet, and then—nothing, but a red haze. An instinct.

Blood.

Beside me, Devon looked up from his paper and tilted his head to one side.

You okay? I read the words in his expression, felt them in the pull of his pack-bond at mine, but I didn't actually hear his voice in my mind. I hadn't heard anyone's, not even Callum's.

Not since Chase.

Not that I'd heard Chase, either. I'd resisted the urge to go looking for him, to close my eyes and sort my way through the mass of interconnected psychic bonds that was Stone River until I found him.

I was being a good little pack daughter, doing everything

Callum asked me to. I'd been biding my time, until he'd allow me to see Chase again.

Blood. Splattering. Burnt hair and men's cologne.

It was all messed up in my mind—Chase and the Rabid who'd turned him, Callum and the Rabid he'd killed the night the rest of my family had died. Stone River. Foreign wolves.

Running and losing myself to the overwhelming, indescribable force of *us*.

I'm fine. I sent Devon the message in feelings, not words, but the set of his jaw—not a single, easy grin in sight—told me that he didn't believe me. I made my best effort at a smile, and with a look that told me that Devon had absolutely no respect for my nonexistent acting chops and that we *would* be talking about this later, he turned his attention back to his own desk, and I did the same.

Failing my algebra final would probably be ill-advised.

May had come and gone too quickly, and the sheet of paper on my desk was the only thing standing between me and summer. Standing between me and Chase, who'd been working with Callum to force the taint of the Rabid out of his head.

Tomorrow, Bryn. Right after school.

That was the sum total of what Callum had said to me the day before, but it was all I'd needed to hear, and if Chase had been on my mind these past weeks, he was in it now.

Before, I loved cars, Yeats, having a bedroom that locked from the inside, and you.

Whether it was my bond with the pack or the fact that he was the first boy to ever haunt my dreams, I couldn't say, but as the days passed and I didn't see him, I started to feel more and more like Chase's words were true. Like I'd always known him.

Like we were the same.

Which was ridiculous and silly and less than no help when it came to graphing the equation for $y = sin\ x$.

Forcing all other thoughts out of my mind, I worked my way through the exam. I willed the numbers to make sense. I matched the sheer force of my will against the power of partial credit, and I forced it to submit.

I forced it to cave.

I dominated that test, the way I couldn't dominate anything or anyone else.

Tomorrow, Bryn. Right after school.

Those five words were all it had taken for Callum to transform from the man who'd promised Ali he'd take care of me to the one who made no guarantees about my safety if I took a single step out of line.

I was Pack and I'd act like it.

I'd *submit*.

If my last visit had been any indication, the pack wouldn't let me get too close to Chase. Wouldn't risk my asking questions the answers to which they either didn't want him to give or didn't want me to know.

Maybe both.

I knew my Rabid was coming. I knew he was bad. I was trapped and I was scared and I ran. Hid.

Was that what it had been like for Chase?

Was that what it would always be like for me?

"Five minutes," our teacher announced from the front of the room, and then, just to clarify the point, he wrote the number 5 in a big loopy scrawl on the chalkboard. On my right, Devon had already started checking his answers. On my left, Jeff of the motorcycle incident had simply given up, opting instead for staring at the sweet, quiet girl who'd dumped him not long after he'd given her my pen.

I stopped writing with forty-five seconds to spare, and even though I didn't have time to double-check my calculations, I couldn't shake the sense that I'd aced it. I certainly should have. On late, sleepless nights, the memory of the Big Bad Wolf waiting for me in dreams, there'd been nothing to do but study algebra and think of Chase.

He'd grown up in the foster care system.

He'd been angry for as long as he could remember.

He appreciated the power of privacy—or had before he'd turned.

He was a living, walking impossibility.

And he was mine.

Pack. Not Pack. Pack. Not Pack.

"Time's up!"

The teacher sounded way too perky for someone who typically took pleasure in our dismay, but given the fact that his summer vacation started the second that ours did, I didn't suppose I could blame him. Once upon a time, summer had meant running around barefoot with Devon and a visit from the only female werewolf anywhere near our age. I could feel it in my bones that this summer was going to be different.

I wasn't ready.

As the teacher came by to collect my exam, I had a single moment of insanity, during which I fought the urge to hold on to my paper. If I didn't turn in the test, it wasn't really summer yet.

If it wasn't summer, I wasn't going to see Chase again.

And if I didn't see Chase again, I wouldn't have to worry about what he might say. What I might find out. What I might remember.

What I might do.

"Ms. Clare?"

The teacher sounded so befuddled that I loosened my grip on the exam and let him have it. Beside me, Devon grinned.

"Did you pass?" he asked, as we gathered our bags and headed for the door.

I didn't respond.

"Come on, Bryn—my summer plans are just as subject to your state of groundedness as yours are. Did you pass?"

With my luck, Dev's summer plans probably involved attempting to organize a werewolf theater festival. I shuddered to think of the number of roles I'd have to play when the surplus of males in the pack refused to don curly blonde wigs and play girls in the tradition of the original Shakespearean plays.

"I passed," I said. "And for the record, I haven't agreed to any of your so-called plans yet."

With Devon, things were easy. Besides Ali, he was the only one I could look at without thinking of the rest of the pack.

"You don't have to go, you know," Devon said, his voice uncharacteristically understated. "If you decide you don't want to, if you'd—for instance—rather hitch a ride into Denver and have a night on the town such as only I can show you…"

My look stopped Devon mid-sentence.

"Sorry. It's just…you smell like him." Devon said the words lightly, but a muscle in his jaw tensed. "You haven't seen him in weeks, you didn't touch him, and you still smell like him."

That was news to me. Self-consciously, I sniffed at my own arm, and a couple of town girls glanced at me and snickered. They probably thought I was checking myself for BO.

"I don't smell anything," I told Devon, ignoring the townies.

Devon didn't reply—he just twirled his pen around his fingers like a tiny, ink-filled baton. "Come on," he tried again. "You. Me. Netflix."

He was every bit as bad as Ali, pulling me back from the edge just before I dove headfirst into the abyss below.

Screw the townies, I thought, and giving them a real show, I butted my head gently against Devon's chest, and he rested his chin on the top of my skull.

"You know I'm going," I said, speaking directly into his shoulder.

He sighed, once quietly and once with the melodrama I'd come to expect from him. "Yes. I know. Nobody puts Baby in the corner, et cetera, et cetera, blah, blah."

The fact that he could attach not one but two "blah"s on the end of a *Dirty Dancing* quote conveyed the true depths of his sour mood.

"I'll be fine."

Devon didn't reply.

"Chase wouldn't hurt me." Even if Chase lost it, even if Callum and the Rabid were duking it out for dominance in his head, if I'd gotten under Chase's skin half as much as he'd gotten under mine, I'd be fine.

Devon said his next words so quietly that I almost didn't catch them. "It's not Chase I'm worried about."

I tried to make him repeat himself, but he wouldn't, and that, more than anything, told me that the person Devon was worried about wasn't me, and it wasn't Chase.

It was Callum.

"You can't honestly be worried about that," I told Dev, but

even as the words left my mouth, I sensed his wolf stirring.

Females were to be *protected*, but the alpha was to be *obeyed*.

"Callum would never hurt me." That had been my litany since the moment he'd rescued me from under the sink. Crooned to me. Talked to me. Banished the haze.

"If you break your permissions, he won't have a choice."

I jabbed my fist into Devon's stomach hard enough to knock the air out of a normal boy. He didn't respond at all.

"I'm not going to break the conditions," I said. "I didn't last time. I'm not stupid."

That statement was met with rather insulting silence.

"I followed instructions last time, didn't I?"

More silence, and then, finally, Devon broke into a song from *Annie*.

"'Hard Knock Life,'" I said. "Seriously?"

Devon shrugged, but I noticed that he didn't step away from me, like his wolf thought that if they just stayed close enough to me, I'd be okay.

"Trust me, Dev. I'll be fine."

My words must have sounded like truth, because he backed off, but in the depths of my brain, I wondered if the future would make a liar out of me. Because the last time I saw Chase, I wasn't fine. I didn't break permissions. I didn't force Callum's hand.

Chase hadn't laid a finger on me.

But I hadn't been fine.

Come out, come out, wherever you are, little one. No sense in hiding from the Big Bad Wolf. I'll always find you in the end. . . .

The only way I was going to be fine—now or ever—was when I knew exactly what had happened to Chase, and knew that it wasn't going to happen to anyone else.

Ever.

Again.

CHAPTER THIRTEEN

"I CAN'T BELIEVE YOU WOULD PRETEND FOR A SINGLE second that you don't know exactly what's going to happen!"

"Alison—"

"Don't you 'Alison' me, Callum. You want to talk conditions, what were my conditions?"

"Ali—"

I recognized the voices from twenty yards away: Ali, Callum, and Casey. They were yelling so loudly that they didn't even seem to be aware of my approach, which was really something, because I wasn't making any attempt to mask the sound of my footsteps, and Callum and Casey should have heard me coming from a mile off.

"This is between me and Callum, Casey. If you can't back me up, keep your mouth closed."

Ali's voice lowered in volume, and I gulped on Casey's behalf. If she'd been using that tone with me, I would have turned tail and run, no questions asked.

"I don't know why I even—"

A low, unidentifiable sound, issued from Callum's throat, stopped Casey's words in their tracks. I wasn't sure if Callum had growled in warning or in threat, but either way, Casey didn't finish what was probably an entirely inadvisable sentence.

I don't know why I even bother?

I don't know why I even try?

I don't know why I even act like there's the smallest chance you might listen to me?

It didn't matter. Even I could tell that Ali wasn't in the mood to hear any of the above. She was challenging Callum. Casey was trying to get her to back off. Our house had somehow become Dominance Issue Central, and I had a sinking suspicion that it was my fault.

Casey was mad at Ali. Ali was furious with Callum. And Callum was talking in low, even tones, like he couldn't have forced both of them to their knees in under a second if he'd taken it in his head to do so.

This wasn't good.

I stopped walking. I stopped breathing. I didn't move.

"I left my family behind. I left my friends. I never contacted any of them again. I kept the pack's secrets, and what did you give me in return?" This wasn't a rhetorical question. Ali was waiting for an answer, and Callum replied, his voice gentle, like he was reprimanding a child instead of facing down the rage of a mama bear. "I gave you Bryn."

"She's mine, Callum. Not yours. Not the pack's. She's *my* daughter, and you swore to me that when it came to her safety, my word would be law, so whatever you know, whatever you've seen—"

And then, there was silence, so abrupt that I wondered for a second if I'd lost consciousness or gone spontaneously deaf in both ears.

"You might as well come in," Callum called, disabusing me of that notion. His voice was dry, like he should have known I'd be hovering at the perimeter of their argument, marking every word. "This concerns you."

I heard Ali mutter something under her breath but couldn't make out what. Slowly, deliberately, I made my way to the house, taking my time with each step, not sure I wanted to see the looks on any of their faces.

I was right to worry.

Ali looked like Ali, Callum like Callum, and Casey looked like he wanted to kill me.

Like any of this was *my* fault. For once, I hadn't done anything. Yet.

"How were your finals?" Ali asked, breaking the silence with a question that sounded so normal that I wondered for an instant if I'd imagined their yelling a moment before.

A glance at Casey out the side of my eye told me that I hadn't.

"Finals went well," I said, keeping my back to the wall, an

instinct that I couldn't shake, even though we were all family here. "I'm pretty sure I aced algebra."

I felt Callum smile beside me, but when I looked over at him, his face was neutral, calm. The face of the alpha, taking care of pack business.

My hands flitted to the waist of my jeans, needing a reminder—a physical reminder—that even when he was alpha, he was still Callum. Even when it came to pack business, I was still his.

"Is this about my seeing Chase again?" I asked. I was facing Callum, but Ali was the one who answered my words.

"You don't have to go. You don't have to do this."

First Devon and now Ali. What did they know that I didn't?

"Nothing," Ali said, and I wondered if my thoughts were *always* apparent on my face. "I don't know anything that you don't, Bryn, but it doesn't take a rocket scientist to figure that this could get ugly."

"Chase won't hurt me."

Ali glanced at Callum, and Devon's words floated back to me—*It's not Chase I'm worried about.*

Callum won't hurt me, either, I thought, but I didn't broadcast the words. The fact that I had to say or think them at all was mind-boggling. I'd approached Callum as a member of his pack, and his actions and mine were equally bound by our agreement. I knew better than to break faith with our entire pack, and I had more inhibition than they were giving me credit for.

Tempting fate was one thing; baiting Pack Justice was entirely another.

"Are you ready?" Callum asked me, ignoring Ali. The look in his eyes told me that he knew me better than she did. He didn't question, even for a second, the possibility that I'd back down.

"He's just a boy," I said out loud. *Just a boy with a Rabid in his head, who claims he loved me before we ever met.* "I'm ready."

Ali sighed, and the sound was unnatural, like her lungs were being deflated, the air sucked out of them by some external force.

"Take care of her, Casey," Ali said, and I couldn't tell if her words were an order or a plea. "Please."

Casey nodded, but not for the first time, I wondered if he'd fully bargained on me when he'd married Ali.

"I'll take care with her, Alison. You have my word." Callum's words should have been comforting, but as an expert at obfuscation myself, I couldn't help but notice what he hadn't said. He hadn't said that he'd take care *of* me. He'd said he'd take care *with* me, and I knew better than to think that those two things were the same.

Casey, Callum, and I walked toward Callum's house in silence. Sora and Lance joined us halfway there.

"You know he's not just a boy," I said, feeling the need to explain myself to someone in Ali's absence.

"I know," Callum replied, and I wondered if he meant for me to hear the slight echo of sadness in his tone.

This visit had nothing to do with Chase being a boy and me being a girl. It had nothing to do with the way he dogged my dreams and haunted my field of vision every time I blinked.

This was about the Rabid.

It was about me.

By the time we got to Callum's house, I'd stopped trying to explain myself.

"Casey, Sora, and Lance are dominant. Your pack-bond remains open. You're not to touch him." With those words, Callum disappeared, and I wondered again why it was that he couldn't or wouldn't stay to watch my interaction with Chase.

"Hello."

Speak of the devil. There was depth to that one word. Even just the sound of Chase's voice made me think of the full moon, silvery and larger than life.

"Hello," I replied, feeling human and small. Someday, I'd run with him, the way I had with the rest of the pack. Not today.

Within seconds, the two of us were positioned just as we had been the last time, me on the sofa, Chase on a nearby chair. He smiled, and in the curves of his lips, I could almost see his wolf: dark fur, light eyes.

"Same rules as last time," Sora said, her impeccably controlled voice breaking into my mind.

No touching.

No talking about my family or the way they'd died.

No asking Chase about the method with which another Rabid had torn him limb from limb.

"How are you?" I asked, feeling even more muzzled than I had the last time I'd been in his presence.

"Good," Chase replied. *I've got control,* he added silently. *Nobody in my thoughts but me. Most of the time.*

His voice was clearer in my mind than anyone else's had ever been, and I knew I wasn't imagining that there was more than a pack-bond between us. I didn't feel him in my hip, in Callum's Mark.

I felt him in my stomach and in my lungs. I breathed him in and out and saw him in my mind, in memories he'd had no part of the first time around.

"I had finals today," I said. The words were insufficient and irrelevant, but as they exited my mouth, my guards relaxed. They didn't mind me talking to Chase the boy. They just wanted me to stay away from his wolf. Away from the night of its birth, bloody and cruel.

"I don't miss finals," Chase said. "Come to think of it, I don't really miss people, either."

"You don't miss being human?" I asked. It was one thing to watch the Weres lose their human selves on the day of the full moon, to watch the wolf slowly taking hold of Callum's body, or Devon's, but it was another thing altogether to imagine going from being what I was to the thing that Chase was now.

It could have been me. The thought broadsided me. Chase sat on his chair like a lion lounging on the savannah. Like a wolf, sprawled across wet forest ground. His limbs dangled off the side. His eyes took in everything, flitting between my body and that of my guards.

It could have been me.

"I don't miss being human." Chase paused, the human holding back words that his wolf wanted him to say. "I miss you."

The air between us turned to static, and I felt his pull—magnetic and uncontrollable. On edge between human and not.

Concentrate, I told myself. I hadn't come here to picture his life before he'd changed. I hadn't come here to commune with his wolf or wonder if it was a feeling like this that had coerced generations of human females to leave their families for a chance at dying while giving birth to werewolf pups.

I'm not that kind of girl, I told Chase silently.

He shrugged, and I wondered if he even knew what I was talking about, if he had even the vaguest measure of the power calling to my body from his.

"Callum said not to touch you," Chase remarked. "You don't smell like meat anymore."

I wasn't sure what to make of either of those observations,

but I saw other things in the blue of his eyes: control that hadn't been there the last time we met. And loneliness, the kind that had no business existing in the middle of a werewolf pack.

"What happened to the wolf who attacked you?" Every time I wanted to ask him a question about the attack, I asked him about his life instead, and now that I wanted to tell him that he wasn't alone, the other questions slipped easily off my tongue.

"He ran off."

"Is he dead?" I addressed this question to my guards. "Did we hunt him down?"

Sora's response came almost immediately. "You don't need to concern yourself with that, Bryn."

That wasn't an answer. It was an order. They were ordering me not to concern myself with the Rabid—the reason I'd come here to Chase in the first place.

"I call him Prancer." Chase saved me from complete and utter frustration. At least *he* had the ability and force of will to stay on topic.

"You call the werewolf who attacked you, almost killed you, and Changed you *Prancer*?" I asked.

"I had to stop being scared sometime. Give the boogeyman a name, and he goes away." Chase shrugged and then continued on in my head. *Callum taught me how to keep him out of my mind, but you can't change the memories. I sleep, and he's there. When I dream, he's got me exactly where he wants me, and there's not a blessed thing I can do about it. But then I wake up, and he's Prancer. He can't control my thoughts. He can't make me scared. Not without my permission.*

"Is Chase talking to you?" Sora asked me. "Silently?"

I wasn't sure how she could tell. Maybe she read it in my change in posture, as my body shifted itself toward him, all of its own accord. Maybe she saw it in my face, or felt it through the pack-bond. In any case, I didn't want to answer the question, but Sora pushed at me, coming forward and placing her hands on my knees, leaning over me in a way that made me lean back.

She was dominant. It wasn't just a word. It wasn't just a concept. It was real, and at the moment, I couldn't have lied to her if I'd wanted to, agreement or no. "Yes."

"He shouldn't be able to do that," Casey said, startled. "Not yet."

Sora snorted and looked at me. "Neither should she."

They're going to tell us to stop, I realized.

And then we'll have to stop, he replied.

Neither of us wanted to. I wanted him in my head. I wanted to be in his, and in the second before Sora made the order official, the two of us joined together mentally, images passing from his mind to mine.

Dark alley.

Grease stains on his pants.

Shadows behind him.

Low, silky voice.

Who's afraid of the Big Bad Wolf?

My thoughts bled over to his. The man I'd called Daddy. The woman who'd been my mother before Ali. And siblings—I'd had siblings, hadn't I? And then came the knock at the door, and a man.

A man with a wolf.

Man killed Mommy.

Wolf killed Daddy.

And then they started looking for me.

Who's Afraid of the Big Bad Wolf?

"Stop it. Both of you. Anything that is said will be said out loud. That's an order."

Radio silence fell between me and Chase, but my head was still a mess of his thoughts and mine and the things I'd shown him, because the orders I'd been given forbade me from talking about them out loud.

"So," I said out loud. "Prancer bit you. You survived."

"That about covers it."

"And I think we're just about done here," Sora said.

"Callum said we had an hour," I reminded her.

"Trust my judgment on this one, Bryn. You don't have much of a choice."

It's for your own good, silly girl.

I was pretty sure that she didn't mean for me to hear that.

"He had a white star on his forehead," Chase said, and

his voice took on the tone of the shadows missing from his eyes. "It was the last thing I saw before I blacked out. Prancer's star."

I was paralyzed, my heart pounding viciously within my frozen body. I was suddenly very aware of my own blood, the way it pumped through my veins, and how easily it would have been for my position and Chase's to be reversed.

He had a white star on his forehead.

Who's Afraid of the Big Bad Wolf?

I thought I would throw up, but I didn't. "They're the same. Prancer and the Big Bad Wolf."

"Bryn," Sora warned, but that wasn't an order. It wasn't. And I didn't have to listen to it.

"The man who hurt you and the man who hurt me—"

"I told you not to talk about that, Bryn." That, from Casey, who seemed terrified of giving me another order, for fear that I would disobey.

I'd promised Ali, and so had he. I wouldn't do anything stupid. Casey wouldn't let me get hurt. But I was hurt.

I was hurting.

Come out, come out, wherever you are. . . .

And then they were there in my head. The pack. All of them—they were there, tugging at my psyche, drowning out Chase, willing me to submit, to take my place, to be their daughter, their sister.

Controllable.

Their pawn.

I'll be fine, I'd promised Ali. *I won't do anything stupid*, I'd sworn to Devon. But they hadn't known—I couldn't believe for a second that either of them had known the full truth of what Callum had been hiding from me these past few months. He hadn't just been keeping me away from Chase, making me work myself to the bone for a few minutes in his presence.

He hadn't been preparing me for *anything*.

He'd been masking the big picture, hiding the truth. I could feel my body going numb, my brain detaching from it, as the ball of things I'd once been exploded in my mind, drowning out everything else. The man who'd attacked Chase and the one who'd killed my family were one and the same. It was eight kinds of impossible, and every single one of them urged me forward.

Fight.

I could fight this. I could fight everything Callum had forced on me in the name of keeping me safe. I could pull against the leash choking me back, the orders Sora was yelling at me.

Trapped.

A familiar haze descended on me. Uncontrollable. Unknowable.

Trapped.

Fight.

Blood.

"This meeting is over," Sora said, reaching for my arm, and

that was the last straw. She couldn't touch me. Not to keep me from Chase. Not to keep me from thinking thoughts that the pack didn't want me to think.

Not to keep me from the truth.

Not now. Not ever.

Obey. Obey. Obey.

Submit. Submit. Submit.

My pack-sense went into overload, but when Sora tried to haul me to my feet, she made a critical error, because there was only one thing stronger than my tie to the pack, and that was the drive to be safe. To escape.

I sensed him coming. I sensed him coming, and I ran, and I hid.

And now Sora's hand was on my shoulder, and they'd lied to me. All of them. My peripheral vision went first, and then the darkness circled in, red and rough, like blood splattered on the wall, as I watched from under the sink.

Obey. Fight. Trapped. Submit.

Survive.

There was the order that mattered. The only one. I leapt from the couch, the darkness closing in all around me, and my guards were so surprised at the show of outright disobedience that they didn't react quickly enough. Not quickly enough to press their will onto mine, or quickly enough to keep me from bashing through one order after another after another, with the fury and ferocity of an animal cornered and caged.

I leapt at Chase, barreling toward him, and he caught me

and held on so tight that I could feel my arms bruising, but it didn't matter.

We were touching.

They'd told us not to touch, and we were touching.

My parents got bit. They didn't survive. Callum killed the wolf who did it before he got to me. Only I guess he didn't. Kill him. Not really.

More passing between us. Feelings: anger-hate-fear-love-hope, words, and scattered images. I was in Chase's mind. He was in mine. I couldn't see a thing. Not even his face.

Trapped. Fight. They're going to take me away. Have to— have to—

Sora, Lance, and Casey jumped to their feet—I couldn't see them, too red, too much red—and Chase pulled me closer. "Mine," he growled.

"Let her go."

"No," I said, forcing my body to follow my commands, grinding my jaw and forcing the world to settle back into place in front of my eyes. "Don't."

Everything I'd known my entire life was a lie. The person—the monster—who'd killed my family was still out there, and Callum knew. He *knew* and he'd kept it from me, kept Chase from me—not because he was dangerous, not because of the Rabid in his mind.

Because together, we would have figured it out.

"Let her go. Now."

The air crackled with Lance's dominance. I hadn't realized how strong he was, how close to alpha himself, and the fact that he rarely spoke gave his words more power than they would have had otherwise. Chase's wolf responded to the order, pausing, growling, backing down.

His fingers loosened around my arms.

OBEY. OBEY. OBEY.

It was overwhelming. Suffocating. Crushing. I felt Chase's panic, and somehow, that rid me of mine. My vision was perfect, because his was becoming cloudy. My thoughts weren't scrambled, because his were.

Trapped, I could hear him thinking. *Fight. Bryn.*

I recognized the madness, saw him losing control, bit by bit and piece by piece, and I remembered what I'd done to Devon when I'd lost myself to a similar directive. When I'd been trapped with nowhere else to go.

If he attacked Lance, they'd kill him.

Fight.

I couldn't lose myself to the adrenaline, the need to get the two of us out of there and away. One of us had to stay in control.

It had to be me.

Look at me, I thought, fighting back my haze and his. *Only at me, Chase.*

I could have shut down my bond to the pack, could have put back up some excuse for a mental block, but I didn't. Instead, my body threatening to seize with the effort it took to keep my basest, most vicious instincts from taking over, I gathered everything that existed between me and the pack, everything that made me one of them, every invisible tendril that tied me to my wolf-brothers, and I shoved it toward Chase.

Mine, I thought.

Trapped. Fight. Survive.

Mine.

There was a *whoosh*, like all of the air had been instantaneously sucked out of the room, and then there was silence, the pack roaring at me from a great distance, unheard. Silence.

Silence, and Chase.

CHAPTER FOURTEEN

"WHAT DID YOU JUST DO?" CASEY'S WORDS WERE sharp, but the expression on his face was closer to horrified. "What did the two of you do?"

Chase looked at Casey and then at me. My panic and Chase's were gone, and in its place, there was something dynamic and warm weaving its way through my body and through his, pulling us together, inch by inch.

"I don't have to answer," Chase said, puzzled. "Normally, when they ask me something, I have to answer." He flicked his head to the side. "It's there, still. I can feel them. Callum. Wolf. Pack. I can almost hear them, but it's different." He leaned forward and buried his nose in my hair, breathing me in. "It's you."

"She reformed their bonds." Sora's voice was dull. "They're each other's first, and Pack second." I felt her prowling near me psychically, testing the limits of our bond, trying to undo whatever it was that I'd done.

"That's not possible," Lance said, exchanging a look with Sora, one that reminded me that they had hundreds of years' experience reading the ins and outs of each other's expressions. "Is it?"

"Mine," Chase said, rubbing his cheek against the side of my neck. I shivered, the touch between us electrifying.

"Mine," I agreed, burying my hand in his hair, "but in a non-freaky, non-ownership, we-both-retain-our-independence kind of way." I nudged Chase. "Right?"

He shrugged. "Sure."

In retrospect, it was probably a very good thing that he hadn't been born a Were.

"They're coming." Sora again, her voice just as emotionless.

"Who?" I asked.

"Anyone close enough to feel what just happened," Sora replied. She closed her eyes, sensing them, and I wondered if I could still do the same—if I tried. "Marcus. The Collins brothers. Everyone your age but Devon. Some of the wives."

Casey breathed in sharply. "This is bad."

A low, rumbling sound emanated from Lance's chest.

Very bad, I translated for Chase.

Holding me this tightly, he couldn't understand how anything between us could be bad. Not when it felt so right. Unfortunately—or maybe fortunately—I was human enough that the warm hum between us, the feel of his skin on mine, didn't convince me that we were safe. We were together, but we were also screwed.

Especially me.

The survival instinct that had led me to do whatever it was that I'd just done wasn't worth much more than spit. How many of Callum's conditions had I broken here? I'd not only disobeyed the wolves I was supposed to be submitting to, I'd challenged their dominance over me and over Chase and somehow rewired things to weaken it. I'd taken the bond—which I'd agreed to open so that I could come here—and instead of shutting it back off, I'd channeled it into something new. The pack was still connected to me, and I was still connected to them, but that was filtered through the overwhelming, all-absorbing sameness that flowed from me to Chase and back again.

I'd approached Callum as a member of the pack, I'd disobeyed him as a member of the pack, and from the slightly green tone to Casey's skin and the fact that Sora wasn't yelling at me, I knew what that meant.

I was dead.

Ali and Devon would never, ever forgive me for this. Worse, they'd never forgive Callum.

"No," Chase growled, standing up and shoving me behind him. "They won't hurt you. I won't let them."

"You don't have a choice, son." Callum came into the room, stone-faced and weary. And even though the bond between us was muted, drowned out by what I now shared with Chase, I struggled to read him, to sense him, to know what he was thinking, and it came to me.

You don't have a choice, son. And neither do I.

Pack Justice wasn't pretty. Like wolves in the wild, Weres who challenged the alpha had to be beaten into submission, or removed altogether. I'd seen grown men torn nearly to pieces for doing less than I'd done here today. They healed. Eventually. Because there wasn't much beyond a silver bullet or decapitation that a werewolf couldn't heal from.

But me?

Not good. So, so not good.

"I don't regret it." I whispered the words and thought Callum would have a coronary. "You should have told me."

Of all people, Callum should have told me. He knew me. He'd seen what the Rabid had done to me, and he'd let me go to bed each night, year after year, thinking the monster who'd killed my family was dead.

I shouldn't have had to find out from someone else that the safety I'd felt in this pack was a lie. That the Rabid was still out there, attacking people. Attacking Chase.

My Chase.

Callum didn't respond to me. He ignored me. Looked right through me, like I wasn't even there. Like I was already dead.

"Sora?" he said, his voice deceptively mild. "A moment, if you please?"

Sora nodded, her face a match in every way for his. Callum's eyes flicked toward Lance and Casey. "Let no one near her. We'll have justice, but I'm the alpha here, and it will be on my word. Anyone who puts so much as a single mark on her before I say to dies."

The words knocked the breath out of me.

Bryn? Chase's voice was tentative in my mind. He wanted to protect me. His wolf wanted to protect me. They wanted to be near me. They didn't understand why Callum's words shocked me to my core when *my* life was already at stake.

"He's bound by his word," I murmured, leaning into Chase's back, pressing my face into his shirt. Callum couldn't make idle death threats. If anyone harmed me, he'd have to kill them.

Good, Chase's wolf snuffed. He would help Callum kill anyone else who touched me.

"You couldn't just leave well enough alone, could you? You couldn't trust—even this once—that somebody knows better than you. You act without thinking, you always act without thinking, and now—" Casey cut off. "Do you know what this is going to do to Ali?"

Tears sprang to my own eyes, but I couldn't keep the smart-mouthed answer off my lips. "Well, I think it's a safe bet that you'll be sleeping on the couch."

Casey turned and slammed his fist into Callum's coffee table, and it split, right down the center. Chase growled, his upper lip curling, his eyes dilating into a swirl of colors.

"It's okay," I told him. *We're okay.*

He didn't like Casey yelling at me and wanted to tear into

him for violence—even directed at a piece of furniture—so close to...

Oh no, I thought. *He did* not *just think the word* mate.

Then again, I kind of had bigger things to worry about than defining my whatever-this-was with Chase. Like the fact that the front door had just been kicked inward, and Weres were already pouring in.

"Outside!" Lance yelled, and even though his dominance no longer had an effect on me, I could sense it, and I could see the effect it had on the others. The others—all of them, yelling and growling and muttering—backed out of the house.

"Anyone who hurts the girl without Callum's specific permission dies," Lance said. "This is the word of the alpha."

"I can't believe this." Marcus sneered from just outside the threshold of the door, bloodlust in his eyes, his face flushed. "She broke faith with the pack, and he's protecting her!"

"He's doing what needs to be done," Lance said. "He always does. That's why he's the alpha. Do you doubt his authority?"

I read the words unspoken in that question—*do you want to challenge him?* Marcus was questioning Callum's judgment. He was playing hopscotch with the line of insubordination, and if he so much as blinked, that would be enough for Callum's dominance to be called into question.

Enough that Callum would have to kill him to prove a point.

"No," Marcus snarled. "I don't doubt the alpha's authority."

"Do you challenge it?" Lance took a step toward him, and Marcus bowed his head slightly, his neck arching into a rounded hook.

"No."

Beside me, Chase was vibrating with fury, his muscles held in check as much by my control as his. Marcus wanted to hurt me. Chase could smell it. His wolf could taste it in the air. And—I pressed further into his mind—there was something familiar about Marcus. About his hatred. About how much he would have enjoyed hurting me.

Chase knew these things. He'd seen them before, in other people, back when he was human.

What Chase knew, I knew. The sensation would have been overwhelming, had I had the luxury of being overwhelmed. Chase was doing a decent job at keeping his wolf under control, but I could feel the charge on his skin, could feel his anger as millions of pinprick shocks on my own, and I could feel his beast stirring.

Chase arched his back, and if I'd thought he was luminescent before, that didn't hold a candle to the power pouring off him now.

"Shhhhhh," I found myself murmuring to him. "Just breathe. You're okay. I'm okay. We're okay."

I needed him to hold it together. I needed, I realized, for him to be safe, no matter what happened to me.

You can't fight them, I said. *No matter what they do to me, you can't fight them.*

He whirled around to face me, zero space in between us. "Can't I?"

"No."

No.

The two of us fought our own little dominance battle— Chase and his wolf on one side, me on the other, the bond between us heating up and bringing us closer in conflict than we'd been up to now.

I didn't stop to think about what I was doing. I just stared him down. If I'd had a moment to think on it, I probably would have realized that challenging a Were was a bad idea, even if you wore his skin nearly as tightly as your own. The last time I'd seen Chase, Callum and the Rabid had been battling it out for control of Chase's mind. Now he was mine, and I'd been Pack long enough—*Callum's* long enough—to know that in my family, we protected what was ours.

"You have to promise me." Silently, I set my will against his, intent on having my way on this one thing. This last thing. Out loud, though, I pleaded. And finally, either because of the desperation in my voice or the unmoving, uncompromising steel baring down upon him from my side of the bond, he nodded.

It cost him everything to make the promise, and his pain hit me like a physical blow. I wanted to curl up next to him, to be closer to him, to make the pain go away. He wrapped his arms around me.

"This just figures," Casey muttered. "Never had a boyfriend, never wanted one, forgets to even brush her hair unless Ali reminds her, and now, this. There's just no in-between with you, is there?"

I was minutes away from being on the receiving end of terrifying and unquestionably physical retribution. Was now *really* the time for Casey to be complaining about my dating habits, or lack thereof?

But at the same time, he was right. There wasn't an in-between for me. I lived at extremes. And maybe I'd die at them, too.

Right. Now.

Stupid, stupid, stupid!

I was stupid, and I'd been betrayed, and I wasn't at all sure which one was worse. I felt Callum come into the room behind me, and as he crossed it, I turned, averting my eyes to keep from looking straight at him. A second later I realized that I needn't have bothered. It wasn't like he was looking at me. His movements were stiff, his face unreadable. For what I could only assume was the first time in a thousand years, he looked old.

Callum said nothing to me. He just nodded at Sora, and she walked over and told Chase to move away from me.

He didn't want to.

He wanted to stay.

To protect.

But he'd promised, and so he let go of me and I of him. "He's safe?" I asked Sora, knowing deep down that Callum wouldn't respond.

"Safer than you are," Sora replied. "His disobedience was mild."

Chase hadn't reneged on a pact with our entire community. I had. Message received.

"What's going to happen to me?" I didn't want to be asking those words, but there they were.

Sora didn't answer. She just dragged me from the house, out onto Callum's front lawn. Callum followed, but didn't step past the threshold of his door.

"Permissions were granted and conditions were set," he said, loud enough for everyone to hear. "Those conditions weren't met. Justice demands blood."

This from Callum. The closest thing to family I had, next to Ali. The man whose Mark I bore—and would always bear—on my flesh. The man who'd lied to me for years and years. The person who for the longest time I'd looked up to most in this world.

"However," Callum said, and that provoked a hum of grumbles that settled when the alpha demanded silence. "However, the girl is human. Her body would not recover from that which she has rightly earned, and our justice—if it is to be justice—cannot be blind. Sora will serve in my stead. She will extract our pound of flesh."

I really, really hoped he was talking about a metaphorical pound. Ice-cold terror filled my veins, and from head to toe, I froze.

"But Sora will do so in human form, and only until the girl's body gives out."

Gives out?

Gives out how?

"And how will Sora know when it's enough?" Ironically enough, that question—which was on the tip of my tongue, too—came from Marcus, his lips twisted into a colorless sneer. "Who is she to judge? The pack *will* be satisfied. This cannot be a slap on the wrist." He paused and then added, "Alpha," with what sounded like respect—probably to stave off a lesson in what challenging the alpha really meant.

"Sora will know," Callum said, and that was all the warning I got. One moment, things were still being debated in the abstract, and the next, a circle had formed around me and Sora—*Devon's mother, pack, protector*—had thrown me to the ground. I scrambled to my feet, but the next second, she came flying at me, a kick delivered to my chest. I flew backward, and there was a popping in my ears. It took me a second to recognize the sound as the cracking of my ribs.

I was lucky she hadn't broken them in half. But somehow, I didn't feel lucky. Again, I made my way to my feet, and again, she was upon me. Instinct said to draw my knives, but even I had more sense than that. This was as much of a reprieve as Callum could give me. If I touched silver, I'd lose it.

I'd die.

And I owed Chase more than that. I heard him howling, as if from a great distance, and I knew that he'd lost the battle for control, that he'd Shifted and that it was the wolf and not the boy who was bound now by the promise he'd made me not to interfere.

I lost my tenuous grip on that fleeting thought when Sora backhanded me, strong enough to send me down again. She rained blows down upon me, and I could feel my eyes blackening, my lips swelling, my body hopeless under the barrage.

All of Callum's training, and this was what I was reduced to. I couldn't fight, couldn't resist, couldn't do anything but let her beat me.

Survive.

The word was a whisper at the back of my throat, a ghost in my mind, maybe even an echo on the wind. I'd given into it before. I'd absorbed it, acted on it.

Survive.

I don't know how to survive this, I thought. This was me losing my family. My friends. Every illusion of safety I'd ever had. Every promise I'd ever made myself that nobody would make me a victim again.

Survive.

Sora moved to drive a deceptively dainty foot into my side again, but she must have misjudged my position, because she lost her footing and stalled, her elegant, angular face completely blank of emotion and strain. Before she could regain her balance and momentum, I scrambled backward and forced myself to my feet.

My face was wet, warm, and sticky, and I could taste the blood in my mouth. But even then, I knew that I could take much, much more. That this could go on. And on. And on.

When would the pack be satisfied?

How would Sora know when to stop?

Trapped. Fight. Blood. Run.

I could feel the need building inside of me. Could feel the fury threatening to overwhelm my mind, take over my senses.

No.

If I fought back, it would only be worse. I couldn't fight. I couldn't run. But I had to. My heart was pumping. My ribs were throbbing. There were no sinks to hide under, no strangers to save me.

Fight.

I stood ramrod still. I didn't move. I didn't run. I just stood there, hurting, fighting off the haze and the need to taste blood myself.

The need to get out of there alive.

Who's afraid of the Big Bad Wolf?

I was. I was desperately afraid, and this time, the Big Bad

Wolf wasn't Rabid. It was Sora. Her fist connected with my jaw. My head snapped back.

Danger. Fight. Blood. SURV—

No! The word exploded in my brain, and with it came paralysis. It washed over my body, taking first my legs and then my torso, my arms, even my lips, until I couldn't manage a single cry when Sora's fist crashed into my face again.

I wouldn't fight this.

I couldn't.

My field of vision exploded, first into red, then into black, and then into nothing. Blessed nothing, and numbness, and as black faded to star-tinged gray, I crumpled to the ground.

Unconscious.

CHAPTER FIFTEEN

FLOATING IN DEAD MAN'S CREEK, I STARED UP AT *the night sky. The dark expanse and the bright stars took turns dominating my visual field, but the oscillation between inky blackness and white-hot light didn't hurt my eyes, just like the water under and around me didn't chill my skin.*

I didn't even feel wet.

It was quiet, and I was alone. Until I wasn't.

He wasn't there with me physically, but I could feel him, next to me and inside of me, and in the distance, I imagined that I heard his wolf howling. For me.

I closed my eyes, letting the sound rush over me, bringing with it chills and warmth and the unerring desire to howl back. Gone was the night sky, gone was the creek, and when I opened my eyes again, it took me a moment to realize that they weren't my eyes.

They were his.

Ours.

My vision was sharper now, and the tiny details of the world—each blade of grass, each hair on each head—were so vibrant that I couldn't see the bigger picture. And then I heard him.

Heard me.

Heard us.

Howling. Screaming. Fear-anger-desperation-NO.

Saw the girl lying on the ground, and then realized that it was me. Blood pooled at her—my—mouth, and the scent was tantalizing. Terrifying.

We needed to go to her. Our vision began to go, overwhelmed by something More.

Rough hands grabbed our wolf body and hauled us backward, and even though we'd promised not to, we fought—not to injure the one who held us but to escape their grasp, to run to the girl, to curl our body around hers and will her to be well.

A whimper escaped our throat. We needed to fight but had promised not to.

"Chase." Callum's voice. Alpha voice. But it didn't have the same effect it used to.

Bryn.

"Shift back. Shift back, and you can go to her."

The words somehow permeated our head, and for a moment, Chase and his wolf seemed to consider them, but the fury and fear radiating through their body was too feral to be contained by human skin.

They wanted to kill.

No, I thought, *and my voice sounded loud in my ears, loud in his. In ours.*

Bryn? His voice was hesitant, his wolf whining.

I'm here, I said. With you. I'm fine.

The body on the ground seemed to argue against that point, but my presence soothed Chase. As he calmed, his beast stilled, and for a split second, the three of us were in perfect harmony. His mind should have felt crowded with all of us there, but it didn't.

"*Change,*" *Callum ordered again.*

The wolf in Chase was opposed to this idea, and I wanted to agree with him, to run away and enjoy being part of Them, not stuck in a human form that would never fit quite as well as this fur. But Chase refused to run, refused to turn tail on this fight, or to leave me—or even my body—behind.

Am I dead? I asked.

The question sent a growl into Chase's throat, and I was struck by the way it felt, by the way everything felt in this body that was Wolf.

"*She's not dead,*" *Callum said, and Chase and I both paused, wondering if he'd read our mind.* "*Smell her. She's just unconscious. Shift back, and you can go to her.*"

Smelling. Pine needles and cinnamon. Bryn.

Good. I was alive. Maybe I was dreaming. Maybe this was my dream.

The pain of white-hot metal cutting through bone shook me from my musings, and a horrible crunching sound, like gravel under work boots, echoed through my—our—his—flesh.

And that was when I realized that Chase was Changing back.

In human form, he crouched down to the ground in a motion more befitting the animal than the man.

Smelling. Seeing. Needing.

Bryn.

Why don't you put some clothes on first? I suggested mildly. Now that we were human again, I found myself more clearly able to think. And also, a little uncomfortable with the fact that I was inside the mind of a naked boy who wasn't human enough to realize that he was naked.

"Why don't I put some clothes on first?" Chase echoed out loud.

Callum looked at him very strangely—naked and crouching, ready to attack, but speaking utterly human words.

My words.

And suddenly, I was back in Dead Man's Creek, floating. Peaceful. Alone. And then a piercing white light split the night sky, and a wave of pain crashed into my body, splitting it into piece after piece.

My eyes fluttered, but I couldn't open them. The vague sensation of hands under my arms, hauling me up into the air, took me by surprise. And just before I descended into darkness again, I heard Callum barking out an order.

"Bring her inside, Marcus."

Floating again. Numb. Nothing hurt. Blessed darkness.

I turned over onto my side, submerging half of my face in water, and I realized that I could still breathe—could breathe right through the creek, like it wasn't even there. Completely accepting of this development—and delighted—I took a deep breath and dove under the water—

"Put her on the couch, Marcus."

Back in Chase's body—clothed, thankfully—I saw Marcus, stiff-faced as he followed Callum's orders and gently laid my broken body down.

"Are you satisfied that she's had enough?" Callum asked him.

Marcus looked at me, and Chase's need to rip his throat out became palpable in our joint mind. Chase did not want Marcus looking at me. He did not want him near me. He could not let them hurt me more.

"She's not faking," Marcus said begrudgingly.

"No," Callum agreed. "Sora beat the girl until she lost consciousness."

Chase hated Callum for the dispassion in his voice, hated him for doing this to me. To both of us.

"Humans are weak," Marcus said finally. "Females even more so. It is enough." Marcus turned his head from my body. "Pack Justice has been satisfied."

Callum simply nodded, and it occurred to me that it was probably no coincidence that he'd chosen Marcus to carry me inside. If Marcus's thirst for my blood had been quenched, no one else would argue.

"Leave us now," Callum said. "I'll tend to the girl."

Marcus left, and he was barely out the door before Chase growled. "Bryn. Her name is Bryn, not 'the girl.' And one day, I'll kill you for doing this to—"

Back in the creek, underwater. I barreled toward the surface and broke through, rising up into the air like a humpbacked whale or a mermaid child, and for a long time, things were quiet.

By the time I woke up for real, I'd been flitting in and out of consciousness—and, when unconscious, in and out of my own mind and Chase's—so much that I wasn't sure where I was, or who I was, or what had happened. As I opened my eyes, feeling flooded back into my body, and I really wished that it hadn't.

Moving carefully, I sat up, and my body lodged its various objections, from a groan in my ribs to a hissing scream in my lip. The rest of me just throbbed. After the shock of it waned, I was able to move my arms, running my fingers over my legs, arms, and torso, probing the damage and expertly checking for broken bones.

A werewolf who'd committed my crimes would have had his entrails torn out for display. I had a host of bruises, a few cracked ribs, and a face that—if it looked as ugly as it felt—probably wouldn't be winning beauty pageants anytime soon.

"It could have been worse," I said, and I winced, deciding that moving my sore jaw wasn't so easy that I could justify talking to myself.

The door opened, and my first instinct was to flinch or to flee, but I had nowhere to go. My body relaxed—warm, like butter—when I realized that it was just Ali, and that no matter what the pit of my stomach might be telling me, I wasn't going to wake up any second, back inside the circle of justice.

"You're up."

Ali had never been one for stating the obvious. Or using short sentences. Or staring just over my shoulder instead of looking me in the eye.

"I'm up," I confirmed.

The dark circles under her eyes were uneven and oddly shaped, like inkblots on a note card, and though I was pretty sure that I looked worse, the wage this whole ordeal had obviously taken out of Ali hit me hard.

"How long have I been out?" I asked, determined not to let her see how painful speaking was.

"Three days. Doc couldn't explain it. Nobody could."

Three days? I'd been unconscious for three days with a battered face and handful of cracked ribs? That wasn't normal, was it? Given that I'd never been beaten before, I wasn't sure. The only thing I did know was that I hadn't blacked out from the pain Sora had rained down on my body, fist after fist, kick after kick. I hadn't lost consciousness bit by bit, piece by piece. It hadn't closed in on me. I hadn't taken a particularly hard blow to the head.

I'd blacked out because I'd refused to fight back.

The conclusion made no sense and complete sense at the exact same time, and my face was throbbing too much to question it. Memory of the haze—the need to protect myself, the solar eclipse in my brain when I'd refused—grounded me in place and rendered me speechless for a moment.

"Where am I?" I recovered, not wanting to think about it. About how inhuman I felt when I gave in to the whisper in the back of my brain to *fight, fight, fight, survive.*

Ali's brow furrowed at my question. "You're in your room."

For a second, I thought that maybe I'd suffered permanent brain damage, because the answer seemed so obvious, but then my mind processed the fact that I'd had very good reason not to recognize my own room.

It was bare. Absolutely bare. My desk was empty. My closet doors were open, and there were no clothes inside. My books were in boxes beside the shelves, and even the bedding that I was sleeping on wasn't mine.

"Where's all of my stuff?" I asked.

"Packed," Ali said.

"Packed?" I repeated.

She didn't say a single word.

"Why is all of my stuff packed?" Was she kicking me out? Was Callum taking me from her? Were they sending me away?

Bryn had been a bad girl, and now they didn't want her anymore.

I stopped breathing, the tightening in my chest drowning out the ache in my ribs.

"Your stuff is packed because we're leaving," Ali said, matter-of-fact.

"Leaving? For where? Who?"

"Yes. Montana. You. Me. The twins."

What was she talking about? Montana? That was the very rim of Callum's territory. Only peripherals lived there.

"We're leaving?"

"Well, after what they did you to, we're certainly not staying here."

I remembered the set of Ali's jaw and the ferocity in her voice when she'd said that I was hers first—her daughter, her responsibility, her charge.

When it comes to her safety, my word is law.

"Casey?" I wasn't sure I wanted to know the answer, but I asked anyway.

Ali's expression—already hard—went completely blank. "Casey," she said in a tone that seemed to communicate that she couldn't be bothered with elaborating further, "is gone."

"Gone as in dead?"

Ali shrugged. "Might as well be."

"You're leaving Casey," I said, my voice going up an octave. "You're leaving Casey and taking me and the twins and we're moving to Montana?"

Ali nodded. "That about covers it."

"But, Ali—"

"This isn't up for discussion. It's decided. The station wagon's been mostly packed for two days. We've just been waiting on you to wake up. Now, can you get out of bed?"

No, I could not get out of bed. I couldn't even process what was happening. I'd known that Ali wouldn't take the whole Pack Justice thing well, but this...

"Bryn. Can you get out of bed? Can you walk?"

I swung my feet over the side of my bed and stood up. All things considered, it was easy. Even my ribs didn't protest too much.

"Doc said you did a lot of healing while you were unconscious," Ali told me. "You're still banged up, but your pupils aren't dilated, and he said that unless there were signs of a head injury, you should be fine to travel."

Travel.

As in leave.

Leave our home.

Leave our family.

Leave the pack.

"Ali, we can't go."

She turned around and walked toward the door. At first, I thought she was going to walk out without answering me at all, but instead, she spoke in a tight, strangled voice that made me wonder if she'd turned around because she didn't trust herself to maintain steely control over the muscles in her face.

"They beat you, Bryn. *Callum* beat you. He had you *beaten*. When they brought you back to me, you were bleeding. You had fourteen bruises, six lacerations, two black eyes, and you were *unconscious*. They did that to you."

"I broke the rules," I said. "Pack Law, I—"

Ali whirled back around. "Don't you dare say this is your fault. Don't you think it, don't you even come close to making excuses for them. They hurt you. And everyone just stood there and let them—my friends, your friends, my *husband*—"

Ali's voice cracked and her body hunched over. For a moment, I thought she'd collapse inward and crumble to the floor, but instead, she straightened and threw her head back. "I don't care what you did. I don't care who they think they are, or what Pack Law says, or who's dominant to who." She took a long, ragged breath. "All I care about is *you*."

"I'm fine."

She crossed the room and hauled me up in front of a mirror. "Tell me again that you're fine."

The unforgiving surface of the mirror told me in no uncertain terms that although the bruises on my face were beginning to yellow and fade, I still looked like I'd been tie-dyed in a vat of black, blue, green, and corpse-colored paint.

"Ali, I'll be okay," I said, trying to convince her to take a step back and think about this. "It could have been so much worse."

She snorted. "If you think you're making a convincing case for staying, you're mistaken. Just listen to yourself, Bryn. 'It could have been worse.' Who's to say that it won't be in the future?" She paused. "Do you think I want that for you? For Katie and Alex?"

Katie and Alex.

Up until now, I'd been dazed and stressing. Now, I was panicked. "They won't let you take the twins. The pack, they'll never let Katie go. You've seen the way they—"

"Oh, rest assured, I'm dealing with the pack." The tone in Ali's voice left very little doubt in my mind that when she said "the pack," she meant "Callum."

Callum, who'd given me to her in the first place.

Callum, who'd ordered my punishment.

Callum, who hadn't looked at me or said a word to me since I'd touched Chase.

"It's not Callum's fault," I said, wanting desperately to believe it. "Ali, he took care with me. He gave me the only chance that he—"

"I am not having this conversation with you, Bryn. I'm just not. I can't." She ran a hand through her hair, and for a moment, she looked very young. "The fact that you don't hate him for this breaks my heart. And if we weren't leaving because of what they'd done to you, we'd be leaving because the pack has twisted you enough to make you think that it's okay for someone to treat you that way. It's not, and we are. Leaving."

There was no arguing with her. I would have had better luck convincing Devon to don knockoffs.

With gentle hands, Ali took hold of my waist, careful of my tender body, and she pulled me close, burying her face in my hair. Her shoulders shook, and I realized that she was crying. Sobbing. Clinging to me in a way that made me think she'd never let me go.

"You didn't wake up," she said. "I waited, Bryn, and I waited, but you didn't wake up."

"I didn't mean to," I whispered. I didn't mean to do any of this. I didn't mean for any of this to happen.

This was my fault. Mine.

Without warning, Ali let go of me and straightened back up. She wiped the tears off her own face and then off mine with the same gentle, brisk motion, and then she walked over to my bookshelf, picked up the box there, and turned to leave.

"Be ready to go in an hour."

An hour. How could a person get ready to leave their entire life behind in one hour? I sat back down on my bed, not even caring about the way my bruises protested and the pain radiated outward from them like liquid spilling over the edges of a pool.

Devon. I had to call Devon.

And Chase.

Chase.

All of a sudden, the air around me felt very warm and the room felt very small. My breath caught in my throat and my stomach dropped, like someone had unlatched a trapdoor in my intestines.

If Ali followed through with this, if we left, I'd lose him.

Bryn?

His voice in my head calmed me, even as my rational self blathered on that the last thing I should have been worrying about when my entire life was being ripped out from underneath me was a boy I'd seen exactly twice.

I'm here, I replied silently. *I'm awake. And Ali's going to take me away.*

Chase didn't reply immediately, and for a moment, I was terrified that he had gone. But then, slowly, images began to make their way from his consciousness to mine. They danced at the edges of my mind, and like a butterfly, every time I tried to latch on to one, it flew away.

He took it away.

My mouth set in a firm line, I pictured the bond between us and pulled. Growing up, I'd never been a match in strength for the other kids in the pack, but I could hold my own at tug-of-war based on the fact that I never let go. Once I got a grip on that rope, if someone wanted to get it back from me, they would have had to pry it out of my limp, dead arms. Even once they'd pulled me across the line, I didn't stop fighting.

Chase never stood a chance.

The images flashed into my mind, and I managed to hold on to them long enough for a concrete picture to form in my brain.

Bars.

Steel.

Cage, I realized. They'd *caged* him. My lip curled upward with fury. Didn't they realize how awful it was, to be trapped there? I could feel him pacing back and forth.

He wanted out.

I won't let them do this to you. I'll—

Nothing, he said back. *If I can get out, I will.*

A long pause.

They'll let me out when you're gone.

Understanding washed over me, and relief. They weren't punishing him. He wasn't trapped because he'd disobeyed. He was there because I was leaving, and for whatever reason, they didn't want him trying to stop me.

Another vague image, a half-completed thought he didn't want me to hear—

"Ali." I said her name out loud, and things became very, very clear. *Ali* had asked them to cage Chase, and they'd agreed. If I'd been in my right mind, I might have wondered what exactly Ali had been forced to sacrifice to get them to grant her request—not to mention permission to leave—in return. But I was too angry to think about anything other than the fact that despite Ali's ranting and raving about the way the pack had treated me, they were treating Chase like an animal on her bequest.

I couldn't let her do this. I wouldn't. In fact, I wouldn't let her do any of this. I wouldn't leave. I wouldn't step foot in that car, and she couldn't make me. It was going to be a cold day in July before I let her do this to me. To him.

To herself and to Casey. To the twins.

She wasn't doing this.

End of story. *Finit.*

CHAPTER SIXTEEN

"I'D TELL YOU THAT YOU CAN'T STAY MAD AT ME forever, but I have a feeling you'd take that as a challenge."

Exactly two hours after I'd sworn that Ali would drag me kicking and screaming to the car over my own dead body, I was sitting shotgun, alive and not bloody in the least. I'd been giving her the silent treatment for the past hundred miles—not that it was doing any good.

Part of me understood why she was doing this. If Ali hadn't been so icily furious on my behalf, I might have hated the pack—and Callum—but *if* was a luxury for another time. Right now, I could handle being mad at Ali, but I wasn't sure I could handle anything else, and I wasn't going to risk the dense vortex of emotions in my gut working their way to the surface. I was not about to break down. Not in this car, not once we got to Montana, not ever.

"You would be doing the same thing," Ali told me. "If something happened to me, if you were in charge of Katie, and if the pack had attacked her—whatever the reason—you would do the exact same thing."

"Shut. Up." I broke my silence.

"I'm doing this, I'm not sorry I'm doing this, and I'm not going to undo it," Ali said. "Live with it, kiddo."

"You didn't even ask me what I wanted," I shot back. "What happened—it happened to *me*." It was bad enough that Callum had taken it upon himself to decide what I could and could not handle knowing with respect to The-Night-That-Shall-Not-Be-Named. I wasn't about to let Ali take this away from me, too. "*I'm* the one they hurt. *I'm* the one who bled, *I'm* the one whose body is so bruised that I might as well start answering to the name 'Patches,' and *I'm* the one who had to watch Callum—"

I broke off. Didn't want to go there.

"Watch him what?" Ali said evenly.

"Nothing," I said through clenched teeth. "He did what he could."

I knew it was wrong to be mad at Ali for trying to protect me, but not Callum for hurting me in the first place. I just didn't care.

"Do you honestly think that Callum didn't know what would happen, Bryn? From the moment he left you alone with Chase?" She stared out at the road before us, and I leaned forward and flipped on the radio, hoping to drown out her words.

Her face tightened and then her hand lashed out. My arm,

like a creature possessed, jerked upward, throwing up a block to protect my face before my conscious mind had time to realize that all Ali was doing was turning the radio back off.

Unsettled, I lowered my arm and hugged it tight to my chest, feeling small and stupid and laid painfully bare.

If Ali noticed my reaction, she at least had the decency not to call me on it. Instead, she pressed on with the current topic: Callum, justice, and me.

"How many times in your life have you gotten the drop on Callum, Bryn? How many times has anyone? He knew damn well you'd break the conditions before he set them down."

Callum had always known what I was going to do before I did it. I'd spent my entire life trying to get the drop on him.

He knew me.

No. I didn't want to hear this. She couldn't make me. Radio. On.

In the backseat, Katie whimpered from her car seat. Both twins had cried solid for the first hour, and about fifteen minutes back, they'd finally cried themselves out and fallen asleep. My brother and sister weren't any happier to be leaving than I was.

Shhhhhhh, I told Katie silently. *It's okay. I'm here.*

The farther we drove away from Callum's stronghold, the weaker the twins' bond to the pack grew, and the more they latched on to Ali and me. Especially me. I was pretty sure that Katie had yet to figure out that I wasn't a wolf. The night I ran with the pack confused her. Even now, with my own pack-bond muted, I was the closest thing she had to Pack.

To home.

"I can't feel them anymore," I muttered, my words lost to the song blaring from the speakers.

It began to rain, and Ali turned the windshield wipers on and the radio off.

"You can't feel who?"

"The pack. Even after...what I did...they were still there. Faintly." Chase was just more there. But as the mile markers ticked by, everything was getting fainter, and now I couldn't feel any of the Weres at all, except for Chase—and I could barely feel him. He existed only as an image, a sound, a feel in the recesses of my brain, but even that was getting harder and harder to hear.

"Chase didn't do anything wrong," I said, allowing my ire to take the place of the holes in my soul. "You made them lock him up, and he didn't do anything wrong."

"Believe it or not, I'm not a monster, Bryn. I asked Callum to lock him up, because Callum issued an edict that no one was to stop us from leaving. Based on the way that boy stood guard over you while you were unconscious, flashing from one form to another, daring us to move him from your side, I inferred that he might not be able to keep himself in check when we left, and that you might not want him to face the kind of *justice* that had been visited upon you."

For a single second, that took the wind out of my sails. "Did you have them lock Casey up, too?" I sneered, once I'd recovered.

"As a matter of fact," Ali replied, her grip on the wheel tightening, "I did."

Radio. On. Only this time, it was Ali's decision, not mine, and she turned down the volume and changed the station. In the backseat, Katie closed her eyes again, and for the next hundred miles, the four of us drove in near-silence, the gentle warble of country music the only sound in the car.

Ali drove straight through the night. At some point, I fell asleep, and in my dreams, Chase came to me in wolf form. His fur was black, his body lean and muscled, and his eyes were lighter even than their human counterparts: two orbs of ice blue in a sea of darkness. I didn't say a word, and he didn't make a sound. The two of us just sprawled out on the ground about a foot apart. I could feel his warm breath on my face, and after an eternity of the two of us staring at each other, I buried my hands in his fur, which should have been coarse, but felt silky soft in my hands. His chest rose and fell as he breathed, and I could feel my heart beating in unison with his.

"This doesn't mean we're mates," I told him.

He opened his mouth very wide in a mischievous, wolfy yawn.

"Women's liberation and all that," I continued, catching

his yawn and trying to push it down. "No Mark. No lifetime commitment. No 'property of' signs. We just have a bond, that's all."

His tail beat quietly against the dirt beneath us, and a smile worked its way onto my own lips.

"Loser," I said, playing my fingertips over his rib cage, oddly compelled to scratch his belly.

In response to my insult, Chase bared his teeth in mock threat, but scooted closer toward me, and after a long moment, I laid my head on his neck, and the two of us—girl and wolf—fell asleep, into a dream within a dream.

I see you.

Words dripped, sing-sung, from a crooked mouth. No face. No body. Just a mouth—bones cracking, jaw breaking.

I see you.

Sharp smile, fanged and smeared with red.

I recognized the voice. I recognized the blood, but this wasn't my nightmare. It was Chase's.

Like a strobe light, images flashed in rapid fire in front of me. A man: brown eyes, open face, never aged past thirty. Red teeth. Gray wolf, white star. Jaws snapping.

So much blood.

I looked for Chase, called to him, but I couldn't find him. I was too far away.

Wolf. Fight.

Not my dream. Not my instinct. Not my haze, but the whole world went blood-red nonetheless, almost purple. Rotted. Congealed.

Chase. I had to find Chase.

I could feel his eyes opening. Lightning in his stomach, jaw aching as he Shifted back to human form.

Look at me, Callum whispered to him, a ghost on his shoulder.

You're mine, said the mouth with the wolf attached. *I made you. You belong to me.*

And that was what did it, because Chase didn't belong to blood and panic. Didn't belong to a Rabid rotting from the inside out. He didn't even belong to Callum, steady and sure.

He belonged to *me*.

Light surged all around us in a starburst, halfway between the moment of detonation for an atomic bomb and the skyline on the Fourth of July.

Warm.

Safe.

Mine.

And just like that, Chase and I were back on a bed of wet leaves and grass, the smell of dirt and autumn reminding me that this was a dream. Only a dream.

In human form, Chase curled beside me, his forehead damp with sweat, and I ran my fingers through his matted hair, as naturally as I had his wolf fur. I folded my body against his, keeping watch until his breathing slowed, and mine slowed, and together, we faded into sweet, blissful nothing.

"Wake up, Sleeping Beauty."

My first instinct when I heard Ali's words was to growl, but as the real world settled back into place and the protective instinct my dream had awakened slipped from me, I remembered two things. First, I wasn't actually a werewolf and therefore didn't have the possessive-protective gene dictating my every move, and second, I wasn't talking to Ali at the moment. Feeling awkward in my own body, I rubbed the sleep out of the corners of my eyes and instead of growling, settled for a pointed glare.

Ali ignored me. She just unbuckled her seat belt and climbed out of the car, shutting the door on me and my mood. While I was still trying to get over the insult, she opened the back door on the driver's side and unhooked Katie from her car seat.

"I take it we're stopping?" I asked.

"We're here," Ali corrected me. "You slept like the dead and missed breakfast. I'm sure someone can rustle you up some food if you're hungry."

Settling Katie on one hip, Ali gestured toward the other car seat. "You mind?" she asked.

I wanted to say yes, but the look on Alex's face—scrunched up and lopsided—kept me from being difficult on principle. I unbuckled my seat belt, opened the door, and slid out of the car. I was halfway through liberating Alex when my mind caught up with my body enough to wonder where *here* was.

The air was crisp and cool for early summer and smelled like snow in my nose, even though there wasn't a hint of white on the stretch of grass under my feet. Hoisting Alex into my arms, I turned and looked away from the car, and the way the earth stretched out before me—green and flat and untouched— threw me back.

Turning slowly, I took in the 360 view. There was a large, wooden building up ahead of us—a restaurant, or maybe an inn—and from the distance, I could see a crooked sign hanging over a small porch but couldn't make out the words. Other, smaller buildings dotted the horizon, looking like they'd been carved from the land itself. There were scattered trees, and in the distance, I could see a denser forest and a hint of blue. Water. Possibly a lake.

And that was the exact second I realized where we were— and who lived in Montana.

Sure enough, as Ali and I moved toward the largest building, the sign came more clearly into view and a man—tall, with a scruffy beard and a deceptively unassuming air—came out onto the porch.

"The Wayfarer," I said, reading the sign.

"Did I not mention that this was where we were coming?" Ali asked.

"No. You neglected that detail."

"Oh, right. Because we weren't talking."

Sometimes, Ali could be just as much of a brat as I was—the downfall of having a guardian barely twice my age.

"Ali," the man on the porch greeted her.

"Mitch," she returned, her tone more or less identical to his—mild, warm, and unsurprised.

"These your little ones?" Mitch asked, his eyes going to the twins.

Ali nodded. "Kaitlin and Alexander. They're almost four months."

"Little girl likes her wolf," Mitch said with a smile. "She's growing faster than her brother."

Ali blew a wisp of hair out of her eyes, and Katie, as if she knew exactly what the adults were talking about, arched her back, her pupils dilating.

"Oh, no, little missy," Ali said. "You wait until Mama's got you out of these clothes and—"

Katie's body trembled with the pre-Change, and Mitch came to Ali's rescue.

"Here," he said. "I'll take her."

Katie went to him willingly, and for a moment, it was like she'd forgotten about changing altogether, which was a minor miracle that wouldn't last. Since the day she was born, Katie had never been this long in human form, and now—with the wilderness spread out before us—her urge to Shift would win out, without question or doubt. It was only a matter of time.

"Bryn," Mitch greeted me. He didn't look twice at my battered face. He didn't seem surprised that we were here.

He knew.

I felt like I was back at the Crescent in front of the pack, stripping down my mental defenses, letting them in just so they could beat me later.

Screw that.

What had happened was no one's business but mine.

"Hey, Mr. Mitchell," I said.

"Mitch," the man corrected gruffly, but he had to have known it was useless. Something about him always kept me from calling him by his preferred name. Maybe it was the fact that though he was a part of our pack, he visited the stronghold rarely.

Or maybe it was because he was Lake's dad.

"Is Lake...?"

"She's out back," Mitch said, his voice a low, rumbling hum. "No idea what she's doing. Pretty sure I don't wanna know, but I suspect she wouldn't mind some company." Mitch paused, for a fraction of a second. "Don't let her shoot you," he grunted.

With Lake, chances were that was pretty good advice. Maybe she would loan me a gun. At the moment, I kind of felt like doing some shooting myself.

"Should I cut through?" I asked, gesturing to the door of the Wayfarer.

"If your mother don't mind you taking off before you four are settled—"

"It's fine," Ali said. At this point, she was probably glad to be rid of me.

"Go on, then," Mitch said, jerking his head toward the door. "Git."

I got.

The restaurant was nearly empty. There were a couple of people sitting in a corner booth, and there was a towheaded woman in her mid-thirties or so behind the bar, wiping down the counter. When I walked in, she leaned forward on both elbows, with a look on her face that told me that she was probably the kind of bartender that people poured their hearts out to.

I wasn't buying.

The bartender caught me staring at her, and I turned my head away, averting my eyes and slumping my shoulders. The reaction was completely reflexive, but foreign, and I found myself wondering when I'd become a good little pack girl who averted her gaze and didn't cause trouble, and—for that matter—when I'd started submitting to humans, even as I silently wished they'd take their prying eyes and quiet sympathy elsewhere.

I had to get out of there.

The back door of the Wayfarer was only about twenty feet away from the front, but I found that despite all efforts to the contrary, I couldn't walk toward it quickly. I'd heard so much about this place over the years. I knew which boards in the floor I could remove to find packets of gum and stashes of childhood treasures, I knew that the whiskey behind the counter was sometimes watered down because a certain someone occasionally snuck a glass and replaced it with water, and I knew that the pool table leaned slightly to the right—a fact that helped if you were the type to hustle the clientele.

By the time I made it to the back door, I felt like I'd been inside forever. The need to get out and away and to be by myself was overpowering, but the moment I stepped outside, the fresh air hit me in the face, cooling my bruises, and the muscles in my stomach loosened enough to remind me why I'd come this way in the first place. About fifty yards away, there was a wooden fence, and on top of the fence sat a girl with long legs, long hair, and a double-barreled shotgun. The legs were tanned, the hair was wheat-blonde, and the shotgun was aimed directly at my left kneecap.

Sora's blank face. Ribs popping. Flying backward.

I physically shook the memory from my head. Lake wasn't Sora. Sora wasn't the Rabid. Nobody was going to shoot me here.

"Too scared to face me up close?" I called, forcing the knot of anxiety from my chest. "Don't tell me you've gone soft, Lake."

Lake snorted and bared her teeth in a wicked grin, and then she was off the fence, shotgun on the ground, running toward me. I started running toward her, too, but barely got three steps before she crashed into me and tackled me to the ground.

"Hey, bruised ribs here," I said.

"Oh, you yellow-bellied crybaby," Lake replied. "Did poor wittle Bwyn fall and go *boom* again?"

"For the last time, I didn't fall out of that tree—you *pushed* me."

"Snitch," she said amiably.

"Mutt," I replied, and then I threw myself at and into her, hugging her hard.

Besides Katie, Lake was the only female born in Callum's territory in the past hundred years. Maybe longer, depending on how old Sora was. Lake and her dad didn't come to our neck of the woods very often, and for whatever reason, Callum never forced their hand, so growing up, Lake and I had developed a relationship that I suspect is similar to what happens to humans who go to summer camp. When we were together, we were inseparable. From sunup to sundown, if you found one of us, you found the other. Devon was my best friend, but when Lake was in town, our duo became an easy trio: the human, the purebred, and the female Were, freaks all.

Lake, ever unaware of her own strength, squeezed too hard as she returned my hug, but despite the hug-with-a-vengeance, my ribs didn't so much as twinge, and I took that as an omen that maybe coming here hadn't been a mistake on Ali's part. Maybe I just needed time to regroup.

Come up with a plan.

After another long moment, I pushed Lake back, and even though I could never have broken her grip of my own accord, she let loose of me immediately. The two of us sat up, and I surveyed her, comparing her appearance and mine out of habit. I was wearing jeans, a sweater, and boots. Lake was barefoot and the only reason she was wearing even a tank top and boy shorts was that she'd outgrown streaking when she was about seven.

Except for that one time the summer when we were twelve, but that was completely beside the point.

"Aren't you cold?" I asked her.

Lake grinned. "Nope."

On the heels of the coldest spring we'd had in years, Lake was sun-kissed and tanned, color in her cheeks, highlights in her hair. I couldn't imagine her ever letting someone else beat her, no matter the cause.

As if she sensed where my thoughts were going, Lake set about distracting me. "How much you wanna bet I can put a bullet through that guy's Coke?" She gestured back toward the Wayfarer, and I noticed that a new group of people had taken a seat in one of the booths. From this distance, I could barely make them out through the dusty window, but I didn't doubt for a second that Lake's view of them was much clearer.

"No deal," I told Lake. I'd learned not to bet with her—about anything—by the time we were eight.

Except for that one time the summer when we were twelve, but again—completely beside the point.

"Besides," I said, "Matilda's over by the fence." I'd never actually met Lake's favorite shotgun, but I'd heard enough stories to make an educated guess.

"She's fickle, is Matilda," Lake admitted. "But boy, can the old girl get the job done."

"What'd this guy do anyway?"

As a general rule, Lake didn't shoot people without a reason or some assurance that they would heal almost as soon as she shot them.

"Jerk cheated on his girlfriend," Lake replied. "And stiffed me on my tip the last time through."

Lake had been waiting tables at the Wayfarer since she was about twelve. Anyone who'd been to the restaurant more than once knew that you didn't play pool with Mitch's daughter expecting to win and you didn't skimp on her tip. I'd never been here before, and even *I* knew that. I also knew that if you had a secret, you didn't come to the Wayfarer in the first place. There were no secrets with Lake Mitchell. None.

"So you asked for permissions, broke the conditions, and Callum had you beaten, huh?"

My first instinct was to pull back, but before my upper lip had worked itself even halfway into a good snarl, I let it go, the tension melting off my face. Lake was Lake. She couldn't help asking. It probably would have sucked more if she hadn't, but that didn't change the fact that if and when I said a word about any of this to anyone, it would be on my terms, not theirs.

The next time Callum's name crossed my lips, it would be because I wanted to say it, not because someone had asked.

Measuring my response, Lake plucked a strand of grass from the ground and chewed on it, deceptively insightful. "Don't want to talk about it?" she guessed, nonchalant.

Did I want to talk about the fact that I'd disobeyed the pack? That Callum had betrayed me, over and over again; that every day, he'd let me go on believing one thing when reality was another? Did I want to talk about the fact that together, Callum and I had destroyed Ali's marriage, torn my family apart, and brought life to a screeching halt?

"Not particularly."

"You want to race me to the dock?" Lake asked in the same casual tone.

I thought about running with the pack—how connected I'd felt. How invincible.

"Ten-second head start?" It helped to barter with Lake.

"Five."

I took off the moment the word was out of her mouth, ignoring the pain in my side and the way the bruises on my face and shoulders throbbed as my movements pulled skin tight across muscle.

I was *fine*.

Lake tore past me in a blur, never one to hold back on super-speed just because her opponent didn't have it. Jaw set, teeth clenched, I pushed myself to keep up, keep her in sight, and in the edges of my mind, I felt him.

Chase.

He and his wolf wanted to be here. They wanted to run with me, and as I pushed myself harder and harder, I pretended that Chase was there beside me, his hand looped through mine. In my dream, I'd kept watch over him. Protected him. I'd been the strong one.

I hadn't been the one crumpled on the ground.

With the Wayfarer behind me, I ran, trying to leave everything but that memory in my dust. My feet beat into the ground again and again, punishing it and punishing my body for its human weakness.

If what I'd seen the night before was real—and every instinct I had said it was—then a Rabid was still stalking Chase's dreams. The same Rabid that had hunted him down as human prey. *The* Rabid.

It didn't matter if my ribs hurt. It didn't matter if every time I blinked, I saw Sora's fist coming toward my face. I needed a plan. I needed to be strong. So I just kept running, because come hell or high water, a girl couldn't afford to be weak or human at a time like this.

CHAPTER SEVENTEEN

By the time I got to the dock, Lake was already lounging, her head thrown back and her feet dangling just above the surface of her namesake. The way I saw it, I had two choices: deal her in, or lie to her face. Experience—and my acquaintance with her trigger finger—told me that she made a better ally than an enemy, and if there were some things that were mine and mine alone, to play and replay in my head as I stared at my ceiling each night, there were others that I needed a second opinion on. And if that second opinion happened to come from a waitress with no compunctions whatsoever about eavesdropping on any and all Weres who passed through her territory, all the better.

"You heard anything about the new wolf?" I asked, plopping down next to her on the dock. Even with my ribs protesting so much that I wondered if they'd poked a hole in my lungs, the question made its way easily off my tongue. Things were always easy with Lake and me, even though Mr. Mitchell always swore that "doing things the hard way" was her middle name, the same way "pack business" could have been mine.

"I heard my dad talking to Ali on the phone," Lake said, staring out at the water. "Mama Bear was spitting nails— something about you and this new boy."

"Chase." Supplying his name didn't make me lose track of reality, but when I blinked, I kept my eyes closed for a fraction of a second longer than I would have otherwise, waiting for Chase or his wolf to appear, emblazoned on the inside of my eyelids. Now that I wasn't running anymore, it was harder to picture him, harder to feel him on the other side of the bond I'd forged.

"Ali didn't say the boy's name," Lake continued, closing her own eyes and tilting her head back, offering her face up to the sun. "She just said that he was bad news—for you. That Callum was hiding something. That you'd end up hurt."

At first, I'd assumed that the conversation Lake had over-heard was the one that had directly prefaced Ali dragging me and the twins off to the Wayfarer, but her words made me ask for a clarification on that point, and it became apparent that Ali had been in contact with Mitch long before I'd broken the conditions of my permissions.

Ali's lack of confidence in my ability to stay out of trouble was astounding. Or it would have been, if I'd proven her even the tiniest bit wrong.

"Did Ali or your dad know that the Rabid who attacked

Chase was the one who killed my family?" I was fairly certain I knew the answer to that question, but I had to ask. A week ago, I would have sworn that Callum couldn't have kept something like that from me, either.

To my relief, the second the word *Rabid* left my mouth, Lake's eyes flew open, and she almost fell off the end of the dock, supernatural grace and balance the only things that saved her from taking a nosedive I wouldn't have been able to avoid.

"The Rabid who killed your... I thought Callum killed that scum-licking, dirt-sucking, mother—"

Sensing that Lake could provide an infinite number of adjectives to describe the man Chase called *Prancer*, I cut her off. "I thought so, too, but no. The Rabid got away. Nobody thought it crucial to tell me. Flash-forward eleven years, and what do you know, Chase gets bit."

Lake digested that for a moment. "And I'm guessing the alpha didn't particularly want you to figure that one out."

I was grateful that she hadn't said Callum's name this time. "He let me see Chase, knowing I'd figure it out, and then he had me beaten for doing it."

Ali's logic had crept into my thoughts enough that my mouth was verbalizing it to Lake. If I could run with broken ribs, I could force myself to part with one or two ugly truths and to silently say the words that cut me most.

Callum. Pack. Stone River. Permissions.

I thought the words and thought them hard, pushing through it like the pain was nothing.

Callum.

Pack.

Stone River.

Callum.

Under the waistband of my jeans, the Mark was still there. I placed my hand over it, lining my fingers up with the grooves that Callum had carved into my skin.

"The Rabid is still alive. He's been alive all this time, and now, he's messing with *my*—" The possessive seemed more important than the noun that followed it. I wasn't sure what to call Chase—my friend? My wolf? My other self?

"So it's true," Lake said, saving me the trouble of finishing my sentence.

"What's true?"

"You and this boy. You Marked him."

When she put it like that, the impossibility of the situation became a magnitude more difficult to ignore. I wasn't a were wolf, and I certainly wasn't the Stone River Pack alpha. Callum hadn't been present when I'd thrown my pack-bond at Chase. The alpha hadn't forged a new connection between us, I hadn't bitten Chase, he hadn't bitten me, and what we shared was nothing like the bond between a werewolf and his mate.

It also bore no resemblance to the bond between Callum and me.

"It wasn't like that," I said. "It was—" How could I possibly describe what had happened, even to Lake? "We'd just figured out that his Rabid was the same as mine, and they were going to separate us."

We'd panicked. Both of us. "I had to calm him down. I couldn't let them take him away. I had to—"

Had to what? I wasn't explaining this right. Lake was sitting very still, an odd light in her eyes that I couldn't quite diagnose.

"I had to protect him. And me. So I took everything I felt for the pack. I saw the bond, and instead of closing myself off to it, I pulled. I pulled at it and I thrust it toward Chase."

I expected Lake to tell me again that what I'd done was impossible, but instead, she looked down at her knees, and in the softest voice I'd ever heard her use, she asked me the last question I ever expected to hear from her lips. "Could you do it again?"

For a second, I thought she was asking if, given the chance, I would go back in time and do the exact same thing again, knowing the consequences, but there was something between us—a light shifting of air, a pulsing in her bond with the pack and the muted power of the Mark on my side—that told me that wasn't so.

She was asking if I could rewire someone else's pack-bond. She was asking if I could rewire hers. Lake and her dad were peripherals. Callum didn't require their attendance at the

Crescent, but they were still a part of Callum's pack. He was still her alpha.

"I don't know, Lake."

Could you try? I didn't hear the words, the way I would have if my bond with Chase didn't stand between Callum's pack and my mind, but I could see the question on the tip of her tongue. After a moment, she bit her lip, and whatever I'd imagined I'd seen disappeared, replaced by a look I associated with Lake's reaction to being dared to do something.

An alarm sounded in the back of my head, because that look was trouble. Lake Mitchell didn't turn down dares.

"I suspect you're wanting to know why Callum didn't kill the Rabid," Lake said.

Cautiously, I nodded.

"And I suspect you're wanting to know if he has plans to kill the Rabid now that he's back?"

This was why I had dealt Lake in. She had no inhibition, no sense of propriety, and she was fearless. Pack or not, she wouldn't shy away from pressing Callum's buttons. Growing up removed from Ark Valley had given her the luxury of following her own will more than the alpha's, and right now, Callum's privacy and hallowed judgment didn't command her respect nearly as well as my need to make sure that this Rabid was put down.

"If Callum's not going to kill the Rabid, I will." I said those words out loud for the first time and knew that it wasn't a bluff.

It wasn't me blustering or running off at the mouth without thinking. It wasn't foolishness, and it didn't matter that I was human and the Rabid was not.

He'd messed with what was mine. He'd killed my family. He'd hurt Chase. And the only way to get him out of Chase's head forever was to see him dead.

I told Lake as much, and she didn't even blink. She didn't ask me how exactly one human girl was going to take down a Rabid that had been evading our entire pack for over a decade. She just took me at my word and moved on to the next order of business.

"What do you need me to do?"

I looked out at the water, working my way through the situation, taking into account everything I knew about Lake, the Wayfarer, and her brand of persuasion. I thought of the human bartender, with her talk-to-me face and eyes that didn't look like they missed much, and I thought about the kind of clientele that a place run by a peripheral male would naturally attract.

Wolves weren't solitary creatures. Where there was one werewolf, sooner or later, there were more, and Mitch and Lake weren't our pack's only peripherals.

"I think I need you to talk to the bartender," I said, turning the idea slowly over in my mind. If any of Callum's other wolves had been here, the bartender would know, and if she'd gotten them drunk enough, they might have talked. Lake didn't ask for the rationale behind my request. She just stood up and made her way back to the restaurant, because she knew as well as I did that any good plan started with recon.

It wasn't until Lake and I were sitting on stools in front of the bar that I thought to wonder how exactly a human female had ended up working for Lake's dad. Looking for answers, I closed my eyes and let my senses take over. The woman in question smelled like Walmart soap and evergreen trees. She bore no Marks and had no connection to the pack. Not to Stone River, and not to any of the others. She wasn't on edge and there wasn't the slightest whiff of fear in the air around her. From somewhere behind us, I heard a rustle, and my fingers curled reflexively into fists.

Wolf.

And not one of ours, either.

"Easy, girl," Lake said, even though I got the feeling that the intruder's presence sent her hackles up, same way it did mine. "This here's neutral territory. We welcome all types."

Technically speaking, this wasn't neutral territory, and it wasn't Lake's. Montana was Stone River territory. It belonged to Callum, and the wolf behind us did not.

"He's a peripheral," Lake told me. "One of Shay's."

I hadn't had much practice identifying other packs by smell, but I recognized the name. Shay was the youngest alpha in North America. He'd challenged the former leader of the Snake Bend Pack around the turn of the century and won. Like Devon, Shay was a purebred Were, and Sora was his mother, too. Technically, that made him Devon's half-brother, but since neither of us particularly cared for him, we didn't think of him that way. Shay had broken all ties with his family—and Callum—long before either Devon or I were born.

"Your dad lets Shay's wolves eat here?" I asked. It was unfathomable.

"Only the peripherals, and only the ones that can mind their manners," Lake said. "It doesn't hurt to have friends."

I tried to see the sense in that, however much my instincts were telling me it was wrong-wrong-wrong. I'd thought that the Wayfarer was a resting point for Stone River peripherals, but given the host of smells in the air, its clientele was far more eclectic than I'd given it credit for.

All the more reason to talk to the bartender and find out what she knew.

"I'm Bryn." I opened my eyes again and met hers, and if she noticed that I'd been smelling her, she didn't comment on it.

"Keely." For a long moment that was all she said, and then she turned and narrowed her eyes at Lake. "You up to something?"

Lake's lips worked their way into an easy grin. "Always. You heard anything about a Rabid?"

I'd expected her to finesse the question more, but who was

I kidding? This was Lake. Keely paused for a moment and then snorted. "If I lied, you'd smell it, so I'll stick with *that's no concern of yours* and suggest you leave it at that."

Lake opened her mouth to argue, but I pinched her leg in the age-old sign for *shut up and let me do the talking.*

"You know about werewolves," I said, meeting Keely's gaze.

"I expect I might," Keely allowed.

"And you're not dead."

Keely snorted. "This one sure knows how to sweet-talk a girl, doesn't she, Lake?"

I wondered if Callum knew that there were humans in Montana who knew who and what we were, but if he didn't, I wasn't going to be the one to tell him. "The fact that you're alive means you know how to keep your mouth shut. I can respect that."

Lake pinched my leg. I ignored her.

"So I won't ask you about any Rabids or any secrets."

Another pinch. Harder this time. I swatted Lake's hand away.

"But I am going to ask what you've heard about what it takes for a human to become a Were."

My logic in asking that question wasn't so much a rationale as an instinct. Any human who'd been within five feet of a werewolf and known him for what he was had thought about it. What it would be like to Change. What it would take to trigger it.

Ribs popping. Head throbbing. Punch after punch after punch.

I forced the swell of fear down before Lake could smell it, before the peripheral in the back right corner could get a taste of me. Keely and I weren't talking about a beating. I had no reason to be thinking about that. None. We weren't talking about Marks or being bitten.

We were talking about slaughter.

"I asked about that," Keely said. "When Mitch told me what he and Lake were and warned me that things could get rowdy here. He said he wouldn't let a soul touch me, but even so, I asked what would happen if I got bitten or scratched—if I would change or just keel over. Never hurts to be informed."

"Humans becoming Weres is supposed to be impossible," I said, thinking that instead of celebrating birthdays, I should start marking my life by its impossibilities. One for a four-year-old escaping a Rabid. Two for being Marked by a thousand-year-old alpha. Three for closing my mind off to the pack so completely for so long. Four for a boy who should be dead.

Five for the way I'd claimed him above and beyond our allegiance to Callum's pack. Six for the way Chase had come to me in my dreams.

"It's not impossible," Keely said, leaning forward on her elbows. "Just unlikely."

Now that was interesting. In silent agreement with my assessment, Lake finally stopped pinching my thigh. "That so?" she asked Keely, her voice a low rumble that reminded me of her dad's.

Keely nodded. "The way I've heard it, in the past thousand years, a human being changed has happened three or four times. Mostly, they just die. If anyone could figure out how to bring humans over without killing 'em dead, I suspect there'd be a lot more of you wolf-types than there are."

There was power in numbers. The larger the pack, the more powerful the alpha.

I digested the information Keely had given me slowly. Chase's situation wasn't impossible. It was *improbable*. I filed that information away for future knowledge.

"You know anything about the other times it has happened?" I asked Keely, not really expecting an answer. She shook her head and then excused herself, as the Were I'd felt earlier came up to the bar.

"I thought you wanted to find out about the Rabid," Lake said, dropping her voice to a whisper.

"I do," I whispered back, "but Miss Keely over there wasn't talking, and right now, our best lead on the Rabid is Chase."

I had no idea where the Rabid was or what he was doing, but I did know that a part of him was in Chase's head.

Burnt hair and men's cologne.

Banishing the memory of the smell, I told Lake about the first time Callum had taken me to see Chase. About the way that, for a few moments, the Rabid's claim to his prey had outweighed Callum's. About the way I'd seen Chase in my dreams and followed him into his own enough to know that the Rabid was still playing games.

"Let me get this straight," Lake said when I was done, leaning back on her bar stool in a position I would never have been able to manage. "You and the Stone River Pack alpha and *El Rabido* are fighting it out for dominance in lover boy's head."

There were so many things wrong with that sentence. The casual way she'd referred to the Rabid. The words—*Stone River, Pack, alpha*—that brought Callum's image to my mind and made me wonder how long thinking of him would feel like pressing on a bruise, just to see if it still hurt. And then there was the fact that Lake had referred to Chase as "lover boy," when really, he was just a boy. My boy.

Mine.

Mistaking my reaction for offense, Lake quickly added a second incomprehensible sentence onto her first. "Between Callum, the Rabid, and the infamous Bronwyn Clare, my money's on you."

Yeah. Right. The pain from my ribs, dull and aching, called the wisdom of that bet into question.

"Seriously, Bryn. You may be human, but I know you. You fight dirty."

The vote of confidence made me smile, but the movement hurt my face, reminding me again that I wasn't invincible.

I wasn't even that hard to break.

"I'm going to go," I said. "See how Ali's doing. Get settled."

Lake narrowed her eyes at me, trying to see past the surface of my words. I stared back at her, holding her gaze until she looked away. Realizing what I'd done—and what it would have meant in her wolf's eyes—I offered up an olive branch.

"I'm not giving up, Lake. I'm just regrouping."

I needed to think. I needed a plan, and as far as I was concerned, *recon* had just begun.

CHAPTER EIGHTEEN

"ALI?" I WASN'T ENTIRELY SURE THAT I WAS IN THE right place, so I called out as I opened the front door. The word bounced off the walls, and even though everything about this cabin—three bedrooms scrunched side by side, a combined living and kitchen area twice as big as I was used to—screamed *not home*, it was the difference in echoes between this house and Ali's that did me in.

Regrouping was one thing. Recon was good, and the Wayfarer wasn't a bad place to do it. But this wasn't home.

Thinking about Ark Valley made my mind go quiet, and my pack-sense surged. Chase came first, and I saw him running, the way Lake and I had earlier. I felt his stride in the muscles stretching down my own thighs and the urge to run, to be with him, almost devoured me whole.

Next, I felt the twins, two rooms over. Devon, Callum, and all of the other members of our pack were too far away for me to feel, except for Lake and her dad.

"Ali?" I called again, keeping my voice down this time,

because my connection to the twins hummed with the low buzz of sleep. She didn't reply, and I found all three of them sleeping on the same king-sized bed on a comforter that wasn't ours. Alex was on his tummy, his tiny human hands buried in Kaitlin's fur, and Ali's entire body was curved around the two of them. The moment I walked into the room, Katie stirred.

She blinked. Once. Twice. Three times. And then she wriggled. Glancing at Ali, dead to the world, I walked quietly to the bed and picked Katie up. She burrowed into my body, like she thought she could carve out a puppy-sized space in my side.

"Hey there, baby girl," I whispered.

Katie snuffed, and I realized she was smelling my breath. I wondered if I smelled like home, and if she could make out the faint scent of blood from my bruises.

Katie whined and then licked me.

"Shhhhh," I told her, settling her puppy form in my arms. "Mama and Alex are sleeping."

Katie stilled, and I brought my eyes back to Ali. She'd driven through the night to get us here. I doubted she'd slept much the three before that, when I'd been wafting in and out of consciousness.

"Mama's tired," I told Katie, my own stomach twisting. "Mama's had a hard day."

Week.

Month.

And me being me probably hadn't made it any easier for her.

Katie, well and truly bored with my revelations, yawned, her puppy-mouth opening so wide that if she were in human form, she probably would have dislocated her jaw.

"Did you wake up just for me, baby?" I asked her. She snuggled into my side again, and I took the cue. Gingerly, I slid onto the edge of the bed. I propped myself up on a pillow and let Katie sprawl out on my stomach. She laid her nose just under my chin, let out of a whoof of puppy-fresh breath, and fell asleep. I curled toward Ali, careful not to squish Alex, willing the three of them to sleep well.

Willing all four of us to be okay.

Sleep came. The clearing. The forest. The smell of early autumn—but no Chase. I knelt down to the ground, and with the motion, I lost my awareness that this was a dream. That maybe Chase's absence just meant that he wasn't asleep. Instead, I dug two fingers into the dirt and brought it to my nose.

I couldn't smell him. I couldn't smell anything. A sluggish worry wrapped its way slowly around the base of my spine, and like a snake, it slithered up my back, one vertebra at a time. I couldn't smell *anything*. It was worse than being blindfolded, worse than small spaces, worse than opening my mouth to scream, knowing the sound would never make it from my throat.

I couldn't *smell.*

I hugged my knees to my chest, unable to rise into a crouch, unable to ready my fists or reach for my blade. And then the world around me folded in on itself, like someone was making origami. Like I was a test paper and someone had crumpled me up and thrown me away.

And then the world was being uncrumpled, and the forest unfolded into something new.

Something small.

Something that smelled like wet cardboard and drain cleaner. I would have taken comfort in the fact that I could smell again but for the memories that combination brought with it.

Teeth ripping into flesh. Skin tearing like Velcro. Blood splattering. Again and again, vicious, relentless, thorough. Blood-blood-blood-blood-blood...

Jaws. Daddy. No! I wasn't back there. This wasn't real. I was big now. I was strong.

"Come out, come out, wherever you are, little one. No sense hiding from the Big Bad Wolf. I'll always find you in the end...."

Even though I was big now, even though I knew that this was impossible and that it wasn't happening again, I couldn't stop myself from walking through the old, familiar motions. I peeked out of my hiding space under the sink, saw the man.

I couldn't smell him.

I saw him Change.

Star on his forehead. Gonna find me. Blood. Blood-blood-blood—

I closed my eyes, the same way I had when I was four. I closed them, but I could hear the monster breathing—*right outside.*

It was gonna get me. The Big Bad Wolf was gonna get me.

Wood cracked, splintering. It was the front door—the door the wolf had locked behind him, back when he had been a man. And in came others—so many others. A man with exactly three lines on his face: one from smiling, two from frowning.

Callum, the grown-up me realized, even as the four-year-old inside me watched, unable to move.

A woman with a sleek dark ponytail—*Sora*—dove across the room, tackling the Big Bad Wolf away from me.

"I've got you, Little One." Hands reached in to grab me, but I didn't resist. "I won't let anyone hurt you."

Blood-blood-blood-blood.

"Shut your eyes."

I couldn't follow Callum's gentle command. Couldn't then. Couldn't now. The first time, I'd seen Sora change to wolf form and go for the Rabid's throat. Then Callum had turned

244

my head away. Only this time, he didn't. He let me watch, and there was nothing to see.

No Big Bad Wolf.

No house.

Nothing but the forest, outside of Callum's house. I turned back to face him in his arms, and he dropped me. I hit the ground hard, and Sora, still in human form, lashed out at me. She was too fast. I was too slow.

Bryn.

No. Not again. No-no-no-no—

Bryn. It wasn't Callum in my head. It wasn't the pack. It was Chase, and the moment I realized that, the world shifted on its axis, and I was back in the clearing, crouched down, smelling the dirt.

"Chase." I said his name out loud, and in wolf form, he nuzzled me, pushing his head under my hand.

Chase.

He butted my chest with his nose, and I fell over back onto my butt. "Jerk," I said.

He laughed, as much as any wolf could. Then, without any warning, he was human, and he was holding me. Rubbing his cheek against mine. Smelling my hair.

This time, I pushed him away, and he fell back. "Jerk," he said.

I smiled. "It really is you," I replied. "Isn't it? It's not just a dream."

Chase snorted. "I wasn't even asleep." For a moment, he sounded human, but then his eyes began to yellow, and the diameter of his pupil doubled within a single beat of my heart. "You needed me," he said, a deep vibrating hum in his voice. "I felt you. *Protect.*"

The last word didn't sound human. It didn't sound human at all. Chase had claimed me every bit as much as I'd turned my pack-bond to him, and what was an itch in the back of my mind when I was awake was all-encompassing now.

Chase wanted to protect me.

He had to protect me.

His wolf wanted out, wanted to smell me again. Make me okay.

"It was just a nightmare," I said, my voice low and calming. "No interference. No Rabid in my brain. No Callum. Just me."

I didn't mention that my brain wasn't the safest place to be these days. Without a word, Chase brought his hands up, ran them lightly over the bruises on my face, one by one.

"Scared," he said.

It was easier to admit it here. I nodded.

"Angry," he said, the wolf sneaking into his tone.

I nodded again.

"Sad."

These were things that the wolf inside Chase understood. Simple things that a human wouldn't have been able to diagnose with one-word sentences. Emotions were complicated for humans. They were complicated for me. But for Chase, liquid and feral and always a moment away from changing, they were simple.

I was scared and I was angry and I was sad, and there wasn't a thing I could do about any of it.

Chase cocked his head to the side, and for a moment, I thought he would Change again, but instead, his body went abruptly still in a jerky, violent motion, like someone or something was holding him back. He dropped to his knees, then to his stomach, and as I reached for him, a foreign smell filled the air.

Burnt hair and men's cologne.

The Rabid. I pulled Chase up, forced him into a kneeling position, and put my hands on his shoulders the way that Lance had when the Rabid had flooded Chase's waking mind.

"Look at me, Chase. Look only at me."

For a moment, it wasn't Chase looking back from those eyes. His lips curled into an ugly smile, serpentine and sharp.

Come out, come out, wherever you are. . . .

No.

"Look at me, Chase. *Look at me!*" I forced myself into his mind, brought his eyes to mine with my strength of will. I let my mind flood every corner of his. And I saw the Rabid.

He couldn't get to me.

Couldn't get to Chase when he was awake.

Callum had put up walls. And it was even harder now. Now that the boy had changed.

Looking at Chase, I got a sense of the Rabid. I could almost see the floss-thin line that connected the two of them. Nothing like the wall of light shining out of my body, connecting every part of Chase to every part of me.

Chase was *mine*. And the Rabid didn't even know it. Didn't know that anyone who hurt Chase was *dead*.

Warmth. Safety. Home.

The smell of burnt hair receded as Chase buried his hands in my hair and mine found their way to his. I stared into his eyes as they faded back to blue, and in them, I saw a reflection of an image Chase had seen when the Rabid had taken over.

"Girl." Chase said the word out loud.

A girl. My mental image of her was complete, the bond between Chase and me pulsing full force. Like we weren't hundreds of miles apart. Like he was standing right there beside me. Like this was real.

"Girl," I repeated. "Four years old, maybe five. Light hair. Gray eyes. Blood."

Only this time, the girl wasn't me, and she wasn't covered in someone else's blood. It was hers.

Girl.

There was a name on the tip of Chase's tongue, on the tip of mine, but before I could say it, I felt a sharp pinch in my ear. And another in my toe. And then—

"Ow!" I sat up in bed. My heart was pounding. My throat was dry. Chase was nowhere to be seen.

"Pleasant dreams?" Ali asked.

Not exactly, but I wasn't about to tell her that. I brought my hand up to my ear. It wasn't bleeding. Neither was my toe. But Alex, who was in his wolf form for the first time in I wasn't sure how long, looked quite pleased with himself, and Katie licked the side of my face.

"What time is it?" I asked Ali.

"Morning." For a moment, that was all she said, and then she looked back at me from the foot of the bed, where she was unpacking the twins' onesies. "You slept through the night. We all did, even Nibbler One and Nibbler Two over there."

Ali had slept. The twins had slept. What I'd done—at least the latter half of the night—wasn't sleeping.

It wasn't human, either.

"How are you feeling?" I could tell by Ali's tone—forced casualness—that she expected me to jump down her throat for asking the question.

Scared. Angry. Sad, I thought. But all I said out loud was, "A little better, maybe."

Ali wrinkled her forehead and cocked her head to the side. Clearly, she hadn't prepared herself for me to be pleasant. After a moment, her eyes narrowed. "What exactly did you and Lake do yesterday?" she asked, like we might have held up a gas station and gone on a crime spree across the country, all in the span of just a few hours.

"We went to Mexico, had some tequila, eloped with a pair of drug smugglers, and took part-time jobs as exotic dancers. You know, same old, same old."

Ali snorted.

"I'm torn on stripper names. It's either going to be Lady Love or Wolfsbane Lane. Thoughts?"

Ali threw a onesie at me. "Brat."

Considering I'd cost her a husband and her home, that was probably putting things lightly.

"Talking about it might help," Ali said, seeing a tell on my face to the guilt sloshing around in my stomach. "You're going to have to talk to someone eventually, Bryn."

I thought back to the dream. Back to Chase. Back to the screaming girl and the name buried in my mind.

"I am talking to someone," I said, making the executive decision that Ali didn't need to know that the person I was talking to was a teenage werewolf haunted by the psychopath who'd murdered my birth parents. "And you're right, it helps."

Ali was dumbfounded. Obviously, this wasn't the response she'd been expecting. Before she could formulate a reply or press me for answers, I bounded off the bed and went in search of clean clothes.

"Where are you going?" she called after me.

"First, I'm getting dressed," I called back. "And then I'm going to see what Lake is up to. I have a project for her."

The day before, our best lead to the Rabid had been Chase, but today, I had more. I had a mental image of a girl. I had a name. And I had a deep and abiding suspicion that if my family had been the Rabid's first set of victims, and Chase was his most recent, they weren't alone.

Somewhere along the line, the Big Bad Wolf had attacked someone else, too. Her name was Madison.

CHAPTER NINETEEN

LAKE AND I SET UP SHOP IN THE RESTAURANT. I ordered cheese fries; Lake got a triple-bacon cheeseburger. Breakfast of champions, all the way.

"I take it you have a plan, Picasso?" Lake asked, after she'd had her way with the burger. I ignored her for a few seconds, putting the finishing touches on the face I was sketching on a napkin. Given the limitations of (a) my skill and (b) my current medium, the likeness wasn't a bad one.

"This girl," I told Lake. "The Rabid was thinking about her last night. I think she's one of his victims."

When the Rabid attacked my family, I'd gotten away unharmed. Chase had nearly died.

Somehow, I didn't think that the Rabid's other victims had been so lucky. In the past thousand years, only a handful of humans had survived a major werewolf attack long enough to go Were themselves, and Chase was a lot older than the girl I'd seen in his mind and in the Rabid's.

Stronger.

"Okay," Lake said cheerfully. "We've got a face on a napkin." I could practically hear an unspoken *is it time to shoot someone yet?* on the end of that sentence, but I pressed on.

"We have a picture, and we have a name."

MADISON, I wrote in all capital letters on the napkin.

"And," I continued as I wrote, "if she's one of this guy's victims, her body was either found torn apart by wild animals, or he hid her bones after eating the rest of her."

Anyone else probably would have balked at my bluntness, but Lake just twirled her blonde hair around her right index finger and nodded.

"Google?" she asked.

"Unless you have a better starting place," I replied, "then, yes. You guys have wireless in here?"

Lake leaned back and grinned, slinging her arm over the back of our booth. "What do you think we are, heathens? Course we have wireless."

Most of the older Weres were technologically resistant, but I'd grown up with the internet and so had Lake. Together, we probably knew more about technology than the entire old guard of Stone River combined.

We also had laptops.

It was early enough in the day that the rest of the restaurant was empty, save for Keely, and if she thought the sight of two teenagers surfing the internet in a werewolf bar was a bit odd, she certainly didn't say so.

"I'll start by searching news stories. You see if you can find some kind of missing-persons database in case our girl's body was never found."

"Anybody ever tell you you're bossy?" Lake asked.

"That a rhetorical question?" I returned, while entering the words *Madison, wolf attack, dead OR missing,* and *girl* into the search field.

"Nope," Lake replied, her own fingers moving lazily across the keys. "Not a rhetorical question."

"In that case, yes. I've been told on occasion that I'm bossy."

"Thought so."

The two of us fell into silence as we combed through our search results. Fifteen minutes later, I reached for a cheese fry, only to find the plate empty. I shot arrows at Lake with my eyes, but she just grinned.

You snooze, you lose. It was practically wolf law.

"You finding anything?" Lake asked.

I shook my head. "Nope. You?"

"I've checked two missing-children databases and none of them have a Madison that looks a thing like your girl there." Lake paused, the perpetual motion of her body stilling. "Lot of missing kids out there," she added.

Frustrated that my plan hadn't yielded even a smidgen of a lead, I switched from surfing news stories to searching images. Since the missing-children databases hadn't turned up our girl, I tried a new combination of words.

Madison, in loving memory

A couple of clicks had the search engine displaying a hundred images per page, and fourteen pages and half an hour in, I saw her. Hands shaking, I clicked on the picture and followed the link.

Madison Covey, age six

She had light blonde hair, tied into pigtails for the picture. Her eyes were bluer and less gray than they'd been in my dream, but the resemblance was unmistakable. Someone had erected an online shrine for our Madison.

Ten years ago.

"Find something?" Lake asked.

I didn't answer, not right away. I just did the mental math. If she'd lived, Madison would have been a year older than me.

"I'll take that as a yes." Lake swung over to my side of the booth, and she leaned her head over so that the side of her forehead touched mine. Together, we scrolled down the page. It wasn't the kind of information I'd hoped to find. No police reports. No detailed descriptions of her body after the attack. Just a picture of the girl and information about her favorites: favorite colors (orange and blue), favorite foods (macaroni and cheese), favorite thing to do with bubble wrap (pop it).

We miss you, Maddy.

I closed my eyes, seeing Chase and seeing this girl through the Rabid's eyes.

"He killed her." I tried to pull myself away from the little girl's face, tried not to wonder if she'd been hiding under a sink when he found her, or if he'd dragged her body into the forest to celebrate his kill.

"She lived in Nevada," I said. "Not Callum's territory."

"Odell's," Lake supplied. "The Desert Night Pack. They smell like sandstone and fish."

Not a pleasant combination, or one that made any amount of sense, but that's the way it was with foreign packs. None of them smelled good. They weren't supposed to. They were foreign. They were threats. Wolves from our pack probably didn't smell any better to them.

"Looks like this Rabid is an equal-opportunity hunter," I said. "I was attacked in Colorado. Chase is from—"

Where was Chase from?

Kansas.

The answer was enough to make me close my eyes, letting a blink last longer than it otherwise would have.

Somewhere in Ark Valley, Chase was awake.

"Chase is from Kansas," I said. "Rim of Callum's territory."

"You and Madison were both little girls. Your parents were obviously adults. Chase is a teenage boy. What's the pattern?"

There were few things in life more frightening than a werewolf who watched *Law and Order*.

"Multiple states, multiple territories. There is no pattern, unless…"

I didn't finish my sentence, and I didn't have to. Lake was already there.

"Unless there are more."

Not just Chase and Madison and me. What if there had been others? If this Rabid hunted across territories and never stayed in one place for long, he could have been doing this for years. But how was that even possible? Weres just didn't think like that. Wolves had territories. Even lone ones.

Even Rabids.

They didn't just drift from state to state, hunting humans unnoticed.

My fingers made their way back to the keys, and I opened a new window. Now that I had a last name and a town, maybe I could track down a news story, a police report, anything.

Lunch came and went. I had another order of cheese fries. Lake had another triple-bacon cheeseburger. Keely didn't say a word. Slowly, the restaurant began to fill up. Humans, mostly. The peripheral Were from the Snake Bend Pack. Another Were that I recognized as one of Callum's.

By late afternoon, Lake and I had an MO. Hundreds of people had been killed by wolves in the past decade. A small subset of them—all children—had been attacked in cities or towns where there were no native wolf populations. Many of the victims had died on the spot. Others, like Madison Covey, had been dragged off into the woods, bleeding all the way, no more than scraps of flesh recovered to identify their bodies.

And then there were the thousands of missing children about whom nothing was known. There one day, gone the next. For all we knew, some of them had fallen to our Rabid, too.

One thing was certain: Chase and I were outliers. He was the oldest. At four, I would have been the youngest, and my parents were the only adults.

At one point, Lake rustled up a map and a pen. We spread it out over our table, marking each of the attacks that fit our Rabid's pattern.

Maybe we didn't know what we were doing. Maybe two kids with an internet connection and a lot of time on their hands couldn't track a serial killer, even if they knew what to look for better than any police department would.

But maybe we were right.

I had no idea what to do about it. For minutes at a time, maybe hours, I stared at the map. We'd marked kills in every territory, but the most were in Callum's and the two adjacent territories: those belonging to Odell and Shay. The attacks zigzagged out from some invisible central point, and I cursed the fact that I'd taken algebra instead of geometry this year in school.

Tell me where you are, I said silently.

There was no reply. I hadn't really expected one.

"You girls hungry?" Keely asked, wrapping back by our booth, the way she did every hour or so to check on us.

I nodded. Lake grunted.

"The usual?" Keely asked, her voice dry.

I shook my head. "Pie?" I asked Lake.

She nodded. "Pie."

Five minutes later, we had our pie, but this time, Keely didn't disappear after delivering it. "Do I want to know what you two are up to?" she asked.

"No."

"Probably not."

Keely put a hand on her hip. "This about that Rabid?"

"Yup."

"Sure is."

Lake and I paused, meeting eyes and wondering how exactly it was that Keely had tricked an honest answer out of us. I, for one, hadn't had any intention of telling her a thing.

Keely held up a hand. "You know what? I don't want to know. Lake, you have company. Let me know if you need help disabusing him of any notions."

I was still stuck on wondering how exactly Keely had pried the truth from our lips, when her words sunk in. Company? What kind of company?

And that's when it washed over me: *wolf. Foreign. Wrong.*

I straightened in my seat, hackles raised. Lake didn't adjust her posture at all, but underneath the table, I saw her hand move, and for the first time, I noticed that she'd brought Matilda with her this morning.

"Now, why do you have to go and reach for the gun?" the

peripheral from yesterday asked her. He was tall and broad, and I deeply suspected that in wolf form, he'd be almost as large as Devon. "And here we've been getting along so well."

Lake smiled, slow and sure, a look that meant she was getting ready to either flirt or attack. I braced myself for either or both.

"You're just sour because I beat the tar out of you at pool." Lake smiled, tossed her hair over her shoulder, and in a motion too quick for me to track, whipped out her shotgun, aiming it squarely at the foreign wolf's nose.

"I thought you said it paid to have friends," I reminded her.

Lake didn't blink. "It does. If Tom and I weren't friends, he might be trying to prove that he's the stronger wolf, and I might be making the reverse argument with the help of my gun."

He blinked twice and then laughed, but didn't sound entirely comfortable. There was an edge in Lake's voice, one that told him to take her threat seriously. He was male, he was bigger, and he was probably stronger—but she was armed.

I really hoped this wasn't going to degenerate into a dominance squabble, though in retrospect, it was probably too much to hope that I'd left that behind.

As if sensing my thoughts, the foreign wolf turned his attention to me. "You're Callum's Bryn," he said shortly.

I met his gaze. I refused to look away. I managed not to think about Sora. I managed not to think about the fact that if he wanted to, this man could squash me in a second.

"I used to be," I replied.

"Hey, buddy. Eyes on me." Lake was the protective type and the jealous type. I wasn't sure which had her forcing the foreigner's eyes back to hers. If he challenged anyone, her posture seemed to be saying, it would be her.

Personally, I wouldn't have laid money on his odds.

"The alphas have been called," he said after a long moment, never moving, never taking his gaze from hers. "Stands to reason some of them will be passing through on their way to Callum's."

Lake didn't blink. She didn't move. She also didn't cock the trigger of her gun, and her "friend" took that as encouragement. "I thought you'd want to know."

Lake didn't reply, but after a long moment, she put down the gun, her suntanned face going ashen white.

"Why's the Senate going to Ark Valley?" I asked, even though I deeply suspected we had the answer spread out on the table in front of us, marked with Xs and stars.

"Callum called 'em," the Were replied, taking his eyes from Lake to look back at me.

I tossed my ponytail over my shoulder. I knew how to do this. If you needed answers, you had to stand your ground.

I could do this.

"And why did Callum call 'em?" I asked.

The Were shrugged. Keely took that moment to refill my coffee, and as her shoulder brushed the man's, he shrugged again and started talking. "Who knows? With the old man, chances are as good as they aren't that it's for something that hasn't even happened yet."

The old man. Even among his own kind, Callum was older than most. Stronger, too. But the last part of that sentence...

"Why would he call a meeting about something that hasn't happened yet?"

The man shrugged, like it was becoming a compulsion. "Because he knows it will."

I still wasn't following. Fortunately, someone was.

"Are you saying Callum's psychic?" Keely asked quietly, sounding a measure less incredulous than I felt when I heard the question. Alphas were connected to their packs. They saw through eyes that weren't their own. They were strong.

But they weren't psychic.

"I'm not saying a thing," the Were said as if he couldn't figure out how exactly he'd managed to say as much as he already had. "But, yeah. You don't get to be Callum's age or have a pack that big without an edge."

Keely set my coffee cup back down and then moved on to the next table, and the Were stopped talking. His forehead wrinkled as he took in the full sight of our table. "What are you two doing anyway?" he asked.

I expected Lake to reply, but she didn't. She'd gone ashen at the announcement about the alphas and hadn't yet recovered.

"We're plotting world domination," I said, covering for her, wondering what was wrong, even as my own mind was muddled with possibilities I'd never considered. About Callum. About Ali's assertion that Callum had known what my permissions would lead to, long before he'd ever granted them. "It takes more planning than one might think."

Werewolves could smell lies, but most of them were significantly dicier on the subject of sarcasm.

"I should go." Lake rushed the words into each other, and then, in a blur, she was gone, shotgun and all. The moment she left, I became aware of how close this foreign wolf was to me, how awful he smelled, how jarring his presence was to my pack-sense.

I didn't show it. I just sat there, and after four seconds, or five, and one hard look from Keely, he backed slowly away. I reached for my coffee cup and didn't notice until I picked it up that my hand was trembling. I reached out my other hand, steadying the cup, and then I brought it slowly to my lips, digesting what I'd just heard.

The alphas were coming. The Senate had been called.

Callum may or may not have been psychic.

And Lake was nowhere to be seen.

CHAPTER TWENTY

GOING AFTER LAKE WAS EASIER SAID THAN DONE. I dropped our stuff back at Cabin 4, where my family and I were staying, and then I tried to figure out which of the other houses dotting the horizon was hers. Based on the number of them on the property, Mitch was either an impressive businessman or really bad about picking up strays. At some point, the Wayfarer appeared to have evolved from a restaurant/bar to some kind of inn.

Or possibly a halfway house.

None of which told me where Lake was, or why she'd run off in the first place. Either I'd missed something in her interaction with the wolf named Tom—and I didn't think I had—or she was upset about the Senate meeting. Or what Tom had said about Callum.

Or both.

Until I knew what had upset her and why, I couldn't judge whether it would be better to give her space or hunt her down, keep her out of trouble or get into some with her. Looking for her gave me an excuse not to think about the bombshells Tom had dropped.

Tracking had never been my strong suit, but I knew enough to start where I'd lost track of my prey to begin with. The dirt path up to the restaurant was well trod, and I wouldn't have been able to pick out Lake's tracks were it not for the fact that most of the other patrons of this fine establishment followed the trinity of instructions on the front door: No Shirt, No Shoes, No Service.

That had to have been Keely's doing. Werewolves weren't particular on the topic of dress, or lack thereof.

Lake's imprint was light in the dirt, which told me she'd been running full speed, her feet barely touching the ground as she bolted. When the drive gave way to fields of grass, I followed the trajectory she'd been taking before until I hit a more densely wooded area. I found her clothes in shreds, scattered with the force of her forward momentum, her shotgun abandoned beside them.

Knowing what the torn tank top meant, I knelt to the ground and looked for confirmation. I didn't have to look far.

Paw prints.

"She Shifted."

The mild voice took me by surprise. I'd been so caught up in tracking Lake that I hadn't noticed someone else tracking me.

Mitch had the grace not to mention just how easy that task had been. "Lake just needs to run it out for a bit. She'll head for the mountains, always does. 'Bout halfway there, she'll turn back."

It was already getting dark outside.

"Don't you worry about her, Bryn. I've never seen a girl for running like that one. For that matter, haven't seen many wolves even half as fast. She'll be back by sunrise. Always is."

"Why's she running?" I asked, slipping into the gentle cadence of Mitch's ambling tone.

"Senate's coming through," Mitch commented, sounding for all the world like he was commenting on the weather. *Storm's comin'. It'll pass.*

"But what does the Senate meeting have to do with Lake?" I asked.

Mitch stared at my face, long and hard, taking measure of whatever he saw there before speaking again. "Nothin' that I know of. I suspect they'll be talking about this Rabid the two of you have been nosing around at all afternoon."

And here I'd thought that getting away from Callum meant that I'd have some privacy—and the chance to get the drop on someone, every once in a while.

"Is Callum psychic?" The question slipped off my tongue before I'd even thought about asking it.

"Psychic?" Mitch repeated, biting back a smile that made me feel younger than I was. "Not a word you hear much in our world, Bryn."

By some definitions, we were all psychic. Pack-bonds

connected the Stone River wolves to each other, to their wives, and to me. I could speak to pack members without opening my mouth, and for the past two nights, Chase and I had shared dreams.

We'd pulled the image of a girl from the mind of the Rabid.

"Does Callum know that things are going to happen before they happen?" I asked, rephrasing the question in terms of specifics, as Ali's question to me in the car floated back into my mind: *How many times have you gotten the drop on Callum, Bryn? How many times has anyone?*

"Callum's got good instincts," Mitch said.

"The kind of instincts that let him see the future?" All of a sudden, I had to know. How it worked. How much Callum knew.

If he'd done this to me on purpose.

"Let's just say he has a knack for knowing what's going to happen before it does and leave it at that."

"A knack?" I snorted. "Like you have a *knack* for turning into a wolf?"

Mitch ignored my sarcasm. "Something like that."

"Is it because he's an alpha?"

"No."

"Is it because he's a Were?"

"No." Mitch put his hands into the pockets of his jeans. "It's just a knack, Bryn. Some people have 'em. Most don't."

He made it sound so simple. So matter-of-fact that I

wondered why it had never occurred to me before.

"Some people are fast. Some people are strong." Mitch grinned. "Some people are just real easy to talk to."

I recognized that grin and knew it meant something. He was teasing me. *Real easy to talk to . . .*

"Keely," I said, my mind spinning. Lake and I had told her what we were doing without even meaning to. The peripheral male who'd warned us the other alphas were coming hadn't spilled the beans about Callum's reputed power until Keely had come over to pour my coffee, brushed her shoulder against his, and then, he couldn't tell us everything we wanted to know fast enough.

No wonder Mitch had a human bartender, if that bartender had a *knack* for getting secrets out of anyone who passed through.

Knacks. Some people have them. Most don't.

I saw the next question coming a mile off. I took my time asking it, because I didn't want to sound as ridiculous as I had when I'd called Callum *psychic*. "Do I have one?"

Mitch shrugged. "You'd know that better than I would."

I thought of fighting Devon. Of hiding under the sink. Of forcing my pack-bond onto Chase.

Of fighting back the Rabid in his head.

Was that *something*? Or was I just lucky and stubborn and everything that any human Marked by an alpha and raised by werewolves would have been?

For his part, Mitch reached out and patted my shoulder as if he were consoling me for all of the knacks I didn't have. "Way I see it, Bryn, you've always been mighty scrappy."

Scrappy? *Scrappy?*

Some people could see the future. Some people could loosen other people's lips just by looking at them. And me?

I was *scrappy*.

Lucky me.

"Will the alphas stop in the restaurant on their way through?" I asked.

Mitch's smile hardened. "Some will."

"Will Keely . . . use her knack?" The phrasing sounded ridiculous, but I wasn't sure how else to put it.

Mitch took my meaning and shook his head. "Keely'll take tomorrow off. I'll man the restaurant myself."

I got the feeling he didn't want any of the alphas to know about Keely or what she could do. Especially since the Wayfarer played host to some of their peripherals.

"And Lake?" I asked. I still didn't understand why she was running or what exactly she was running from.

"Those alphas won't see hide or hair of Lake, Bryn. She'll stay far enough away, they won't even smell her."

There was something in his tone that made me think that if Lake hadn't been inclined to stay away on her own, he'd have seen to it that she did. Given my own mixed feelings about the Senate, I understood the impulse, but not the hardness around Mitch's eyes.

"Why?"

Mitch sighed, and I wondered if he'd tell me I asked too many questions. Finally, he looked down at the ground and then, as if his shoes had given him the answer, he turned back to me. "Some Weres, especially the dominant ones, get real funny around females, and Lake's not a kid anymore."

Our pack had three females. Sora, who was mated to Lance. Katie, who was a baby.

And Lake.

"Usually isn't too bad, unless there are a bunch of men and only one female," Mitch continued.

But of course, in our world, that was the way it always was. Most Weres took human mates. Whoever ended up with Lake wouldn't have to worry that she'd die in childbirth. If she married a werewolf, her children would be pure-blooded Weres.

"She's fifteen," I said.

Mitch nodded. "That she is." He didn't say anything else, and I felt an overwhelming urge to change the subject and an abject inability to do so. After a long, torturous silence, Mitch patted my shoulder again and then shoved me back toward the restaurant.

"It's almost dark, and if I know Ali, she'll be worrying."

Just like Mitch would, waiting for Lake to come back.

"Go on," he said gently. "Git."

With one last glance at the forest and Lake's shredded clothes, I did as I was bid, and got.

When I got home, Ali didn't harass me about what I'd been doing all day, because I preempted any questions on her part by throwing some of my own at her.

"Did you know Callum sees the future?"

Ali opened her mouth and then closed it again. "Mitch?" she said finally, her mouth settling into a tense, straight line that told me she'd be giving him a piece of her mind in the near future.

"Peripheral from another pack," I said, figuring that I'd save Mitch a confrontation or two.

Ali nodded and after a few seconds of silence, she spoke, "I've always known. Callum told me the day I decided to join the pack."

"Before or after you decided to join?" I asked.

Ali didn't answer me, and I read the meaning in that. Callum had put his cards on the table and told Ali he saw the future before she'd chosen to become a part of his pack. The only reason he would have done that was if something he'd seen played a pivotal role in causing her to stay.

"What did he see?" I asked her.

Ali shook her head. "Doesn't matter. I changed it. It didn't happen."

"Ali?"

But she wouldn't budge, and I filed the exchange away as

a mystery for another time. Right now, I had other questions. "Did everybody but me know?" I asked, trying not to sound as put out as I felt. Ali had earned herself a few buys. I'd given her enough venom she didn't deserve over the past few months to forgive her for keeping this a secret.

The rest of the pack, however, was another story.

"Most of the oldest wolves know," Ali said. "None of the wives do. Devon doesn't."

She knew me well enough to know that Dev was the one who mattered the most.

"I take it Lake knows now?" Ali continued.

"Maybe."

Had Lake even heard that part of Tom's confession? The moment he'd mentioned that foreign alphas would be passing through the Wayfarer, she'd gone quiet and pale.

"The Senate is meeting," I said.

"*Senate*," Ali scoffed, purely out of reflex. "There's nothing democratic about werewolves. *Nothing*."

She was right. This meeting would be like throwing a bunch of champion gladiators into a ring and telling them to talk out their differences over tea. A democracy sounded good in theory, but every time the Senate met, it threatened to be the last.

All it would take is one alpha to decide that he was above it. Below it. Whatever. One dominant wolf curious to see if he could force his will on one of the others, absorb that territory into his own. Grow his pack's numbers and power by taking someone else's.

By force.

"Lake's gone," I said, thinking of those same men and the way the thought of them had sent her running—not because she was running away, but for the same reasons I'd forced myself to race her to the dock. To prove I was faster. Stronger. Tougher than anyone thought I was.

Even me.

"Gone?" Ali was startled. "Gone where? Does Mitch know?"

I nodded. "She Shifted and took off for the mountains." It was easy to picture Lake running. She was a honey-blonde wolf, a color you never would have seen in nature, and she was fierce. If I'd wanted to, I probably could have reached for her through my pack-bond, but I knew when to leave well enough alone.

When Lake was ready to talk about it, she'd come back.

"The Senate," Ali said, and this time, her voice was tighter. Less sarcastic, more pained. "Some of them will have to pass through here to get to Callum. I take it Callum is the one who called them?"

Callum was more or less the only one who ever called the Senate. The others were content to live as kings in their own territories. He was the one who'd declared them a council. This whole democracy thing was his idea. Given what I knew now about his so-called knack, I had to wonder if there was a reason for that move.

Callum never did anything without a reason.

"Lake doesn't want to see anyone who passes through," I said, refusing to think about Callum any more than I had to. "Mitch says male werewolves can get weird around females."

Ali's silence wasn't a surprised one. She'd known, then. I probably should have figured it out when Lake's visits to Ark Valley had become fewer and further apart, the older we got.

"Nobody will touch Lake without Callum's say-so," Ali said. "Not unless they've lost their minds."

Considering that Lake and I were currently tracking a Rabid, that was less than comforting. Disturbing, too, was the idea that some of the other alphas might be unstable enough to fall under the same classification, at least where female werewolves were concerned.

"Callum wouldn't let anyone hurt her," I said.

Ali tried to hide her incredulous look, but I saw it anyway, the way her mouth twisted to the side and her eyes widened, reminding me that he'd done more than let Sora hurt me.

He'd told her to do it.

"Callum's more of a big-picture person, Bryn." Ali's voice was soft, and I got that she was trying to be gentle with me, trying to make me understand the situation in a way that would hurt me less, even though she had no desire to *understand* it herself.

"Sometimes, for the future he wants, the details have to give."

The details. Like *me*.

"I'm going to go," I said. "To my room. It's been a long day."

Ali nodded. "Love you, kiddo."

"I love you, too."

By the time I got to my room, I needed something to do—half so I could stop thinking about Callum and his so-called knack, and half so I wouldn't start thinking about the fact that this *wasn't* my room.

The map provided a convenient distraction. I spread it out over my bed and stood on my knees over it. There had to be some pattern to the killing. If I'd had a ruler, I would have measured the distance between each of the kills. Instead, I played connect the dots, drawing a line from the first attack—the one against my parents—to the next chronologically, and then the next. I stopped when I got to Chase's, and still, there weren't any answers.

There were more attacks in the West and Midwest than in the East. More in the North than in the South. But that still left a quarter of the country.

A quarter that was divided among alphas, none of whom would have tolerated a lone wolf, let alone a Rabid, on their land.

Maybe if he was at the edges of the territory? I thought. Things were certainly different at the Wayfarer than they were in Ark Valley. Using the same pen, I drew an outline over each of the territories. Callum had Kansas, Colorado, Wyoming, Montana, Nebraska, and the Dakotas. California, Nevada, Oregon, Idaho, and Utah were part of Desert Night territory. Snake Bend zigzagged from Arkansas up to to Wisconsin, looping back down for Illinois.

As I finished tracing Shay's territory, I paused, looking closer at the map. It was the kind that had geographical information on it as well as official boundaries: rivers, mountains, that kind of thing. I thought briefly of Lake, running for something she wouldn't reach, but then I forced myself to concentrate.

Callum had been in America longer than Colorado had been a state. I grappled with my memory, grasping at straws. Somewhere in my "surviving pack life" lessons, there'd been pack history.

Rivers. Mountains. Lakes.

That was it. Once upon a time, territories hadn't been drawn along state lines. They'd been drawn along natural ones, and I remembered—almost remembered, couldn't remember—*something*.

Something Callum had told me about the borders of our territory. Of all territories.

I forced myself to close my eyes. I pictured Callum and ignored the stinging in my throat. The phrase, if I could just remember the phrase...

No-Man's-Land.

Triumph was sweet, the aftertaste bitter. I couldn't have

been older than six or seven when Callum had told me about it. There were places where the natural cutoffs didn't line up well with state lines. A tiny slice of one state might be cut off from the rest of a territory by a river or by mountains. Hardly worth fighting over, but fighting was what Weres did about territory disputes, so in certain cases...

The alphas had a gentlemen's agreement to leave the land alone.

The answer was so obvious that if I'd been any older during Callum's little tutorial, I would have berated myself for not thinking of it sooner. With a smile, I took my pen and circled the tiny slices of the map that fell between boundaries, grateful that I'd managed to remember and that Callum had told me in the first place.

In retrospect, though, it seemed like a weird thing to teach a kid who just wanted to learn how to tell a few lies and not get eaten.

Sitting back, I examined my work. It wasn't an answer. There were five relevant pockets of land that fell in the center of the Rabid's attacks, each one so small that they weren't labeled with any city names on the map. Now, I just needed to figure out which one the Rabid was using as his base of operations.

A funny feeling wormed its way through my insides. It wasn't entirely dissimilar to what I'd felt the night I'd run with the pack, or the starburst of determination in my brain when

I'd realized that I needed to touch Chase, even if it meant breaking every rule.

I was a predator, tracking her prey. I was hunting, the same way Weres took down smaller game.

"I don't *need* to hunt this Rabid." I said the words out loud, trying to convince myself that they were true. Even if I knew where he was, killing him wasn't my job. I wasn't as well equipped to do it as Callum and the other alphas were, and this was what they were meeting about.

The last time I'd rushed into something, things hadn't ended well. I thought of Ali in the other room, thought of everything she'd given up for me. If I got myself killed, she'd be the furthest thing from okay, and the twins needed their mother.

I had to wait. I had to let the Senate take care of this. If they knew what I knew, that this Rabid had been hunting on all of their lands, they'd want to take care of him as badly as I did. Any werewolf with even a lick of sense knew that challenging an alpha on his own turf was a good way to get yourself *dead*.

I looked back at the map, and thought back to the words I'd sworn to Lake. *If Callum's not going to kill the Rabid, I will.*

Until and unless that happened, I needed to get rid of this feeling. I needed to step back, even if the part of me that had grown up Pack felt like stepping away from a kill was wrong. You didn't come between a wolf and his prey, but I forced myself to let go of mine. Folding up the map, I wondered if I should share what I'd managed to uncover so far. I had no way of knowing if any of it was valid. No way of knowing how much of it—or how much more—Callum and the other alphas already knew.

Exhausted, but knowing I wouldn't be able to sleep, I leaned back in my bed. My breathing slowed, but my eyes didn't close. I cleared my mind until Chase's scent filled my nose.

If my eyes hadn't been open, I would have sworn he was there in the room with me, but he wasn't. Even with five hundred miles between us, we were connected. It wasn't all-consuming the way it had been in the minutes after I'd formed the connection, but it was there, and as I stared up at the ceiling, I became aware of the fact that somewhere, Chase was staring up at a starlit sky.

I breathed in.

He breathed in.

As long as we were awake, there was no Rabid to haunt his mind, no memories to plague mine. There was just Chase and me and the uncannily comfortable silence of two people who felt as if they'd known each other for much longer than they actually had.

I saw through his eyes. He saw through mine. And for the first time since we'd come here, I felt like I was home.

Eventually, I did fall asleep, and in an ironic twist of fate, Chase wasn't in my dreams and I wasn't in his. In fact, my sleep was dreamless. Peaceful—until the sound of a heavy weight dropping onto my bedroom floor woke me up.

Four-legger. Wolf.

That was all it took for me to jump out of bed. I landed on my feet, and since I'd fallen asleep fully clothed, my knives were still sheathed to my calves. I had a silver blade in each hand before my eyes had even adjusted to the darkness. Moving on instinct, I put my back against the wall, scanning for the threat, and the moment I found it was the exact moment that the wolf in question slumped to the floor and melted into human form.

Lake. Worn-out and naked. I couldn't do anything for the former problem, but for both of our sakes, I shielded my eyes and rifled around in my suitcase until I found something that would fit her. The sweatpants were short on her and the tank top was too tight, but she didn't complain.

She didn't say anything.

"Have a nice run?" I asked her. I would have asked her if she was okay if I hadn't known for a fact that the answer was no. There was no sense in making her say it.

"I'm tired," Lake said. "Mind if I crash here tonight?"

I doubted she was too tired to make it the additional hundred yards to her house, but I wasn't about to turn her away. Lake needed a friend, and she needed Pack. Right now, I was pretty much the only person in the world who qualified as both.

"*Mi casa es su casa,*" I said. "Literally. I'm pretty sure your dad owns it."

Lake managed a grin. "That make me your landlord?"

I snorted. "Not hardly." I sheathed my knives and sat back down on the bed.

"Scootch over," Lake told me.

I obeyed. Part of me wanted to wait for her to say something, but given the fact that she'd come right out and asked me about the Callum situation, I figured I owed her the same courtesy.

"So. Alphas passing through on their way to Callum's, and that peripheral thought you should know because they might decide you're worth fighting for."

Lake blew out a breath of air with so much force that her lips actually made a popping sound. "If they tried anything, I'd kill 'em."

"Still sucks, though," I commented.

Lake snorted.

"Don't want to talk about it?" I asked.

Lake shook her head. "Sorry about crashing here. Was feeling kind of lonesome. When we were little, I used to sneak into Griff's room all the time. Drove him nuts."

The rare mention of Lake's twin took me by surprise. Anyone with the power of inference could tell just by looking at her that she'd had a brother once, since by definition, female Weres were always half of a set of twins. Sora's was a male in our pack named Zade. Katie's was Alex. Lake's was dead.

Thinking back, I couldn't remember the last time Lake had mentioned Griffin, but I knew better than to comment on that fact.

"I don't mind the company," I said instead. "I get it. You run to be alone. And when you're done…"

You don't want to be alone anymore.

I didn't say the words out loud, but I pushed them toward her, not knowing if she'd hear them, since I was Chase's first and Stone River's second.

"You figure out anything else about the Rabid?" Lake asked.

"Maybe," I said. "There are some places that don't technically belong to any of the alphas. He could be hiding out in one of those."

"You think the Senate knows where he is?" Lake asked.

I didn't answer. If they didn't now, they would soon. There wasn't a place in the country someone could hide from a dozen alphas once they had his scent.

Burnt hair and men's cologne.

"We need to know what the Senate knows," I said. "We need to hear what they say in that meeting."

Even in the dark, I could see Lake go sardonically wide-eyed. "Really? I never would have thought of that!"

I folded my arms across my chest. "Well, if you're going to be that way, then I'm not going to tell you my plan for eavesdropping."

"No more sarcasm. Scout's honor."

I snorted. The idea of Lake in the Girl Scouts was something else. She'd have earned all of their badges and single-handedly destroyed their reputation within a week.

"Bryn," she prodded, her voice coming closer to the high-pitched whine of a dog begging to be let inside.

Being the generous soul that I was, I gave in and provided her with the key to all of this. The thing I'd discovered earlier tonight. "Chase."

The two of us didn't have to be asleep to enter each other's minds. We just had to be still. If he could get close enough to overhear the alphas talking, I could eavesdrop on them myself.

Two days. One for the alphas to get to Ark Valley. One for the meeting. Two days, and I'd have answers. Glancing out the side of my eye at Lake and thinking about everything she had and hadn't said tonight, I decided it wouldn't kill either one of us to stay inside and hidden until then.

CHAPTER TWENTY-ONE

~

AFTER TWENTY-FOUR HOURS INDOORS, LAKE WAS SO twitchy I thought she'd implode, or, more likely, explode, leaving a variety of casualties in her wake. Since I had no desire to be blown to Bryn bits, I was as relieved as she was when Mitch declared the coast clear. Unfortunately, unlike Lake, I couldn't take a romp through the forest in celebration, and I couldn't follow her to the restaurant and lend a hand waiting tables.

I had bigger fish to fry.

If the coast was clear at the Wayfarer, that meant the alphas had arrived in Ark Valley. And that meant it was time to put Operation Eavesdrop into play. Like the old pro I was, I faked the stomach flu and talked Ali into letting me stay in bed all day. The secret to success, as it turned out, was oatmeal—even *I* thought I was throwing up as I hurled three quarters of a bowl of cooked oats into the toilet.

After a little bit of wheedling and looking pathetic, I managed to convince Ali that she didn't need to worry and that all I needed was the solitude and quiet to sleep off the flu, so—with a trash can beside my bed and the evidence/oatmeal hidden away from prying eyes—I bought myself a ticket to slumber land. Or, more precisely, to Chase.

I told myself that it would be simple, that I'd just slip into his mind the way I had on numerous other occasions. I'd done it without even meaning to when I was unconscious; we'd done it in our dreams. But even as I tried to convince myself that this was nothing, a traitorous part of my brain whispered that the second I came within a hundred yards of this meeting, Callum would know—not because of his knack or because he was alpha, but because staying away had been one of the conditions he'd laid down. Long before I'd had any reason to want to attend this meeting, Callum had forbidden me from going. He might as well have dared me to be there.

He had to have known that.

As I lay back, my eyes on the ceiling, I wondered if double jeopardy applied in Pack Law. I'd already broken my permissions. What more could they do?

"Deep breaths," I muttered, willing my heart to quit bludgeoning my chest from the inside out. "You're going to be fine."

What would they do to Chase if they caught us? What would they do to me?

For a moment, I considered backing out, but like a neon sign, the image of a pigtailed little girl lit up in my mind. *Madison.*

This wasn't just about me anymore, and it wasn't just about Chase and the way the Rabid stalked him through the night, refusing to let him forget even for a second who had the power and who'd been left gutted on the pavement.

This stopped now. The attacks. The aftermath. The victims. It had to stop, and the alphas would take care of it. Once I heard it from their own mouths, maybe the ever-present roar in my gut—*kill the Rabid, save them, fight, protect*—might dissipate and die, and I could go back to being the girl who loved playing in other people's trash and didn't care much for dominance hierarchies and inter-pack relations.

Maybe I could go back to being Bryn.

"I'm calming down. I'm breathing. I'm ready."

My body rebelled against those orders, but I ignored it, closed my eyes, and let myself be pulled into thoughts of Chase.

Dark hair. Blue eyes. Lopsided grin.

Chase.

He had a small, sinewy scar that pulled at one edge of his mouth. He appreciated rooms that locked from the inside and despised being caged. He moved like flowing lava. He thought he loved me, even though I could count on one hand the number of times we'd actually met.

Chase.

My body relaxed. My heartbeat slowed until I could only imagine the low, soothing whoosh of blood through my veins.

Chase's scent enveloped me, and as I breathed it in and out and felt his presence all around me, I lost myself to the pull of his psyche at the edges of mine. Like a sand castle at high tide, I broke, dissolved, and drifted slowly away.

"They want to see you."

As my mind settled into Chase's, and we became *Chase-Wolf-Bryn*, the senses we shared flared to life. Smell came first, the way it always did, and I recognized the person speaking to Chase because underneath the familiar scent of Stone River, he smelled angry. Not the fresh rush of adrenaline that came with fury, but the rotting irritation of bitterness as it decomposed.

Marcus.

If he'd found my adoption galling, the fact that the entire Senate wanted to see Chase, who hadn't even been born a Were, must have chafed, too.

Senate? Us? Now?

On one level, I was aware that this was why I'd come here, but going to the meeting hadn't been part of the plan. We were supposed to eavesdrop. We weren't supposed to venture into Alpha Central ourselves. My thoughts blended into Chase's, my questions into his.

Why did the Senate want to see Us?

Deeper in Chase's mind, his wolf was anxious, antsy about

going into a room filled with Others. Wolves who weren't Pack. People he didn't trust.

We have to go, I thought, even though, like the wolf, I didn't want to. Chase nodded to Marcus, not bothering to conceal his dislike of a man who'd always hated me. If I'd been in my own body, I might have made a comment specifically designed to press werewolf buttons, but instead, I let Chase's thoughts guide mine. We were about to walk willingly into the wolf's den. Literally. We couldn't afford a divided front at a time like this.

Chase pushed forward, and as we neared Callum's house, his fists clenched. From the depths of his mind, I tried to prepare him for the rush of power that slammed into Our body the moment we crossed the threshold of Callum's door. Each alpha in this room carried with him the weight of an entire pack, and it nearly brought Us low. These men played at being human, sitting around a table in Callum's living room, but the air between them was so saturated with primal instincts that Chase almost couldn't breathe.

Jaws should have been snapping. Bodies should have been pinned to the ground. Heads should have been bowing, blood should have been spilled, and one man should have ruled them all.

That was what the wolf inside of Chase said. That was the only conclusion supported by the pulsating, electric, *lethal* undertone in this room.

"I take it this is the boy?"

Chase took two steps back. Wolf wanted to come out. We had to get out of there.

No, I said softly, finding my own voice in Chase's thoughts. *Keep your head angled at forty-five degrees to the ground, but stand up straight. Don't back down, don't challenge. Don't even move.*

There wasn't another wolf within a mile of Callum's house at the moment. The power in this room would have been too much for them, and the Senate didn't deal with packs. The alphas didn't touch wolves that weren't theirs. So why had they called for Chase?

"Come in," Callum said evenly. Chase could have resisted the order. He was mine more than he was Callum's, but I echoed the sentiment. *Step forward. Keep your head tilted downward, but don't look at the ground. Look at Callum. Keep your mouth closed. Whatever you do, don't show your teeth.*

The closer we got to Callum, the more we could feel the others, prowling just outside our thoughts. They didn't push. They didn't attack. But they were there.

"He isn't Rabid."

For a second, the voice sounded so like Devon's that I wondered if he was pulling a ventriloquist act from somewhere in the depths of Callum's house. And then I realized—

Shay.

"He hasn't Shifted yet, which means he has more control than most young ones. Impressive, Callum."

There was something irreverent in Shay's words, a tone that told me that Shay remembered being under Callum's rule and wanted everyone else to forget it. In his own domain, Shay was king, but here, he was young, foolish, and couldn't hold a candle to Callum's years, his experience, or his power.

Perfectly contained. Understated. Overwhelming. That was Callum.

Bubbling, roaring, biting at the bit. That was Shay.

"Chase." Callum's words brought our eyes to his, and inside of Chase, I almost flinched. If I'd been me instead of Us, I would have.

I knew those eyes. I knew Callum. And he knew me.

Bryn.

I felt the call. I wanted to respond but didn't. I wasn't Callum's anymore. He couldn't tell me what to do. I wasn't even sure if he knew I was there, or if he simply saw me every time he looked at Chase, thought about me almost as much as I thought about him.

There was no room for questions like these in a room full of the most dominant wolves in North America. We had to stay in control.

"Callum." It was Chase's voice and Chase's response. I guided his body language, but I couldn't guide his words. I couldn't respond to the look in Callum's eye or wonder what it meant.

"The Senate would like you to describe the Rabid, his

attack, and your recovery." Callum didn't phrase the words as an order. He kept his voice low and soothing, but I saw the way the other alphas' eyes lit up at the question. They had a vested interest in finding out more about this Rabid, about what had happened to Chase.

Sandstone and fish. Cedar and sour milk. Ocean salt and sulfur.

Their scents flooded Chase's senses, making it hard for him to concentrate on anything else.

Don't let your lip curl up. Don't growl. Don't show your teeth, I told him.

He didn't, but inside him —inside Us—his wolf was awake and ready. It wanted to take control. I wouldn't let it.

Wolves, it argued back. *Not Pack. Protect girl.*

If my presence here caused Chase to lose it, I would never forgive myself, so I channeled everything I had into keeping him calm. Soothing his wolf. Guarding his mind as his story spilled in monotone from his lips.

The alphas asked questions—more detailed questions than I'd ever thought to ask. What was the length of the duration of the attack? How long had Chase lain on the pavement before Callum's wolves had found him and brought him back? Did he have any insight into how he'd managed to survive? How did he guard his mind from the Rabid? Did the Rabid ever take control of his physical body? Had it ever asked him to attack Callum? Could that happen?

No, Chase explained. Callum had brought him into the pack and trained him to use his pack-bond to guard against the Rabid's psychic advances. Chase refrained from mentioning that I'd manipulated that bond, that I was the one who chased away the Rabid's presence in his dreams now.

Finally, the questions stopped. One of the alphas, the one who smelled like sea salt, had the last word. "You've done well with him, Callum. You're a strong boy, Chase, and you'll been an even stronger man. Stone River is lucky to have you."

That didn't sound like a compliment. It sounded like a complaint, but I didn't have time to process that fact, because the next instant, Chase and I were dismissed.

"You can go now," Callum said. Chase wanted to argue. He wanted to stay. And for a moment, I wanted to let him, but the older, wiser part of me, the part that had learned about surviving in a werewolf pack from the very best, couldn't let him.

Go.

I read the order on Callum's face. I might have imagined that he knew, on some level, that I was there in Chase's head, but I wasn't imagining the compulsion behind his request that we leave.

I wasn't imagining the promise of violence if we didn't.

Go, I told Chase. *Leave the house. Go as far away as you can and still hear.*

After all, Callum hadn't specified *where* we had to go.

As the door closed behind us, Chase's body relaxed. He

walked quickly, keeping one ear to the conversation in Callum's house.

It was silent.

They wouldn't talk as long as they could hear us. There wasn't a single man in that house who had become an alpha by virtue of their stupidity. The alphas didn't trust Us, and they weren't taking any chances. I wanted to scream. Chase wanted to scream. His wolf wanted Out.

The incessant plea—*Out, Out, Out*—gave me an idea.

Are your senses better in wolf form? I asked Chase silently.

His response told me that he wasn't sure of the answer. In wolf form, Chase always had trouble thinking. Trouble remembering.

Shift anyway? I asked him. *I might be able to think for both of us.*

Yes, the wolf inside of Chase said. *Yes!*

Chase shuddered. The muscles in his neck relaxed. His head rolled to the side, and then pain, white-hot and bone-shattering, enveloped his body.

I felt it. I welcomed it. And as Chase's human form gave way, a rush of power washed over the pain, turning agony to ecstasy and back again.

Run. As a wolf, Chase wanted to run. It would have been so easy to lose myself to the same overwhelming need, but I didn't. I couldn't. In wolf form, Our senses were doubled, and as We padded away from Callum's house on all fours, the alphas finally began talking. We could hear them, but they couldn't hear Us.

Wolf didn't want to listen. Wolf wanted to run.

No. Unlike Chase, whose conscious thoughts were scrambled and wordless post-Change, I was still me. I could still remember why We'd Shifted, and I could still make out the meaning in the words the Senate was saying, even if I could only decipher about one in every three.

"...Change...powerful."

"...miscarriage..."

"...five in the entire country! Five!"

Five what? Five Rabids? I hoped to God that wasn't true.

"Two in your territory, Callum." Shay's voice traveled better than the other alphas'. He talked more loudly, putting more power into his voice, because of all of them, he was the youngest and he had the most to prove. Wolf understood this better than I did, and I pulled my understanding of the situation from instincts that weren't mine.

"Your numbers are growing. Two babies, one new wolf. Stone River is already the largest pack."

Wolf knew what this meant, his innate grasp of the intricacies of Were politics putting mine to shame. More babies, Wolf said, meant more wolves. More wolves meant a bigger pack. A stronger pack.

A stronger alpha.

I got the message loud and clear: in the wild, math was

simple. The strongest alpha was only as strong as the force of his pack. And right now, Stone River was the biggest pack.

Alpha. One alpha. One pack.

Wolf growled the words, and I absorbed them. To werewolves, dominance was everything. The most dominant wolf had all of the power. The strongest wolf was meant to dominate them all.

Unite the packs. Unite the power.

That was the siren's call that set each and every alpha on edge when the Senate was called. They needed to challenge each other. One of them needed to dominate, the others needed to submit. Wolf's instincts gave way to my explicit knowledge of the situation, and I did the math.

Callum had the biggest pack. Callum had a knack for seeing the future. I would have bet my life that Callum was older and stronger and more *everything* than any other person in that room.

Callum was the biggest threat, and the fact that his pack was growing faster than the others did nothing to assuage the others' fears, their instinctual suspicions that if Callum had wanted to, he could have been their alpha, too. The realization startled me, but it didn't surprise me. It took me off guard, but it made perfect sense. Callum was experienced. He was powerful. He was smart.

He was *Callum.*

"Five births, and two of them yours." Shay again. I hated

him, but appreciated his enunciation, because the rest of the alphas' voices blended together in a blur.

"...no births..."

"Only one..."

The other alphas didn't like the idea of Callum's pack growing while theirs shrank. They had to have known, the way Wolf did just being in the room with them, that if Callum tired of democracy, the entire North American continent could be his.

"...Rabid..."

At that word, Chase's wolf ears literally perked up. Even with his mind jumbled, he recognized it.

This was why we were here. Why we were listening.

"Answer...not that simple..."

"—prerogative—"

I could only catch bits and pieces of words, but even that shocked me because they weren't the words I'd expected to hear. The alphas should have been talking about strategies for hunting the Rabid. They should have been sharing what they knew of his potential location. They shouldn't have been saying...

"...unless...we need..."

"...turn...blind eye—"

Blind eye? Blind eye? They couldn't have just said those words in a discussion about a rabid wolf. They *couldn't* have. The men in this room were a twig's snap away from attacking each other in one giant dominance struggle. This Rabid had killed in their territories. His very existence was a challenge, and alphas didn't abide challenges.

Alphas were strong. They kept their packs safe. They eliminated threats.

"—in exchange...desirable..."

"So we barter with murderers now?" Callum's voice carried, for the opposite reason as Shay's. He had nothing to prove. It was power, not volume, that carried his words to my ears, and Wolf crouched, belly brushing the ground at the sound of the tone.

Callum wasn't Chase's alpha the way he used to be. But even now, that tone, that power—

There was an instinct to obey. To fold. To give in to the power of his words.

But Shay didn't. "Is that your final word on the matter, Callum?"

"It is."

For a moment there was silence, and then Shay spoke up again. "And what are you going to do about it?"

Nobody spoke to Callum like that. Not the other alphas. Not his own wolves. Not even me...most of the time anyway.

Shay wasn't challenging Callum. Not exactly. He was daring Callum to challenge the rest of them. To force his will on them. To prove he could.

To do it.

One pack. One alpha.

"Are we a democracy or aren't we?" Shay threw down the gauntlet. "Do we vote or do you decide?"

Vote on what? Decide what? To barter? To turn a blind eye?

Challenge them, I screamed silently at Callum. *Do it. Take them. Take it all.*

He could have. Every part of me, every memory, every instinct I had said that Callum could stop this. He could make them understand.

He could make them *submit.*

But he didn't. "We're a democracy," Callum said, his tone never changing, his surety never called into question.

Wrong. Wrong-wrong-wrong. Wolves weren't meant for democracy. Werewolves weren't meant to vote. Callum was safe. Callum was strong. Callum should have done something.

He didn't.

"All in favor?"

In favor of what? I couldn't hear the vote go down, didn't hear anyone's answer but Callum's, but I knew based on the tone of his voice that it must have been in the minority, that the others were voting to do the unthinkable.

I tried to wrap my mind around it but couldn't. The Senate wasn't going to hunt the Rabid. They were going to make him a deal.

CHAPTER TWENTY-TWO

"NO!" I SAT UP IN BED, THE SCREAM TEARING ITS WAY out of my throat. On the other side of our bond, Chase was going wild, his wolf giving in to bloodlust, hunting. Rabbits. Deer.

Chase needed to kill something.

I could relate. My own fingernails dug into my pillow, and I came dangerously close to tearing it apart. As I extracted myself from Chase's mind, I was hit with two pangs of withdrawal. One was his. The other was mine, and they mirrored each other so perfectly that at any other time, I would have turned the feelings over and over in my head, remembering the feeling of his skin and being inside it and hurting in sync with his loss.

With the way that we'd both just been betrayed. Again.

Callum could have fought the other alphas. He could have fought them, and he could have won, but we just weren't worth it to him. Chase and my parents and Madison Covey and who knows how many other children who'd been torn to shreds— they weren't worth it.

I wasn't worth it.

"Bryn!" Ali came rushing into the room, a knife in her hand. The image seemed wrong. Ali wasn't a fighter, and I could take care of myself.

I was the one Callum had trained to fight, not her.

"Are you okay?" Ali's eyes were wild, and for the first time, I felt her pack-bond brushing against what was left of mine.

Ali was Pack, and I'd scared her to death.

"I'm fine," I said, thankful that she didn't have a Were's ability to smell the truth. "Bad dream."

Except it wasn't a dream. It was real. The Rabid was alive, and if the Senate had their way, he wouldn't be experiencing a shift in condition anytime soon. And Callum had just stood there and let it happen in the name of *democracy*.

Screw democracy. And screw Callum, too.

Ali sat beside me on the bed. "It must have been some dream," she said, stroking my hair back from my eyes.

I reminded myself that Ali was family. Ali would never have betrayed me like this. But Ali wasn't a fighter, and she wouldn't understand that I had to fight. That if the Senate wasn't going to kill the Rabid, I was.

She'd worry, and she'd yell, and she'd lock me in my room until I turned thirty. And while I sat around doing nothing, other people would die.

"It was a really bad dream," I told Ali, forcing the tremors out of my voice. "But on the bright side, I don't think I have a fever anymore."

"You never had a fever," Ali replied. The tone in her voice reminded me that Ali wasn't stupid, and that oatmeal or no oatmeal, there was a good chance my "illness" hadn't fooled her as well as I'd thought. "You needed to be alone. I get that."

I felt like maybe she did understand, even though her actual words reinforced the fact that she had no idea that this had nothing to do with me struggling to deal with the events of the last few days and everything to do with the events of the last few minutes. It wasn't Ali's fault that I'd neglected to mention that Chase and I could hop in and out of each other's heads at will. There would be time to feel guilty about that little omission later. Right now, I had other things to hide.

Like the fact that the dull roar in my gut—telling me to *hunt*, to *kill*, to *protect*—had gone nuclear.

On the other side of our bond, I felt Chase's approval, felt him tear into an animal's throat with a ferocity that should have scared me, but didn't.

"Are you sure you're okay?" Ali asked, doing a 180 from the moment before and laying a hand on my cheek. "You actually do feel a little warm, and you look…strange."

"Thanks a lot," I replied. It wasn't like I could say, *Well, the werewolf who shares my brain just killed a deer, and the two of us are planning on hunting down the Big Bad Wolf like the woodsman of yore.*

Hmmmm . . . , I thought, the mind bunnies multiplying. *Woodsman. Ax. Silver ax.*

If I was going to hunt a Rabid, I needed weapons, and I needed to figure out where exactly the Rabid was. I'd counted on eavesdropping to tell me the latter, but things hadn't worked out that way. I'd have to figure it out myself. As for weapons...

"I think I'm going to go to the restaurant and harass Lake," I told Ali. "She's waiting tables this afternoon, and I'd kind of like to see her in action."

I didn't mention that the action I most wanted to see Lake enact was the way she'd respond when I asked her if she had any weapons other than a shotgun. If she didn't, she'd know where to find them and she'd take disturbing joy in doing so. I'd be Santa Claus, just for asking.

And while Lake requisitioned supplies, I'd track our Rabid. I wasn't sure how, but I knew I'd do it, the same way I knew that Ali wouldn't object to me going to talk to Lake.

"She doing okay?" Ali asked, transferring her maternal instincts from me to Lake.

"She'll be fine until the alphas come back through, and then she'll be fine again after that."

If I could figure out where our prey was hiding, Lake wouldn't have to stay inside when the alphas came back through Montana. We'd be well on our way to No-Man's-Land by then.

The Wayfarer was nearly empty when I slid into a corner booth. Lake, notepad in hand, slid in across from me.

"Aren't you supposed to be taking my order?" I asked.

"Bite me. And then you can tell me what's wrong." She paused. "Aren't you supposed to be with...?"

She gestured elaborately, and I filled in the blank. Lake had known my plan for this morning. I'd promised to report back, and here I was.

"Been there. Done that. Didn't go so well."

Lake threw her notepad to the side, summarily ignoring the three other occupied tables in the restaurant. "Didn't go so well as in you didn't see anything, or didn't go so well as in you didn't like what you saw?"

"More like heard," I corrected her. "But the second one."

"The Rabid escaped again?" Lake guessed. "They have no idea where he is?"

"Oh, no," I replied, my voice forcefully cheerful, because it was the only way I could keep from yelling. "Nothing like that. Apparently, he has something the alphas want, so they're not going to hunt him. They voted."

"Voted?" Lake asked incredulously. Clearly, she couldn't imagine Callum voting on anything, not when his word was, in her experience, pretty much law.

"Callum was in the minority. They outvoted him. Nothing he could do."

Lies, lies, lies. He could have done something. If he'd wanted to.

"Sucks," Lake opined. "So when are we leaving?"

She didn't even have to ask what I intended to do now. She knew, and she was with me, the same way Chase was. Two teenage werewolves and one human girl against an enemy the pack had chosen not to cross.

This Rabid was going down if it killed me. I tried not to think about the fact that it probably would.

"We leave as soon as I figure out where we're going," I said, concentrating on what needed to be done, right here, right now. "In the meantime, can you rustle up some...?" I didn't want to say the word *weapons* out loud, but Lake took my meaning.

"Supplies?" she asked, her eyes sparkling, but hard. "I might know where we could get some. Just let me tell Keely I'm out of here."

I wasn't thrilled with the idea of Lake "telling" Keely anything—not when I knew that it was disturbingly easy to tell Keely way too much—but Lake couldn't exactly take off without explanation. Not if we wanted to keep Ali and Mitch in the dark.

"Be right back," Lake told me, heading for the bar.

"Excuse me," a man—human—at a nearby table called. "Could I get a refill on my—?"

"Nope." Lake didn't even look for him as she zeroed in on Keely. I hung back, figuring that the less I spoke to the World's Best Listener, the better.

For her part, Keely took one look at Lake and frowned. "Whatever it is, the answer is no."

"But you don't even know what the question is," Lake said.

"I don't have to. I know that look. That look is trouble."

Lake wheedled. "I just need to cut out early today. Bryn needs my help."

Keely blew a wisp of hair out of her face. "Fine, but you breathe a word to your daddy about me letting you out of here without a cross-examination, and you and I are going to have words. Clear?"

Lake smiled in response, and I added Keely to the list of people, including Ali and Mitch, who'd be ready to kill us the moment they figured out where we'd gone.

Five minutes later, Lake and I were outside and on our own.

"Cabin twelve," Lake said.

"What?"

"Cabin twelve. That's where my dad keeps the weapons. The lock on the door is kid's play to jimmy open."

I didn't ask how Lake knew this, and I didn't question the fact that Mr. Mitchell had an entire cabin full of weapons. Under normal circumstances, I would have, because—Lake's fondness for shotguns aside—werewolves didn't need weapons. They *were* weapons. But thinking back to the look on Mitch's face when he'd told me, all calmlike, that male were-wolves could get funny around females, I wasn't surprised.

Against humans, werewolves didn't need weapons. Against other werewolves, being armed to the hilt might come in handy, at least in human form.

"Okay," I said. "So you'll take care of the weapons situation. Now we need to know where we're going and we need a way to get there."

I kept coming up with small problems, like transportation, because no matter how many times I turned it over in my mind, I couldn't come up with a solution to the bigger one: we didn't know where the Rabid was. We'd have only a few hours' head start once we left here, before Ali and Mitch figured out that we'd gone. We couldn't afford to wander around aimlessly. We couldn't act on some unformed hunch.

We had to be sure.

"Transportation is easy," Lake said when I brought up the issue. "My dad got a new car, but he hasn't gotten rid of his truck yet. We'll take that."

"Can you drive?" I asked. I wasn't sixteen yet, and though I'd managed fine with all stolen motorcycles I'd come in contact with, I wasn't sure I could handle a stick shift.

"Bryn, I live in the country in the middle of nowhere. The school's thirty miles away. My daddy's had me driving since I was twelve."

I followed her words enough to know that transportation wouldn't be a problem, but beyond that, all I could think about was the Rabid.

Madison.

"You look like you have an idea," Lake said.

"I might," I replied. Everything we'd discovered about the Rabid so far, we'd discovered because the last time he'd come after Chase's dreams, Chase and I had seen a glimpse into his mind. Marks, bonds, connections—they went both ways. The only reason the Rabid stalked Chase's dreams was because Chase was blocking him when he was awake.

But what if that stopped?

What if Chase opened up the bond with the Rabid, just enough to get inside his head? Just enough to tell us where he was?

"Bryn? Idea?"

"I have one," I said, "but Chase isn't going to like it."

Chase was in human form when I found him, but I could till taste the faint tang of blood on his tongue from the hunt.

Chase?

I didn't come completely into his mind. I pulled myself back from his senses and concentrated on keeping my own.

Bryn?

Just thinking my name seemed to calm him, remind him that he was human, even when he was wondering at what point along the line he'd become a beast.

You went hunting, I said. *Plenty of men do the same.*

Of course, most men hunted with guns instead of their teeth, but that wasn't what Chase needed to hear, so I left it unsaid. Instead, I concentrated on the thing that had sent Chase into hunting mode in the first place.

We're going to kill the Rabid, I told him, my voice steady and calm. *I promise you, he's going to die.*

For a moment there was silence on Chase's end of the bond, and then he spoke again, his words broken, like he couldn't remember quite how to put them together into thoughts. *Prancer—want—dead—protect.*

We're going to kill him, Chase. Lake and I are gathering up some weapons. If we shoot from far enough away, he might not even hear us coming. He'll think he's safe because the alphas aren't coming after him. He won't be expecting us.

Another pause, and this time, when Chase spoke, his words made perfect sense. *I'm tired of fighting him.*

I thought of what I was about to ask Chase to do and blanched. *We need to find him,* I said slowly. *And the only way to do that is to get inside his head.*

I didn't say the next part, couldn't make myself spell out the fact that the only way for me to get into the Rabid's head was for Chase to let him into his.

I won't let anything happen to you, I swore. *We just need a few seconds. Just long enough to figure out where he is.*

He'll want me to hurt you, Chase replied, his voice weary, even in my mind. *He always does.*

I thought of Chase slamming his wolf body into the cage in Callum's basement, because to him, I smelled like food. I thought of his body trembling as the smell of a foreign wolf flooded Callum's living room and of the way Sora's first instinct had been to get me out of there.

You wouldn't hurt me, I told him. *You'd die before you'd hurt me.*

Asking him to do this was killing me. It wasn't fair. I felt like Callum, treating Chase like a detail that didn't matter as much as the big picture. But as much as I wished I could do this myself, I wasn't the one with the connection to the Rabid. I wasn't the one who could track him.

Chase was.

You have to promise to get out of my head, Chase said. *If Prancer takes over, if I can't fight him off . . . you have to leave. I won't let him get to you, too.*

I didn't promise, because I had no intention of abandoning ship the moment things turned sour, not when I was the one asking Chase to put himself at risk.

I won't let him take you, I said, pushing the words into Chase's head with a ferocity that he must have been able to feel from head to toe. *You're mine.*

For a moment, there was a pause, and then Chase's voice went very dry in my mind. *In a non-freaky, non-ownership, we-both-retain-our-independence kind of way?* I could practically see his lips curving upward into a subtle grin.

Yes, I replied hastily. *Exactly.*

Okay.

Okay? I asked him.

Okay, he repeated. *I'll do this. — Don't leave me. —*

He didn't mean for me to hear that last part, but the second I did, I let down some of my own guards, brought myself further into his mind, telling him over and over again, in every way I knew, that he wasn't alone.

He breathed in.

I breathed in.

He breathed out.

I breathed out.

And then, Chase let in the flood. I should have been prepared. I knew more about closing off and opening up bonds than just about anyone, but still, the rush of scent and the oily feel of a snake slithering down the back of Chase's neck took me by surprise. His scars, each and every one, began to burn, and for a moment, he couldn't breathe.

Well, well, well . . . if it isn't the prodigal son.

The voice sounded so normal, so human, but the sound of it hurt Chase's ears. I pictured him bleeding, torn to pieces, the way the Rabid had left him that day.

Not your son, Chase thought. *Not your anything.*

That's right, I echoed, my words for Chase's ears only. He was his own person, and he was mine, the same way that I'd been his from the moment we'd touched. The Rabid thought he knew so much, but he didn't know that I was there.

Change.

The word was a whisper, but also a command. This wasn't Callum telling Katie to change back to human form. This wasn't me asking Chase to become a wolf.

This was domination. And punishment. It was cruel.

You don't have to, I told Chase, even as I felt the pressure the Rabid was applying.

He'll know something is wrong if I don't.

I heard Chase's bones breaking, felt his skin give way as he lost his human form. The Rabid laughed.

Change back.

Shifting took energy. It was painful. Chase needed to recover.

Change.

Change back.

The Rabid didn't let Chase settle fully into one form before forcing him into another.

Stop, I wanted to scream. *Stop!*

But I didn't. Tears streaming down my cheeks, my own body shaking with Chase's burning white pain, I pushed. Pushed my way from Chase's mind into the Rabid's.

Burnt hair and men's cologne.

The smell was overwhelming. Suffocating. I needed to throw up, but I couldn't. I had to do this, because Chase couldn't. Because his body was being forced to break itself and reassemble, over and over again.

Sweat mixed with the tears on my cheek. A white-hot poker pressed into my stomach, my legs, my jaw.

Change. Change back.

I had to concentrate. I had to find out what we needed to know so Chase could throw his walls back up.

Protect, my pack-sense demanded. Chase was mine. I had to protect him. I had to push the Rabid away—

But first, I had to track him.

I closed my eyes. I pictured the wiry bond that connected Chase to this madman. I followed it to its roots. I let damp, overwhelming darkness wash over me, until I couldn't remember what it felt like to be warm.

Blood. The Rabid liked blood. He liked power. His name was Wilson.

The information came all at once, but it wasn't enough. I pushed further.

Where are you? I thought, knowing he couldn't hear my words. *Tell me where you are.*

I saw a cabin. And blood. A forest. And blood. A town—one stoplight. A store called Macon's Hardware.

A path into the woods.

Trapped. The word was a whisper in my mind, and the second I heard it, Chase's own instincts flared to life. *Trapped,* he echoed. He struggled not to fight the Rabid. Not to push him back.

We needed to fight. We needed to get out of there. We needed to take care of each other.

But first, I needed more. A cabin. One stoplight. Macon's Hardware. A path into the woods.

Tell me where you are.

For the first time, the Rabid stopped in his onslaught against Chase. He paused, and I wondered if he smelled me, the way I smelled him.

No time. I had no time. Chase was hurting. If the Rabid smelled me, he'd punish Chase. Hurt him. Hurt him more.

No-Man's-Land. Macon's Hardware. Images flashed from the Rabid's mind to mine. He pulled back, but once I got ahold of something, I never let go until I was ready.

Macon's Hardware. Path into the woods. And then, finally a name. A town.

The Rabid roared, a noise more fitting to a bear than a wolf, and then he laughed a horrible, mad sound that made me picture blood running from his human lips, down his human face, soaking his human hands.

My stomach rolled. This was a man who killed his victims and laughed.

Time to go, I told Chase.

I can't. He's too strong. Walls are gone. Callum helped me. I can't—

You can, I said back. *Think of me, Chase. Think only of me.*

He did. He thought of me, and the Rabid thought of me, and their mental images mixed together in my mind. Wet cardboard and drain cleaner and the smell of little-girl fear. Brash and beautiful and *home.*

That's right, I told Chase. *I'm home. Come back to me.*

I had to protect him. I had to undo this. There had to be a way. The panic rose in both of our throats. I saw Chase's field of vision bleed into a dotty, hazy red.

Trapped.

This time, I grabbed on to the word. Made Chase hear it. We were cornered. We were scared.

We would get out of this alive.

Trapped. Escape.

Survive, I whispered the last word, because Chase couldn't seem to remember what it was, and his own instincts flared to life. He was a fighter. He fought. This man was nothing.

He wasn't all-powerful. He was *Prancer.*

And we didn't have to let him do this.

Chase was mine. I was his. The Rabid wanted us both, and with that realization, I felt something snap inside of Chase. The Rabid could threaten him. The Rabid could torture him. . . . But he had no right to think of me. None.

I felt the hum of power, a shift in the air when Chase

slammed up his mental walls and caught the sliver of power that bound him to this man between his teeth. Like an animal, a hunter, he tore into it. Shredded it.

And as it began to reweave itself, impervious to Chase's attack, the boy I called *mine* took everything that bound him to this Rabid, and in a moment of perfect symmetry, he threw it at me.

I'd felt the sensation before. A tilting of the world on its axis. An explosion in my brain.

Echoing, seductive silence. Silence and Chase.

CHAPTER TWENTY-THREE

"YOU OKAY?" LAKE'S VOICE BROKE INTO MY THOUGHTS and brought me back to the present. To the back porch on Cabin 12, where I'd sat down to contact Chase. "At first, you were quiet, and then you were crying. Your body starting twitching, and then, you got real still."

I caught my breath. "I'm fine," I told Lake. *We're fine.* Back at Callum's, I'd panicked and rewired our pack-bonds, mine and Chase's, and just now, when he'd sensed the Rabid threatening me, Chase had done the same. Only this time, he'd cut his connection to the Rabid completely. The pack was still there in the depths of Chase's mind, in mine, but the Rabid was gone.

"You didn't feel anything?" I asked. When I'd rewired my pack-bond, every wolf in the near vicinity had felt it.

"Nope," Lake said. "Should I have felt something?"

I thought for a moment: of the pack, of Chase, and of the Rabid. "No."

This didn't have anything to do with Stone River. This had to do with Chase and the man who had made him. The man whose name I now knew was Wilson. The man who was residing in a cabin in the woods, a mile away from Macon's Hardware in a place called Alpine Creek.

"Wyoming," I said out loud. "That's where we're going."

Lake heard me. I repeated the message silently, sending it to Chase. He was exhausted physically, and I realized that he wasn't in any shape to travel from Colorado to Wyoming on his own.

He'd recover. Werewolves always did. But he needed time—and time was one thing we didn't have. Sooner or later, the alphas would pay the Rabid a visit to collect on his end of whatever deal they'd made him. Sooner or later, Ali and Mitch would get suspicious about what Lake and I were up to.

Worst of all, there was a part of me that knew the Rabid wouldn't react well to losing Chase. He liked blood. He liked power. And since Chase had robbed him of the latter, someone would pay with the first.

I hated that I'd been inside the Rabid's head. Hated that I understood him enough to know that if the three of us waited, someone else would die.

Lake and I are going to grab some weapons and borrow the keys to her dad's truck, I told Chase. *You can't run all the way to Wyoming. You're going to need some help.*

There was only person in Ark Valley that I trusted enough to ask for help.

Devon.

Chase bristled, the way any male werewolf would have at the sound of another male's name, so I repeated myself.

Please, Chase. He'll help. You know he will.

Chase knew because I knew, and now, more than ever, he was in my mind the way I'd been in his.

Devon, Chase repeated. *Alpine Creek, Wyoming. We'll see you there.*

"You done playing telephone?" Lake asked.

I nodded, pulling back from my bond with Chase as he did the same with me.

"Okay, girlie. Let's weapon up."

The words *weapon up* were slightly terrifying coming out of Lake's mouth, her voice a weird combination of resolve and glee.

I shuddered, but gestured broadly with one arm nonetheless. "Lead on."

Lake didn't take any more urging. It took her less than a minute to jimmy open the back door to Cabin 12, and when the door opened to reveal her father's weapon's cache, my mouth dropped open. I'd expected a couple of guns, an excess of silver bullets, and a knife or two. Instead, I saw a room as large as the cabin that Ali, the twins, and I were sharing. Letting out a low whistle, I took in the 360 view.

One side was clearly dedicated to creating the weapons. I recognized a forge in one corner, and there were a variety of tools, and a few things I couldn't identify that seemed to have a vaguely Frankensteinian feel about them. The other side—and three of the walls—were covered with weapons. Guns. Knives. Axes. Traps. Snares. And several things that I couldn't even identify.

Lake breathed out a happy sigh as she approached the row filled with guns. "Matilda was my first, but, ladies, you know how to make a girl want to stray," she said.

"Lake, could you please stop sweet-talking the weapons? It's kind of freaking me out."

This room didn't look like the cautious work of a dad who was afraid that someone might get a little fresh with his teenage daughter. It looked like the work of a man preparing for a brutal and inevitable war.

Lake stuck her bottom lip out in a pout at my reproach but then shifted into business mode. "Silver bullets are in the chest on your right," she said. Then she paused, picked up a container full of some kind of arrows, and poured them on the ground. "Fill this up. Grab a dozen or so silver arrows, too. I'll take care of the crossbows and guns."

While I followed her instructions and started stocking up on ammunition, Lake hauled a large, empty duffel bag off one of the shelves and began throwing in the big guns. Literally.

And some small guns.

Three crossbows.

"Lake, you do know that there are only three of us, right?"

She snorted. "All of this is just for me. I'm getting to you. Callum taught you how to shoot on a nine millimeter, right?"

I nodded.

She threw several more guns into the bag, moving so quickly that her choices should have seemed haphazard but didn't.

"Is this good?" I asked Lake, after I'd pulled several boxes of handmade silver bullets out of the cabinet and gathered a few of the arrows off the floor.

"Yup. You prefer a crossbow, a longbow, or old school?" Lake asked me.

"I'm better with knives," I said.

Lake nodded, and then she looked at me very closely and said, "Stand up."

I did.

"You've got two on you right now, correct?"

I nodded, not bothering to ask how she could tell. "I don't go anywhere without them."

"You'll be better with your own than you are with mine, but I'll bring a few extras, for throwing. First, though…" She trailed off, thoughtful. "How tall are you?"

"Five-six."

"You're a couple of inches shorter than me," Lake said, "but you've got pretty long arms, so…"

I had no idea where this was going, until Lake walked over to the workbench and picked up two metal wrist guards about the length and width of my forearms, but thin. "Let me put these on you," she said. I complied. The metal was much lighter on my wrists than it should have been.

"Can you lift your arms?" she asked me.

I nodded.

"Can you fight?"

She didn't give me a chance to answer the question—she just attacked me. In a room full of enough firepower to blow the whole reservation to kingdom come.

I managed to dodge her blows and get in one of my own. The weight of the wrist guards didn't slow me down, but I couldn't put the same kind of force behind my blows.

"With these, you won't need to," Lake said. "My dad made them for me. Just in case. Take a step back and then twist your wrists sideways, hard." She demonstrated and, mystified, I obeyed. Four long, thin silver blades popped out of each of the wrist guards.

"If you're fighting something with claws, you might as well have some of your own," she said.

I stared at them and then began to experimentally move my wrists. "Your dad a big fan of the X-Men?" I asked.

Lake shrugged. "Worse comes to worst, he wanted to give me an edge."

"You couldn't Shift with these on," I told Lake.

Lake arched an eyebrow. "I wouldn't need to. Land one or two good hits to a Were with these, and you've bought yourself some exit time."

Mitch had said that he didn't know many werewolves who were even half as fast as Lake. If she took them off guard in her human form, they might not be able to catch up to her as a wolf.

"Twist your wrists the other way, and the claws will retract. Now, let me throw in some explosives and we'll be good to go."

As Lake added the finishing touches to our artillery and slung the duffel bag over her shoulder, I picked up the box I'd loaded up with ammo. "You okay?" I asked her.

Lake snorted. "Do I look not okay to you?"

She didn't look the way she had the other night, as we'd lain in my bed, listening to foreign alphas passing through.

"You look fine."

"I am fine."

I nodded. There would be plenty of time for me to play werewolf Dr. Phil later. Right now, Lake and I needed a ride. Preferably one with GPS. "Ready to commit a felony?" I asked her.

She met that statement with the most serene of smiles. "It's not grand theft auto if the vehicle in question belongs to your father. And b-t-w, if anyone asks you what's in that box, I'd advise you to say, 'Feminine supplies.'"

The box was large and heavy, and there was a distinct clanging sound as I carried it. "As in tampons?"

"Keely's not going to ask questions. Ali's busy with the twins, and everyone else around here is male. Tampons scare the bejeezus out of them, my dad included, but if the person who asks is a Were, they'd smell the lie. Hence, *feminine supplies.*"

"Because we're females, and they're our supplies?" I guessed.

"No. Because weapons are feminine." Lake gave me an insulted look. "Why do you think I named my gun Matilda?"

All things considered, I was kind of surprised that Lake was planning on going into this battle without her double-barrel.

"Matilda maims," Lake explained when I asked her. "She doesn't kill."

"Enough said," I replied, because after what the Rabid had done to Chase this afternoon, after what he'd done to the little girl named Madison, after everything he'd taken away from me, starting with my parents and ending with my faith in Callum, this S.O.B. was *dead*.

The distance between Montana and Wyoming went by disturbingly quickly with Lake behind the wheel, and as the two of us reached our destination, I registered the fact that we'd arrived in record time and absorbed what little sightseeing the Rabid's town had to offer.

Alpine Creek was bordered by a river on one side and the ugly, jagged edge of a mountain on the other. Even a human wouldn't have been surprised to hear it called No-Man's-Land,

and as Lake drove our pilfered vehicle down Main Street, toward the town's single stoplight, déjà vu hit me like a blow to the chest.

Macon's Hardware.

Barren street corners.

A dirt path snaking past the town's lone restaurant, leading into the woods.

I'd seen these things from inside the head of a monster, and at the end of that dirt path, buried miles into the woods, there was a cabin. The monster lived there. His name was Wilson. I was willing to bet that if the townspeople knew about him at all, they weren't sure whether that name was his first or his last.

I didn't care.

"Bryn?" Lake's voice cracked my thoughts open, and reality trickled in. She'd stopped the car in front of a rundown house whose owner appeared to have declared it to be some kind of motel. I took in a long, ragged breath.

Did the Rabid already know we were here? Could he smell us? Could he feel us coming from miles away? Was this a mistake?

"We should get a room." I tried not to let the questions show on my face or in my voice. "Chase will be here soon. We'll need someplace to strategize."

Under other circumstances, I might have spent a good chunk of time wondering what it would be like to see Chase again. For as long as I'd known him, other people had been tearing us apart. But right now, I didn't have time to ponder the way my blood turned thin and hot in my veins just thinking about him. I didn't have time for the repetition, with each beat of my heart, of an all-too-familiar word: *Mine. Mine. Mine.*

Right now, I couldn't be Chase's first and the pack's second. My first allegiance was—and had to be—to what we'd come here to do.

Lake and I paid for a room in cash, and I pushed down the growing sensation that as Chase got closer and closer, I was riding a roller coaster climbing steadily to its highest peak, the anticipation of the world dropping out from underneath me to a screaming, hand-waving, heart-thumping freefall, the moment Chase and I met eyes. I didn't have time for that, any of that. I was within ten miles of the man who'd killed my family. The one who'd broken Chase and laughed at the breaking.

That man needed to die.

That thought in the forefront of my mind—and probably Lake's, too—we passed the time waiting for Devon and Chase by settling into our room: one twin bed, no window, no air-conditioning. To Lake's credit, she didn't say a word about my silence, or the volley of emotions that must have been crisscrossing my face as minutes turned into hours. She just took out two knives and started sharpening them against each other, the rhythmic *ching-ching-ching* of metal on metal providing a fitting sound track to my own violent thoughts.

The Rabid's death wouldn't be bloody. Revenge was a luxury for those who had the upper hand, and we didn't. There were more of us, but Wilson was older. He might not have known we were coming yet, but he'd sense Lake, Devon, and Chase the second they got within a mile of his little cabin in the woods. Mulling our disadvantage over in my mind, I detached from the instincts that told me that this man needed to be torn limb from limb. Werewolves were all about the instincts. The one advantage I might have in this game was that I wasn't a Were.

When I had to, I could think like a human.

I didn't need to see my parents' murderer torn limb from limb. All I needed was to put a silver bullet through his forehead and a matching set in his heart and lungs.

I was so caught up in weaving in and out of the situation's logic that I almost didn't recognize the feel of the world turning upside down, my stomach flipping inside out, every hair on my body standing slightly on end, like I'd found myself in the center of an electrical storm.

"Chase." The moment Chase opened the door to our motel room, I said his name, because from the second I saw him, it was the only sound my mouth agreed to produce.

"Bryn." His voice was deep and thicker than I remembered. He seemed to have recovered, as much as anyone could, from what the Rabid had done to him before.

I was wrong, I thought, as I crossed the room to kill the

space between us, needing to assure myself that, yes, he really was okay—that, no, my brilliant plan hadn't broken him past the point of repair. Seeing him was nothing like the downward swing of a roller coaster. It felt like having my soul pulled out of my nose.

It hurt.

His arms wrapped around me, and I turned my head to the side and pressed my face into one of them, assuring myself that he was solid and real. That the Rabid hadn't destroyed him. That I hadn't failed him in a way that he never would have failed me.

"Oh, I see how it is. Baby finds her Johnny Castle, and all of a sudden, she forgets about the small matter of her BFF?"

There was only one person in the world who could deliver that line with a straight face. Until I'd heard his voice, I hadn't realized just how much I'd missed it.

"Devon!"

Chase stiffened as Dev's name left my lips, and Devon beamed at me, doing a good impression of someone who hadn't been bristling a moment before, when I'd buried myself in Chase's arms.

"In the flesh," Devon said. "When you call, Miss Bronwyn, I answer. Always." It was a testament to the gravity of the moment that he didn't treat everyone present to an impromptu performance of "Ain't No Mountain." Lest Devon decide the situation did call for some tunes, I pushed on.

"You probably shouldn't have come," I told him. When I'd told Chase to go to Devon for help, I hadn't thought through the full extent of what it would mean. Two male Weres, both of whom had some claim to a single girl, in one car for hours on end. If Chase had been born a werewolf, or if Devon and I had ever been more than friends, they probably wouldn't have both made it to Wyoming in one piece. And even if the four of us did survive the next few hours and the Rabid in the woods, Devon would still have to deal with the fact that he'd left Ark Valley without permission to come assist me in blowing a Senate mandate to smithereens.

"Do you have any idea what Callum's going to do to you when he finds out you came here?" I asked Devon, cursing myself for involving him in this and for not being able to think far enough ahead to realize what it would mean.

Devon's eyes flashed at my question, like he knew what I was thinking and resented the very idea of being left behind. Again. "Yes, Bryn, I think I have a pretty good idea of what Callum might do to someone who disobeys the pack."

So much passed between the two of us unspoken then. The fact that he'd probably seen the aftermath of my own punishment, while I'd been unconscious. The fact that his mother had been the one to dispense the so-called justice. The way Devon had been furious at me for putting myself in danger by going to see Chase in the first place. The fact that long before I'd been Chase's, I'd been Dev's.

Which led me right back to the problem at hand. "You're Pack, Dev. You're not a peripheral, you're not otherwise connected—you're one of Callum's wolves. Callum could kill us for this, but it'll be worse for you."

Callum's pack could do more than kill Devon. He was so deeply connected to them that if Callum decreed it, they could use the bond to twist him. They could rip out his mind with their anger. They could make him want to die.

For a moment, Devon said nothing, and then, he ran one hand over his gelled hair and pulled his perfectly groomed eyebrows down into a scowl. "The first time I saw you, you were covered in blood. I heard Callum tell my dad that it must have been from your mother, because by the time the Rabid got to your father, you'd retreated under the sink. You were red and shaking and it was the first time in my entire life that I felt the kind of fear from a human being that an animal sends out just before they die." Devon looked at me. "And then, you looked at me, and even though I was only five years old, I knew that what had been done to you was the worst thing I would ever see. I knew that I would never, ever let someone do that to you again."

Because this was my fight, this was his fight. I didn't have a right to deny him that. Not when I'd left for Montana without a word. Not when I'd broken every promise I'd ever made him to take care of myself.

My throat tightened. Chase put a hand on my shoulder.

Devon didn't react to the gesture, reminding me that when the situation called for it, he was (a) a first-rate actor and (b) capable of showing restraint. I'd brought Devon here, just like I'd brought Lake, when without me, they would have been fine. They would have been safe.

Fifteen different images hit my mind at once: Sora and the ugly face of Pack Justice; Ali locking up Chase so Callum wouldn't have a reason to tear him apart; Lake curled into a ball on my bedroom floor; Mitch telling me that some Weres got funny around females. The madman in the woods.

God, what if he got hold of Lake? What if I couldn't stop him? What if Callum tore Devon to pieces, just for helping me? What if Devon's own mother was the one to deliver the blows?

I couldn't take it anymore. I couldn't take knowing that as much as Lake and Devon had done everything in their power to protect me, always, I couldn't do the same thing for them. Because I was human. Weak. Stupid.

Trapped.

This time, I welcomed the feeling of claustrophobia, remembering that the last time I'd felt it, Chase had cut his bond with the Rabid. The last time I'd let this feeling take control of my own actions, I'd rewired my bond with Chase.

Could you do it again? The question Lake had asked me once was drowned out by the panic, the suffocation—the need—not to survive but to protect.

I brought my hand up to Chase's, and the bond between us pulsed and throbbed. With no warning, I became acutely aware of each of our connections to Devon and Lake, and theirs to us.

Mine.

Ours.

Mine.

I could feel Chase's determination, his willingness to follow wherever I led. I felt my love for Devon in shades of silver, and his for me, equally bright and bittersweet. Mine for Lake. Lake's for Devon.

And Chase's for me.

I felt it coming, the way some people could smell rain in the air—a low, uncontrollable rush of power—and I knew. Our bonds to Callum's pack, to Callum, pulled us back away from one another. They pulled us down and kept us there, drowning, leashed. Inside, I roared, and I saw myself taking the bonds in my teeth, my very human teeth, and ripping through them, the way Chase had torn himself away from the Rabid.

Trapped. Escape. Survive.

Protect.

Beside me, Chase growled, and I felt him, felt Us, *Chase-Wolf-Bryn*. As we threw everything we had at Devon and Lake and took everything they had in return.

Ours, Chase thought, adding his will to mine, because he

knew—he knew I loved them. He knew what it was like to be helpless and completely unable to protect those you loved.

Ours, I replied. Something exploded between the four of us: a wave of knowing. A realignment of the earth. And then, for a moment, there was silence.

Lake was the first to recover. "Huh. You know, I really don't think other people can do that, Bryn. If it was even remotely possible, my dad would've found a way to pull some mojo a long time ago."

Impossibility. These days, it was my strong suit.

"What just happened here?" Devon asked, still sounding dazed.

I cleared my throat. "I. . .well, Chase and I. . .we. . . ummm. . .we redid your pack-bond," I said, hoping Dev wouldn't be mad.

Can you hear me? I asked silently.

Devon nodded. *Like my own thoughts. Your voice—it isn't coming from outside of me, it's not coming through an external connection. It's coming from inside my head.*

"Rewiring bonds. . .it's this thing," I said out loud, "that Chase and I do." This thing we did that, when I'd done it last, had brought Callum's entire pack barreling down on us.

Lake, playing it cool, pushed back the feeling of awe that I could feel from her end of our connection. "There're four of us. Does that mean we qualify as a pack now? Because if we do, we need to think of a seriously killer name for ourselves."

Devon opened his mouth and Lake cut him off. "No allusions to musicals, Broadway boy."

"The lady doth offend my ears," Devon said. "Begone, foul witch!"

Lake snorted. "I've missed you, too, Dev."

I barely registered the interaction between the two of them, because I was stuck on what Lake had said about Chase and I being able to do something that nobody else could do.

On an unconscious level, I'd assumed that what I'd done with my pack-bond, I'd been able to do because I was human and Pack, connected, but different. I'd spent years manipulating my own bond, protecting my mind from Callum's pack. And maybe I'd *made* Chase different, too, or maybe being a turned werewolf instead of a born one had something to do with it. But maybe not. Maybe what it really boiled down to was what I'd known from the moment I first saw him, sprawled in a cage.

Chase and I were the same.

Enough with the philosophizing. Lake's voice. Inside my head—and somehow, it didn't sound the way it did when she spoke out loud. It was quiet. Unassuming in tone, if not in words. Not timid, but understated and cautious.

Vulnerable.

Focus, Lake told me, and I could feel her taking a step back from my mind, folding herself inward and concentrating—to the extent that she could—on hiding from me the things that I didn't normally see.

I nodded and took the reins. "Rabid. Here, in Alpine Creek. There's a cabin in the woods. We'll only have one shot."

Chase pulled me close to him, and I wondered if he'd even realized he'd done it. And then I realized that my hand was on the top of his hipbone, but somehow, I couldn't bring myself to remove it as I continued speaking to my friends. My pack.

"The last time I messed with someone's pack-bond, it set off a psychic flare that brought the entire pack straight to us." I paused, letting my words take hold, my grip on Chase tightening. "If what Chase and I just did has the same effect, we're working under a time limit here, so let's move. Lake and I are set for an attack. I have a plan. Boys, it's hunting season. Weapon up."

CHAPTER TWENTY-FOUR

~

NOBODY LIKED MY PLAN.

"You want us to split up?" Chase asked, his brow wrinkling in obvious bewilderment.

Lake echoed the sentiment, her voice flat. "Why would we split up? There's four of us and one of him." After a brief moment's pause, she amended her head count to better reflect our real odds. "Three and a half of us, one of him."

Three and a half, as in three werewolves, one human. I narrowed my eyes. "For your sake, Lake, I'm going to pretend that Devon is the half."

Dev, unquestionably the strongest person in this room, just shrugged and let me keep my delusions. "It's because of my petite stature," he said. All 6'4" of him.

My sensibilities halfway appeased, I turned my attention back to the crux of Lake's point. "Yes, we have stronger numbers, but we have no idea how old this guy is! Do any of you think for a second that the four of us together could take Callum?"

The fact that Callum was still my point of reference and would probably always be the standard to which all others compared was less than comforting.

"We can take him." Chase said the words quietly, but an echo of them, silent and whispered from his mind to mine, lingered in my thoughts. "Not Callum. Prancer. The four of us together, I think we could take him."

I paused for a single moment before thrusting that idea into the guillotine and dropping the blade. "And how many of us would make it out of that kind of confrontation alive?"

I felt their collective hackles go up all around me. For better or worse, this was our pack now. We couldn't afford to lose each other. I'd die if anything happened to a single one of them.

"Our best chance to get out of this unscathed is to split up. One person goes in and plays sniper. The others rush in once the target is hit."

I could see the logic worming its way into their thick skulls, and I pressed on. "If we all go, the Rabid will know it's an attack. There's no other reason three werewolves would show up unannounced in his woods. If one of us goes in and the others fall back, it won't be considered as much of a threat."

Lake ran a hand through her blonde hair, twisting her ponytail around her wrist. "He won't expect us to be armed to the hilt."

That was a near certainty. Lake was the only Were I'd ever met with a fondness for weapons. Weres rarely fought in human form, and with any luck, the Rabid wouldn't be expecting a long-range attack. One werewolf killing another with a series of well-placed bullets would have seemed as absurd to most Weres as the idea of natural wolves settling dominance disputes with pistols at dawn.

"I'll go," Chase said quietly. "He won't consider me a threat at all."

It cost Chase to say those words, to know that they were true. To the Rabid, Chase would never be a real person, let alone one who deserved to be viewed with any kind of wariness or respect.

"He might not perceive you as a threat, but he'll know you're coming," I said, my voice matching Chase's for lack of volume. "He'll smell you a mile off, and he'll know it's you. He'll be waiting. He'll have something planned."

"He won't expect me to have a gun."

At the word *gun*, Lake leaned back against the dilapidated nightstand, crossing her right foot over her left. "Do you know how to shoot?" she asked Chase.

He shrugged. "Point. Pull trigger. How complicated could it be?"

Dev reached out one arm in a show of holding Lake back, even though she hadn't moved a muscle. "Down, girl! The boy knows not what he says!"

"I'll go," Lake said, rolling her eyes at Devon's theatrics. "I'm the best shot."

Devon echoed her eye roll with one of his own. "And I stand the best chance of coming out of this alive if Mr. Crankypants catches on to the fact that someone has him in their sights."

Dev was young, but he was purebred, and Lance had trained him to fight the same way that Callum had trained me.

For a moment, I let the three of them stare each other down, and then I put an end to it.

"It has to be me," I said.

All three of the others looked at me like I'd suggested inviting Prancer to a Very Special Tea Party.

"If any of you get close to him, he'll know that there's a Were here," I said. "If he senses me, he'll sense a human. Outside of the Stone River wolves, most people can't tell that I'm Pack from a distance." The distinction between my scent and the others' was the difference between someone who'd spritzed themselves with body splash and someone who sweated it from their pores. "I won't even register on this guy's threat meter. He'll probably just assume that I'm some kid from town, poking around the woods on a dare." I knew better than to pause and give them a chance to interject. "Besides, next to Lake, I'm the best shot. If I go, the Rabid won't be on guard, he won't be expecting me, he won't recognize me, and I can hit him first try."

Every single one of my friends knew that I had the best argument, but none of them wanted to admit it.

338

"And besides," I added, "it'll take me three times as long to get to the cabin as it would any of you. If I stay out of range and someone needs me, they're out of luck. Any of you could get there in seconds."

Through the bond, I got the feeling that none of them would mind keeping me out of the range of fire indefinitely.

"No." I said the word and spoke it into their minds at the same time. "I've got guns, I know how to shoot, and I'll be careful. If I can't get him in my sights, then I'll come back. He's not going to want to attack a human in his own backyard. None of his previous victims have lived within a hundred miles of Alpine Creek. He's lived here for more than a decade. He has a vested interest in going on vacay to snack. Unless he realizes that I'm there to attack him, he won't attack me."

And, I promised silently, *I won't shoot unless I'm sure I can kill.*

They still didn't like it. I'd always known that Devon was protective, and it had been perfectly clear from day one that Chase and I hurt more for each other's suffering than our own, but I'd never realized that Lake felt the same way, that every illicit adventure we'd ever been on, she would have thrust me behind her in a second, the instant danger appeared.

I-am-doing-this.

Out loud, all I said was, "You guys."

"Fine." Chase was the first to agree. Even as he did, he lowered his head to mine and nuzzled me—the universal wolf gesture for *Come home safe.*

Lake fixed me with a steely glare. "You die, and I'll find someone with a knack for raising the dead, bring you back all zombified, and kill you myself."

"I'm not helpless," I told her, dropping my gaze to my wrists. She nodded.

Ultimately, Devon was the hardest sell. "I would rather shave my head and mold my personal look after a prison guard named Bubba than let you do this."

Of all of them, Dev had been protecting me the longest. He was also the only one who'd seen me after my first run-in with our Rabid. I could sense that image, of a skinny, blood-soaked child, close to the surface of his mind.

Taking a step back, I twisted my wrists sharply and settled into a fighting pose as the claws came out.

I'm not that little girl anymore, Dev. I'm tougher than I look. If you don't let me do this, you're saying I'm helpless. You're making me helpless, and I'm really sick of playing the victim.

In the back of my head, it occurred to me that I might be able to make Devon agree—the same way I'd forced Chase to promise to stay out of it when Callum had Sora beat me. But Dev had an incredible ability for holding grudges, and I wasn't sure that I could put up with the dramatics inside my head as well as out.

"Fine. But Bronwyn Alessia St. Vincent Clare, I'd not have you endangering yourself on my watch."

I smiled. "My stubbornness is my folly?" I guessed.

"You said it. I didn't."

Somehow, I doubted he was joking this time. Rather than reply, I twisted my wrists inward, and the silver blades whooshed in, hidden again.

And then, I went to kill the Rabid.

Devon, Lake, and Chase were all in my head. My senses—human and therefore dulled—confused them and put them at a handicap for fully understanding what was going on, but I trusted that they'd get used to it. I knew the way into the woods as well as the Rabid who lived there did. I'd seen it through his eyes, and even though the glance had been fleeting, I'd discovered that the knowledge behind it stuck in a way that made me feel closer to my prey than I'd ever wanted to be. For better or worse, I knew where to find the Rabid. The only difficulty was staying downwind and keeping to the upper ground. My Glock ate into my back, a solid reminder that from this point forward, we were playing for keeps.

As silently as I could, I moved toward Wilson's cabin, my path twisting enough that if he did hear or sense me, he might not read anything into it.

Wolf. Close by.

I wasn't sure which of the little hitchhikers in my head had sent that message, but as soon as they pointed it out, I recognized the feeling in my gut for what it was. A wolf. Not Pack, but a wolf.

Burnt hair and men's cologne. Baby powder.

I wondered at the additional component to the Rabid's scent but didn't let it throw me. Even monsters could pride themselves on good personal hygiene.

I crouched, covering my back with a tree, and I looked. From this distance, I could make out the cabin, which was much larger than I'd realized from what I'd seen inside the Rabid's head. The difference gave me the illusion of distance, let me forget how close to this man I'd come in my mind.

Settling into my crouch, I scanned the perimeter of the cabin, identifying each and every point of entry. Unless Prancer decided to do us all a favor and take an early evening stroll, I wasn't going to be able to get a sight on him.

That silent admission had the other three nipping at the heels of my mind, pushing against our bond, willing me to call them in.

But I didn't. I held my position, and I watched.

Wolf, I thought, feeling it. *Baby powder and burnt hair and men's cologne.*

And then there was movement behind one of the windows. With steady hands, I reached for my gun and pulled it out of my jeans. I could almost make out the edges of a person's form, but given my inferior human senses, it could just as easily have been an armchair. And then, I got unbelievably lucky.

The front door opened.

I moved my arms, aiming my gun at the door, and my finger began to press down on the trigger, little by little, as I waited for my target to appear. A mile away, Lake, Devon, and Chase prepared themselves to converge on me. To protect me.

Closer. Closer. Closer.

The door was almost open. I could almost see...there, a body—

No.

The instinct surged up from my stomach, like vomit in the back of my throat. This wasn't right. Something didn't feel right. It didn't smell right. It smelled...

Female. I eased my finger off the trigger, just a hair, as my intended target cleared the door.

It wasn't the Rabid.

The realization shook me, but I didn't lower the gun.

A girl. My age, maybe, or a little older. She had light brown hair and pale gray eyes, and there was something horribly, gut-wrenchingly familiar about the lines of her face.

Madison.

My gun lowered itself. My mind reeled. This was impossible. Madison was dead. She'd been declared dead when she was six years old. The Rabid had torn her so far apart that there was nothing but scraps left to bury.

Nothing but scraps.

No body.

Not dead.

I tried to adjust to that information, to reconcile the waif-like teen in front of me to the little girl, but before I could do that, I was body-slammed with another realization.

She wasn't alone.

They poured out the front door, one after another, and it finally sank in that the Rabid wasn't the only person who lived in this mammoth house in the woods.

He had people with them. Children. And every single one of them was a Were.

Retreat wasn't in my DNA any more than it was in the average werewolf's, but I couldn't stay there, not when I'd almost shot a dead girl who couldn't have been more than a year older than me.

Where had Wilson gotten all of these werewolves?

The answer was obvious. I'd always assumed that the Rabid was killing the targets we'd so painstakingly marked on our map. Hunting them. Feeding his bloodlust with prey more satisfying than a rabbit or deer. I'd assumed that Chase was a mistake, an aberration who'd gotten away and survived.

Apparently, I'd been wrong.

Wilson hadn't been killing the children he'd attacked. He'd been *turning* them. Creating his own little werewolf army. It was sick.

Sick and *impossible*. According to what Mitch had told Keely, there had been a grand total of three, maybe four cases of a human being changed into a Were in the past thousand years. One case every two hundred and fifty years, even though the prevalence of attacks was much, much higher.

Yet somehow, this Rabid had managed to change dozens.

The girl I'd almost shot—the one who'd come outside when she'd sensed me near, the one who was my age and my height and my build almost exactly—*Madison*—she could have been me.

If Callum had arrived at my house a few minutes later, she would have been.

Come out, come out, wherever you are. I won't hurt you. The Big Bad Wolf always wins in the end.

Had I been the first? A trial run? A way for him to test whatever method he'd found for changing humans? Were my parents just in the wrong place at the wrong time? Had they died because of me? Why hadn't they changed? If this Rabid knew the secret to making new werewolves, why had he only used it on children? Did it work on adults? How could a six-year-old even survive the kind of ravaging it took to trigger the change?

My pack—my friends—descended on me the second I came within their range. Their questions pushed mine out of my head, and their touches—soft on my face, my arms, and my stomach—calmed me enough that I was able to make a sound. And unable to keep from crying.

It was supposed to be me.

They heard the words, and they absorbed them. They let

me break, and then they put me back together again, all in a matter of seconds.

I straightened and cleared my throat, but when I spoke, my voice still came out husky with tears. "We'll be needing a new plan. As it turns out, the numbers are in his favor, not ours. And also, we can't kill them." I paused, because the irony of the words I was about to say didn't escape me in the least. "They're just kids."

"One of us should go back to the cabin," Devon said softly, his voice cutting across mine, quiet and insistent. "Just close enough to try to scent their numbers."

"Does it matter?" I asked, meeting his eyes and wondering how exactly the two of us had gone from algebra and the safety of Stone River to here, all in a matter of months. "If Wilson has twelve Changed werewolves, or if he has forty, does it really matter?"

Either way we were outclassed, outnumbered, overwhelmed, and screwed. In that order. Since I'd both been there and done that, I made an executive decision, one I begged the others with my mind and with my eyes to follow.

Retreat.

CHAPTER TWENTY-FIVE

BACK AT OUR TEENY-TINY MOTEL ROOM, I TRIED TO catch the boys up on everything Lake and I had discovered with our internet sleuthing. "It's hard to get a real count of how many attacks this guy has been involved in. There are at least four or five confirmed deaths—with bodies and every-thing—that might fit his profile."

Those would be the Rabid's failures. The people he'd tried, but failed, to change. Or maybe he'd never tried to change them. Maybe he'd just been thirsting for blood.

"We found several other attacks, too, where the victim was either missing or presumed dead. I'm not sure how many. Less than a dozen, more than six, but that doesn't really tell us how many wolves Wilson has in that cabin. Who knows how many of his attacks we missed? This is Google we're talking about here, not science. Lake and I aren't professional profilers. The only thing our research really told us is that there was a very good chance he'd attacked a lot of people in a lot of different territories. The numbers are fuzzier."

I thought of the missing-children database Lake had found online, put up by parents hopeful to get their kids back. How many of those "missing" kids were dead? How many of them were here in Alpine Creek, older and less human than they'd been when they disappeared?

"I saw fifteen or sixteen at the cabin," I said, thinking back. "There might have been a few more inside. The youngest was maybe four or five, the oldest probably about seventeen."

"Were they all female?" Chase asked, an odd expression on his face, like the word *female* had taken on a whole new meaning the moment he'd become a Were.

I shook my head. "About half and half."

Lake laughed, but it was a sad, grating noise. "Half of sixteen is eight. Looks like Katie and I aren't quite so special anymore."

Lake was right. The only way a female werewolf could be born was as half of a set of twins, but apparently, if you knew the secret to making new werewolves, females were just as easy to make as males. I thought about what that could mean for a pack. Fewer human wives, fewer babies lost in childbirth. More purebreds. Stronger wolves.

A stronger alpha.

"I guess we know why the Senate was willing to deal," I said, my voice like sandpaper on my throat.

Werewolves were so long-lived that it didn't make much of a difference for the species if there were years when not a single live birth took place. The birthrate, however low, was still usually higher than the death rate, because Weres were nearly impossible to kill.

But expanding a pack's numbers? Trying to stay head to head with a pack as old and large as Callum's?

That was a real concern.

"The other alphas want stronger numbers." I looked down at my fingertips, like they'd tell me my sickening logic was false. "The Rabid can give them numbers."

Suddenly, I understood why the alphas had really wanted to see Chase. They'd wanted to see how a changed werewolf compared to someone who was born that way, and they'd wanted to know the details of the Rabid's attack, because they were hoping to figure out what the monster knew that they didn't.

"The Rabid isn't going to give up the secret to making new werewolves." I said the words decisively and wouldn't have been able to keep from saying them, even if I were the only person in the room. "The moment he tells the alphas how to make new wolves, he's dead, and we have an even bigger problem."

One Rabid out hunting humans was bad. A half dozen or more alphas doing it was a problem that no amount of trickery on my part would solve.

"So if he's not giving up the secret, what do the alphas stand to gain from letting him live?" Chase asked, sounding more human than I'd heard him in a very long time. If he'd let his wolf take over, he would known the answer.

Numbers were power.

"He's bartering *them*," Lake said, flopping down on the bed and pulling her knees to her chest. "Those kids back at the cabin. Those are his bargaining chips." I reached out to Lake's mind and saw how close this hit to home, how many times she'd wondered if someday, her own alpha might decide to barter her.

Never, I told Lake silently, putting all of my force behind that single word. Callum was an alpha of alphas. His first instinct was always, always to protect.

Except, a tiny voice in my head reminded me, *when it wasn't.*

Still, I couldn't believe, even for a second, that he ever would have treated Lake like a commodity. That he ever would have let anyone harm her, no matter what they offered him in return.

"What if the Rabid isn't trading the kids he has now?" Devon asked, pacing the room with long, angry strides. "There're two things every dominant wolf wants: territory and a pack."

Those were the things that had led Devon's brother to leave Callum's pack and transfer into another, just so he could have the opportunity to challenge and kill that pack's alpha the moment he was accepted as a transfer. The need for territory and for a pack was something that Devon understood, more than he'd ever let on to me before now.

"Dev's right," Chase said, recognizing the instinct, his voice taking on a fluid, reflective tone that told me this conversation was bringing him closer and closer to the edge of a Shift. "Why would Prancer give up any of his wolves when he could...just...make...more."

I felt Chase's control begin to slip and reached out to him, grabbing his lapels with my fists and his mind with mine.

Stay with me, Chase. Stay human.

I had no idea what he'd do in wolf form in a room this small. The last time he'd been this upset, the need to hunt had been overpowering.

Stay with me, I said, repeating the words in a soothing tone halfway between a lullaby and a command. *Stay. Human.*

I could feel his wolf snarling beneath the surface, and for a moment, I thought I'd lost him, but as I spread my hands flat against Chase's chest, willing him to calm, his wolf settled, and Chase nodded.

Bryn.

Chase.

Bryn.

For a split second, I wondered what the two of us would be doing if we were the only ones in this room. Then I forced myself to step back as I realized that Devon and Lake had been seconds away from stepping between Chase and me, willing to protect me at all costs.

The last thing we needed right now was to fight amongst

ourselves. The stakes to killing this Rabid had just shot up, because even more so than I'd realized before, if we didn't kill him, future attacks were a foregone conclusion. Lots of them, probably. New werewolves, made to order.

More kids who lost everything to the Big Bad Wolf.

Why not adults? Was that it? Was that the whole trick to making new wolves? Children could survive, adults couldn't?

I pushed back the ponderings. It couldn't be that simple, or the alphas would have already figured it out. And besides, even if we assumed that the Rabid could change adults, from the alphas' perspective, younger was probably better. Inter-pack dominance, positioning yourself for power amongst the other alphas—the entire process was a long game. To people who lived practically forever, eighteen years wasn't so long to wait for someone to mature, and the earlier a pack got ahold of someone, the more influence they had.

Look at me.

And that brought me back to the fact that I had every reason to believe that what the Rabid had done to Chase was what he'd had planned for me, when I was a kid. On some level, I'd always known it wasn't a random attack and that the monster had come looking for me. That my parents had just been the ones standing in his way.

Come out, come out, wherever you are. . . .

But why me? Why any of us?

I brought my eyes to Chase's and in them, I saw myself. Saw

that from the moment I'd first heard his tortured howl, my gut had been telling me that we were the same. I looked at him, and I saw the red haze of his dreams and of mine. Remembered the fight-or-flight instinct, a wild, feral, merciless, uncompromising need to survive that I'd felt in his mind and in my own.

The alphas had asked Chase how he was attacked. They'd wanted to know, because they'd wondered if it would tell them something more than any previous investigations had. The Rabid had been hunting for more than a decade. During that time, at least some of the alphas must have known.

They must have watched him and wondered how he made the impossible flicker to life.

I wasn't aware of the moment that my thoughts went from silent to verbal, but the others had no problem picking up on the things that had gone unspoken, their minds and their thoughts interwoven with mine. "Maybe the Rabid does something a little different each time," I said, a hot feeling, like steam, seeping over my body in a way that wasn't pleasant in the least. "Lake and I were looking for patterns earlier, but what if there is no pattern, other than the fact that every one of Wilson's wolves should have died? What if the secret isn't about the attack at all?"

No magic sequence. No recipe for how to ravage a body just right.

"What if it's about the *victim*?"

Chase and I were *the same*.

We did whatever it took to get out of a situation alive and

intact. If you blocked us into a corner, we lost it. If you beat us down, eventually, we popped back up. We fought, and we held on, and at the end of the day, we *lived*.

I'd grown up in a werewolf pack where everyone was stronger than I was and yet, until that day with Sora, I'd never really gotten hurt. With training, there were times when I could get lucky enough to get a few good blows in on a full-grown Were. When the Big Bad Wolf had come knocking at my parents' door, I'd known to run and hide. When you broke my ribs, I didn't stay down for long. When I refused to fight, when I resisted the urge to let everything go red and let my inner fury out, I passed out for three days.

When the stakes were high and you tried to force your dominance on me, I rewired the entire hierarchy of the pack.

It wasn't natural. It wasn't normal. It wasn't *human*, and when I'd asked Callum about it, he'd told me that my bond with the Stone River Pack hadn't changed me, that I was *exactly what I'd always been*.

I was a person who had the potential to survive a full-blown werewolf attack.

I was scrappy as hell.

"Don't you guys get it?" I said, the words pouring out of my mouth, one after another after another. "Chase and I, we're the same. We're not normal. We're…"

I refused to use the word *scrappy* out loud and rapidly searched for a suitable replacement.

"We're resilient. Our brains must just be wired differently than everyone else's, because we don't respond to threats the way normal people do. Something happens to us, and we fight. Or flight—fly, whatever. The point is, when the situation is bad, when things are really dicey, Chase and I pull through. And so did the kids in Wilson's cabin. They got bit, and they survived."

I couldn't explain how exactly the answer had come to me, or why I believed it so strongly when there were probably other solutions to be found. But I did believe it, and because I did, the three of them did, too.

"It's not about how you attack them," Lake said, lifting the thought from my mind. "It's about who you attack. It makes sense—if only one in ten thousand people has the ability to survive, and you attack randomly, then only one in ten thousand major attacks will lead to a Change."

"And since Were attacks on human aren't common..."

"It never happens."

I felt Chase again, felt his wolf stirring under the surface of his skin, but this time, he pushed the instinct down on his own, replacing it with icy fury.

"If you know who to attack," he said softly, "if you can figure out what allows someone to survive and selectively attack those people..."

Hunt down those people like animals. Like prey. I brought one hand to the side of Chase's face, needing to touch him, needing him to know that I understood.

"If you know who to attack," I said, finishing his thought, feeling for a moment like we were the only two people in the room, "then making new werewolves really isn't that hard."

I wondered how the Rabid was finding them, the people like us. I didn't have to wonder what alphas like Shay would do if they found out how to track our kind, too.

That couldn't happen.

The Rabid had to die, and the secret had to die with him. Then, and only then, would things go back to normal. Weres would stop attacking humans, because the humans they attacked wouldn't survive, and the risk of exposure wasn't worth it for one new werewolf every couple of hundred years.

The Rabid had to die. It was a variation of the same single-minded thought that had driven me for months.

"We need a plan." For someone who'd once made a practice of rushing into things blind, I was beginning to feel like a broken record with those four little words. Unfortunately, this time, I didn't have a plan, so I was forced to take the situation apart, piece by piece.

Goal: kill the Rabid.

Problem: a sneak attack at the cabin was out, because our target had at least a dozen not-so-human shields. If we fought Wilson at the cabin, we'd have to fight his little homemade pack, too.

Problem: we couldn't fight the kids. Not Madison. Not the others. Not when they were victims in all of this, too.

"We'll either have to catch the Rabid when he leaves the cabin, or we'll have to lure the kids away from him." Those were the only two options I could see, and I wasn't fond of either of them.

"Problem," Lake said out loud. "If we lure the kids away to attack the Rabid, we'll have to split up."

Needless to say, after the last time, none of them were fond of that idea.

"Problem." Chase ran one hand up his arm as he spoke. I doubted he even noticed he was doing it. "We can't just wait for Prancer to leave his house. We don't have time."

I looked down at my watch, as if there was even the slightest chance that it would tell me how long we had before Ali and Mitch figured out where Lake and I had gone, or how long it would take Callum to respond to the psychic beacon that had gone up the second I'd rewired Devon's and Lake's bonds. For that matter...

"Problem," I said. "If the Senate is making the Rabid a deal, they'll probably come here to do it in person." That was the way it was with werewolf bargains. Like my permissions, the alphas' deal with the devil would require a certain amount of ceremony.

"Okay, so we can't just wait it out and hope the Rabid leaves his cabin sometime soon, and we can't risk splitting up to lead his harem on a merry little chase...."

The fact that Lake had referred to the wolves as a "harem"

did not escape my attention, but I wasn't about to touch that issue—or the vibes I was getting from the bond between us—with a twenty-foot pole.

"We'll have to lure him out," I said instead. Chase leaned toward me, the way a plant turns toward the sun. "If we can't go to him, we'll have to bring him to us."

Now.

"Hmmmmm," Devon said. "If I was a psychotic werewolf who had a fetish for turning small, defenseless children into my own personal lapdogs, what would it take to get me to leave my happy little family to come into town?"

In the back of my mind, an answer began to surface, but before I could verbalize my half-formed plan, Lake and Devon both started to glare at me.

I turned to Chase, looking for backup. His face was set, his expression stony. I laced my fingers through his and looked him straight in the eye, folding myself into his mind, absorbing his objections and showing him my need to do this.

"We're not using you as bait," Lake said, pulling me reluctantly back into my own body. "And don't you argue with me, Bryn, because if this guy didn't already have his own little party going on in the woods, you would never agree to let me lure him into town by letting him know there was a female Were there."

She was right, but we also didn't have any other choices. The Rabid didn't need females. He didn't want them. But he was in the business of making werewolves and apparently had a way of identifying the kind of people who could survive the Change. People like me. Resilients.

Naming the knack and those who had it satisfied me, but it did nothing to distract me from the fact that if our Rabid was a psycho, the fact that the Resilient in question was the one who'd gotten away might be more enticing than any of us knew.

"He has a girl out there," I said. "About our age. Her name is Madison, and she died when she was six years old. Not really, but that's what her family thinks, and that's when her life ended. She was six; I was four. As far as we know, mine was the only attack that was ever interrupted by other wolves. Some of the Rabid's other victims might have ended up dead, and Callum's pack found Chase after the fact, but I'm the only one who got away absolutely unscathed. He never even got the chance to attack me, and he really, really wanted to."

No sense hiding from the Big Bad Wolf. I'll always find you in the end.

But he hadn't found me. Not in time. I knew Weres well enough to know that predators didn't enjoy giving up their prey. If Callum hadn't taken me into his pack, the Rabid probably would have come for me again. And again. And again, until he succeeded.

I said as much out loud, and my logic hung in the air.

Who better to play bait than the one who got away?

"I got away, too," Chase said, bringing our joined hands to

my stomach, like all of his problems could be solved by holding me tighter. "First when he attacked me, and later when we severed the hold he had on my mind."

Chase was right. The Rabid would want him. Want to hurt him. Want to make him pay. An acidic, burning feeling flared inside of me at the idea of letting Chase play bait.

"Absolutely not."

"God, Bryn! You are such a hypocrite. At least Chase isn't human! At least he can protect himself. If this guy gets ahold of you—"

"Don't throw my species in my face," I said, facing Lake down. "How would you feel if your dad locked you up in a glass room somewhere because you were female, and male werewolves were always going to be bigger and physically stronger than you were? Maybe this Rabid would come if Chase was the bait, but he'd definitely come expecting a lot more of a fight than he would from little old human me."

Support for my position came from the most unlikely ally. "Bryn's right," Devon said, his voice low and contemplative in a way that made me think his desire to Shift was strong but controlled. "Believe me when I say that I wish that she wasn't, but girlie knows her business on this one. This guy is sick, and if he thinks Bryn is waiting for him in town with a little bow around her neck, he's not going to be able to resist. Not even if he suspects it is a trap."

Chase growled, and the sound seemed to jump from his

throat to Lake's. Neither one of them were happy with this plan, and the electricity in the air told me that we were about to be having a debate of a different kind. Once one of them Shifted, they all would, and then I'd be arguing with their wolves instead of people, and having seen the way Chase's wolf thought of me, I doubted that would go down in favor of my plan.

Protect.

Protect.

Protect.

"Fine, I get it. You guys want to protect me. But what about the kids out there who Wilson hasn't attacked yet? Who would we rather set him up against—me or them? Because if we don't move quickly enough, if someone gets here and stops us, that's what's going to happen. At least I can fight back."

Protect.

Protect.

Protect.

None of them were convinced—not even Devon, who'd spoken up on my behalf.

"I can fight back," I said again, "and you guys can cover me. Lake brought a freaking munitions store with her. We've got every weapon imaginable. You guys stay just out of range, and as soon as he shows, you descend, and we pump him full of so much sterling that he's puking silver."

If they wanted to protect me, they could. They could be my

backup; once we got Wilson into town, I'd even step back and leave the kill to someone else. But first, we had to get him into town, and this was our best chance to do it.

"How's he going to know you're there?" Lake asked finally. "We can't exactly take out an ad."

I glanced at Chase and thought of the way this Rabid had tracked us both, set us up, and moved in for the not-quite kill.

"How did he track us in the first place?" I asked, throwing out the rhetorical question. "Scent, genotype, Craigslist—I don't care. Maybe he just has a knack for finding Resilients. And even if he doesn't, at least one of those kids saw me in the woods. This guy's a hunter, and I'd be very surprised if he didn't already have my scent. He'll come. But if we want to make doubly sure, I'd lay money on someone in town having his number." As segregated as Ark Valley was, it still abided by the natural laws of small towns. Everyone had everyone's phone number, if they had a phone. "I'll go to the restaurant or the hardware store or wherever and ask whoever's in charge to give Wilson a call, something along the lines of 'There's a girl here asking for you. She says her name is Bronwyn.'"

"That'll do it," Dev said. "Crankypants can't possibly know that many Bronwyns."

None of them were happy with the idea, but at this point, we didn't have any other options. It hurt my ego to admit it, but I could do more to hurt the Rabid as bait than I ever would as a hunter. As long as he ended up dead, that was something

I could live with. And as I looked at my friends and at Chase, one by one, they gave me their silent consent, even though I knew that if something happened to me and victory came at too high a cost, none of them could live with it.

"Look at the bright side, guys. He's not going to kill me. Worse comes to worst, he'll attack me, and I'll Change." The words hung in the air, but no one was comforted by my bravado. Not even me.

CHAPTER TWENTY-SIX

"CAN I GET YOU ANOTHER CUP OF COFFEE?"

My cup was still three-quarters full, and the waitress hadn't bothered to bring the pot back with her, so I recognized a fact-finding mission when I saw one. Towns like Ark Valley and Alpine Creek didn't get many visitors, and I was well acquainted with the expression in the waitress's eyes: a particular mix of boredom, curiosity, and suspicion. She hadn't hesitated when I'd asked her to call "Mr. Wilson," immediately replying "The one who lives in the woods?" and letting loose with a sound somewhere between a *hmmm* and a *harrumph*, I couldn't tell which.

"I'm good, thanks," I said. She waited for a moment and then gave me a look, one I'd seen before on a variety of other faces, telling me that I was *different* and editorializing on that fact. Out of habit, I held the woman's gaze, and she made that same hybrid sound a second time. She wanted to look away and couldn't seem to bring herself to do it. Finally, I let her go, decreasing the intensity of my stare without ever taking my eyes from her face. She looked down, and I turned my attention back to my coffee: too bitter for my taste and so rich in smell that I couldn't keep from believing that maybe the next sip wouldn't taste quite so bad.

"Suit yourself," the waitress mumbled, and I could almost hear the admonition—*you're an odd one, aren't you?*—in her tone. "Mr. Wilson said to tell you he's on his way." The emphasis on the Rabid's name told me that I wasn't the only one this woman saw as an outsider, and not for the first time, I wondered why humans seemed to trust their eyes more than their instincts when their gut said something was off.

Wilson wasn't just *odd*. He was a psychopath, and he wasn't human. And there I was, playing bait. I steadied my hands on the coffee cup and let the smell of java stave off the shard of fear that wanted to jab into my stomach and my side and the oldest, most instinctual part of my brain.

Did you guys get that? I asked silently, sending the thought out to the others in the hopes of keeping them from noticing the slight acceleration in my heartbeat. *The Rabid's on his way.*

From the edges of town, Devon, Lake, and Chase replied in the affirmative. It was killing them to hold off, to leave me in this two-bit restaurant alone, but our target might not come if he knew I had backup, so they had to stay far enough away that he wouldn't sense them until it was too late. Once the Rabid got here, I'd stall. Devon, Lake, and Chase would get into position, and then I'd let Wilson lead me outside. He'd feel them coming, but we were banking on the fact that once he saw me, once I was so close to being in his grasp, he wouldn't be able to just walk away.

Protect.

Protect.

Protect.

My pack, as small as it was, wanted to come. They wanted to come *now*. Their wolves were fighting for control, gnashing their teeth, tearing their way to the surface.

Calm. Down, I told them, and with my words, they settled. Waiting. Soon, they would attack.

I sat there for five minutes, ten, fifteen, and two cups of coffee, before a man with brown hair and kind brown eyes slid into the booth across from me. In the corners of my mind, I felt Chase, Devon, and Lake release, sprinting toward us.

Five minutes.

I just had to stall for five minutes.

"You were looking for me, little one?"

I recognized his voice from Chase's dreams—*Change. Change back. Change. Change back*—and it disturbed me that he'd called me "little one," the same endearment Callum had used the night he'd saved me from this man's jaws. It disturbed me even more that up close, Wilson didn't look like a monster. He looked like a man, the monstrous features in my dreams— teeth smeared with blood, sparkling eyes—melding into something almost run-of-the-mill in person. He could have been Callum or Chase or the one I'd once called "Daddy." He could have been Casey, installing a nanny cam in the twins' bedroom.

The monster under my bed, the wolf stalking my nightmares, the person who'd changed the course of my entire life in one night—he looked human, and he wasn't supposed to.

"You hurt me," I said. This wasn't how I'd planned to stall, but I was struggling to remember that this was part of a plan at all.

"Hurting you was never my intention," the man said. "I wanted to give you something. A gift." He paused. "I would have taken care of you."

Teeth ripping into Daddy's throat. Someone laughing. "Come out, come out, wherever you are. The Big Bad Wolf always wins in the end."

"Liar."

I'd been in his head. I'd seen Madison through his eyes, felt his satisfaction in the way that children looked covered in blood, and I knew, just by looking at him, that this was a man who had killed long before he'd discovered the key to making new wolves. Maybe his attack on my family hadn't been his first. Maybe there had been others, and by nothing more than coincidence, one of them had lived. Maybe he'd never planned on anyone surviving, but once someone had, he'd realized that he could have his cake and eat it, too. Kill people and then use them, from that day on, as his personal guard. He could feed his taste for blood and set himself up as king of his own mountain.

I didn't want to understand him as well as I did. I didn't want to be sitting at this table with him. I didn't want him looking at me.

"Why did you want me to come here?" the man asked.

I'd had a story prepared, one that might have distracted him from the senses that would tell him my friends were getting closer and closer to us. That they were almost in position.

Two more minutes, Bryn. Two minutes, and then we're there. Get him outside of the restaurant, and then get clear.

"I've been looking for you because I want you dead," I said, staring into my coffee. Might as well give him a taste of the truth. "For what you did to me. And Chase."

"Ah, yes, Chase. Rather ironic name, don't you think?"

He was trying to be funny. He was trying to seem human. But he didn't mind that I hated him. I think he liked it.

"Why Chase?" I asked him. "Why me? Why us?"

I knew the answer, but I wanted to hear it from his lips.

Instead, he smiled. "I'll tell you at home."

Home.

The word's meaning permeated my mind. This man had come to town to bring me back with him.

"I could scream," I told him. "You wouldn't want to ruin your reputation in town, would you? If they saw you abduct me, it might bring the police out to the woods."

"Ah, but if you screamed, little Bryn, then you'd attract an audience, and that would make it so much harder for your little friends to get their sights on me."

Now, Bryn.

They were ready. They were in position. And he knew it.

"Shall we go outside?" the man asked.

In that moment, I had a choice. If I chose to stay here, I'd be safe, but somehow, I knew that he'd find a way around our plan. A back exit, a human shield, something that would let him waltz off and rob us of the only opportunity we would have to do this right.

So I went with him. He put his arm around my shoulder, and like a caring father, he led me out of the restaurant, leaving the waitress *hmm-harrumph*ing in our wake.

Outside, his grip on me tightened, but I immediately dropped out of his grasp and to the ground, rolling away from him.

A shot rang out, but somehow, Wilson—no, *Prancer*; he didn't scare me—feinted to one side, and it barely grazed his shoulder. He dropped down next to me, grabbed my arm, and made a run for it.

I twisted my wrists, and the blades popped out and into his side, causing him to let go of my arm. I pulled them down and out and drove my fist toward his chin.

Bryn, get out of the way. We can't get a clear shot. You wounded him, now get clear.

He caught my wrist and twisted it, and by some spiteful

coincidence, he did it in the exact motion that drew in my claws. I went in with my other hand, and managed to drag my claws against his chest before—having learned how effective it was with my first wrist—he disarmed that one as well.

Now he had both of my wrists, still and immobilized. I jerked backward, trying to give the others a clear shot at him, and silver bullets rained down upon him: some hitting and some not. He pulled me tightly against him, using me as a shield against the gunfire and against the stares of people beginning to stick their heads out of nearby windows.

"*Fight*," the Rabid whispered, directly into my ear, his voice high-pitched and giddy, his cadence bordering on musical. "*Fight, fight, fight, and everything goes red....*"

His fingers dug into my neck, and they must have hit some kind of nerve, because the next instant—for only the second time in my life—I lost consciousness.

Only this time, I had no guarantees that I'd still be human when I woke up.

Back in Dead Man's Creek, floating, only this time, the water was red, and the sky was blank, not a single star in sight.

I wasn't supposed to be here.

The sense was vague, and I couldn't remember what had happened or why I had come here before, but as I sank down into the red depths and breathed through them, the taste of blood filled my mouth.

Not my mouth. Someone else's—moving and yelling. Chase's. Then Devon's. Then Lake's. One by one, I flashed into their minds and bodies, hopping from one to the other, until I exploded into all three of them at once.

Distance attacks weren't working. Wilson had the body—me—held too tightly, and they couldn't get in a shot. Lake cast her gun aside and grabbed a knife. If the long game wasn't working, they'd bring this up close and personal.

But he was moving too quickly. Running faster than even they could. Chase roared and leaped off the perch from which he'd been shooting, his body changing from man to wolf in a second.

Faster this way. Faster. Save Bryn. Must save Bryn. Bryn-Bryn-Bryn—

The wolf's thoughts were less clear than Chase's, and his connection to Devon and Lake was making it difficult for them to stay in human form. All of them ran for Wilson, but in a moment of confusion and what looked to be an explosion of dust, he disapp—

Floating. Underwater. Can't breathe. Can't breathe. Have to make it to the surface have to—

End.

I woke up tied to a chair, with the taste of blood in my mouth. It took me a moment to figure out that it wasn't mine. Wilson had been injured—badly—and he'd been holding me close.

I spat.

I didn't want any part of him inside of me. But I did want his blood. More of it, anyway.

I looked down at my wrists, which—in addition to being bound—were naked. He'd taken my wrist guards. With a sinking heart, I closed my eyes and a quick survey of my body told me that the rest of my weapons had been removed, too.

And then, there were my clothes.

My bare arms and feet scared me and made me wonder if he'd stripped me of everything, but what little feeling I had left in my body—the ropes were *tight*—told me that I wasn't naked.

But I wasn't wearing my clothes, either.

He must have stripped me to search for weapons, and the clothes he'd put me in afterward weren't mine. I was wearing a dress.

I hated dresses.

It was lacy and frilly, the kind of dress that a very little girl would wear for Easter Sunday, not the kind that should have come in my size.

"He has them made specially," a voice said calmly. "It's what he likes us to wear."

I looked up at the source of the words. "Madison," I said, and she flinched at the sound of her name. "I'm not going to hurt you," I continued, keeping my voice low and gentle, which was ridiculous, considering the fact that I was an unarmed human tied to a chair and she was a weapon in and of herself. "I'm here to help. I just need you to untie me. I know what happened to you, I know what he did, and you—"

"He told me not to," Madison said, her voice empty and dull in a way that made me wonder what had happened to the girl who liked the color orange and popping bubble wrap and macaroni and cheese. "He told me not to untie you, and we have to do what he says. He's in our heads." She paused and when she spoke again, her voice sounded even less like it was coming from a real person. It sounded robotic. Dead. "He just wants what's best for us. He's the alpha. He's our Maker. He protects us."

Callum had brought Chase into the Stone River Pack and taught him how to fight the Rabid in his head, but Madison had never had another alpha to protect her from Wilson. She couldn't disobey him. Arguing with her wasn't going to get me anywhere. "What exactly did he tell you?" If anyone knew how to maneuver around orders and dish out half-lies, it was me.

"He said, 'Don't untie her, don't help her, make her pretty.'" Madison curled her arms around her waist, hugging herself and taking a step back from me. "He said it's your birthday tonight."

"That's right, Madison. Tonight, Little Bryn will be reborn. She'll be your sister. Exciting, isn't it? If things had gone right the first time, she could have been the one teaching you the ropes."

That voice. Gone was the pretense of being a harmless man. Though his words were friendly enough, the tone was sinister. Creepy.

Insane.

"Go tell the others to get ready," he told the girl. "Our distraction will only keep her little friends in town for so long." He paused, and the girl turned to hurry out of the room—like she was trying to escape hearing what she knew he was going to say next.

"When they get here, kill them. Tell the others. It's an order."

For a moment, a familiar expression settled over the other girl's face, and I might have been looking at myself, or at Chase. She wanted to say no. She wanted to rebel. She hated him, but her wolf wouldn't let her disobey, and in the back of her mind was the reminder—always present, never quiet—of the years and years and years of being told that he'd made her. Being taught again and again what happened to you when you tried to fight the impulse to obey.

And then she was gone.

Kill them. Tell the others. It's an order.

I didn't know how many *others* there were exactly, but I knew they had my friends outnumbered and that no one on my side of this little war would attack to kill—not when Wilson's soldiers were his victims, too.

My brain rebelled against the idea that the Rabid had

issued an order for his wolves to kill my friends, half because I didn't want it to be true, and half because it didn't make sense. I would have pegged this psycho for trying to bring Chase to heel and reclaim his mind, or making a stab at claiming Devon or Lake. Then again, as far as Wilson knew, Lake and Dev were still Callum's. He could reasonably kill them for invading his territory, but trying to claim them as his own would be the equivalent of declaring werewolf war. The Senate might have voted to make this man a deal, but if the Rabid stole Callum's wolves, it wouldn't be a matter for the Senate. It would be a direct personal challenge, and Callum would be free to handle it however he wished. In other words, it would be suicide, and I was beginning to suspect that this psychopath was smarter than I'd given him credit for being.

Unsettled, I cast my own mind inward, looking for the others, for my pack. I had to warn them that Wilson's wolves had orders to kill. Their voices crashed over my inner ears like a tsunami—*she's okay   Bryn awake—son of a—these people are— crazy—run—can't hurt them—can't Shift—they're ... human.*

Great. The townspeople must have reacted to the gunfire and fighting, but somehow, Wilson had slipped away with me, leaving my friends to deal with the fallout.

"You must be wondering where your friends are," Wilson said, pulling up another chair and sitting directly across from me, like we were going to have a nice chat over cookies and tea. "You see, after we made our little exit—dirt bombs do wonders for compromising werewolves visuals—your erstwhile protectors got a little caught up in town. People in Alpine Creek don't like me, but they like outsiders even less. Especially the type who come in armed and start shooting up Main Street. I mostly keep to myself. Your friends, on the other hand, well, you can see why someone might think they were dangerous. I can only imagine that someone must have called the sheriff. He's easily bribed, but unfortunately for you, he's more of a shoot-first-demand-money-later type of guy."

An image flashed into my mind. Devon, hands in the air, poised to make a run for it, men closing in from all sides.

"Don't worry," Wilson said. "The sheriff doesn't shoot silver."

I tried to send this information to the others, but their minds were too full. I couldn't get in, couldn't risk distracting them by pulling on our bond. Their problem right now was the humans of Alpine Creek. To come for me, they had to get away from a gun-happy small-town sheriff—and since it had been ingrained in each of us since childhood that Weres didn't hunt humans—they were struggling.

"Good thing we got out of there when we did," Wilson said, bringing one hand up to touch my cheek. I jerked back, and he smiled. "I imagine that's something you know a little about. Escaping against all odds. Coming out of a fight without a scratch when you should be dead."

He searched my eyes, and if I hadn't already figured out that the children in this house were like me, it would have occurred to me then.

"A few of your Callum's wolves tried to kill me once. You were there. I doubt you remember, but suffice it to say, I lived to hunt another day. Some people are just born survivors. They hang on, they get through, and they never give up. You're one of them. So am I."

He caught my chin and forced me to look up at and into him. At first, all I saw was his wolf, lurking below the surface, giddy with the anticipation of the hunt. But then, after a moment, I saw something else.

Felt something else—a flash of recognition. A twinge of familiarity.

We were the same.

"No," I said out loud. "We are *nothing* alike."

But it was still there. Something. There was no connection between us, but there was a pull: like to like, the same magnetism that had brought me to Chase in the basement.

"Werewolves and humans aren't so different," he said. "We share the vast majority of our DNA. Growing up in a pack, you probably haven't been exposed to many humans with gifts, but they're out there, and just like some of our human cousins are gifted, some werewolves are born with a little something extra as well." He smiled. "Most of them become alphas, like your Callum."

Callum, who had a knack for seeing the future. Just like

Keely had a knack for getting people to open their mouths, and I had a knack for getting out of sticky situations. A knack, like this Rabid's, for not ending up dead.

"But I don't want to talk about Callum," the Rabid said, unwilling to lose my attention in the middle of his grand reveal. "I want to talk about us. Do you have any idea how special you are? How rare?"

Did it matter? Did I care if I was one in ten thousand, or one in a million?

"I'm resilient," I said. "I survive things that others wouldn't. I bounce back. I'm hard to kill."

"Is that all you think this is, Bryn? Do you really think that it's just you? That you're just so tough that you come out on top? Come now. Think. Tell me, haven't you ever felt it, creeping up your spine? Whispering to you. Taking over your limbs, your sight, your fear, your rage…"

Wilson spoke about his survival instinct like it was a separate being. Like it was sacred. Like he wasn't a madman reveling in violence so much as the avatar for something primal and cruel. "We're chosen. Tell me you don't feel it. Tell me you don't sense it when you look at me, when you look at the boy that I sent you."

Chase hadn't escaped the Rabid. The Rabid had attacked him and left him bleeding on the pavement, knowing that he was leaving the carnage in Stone River territory and that Callum would clean up the mess. Knowing that sooner or later, if Chase was a part of Callum's pack, the two of us would meet.

Chase hadn't escaped the Rabid. The Rabid had sent him to me.

No. I wouldn't let him taint what Chase and I had. I'd die first.

"I guess this explains how you find them," I said, keeping my voice low and dull. "Your victims."

"I find them the same way you would," he said. "The same way you will, once you're mine. Like to like. I've been waiting a long time for someone strong enough to help me, someone as special as I am." He leaned forward and touched my hair. "You're glorious as a human. So brave. So strong. I should thank Callum for that, I really should. As a Were, you'll be a princess." He sighed. "My princess."

I shuddered and my throat burned, acid working its way from my stomach to my mouth. I fought the nausea as best I could. In my head, the others roared, and the connection between us pulsed, bright like lightning in my mind.

They'd escaped from the sheriff with only a bullet graze to Devon's side that had already started to heal.

Hold on, hold on, hold on, they told me. *We're coming.*

No, I replied. *You don't understand.*

I begged them to come completely into me, to take my thoughts and knowledge as their own and to know what they were up against.

Not just a pack of werewolves. A pack of Resilient were-wolves—capital *R*—who'd lose their minds the moment danger closed in. Of my other selves, only Chase had the same advantage. Devon was a purebred and Lake was a fighter, but their instincts to fight, to escape, to *win* weren't any stronger than the average werewolf's.

"They're coming," Wilson said out loud. "Your friends. I can feel them. I can smell them. They smell like anger. Like blood."

"So do you." I met his eyes, and I smiled. "You may be scrappy," I said, intentionally using the word to demean every-thing he'd just told me, "but you're still allergic to silver, aren't you? You took a couple of bullets. I took a chunk out of your side. You have to be hurting right now."

He slammed his arms into me, pushing my chair over back-ward. My head cracked into the back of the chair, and for a moment, I saw bright lights. Then everything cleared, and I saw him standing over me, his eyes beginning to yellow.

"I'm going to like Changing you," he said. "And once I do, we'll be bonded in a way you can't even imagine. If you think your connection to Callum's pack is strong, you've seen noth-ing. Normal pack-bonds don't hold a candle to what we have. Normal obedience is nothing compared to what you owe your Maker."

He'd had a hold on Chase, even after Callum had claimed Chase as part of the Stone River Pack. I was pretty sure I knew *exactly* how strong that made the bond between a Changed werewolf and the person who brought them over. Chase had broken his, with my help and with Callum's; if this psycho brought me over, I'd have to do the same.

Instead of shaking me, Wilson's words gave me valuable information. They told me that he didn't know what I'd done to my pack-bond. He didn't know that I'd re-carved it, connecting myself first and foremost to Chase. He didn't know that I'd done the same thing with Devon and Lake. This Rabid thought he knew so much about being Resilient, but all he knew was how to fight. Maim. Kill. He didn't know how to see pack-bonds as a threat to his safety, how to attack them, how to escape.

He didn't know that I'd done it before and that if he brought me over, I'd do it again.

He was the one who didn't know the depths of what he was. What I was. What all of the kids outside were.

He was the one who didn't know what he was messing with.

"Your friends are here," Wilson told me. As if I didn't already know. As if I hadn't felt them coming. As if I couldn't see out of their eyes—all of their eyes at once. Bleeding and bloody, they were armed to the hilt, and right now, they didn't care about the fact that the rest of Wilson's wolves were victims.

Anyone who stood between them and me was fair game.

No, I wanted to say, *don't hurt them.* But how could I? How could I tie my pack's hands behind their backs, when the wolves outside were bound to kill them?

Bound to obey.

"You see now," Wilson said, straightening my chair. "You understand. We're all powerful, but the power? It's mine."

Mine.

Mine.

Mine.

The words echoed in my mind, and in that second I knew exactly what to do.

CHAPTER TWENTY-SEVEN

I'D THOUGHT IT MYSELF: WILSON DIDN'T KNOW what it really meant to be Resilient. He didn't know how to use it for anything but blood.

I did.

I closed my eyes and thought of Chase. I thought of Wilson. I thought of Madison, the grinning six-year-old, and Madison, the ghost of a girl who'd greeted me when I woke up. I thought of what it meant to be a survivor myself, and I cast my mind outward, looking for that in them. The power was twisted in Wilson. Ugly. Dark. And that darkness bled onto the others, tainted them.

Madison leapt, and Chase met her midair, their teeth snapping at each other's throats. To their left, Lake took aim and fired at one of the other wolves—small but vicious. My friends and my kind clashed, and their directives pulsed in my head and my veins, until they were all I could hear.

Protect.

Protect.

Obey.

Obey.

Save Bryn.

Kill them all.

I don't know where the burst of strength came from, and I didn't question it. I just shoved my arms outward, straining against the ropes, and they snapped, with the fury of a mother throwing a car off her baby boy. Like a wild thing—a whirl of energy and rage and pulse after pulse of something that I couldn't name—I jumped out of the chair. But instead of going for Wilson's throat, instead of killing him, I ran for the door.

My first order of business wasn't payback. It was salvation, and right now there was so much at stake.

"Stop!" I yelled, issuing the word at top volume with both my mouth and my mind. The bond that connected me to Chase, Devon, and Lake crackled, and all three of them paused. Thrown—and affected by the charge of *something* in the air—their attackers paused, for just a second.

And then their directive was back.

Obey.

"No," I screamed. "You don't obey him. You obey *me*, and I said to *stop*."

I reached for Wilson, for his bond with the others, and I pulled it toward me—pulled their hopes and fears and the people they'd been before he'd stolen that from them toward me—and it sent them as perfectly still as my friends.

"What are you doing?" Wilson growled, gripping me from behind. Slowly, the wolves—his wolves—turned from my friends to face him. A growl broke from Madison's throat, followed directly by a whine.

She was confused. Who was the alpha here—Wilson or me?

"You think you can steal them? Make them yours?" Wilson asked, his gaze losing its focus, making him look unhinged.

"No," I said. "I don't want to make them mine. I want to make them theirs."

You have a choice. The words flowed out of me, and into the wolves I was commanding—Devon, Lake, Chase, and all of the others. *You can choose to obey, to submit, to let someone else make your decisions, or you can decide. You can decide who you want to be, who you want to be tied to. Who you trust.*

I showed them, with my mind, what I'd done to interfere with their bond to Wilson, and what Chase and I had done, when we'd chosen each other and my friends over Callum's pack.

Madison was the first one to melt back into human form. Naked and lying on the ground, she lifted her head, unaware of her own nudity. Broken, but regal.

"Madison, no," Wilson said sharply, like a man talking to a dog.

"Funny thing about Resilience," I said, my heart breaking

for her and for all of them. "Being Resilient doesn't just give you the ability to survive. It doesn't just make you a fighter. It makes you resistant. To injury. To death." I met Madison's eyes, looking only at them and not at the rest of her body. "To dominance."

Being what we were meant that Chase and I—and all of Wilson's victims—played by different rules. That was the reason that at the ripe old age of four, I'd been able to shut Callum's pack out of my head. It was the reason that Chase and I had been able to choose each other over all else.

It was the reason Chase had been able to break his bond to Wilson for good.

"If you don't want to obey him, you don't have to. You don't have to obey me, either. But you can connect to me, or to the others, or to anyone you want. You can choose your family. You can choose freedom. You can choose *this*—"

I showed them what it was like to be part of a pack like the one my friends and I had created. All of us together, our bodies folding into one, our minds connected.

Madison pushed herself to her feet and walked toward us—dirty, bleeding, and bare. "I was six. On a vacation with my family, and he took me. He took me and he hurt me and he Changed me." She looked at Wilson. "You told me that I was yours. You told me how to dress and how to act. You changed my last name. You took away everything, and I. Want. It. Back."

She threw her head backward, and I could actually see the power coming off her body, could see tiny bits of light and power that connected the Changed Weres by their souls. And I could see the girl Madison had been, before he'd taken her, rewiring her connections, writing her own destiny.

One by one by one, the others stood.

I felt them, reaching out to one another and to me, and in that moment, I made a decision of my own.

We were the same.

All of us.

The same.

And for whatever reason, I'd been the lucky one. I'd escaped, and they hadn't. But for the rest of my life, for as long as I lived—whether it was seconds or years—I would be there for them. I would make it up to them. I would help them make it up to themselves.

Mine.

Mine.

Mine.

The whisper came from all corners of the yard as we claimed one another. From Madison and her pack-mates, from Chase and mine, and then, like the birth of a star, there was an incredible surge of light and heat that threw all of us to the ground.

Prancer was the only one left standing.

And as the rest of us got our bearings, only one directive remained in the air and in our bodies.

Kill the Rabid.

I stood and walked away from my nightmares until I reached Chase. I pressed myself into his side, and he buried his head in my hair. He was mine, and I was his. We were the same, and we were more.

I averted my eyes, turning my body into his, and I breathed in his scent, which smelled to me like safety and home. All around us, the others were Shifting into wolf form, and I could feel the power rising in the air. Not just the power of the Shift, not just the power of a pack on the run, but something older.

Deeper.

Primal.

Fight.

For years, Madison and the others had forgotten that they could. Wilson's domination had held their instincts at bay, but now...

Fight.

Fight.

Fight.

An eerie silence descended on the lawn, only to be broken a moment later by a horrible wail, an inhuman sound drowned out by howls and snapping teeth and the sound of flesh tearing like Velcro.

They leapt at him from all sides. Knocked him to the ground. Mobbed his body, a sea of fur and claw and *red-red-red*.

I felt the fury. Felt it like a siren's call, but I breathed through it, holding tight to Chase, the smell of blood so thick in the air that the other smell—*burnt hair and men's cologne*—disappeared into coppery, wet, warm…

Nothing.

It was over.

The feeding frenzy stopped, the haze receding as quick as it had come, and when I lifted my head off Chase's chest to look at the carnage, there wasn't enough left of Wilson the Rabid to bury, let alone heal.

The cries of the pack—our pack—echoed in my head and out of it, as human words and as one united, animalistic howl.

Chase and I let it roll over us, washing away everything we'd been before this moment. Our bodies intertwined.

He was mine.

I was his.

But we weren't alone. Not by a long shot. I melted into Chase's mind, and he came into mine, and as Chase-Wolf-Bryn, for a split second, we saw the world around us with omniscient eyes. Saw our connections to the others—to Lake and Devon and each of the children Wilson had turned. Saw the power we held, saw it well up as the others changed back to human form and turned toward us.

Pack.

Pack.

Pack.

The exhilaration of being Chase-Wolf-Bryn faded in

comparison to the overwhelming sensation of being Us. All of Us. The urge to run, to be free, to be together, was overwhelming, and for the second time in my life, I felt that kind of adrenaline turn toward focusing on a single person. A leader.

They wanted to run. But they couldn't. Not yet. All around me, the whisper of the pack took on a single word. *Alpha, alpha, alpha.*

And that was when we realized—Chase and his wolf and I—that all of the other wolves seemed to be staring directly at me.

CHAPTER
TWENTY-EIGHT

ME? HOW COULD THEY POSSIBLY BE LOOKING AT ME
and thinking a word that conveyed that kind of power? Absolute, unerring, eternal. Protection. Punishment. Justice.

A pack alpha was many things, but human definitely wasn't one of them. And yet, there the others were, staring at me with a kind of palpable expectation, their bodies humming with the energy of the kill. They wanted to run, and they wanted me to tell them they could.

Yours, Chase told me silently, and then, he rested his head on top of mine. His breath was hot on my scalp, and I shivered.

Mine. That assertion came from the wolf inside Chase—battered and bruised from the fight and angry that he hadn't been allowed to take down his prey: the man who had dared to touch The Girl. Chase's wolf wasn't making a claim over any of the other Resilients, he wasn't answering their silent plea to run. He was stating what was, to him, quite obvious.

I was his.

I wanted to burrow inside of Chase, to hide in his mind, to take refuge in his wolf's possessiveness and look away from the dozens of eyes—human and wolf—boring into my own, but I couldn't.

Alpha. Alpha. Alpha.

The words became a high-pitched whine in my mind.

Do what you want, I told them. *If you want to run, then run.*

That wasn't enough for them. It wasn't what they needed. They needed me. They needed the assurance, the answers. They needed what I'd sworn to give them a moment before—anything and everything to help them overcome years of Wilson's abuse.

Run. The word left my mind an instant before it left my mouth, and on both counts, it came from the deepest part of me—from something ancient and pure and utterly confusing. I wasn't a werewolf, but there was something inside of me. Something as raw and primal as the wolf inside of Chase. A survival instinct—and a protective one—and as I told the others to run, gave them my permission, I shuddered, and then I let their joy overwhelm me as I had that day with Callum's pack. I let all of them in, felt each and every one of them through our newly formed bond.

The pack was brutal and beautiful and alive, and overcome with their energy, I threw my head skyward and howled.

I felt, rather than saw, the effect the sound had on Chase.

He arched his back, and the wolf clawed its way to the surface, forcing him to Shift. Instinctively, I dropped down on my knees next to the midnight-black body beside me, and stared into the wolf's eyes. Chase's eyes. I buried my hands in his fur—silky, not coarse—and I felt his heart beat under my palms.

Run. Run. Run, I told the others. This time, my mind-words carried with them joy, as well as power. Lost to the connection and the drive and the urge to move as one, I scrambled to my feet and took off running, an entire pack at my heels, mobbing me. Wanting to be close to me.

The warmth of their bodies kept my skin from chilling, and the adrenaline passed from one member of the pack to another to another, like a stone skipping on the surface of a pond. Lake, tall and blonde even in wolf form, butted my heels with her head, pushing me to run faster, to let go of myself more.

And when I did, when the last of my walls crumbled away, that was when I knew.

The pack was together.

The pack was safe.

The pack was *mine*.

And this time, I'd die before I let anyone take that away.

An hour later, the Weres had settled reluctantly back into their human forms, and I'd managed to remember that I *was* human. Madison and one of the other older Resilients began helping the little ones into new clothes, and for the first time, I realized that some of the children weren't that much older than the twins. The youngest was two, maybe three. Red-haired and solemn, she toddled toward me the second Madison got her into a faded hand-me-down dress. I knelt and let the little one come into my arms, and I settled her on my hip with an ease that I never could have managed before Alex and Katie.

An ease that felt too natural even now, given that this girl should have been a stranger to me.

Lily.

Her name came to me, in the recesses of my mind, like I'd always known it. Her small head leaned contentedly against my chest, and what she knew of life passed into my consciousness. *Wilson—sweet and scary and oh, he'd hurt her once. Red. The bad color. Bad things. Blood. A ratty stuffed bunny whose neck had been ripped out. Cotton in her mouth. Not allowed to cry.*

And then, there was me.

In her eyes, I was beautiful. Tall. Powerful.

I was safe.

Craning my head so that our eyes could meet, I breathed out slightly, and she sniffed like crazy, trying to absorb the smell of my breath.

"Hello, Lily," I said softly. "I'm Bryn."

Lily nodded, and then, with a tentative smile, she turned and pointed, a quizzical look on her face. I followed her finger directly to Chase.

He crossed the room in three broad steps, his motions flowing, as they always did, like water. He brought his face next to mine and rubbed my cheek with his. And then, silently, he turned to Lily, and with a small smile, he huffed out a breath, allowing her to catch his scent.

Through the pack-bond, I sensed that to Lily, Chase smelled like me. *Pine needles and cinnamon.*

I closed the space between my body and Chase's, or maybe he did, and Lily laid her head back down on my chest, content to be nestled between us as my face and Chase's found their way back together. Cheek to cheek. Forehead to forehead. Nose to nose. Then, lip to lip. As the kiss stretched out over a delicious, unbearable eternity, I felt myself folding into his mind and welcoming him into mine. For a single second, the world stopped rotating on its axis and the hum of the rest of our pack went very, very still.

And then, the silence and stillness were broken as I felt the Weres in the room stiffen and heard the beginning of a growl in the back of Chase's throat.

Something's coming.

We didn't get more than a moment's warning, or two, before the front door to Wilson's cabin exploded inward, and Weres began pouring in. I broke away from Chase, and instantly, the sounds of the rest of my pack—*Mine*—were back, louder than ever before.

Ours. Ours. Ours.

This was *our* territory. These men were trespassing. And the wolves inside of each of my pack-mates knew beyond knowing that the pack was to be *protected*, the alpha was to be *obeyed*, and trespassers were to be *killed*.

What started as a low rumble in our bond became audible snarling, and even though I wasn't comfortable with the idea of controlling anyone else—even if they'd chosen, and were still choosing, to let me—I pulled back tightly on my end of the bond, restraining them all with a single word. "Hold!"

"You?" It took me a second to locate the person speaking, and a few more beats to recognize him. He looked more like Devon than he should have, the expression on his face twisting familiar features into something ugly.

Shay.

I stiffened and let my senses reach past the borders of my new pack, my Resilient pack, and when I stepped out from behind the psychic shield of our numbers, the power in the room hit me like a blow to the stomach. I'd felt it before, in Chase's body, but now, I felt something new. Instead of cowering or running away, my instinct was to protect what was mine: *my* territory, *my* wolves, *my* status. This was the Senate. These were alphas, but the roar of the pack I led at the edges of my mind, the way they held back on my command and my command only, forced me to accept an unforgiving, unlikely truth.

These men were alphas. So was I.

"Callum." My eyes sought him out, and my mouth made the word of its own volition. I felt like I'd never said it before, like it was a word in a foreign language that I didn't speak. I wasn't quite sure what it meant. Wasn't sure what—or who— he was. To me.

To the wolves I was bound to protect.

"Bryn," Callum returned calmly. "Seems you've gotten yourself into a bit of trouble."

One of the other alphas snorted. "Where's Wilson?"

"The Rabid?" I asked, seething warmth making its way from my stomach up the back of my throat and out of my mouth as pure venom. "The one who attacked and killed defenseless children in his pursuit of turning other kids into werewolves? The one who was using his ability to do so as a leg up into the Senate's hierarchy? That Wilson?"

"Yes. That Wilson." Shay didn't like me. I met his eyes full-on and didn't even blink. Let him not like me. The feeling was mutual.

"Oh," I said lightly. "That Wilson is dead."

Shay moved forward then, in a blindingly quick motion, and instinct told me that he would have closed his hand around my throat and slammed me against the nearest wall had it not been for the fact that in a move just as quick, each and every one of the wolves in my pack moved to defend me. Chase stepped directly in front of me, so close that my nose almost touched his back. Lake pulled to my side, and the children flanked her—even Lily, who twisted out of my grasp and leapt out toward Shay, her teeth flashing, like she hadn't quite learned yet that they weren't as potent in human form as they were when she was a wolf.

If I'd let her, she would have torn him to pieces.

But ultimately, it was Devon's presence, massive and looming, that stilled Shay's forward motion. The two of them faced off: Dev young and perfectly groomed, even in the middle of chaos; Shay a mirror of everything Dev could have been if he'd cared more about being a purebred werewolf than being a person.

"Back. Off." Devon said the words slowly, giving each of them the weight of its own sentence. A ripple of unrest went throughout the room, the alphas shifting from one foot to another, their eyes on the confrontation.

Challenge.

Dev tilted his head slightly to the side, and I wondered which character he was playing, or if this was 100 percent Devon Macalister, down to the set of his jaw.

Challenge.

Dominance.

"Dev." I said his name quietly, knowing this could get ugly

if I didn't stop it. At the sound of my voice, Devon broke eye contact with Shay and took a step back, closer to me.

"She's their alpha," a man who smelled like sea salt and sulfur breathed, his green eyes flecked with yellow, his pupils widening. "The children think they're hers."

They didn't just *think* they were mine, I wanted to say. They *were* mine. I didn't understand it. I couldn't exactly see the logic behind the choice, but there it was.

I was the one who'd set them free.

I was the one who'd showed them what they could do. I was the person they'd chosen to connect to, and because I'd started it all, I was at the center of the things that connected us all.

I was *theirs*. And even though I was their alpha, even the smallest of my pack-mates seemed to sense that I was also the most vulnerable. The weakest physically. The one that Shay wanted to disembowel.

"I didn't kill Wilson." My voice—barely more than a whisper—echoed with the power of the entire pack, a frenzied blood-thirst that made me sound less human than I was. "They did. The ones he Changed. The ones you *let* him Change."

Lily growled, and coming from a cherubic two-year-old, the sound seemed more demonic than lupine.

"They're free now," I continued, my voice still echoing with power that wasn't mine. "And nobody gets to them except through me."

"You can't honestly believe we'd let you keep them," Shay

said, his tone incredulous. Every instinct I had said that he was challenging me and that staring him down almost definitely wasn't going to get me out of this one. Like flame and tinder, the challenge caught on; I could feel it spreading across the room from one alpha to another. They were stronger than I was. One on one, I didn't stand a chance against any of them. Even surrounded by Resilient werewolves who'd do anything I asked them to, I was outclassed. Resilient or not, my wolves were just kids, and every alpha in this room except me numbered their years in centuries.

I'm not backing down. I tried to let them see that in my face. I may have been outclassed, but if these alphas thought they could take even one of these kids from me when they'd been perfectly content to leave them to a Rabid in exchange for new wolves of their own, they were mistaken.

I won't back down. Not now. Not ever. Even if I was signing my own death warrant.

My gaze flickered over to Callum, and his amber eyes focused on mine in a way that made me wonder if he was seeing me at four or five or six or ten, or any age up until the point that Ali had taken me away.

Bryn. I didn't hear his voice in my head, but I saw that single word—my name—in his eyes. Saw the recognition behind it. The feeling. And something else: a look I knew, one I'd seen many times before. It was a look that pushed me. One that challenged me to take everything he'd ever taught me and *think*. There was a way out of this dilemma, but I had to find it and set it in motion myself.

So I did what Callum's eyes bid me and *thought*. And the answer was there, in everything I knew about the men in this room and everything Callum had taught me about maneuvering my way around werewolves.

"Actually," I said, finally responding to Shay's words, my eyes still on Callum's, "I do think you'll *let* me keep them. Because this isn't Europe. This isn't Asia. And in North America, alphas don't take other alphas' wolves. We don't challenge each other, and if you want to take what's mine, you're going to have to challenge me."

You're going to have to kill *me*. Those words went unstated, but every single person in the room understood that they were there, and a wave of static energy pulsed through the air. Alphas didn't like being challenged. Especially not by females. Especially not by humans.

Especially not by me.

"Seems to me the girl has a point," Callum said, his face neutral, his body perfectly relaxed in a way that would have scared the daylights out of anyone with enough sense to know that Callum wasn't the type to get mad.

He got even.

"By Senate law, if a wolf wants to transfer packs, both alphas have to sign off on it, and Bryn seems a bit resistant to that idea," Callum continued.

Shay growled. "You can't be serious, Callum. She's human! She's weak. If we want what she has, we'll take it. *I'll* take it."

Callum didn't growl, but he must have stopped holding back, stopped shielding his power from the others, because in the next instant, something ancient and undeniable flooded the room. *This* was what it meant to be alpha. *This* was what real power felt like.

Each and every one of the men in the room stumbled. I didn't even blink.

"Now, see, that depends," Callum said, his voice still neutral, his face still blank. "On whether or not we consider ourselves a democracy."

I couldn't help the satisfied smile that spread slowly over my lips. I'd seen this coming. I'd set him up to say it. If the Senate was a democracy, none of the alphas in this room could challenge me or take a single wolf that belonged to me. And if we weren't a democracy, well...

In that case, Callum had no reason to hold back. No reason to recognize anyone else's claims to their wolves.

"Well, Shay, are we a democracy or aren't we?" I took great pleasure in throwing those words, the exact words Shay had used to force a vote on the Rabid, back into the Snake Bend alpha's face.

Game. Set. Match.

No one wanted to challenge Callum, and to take what was mine, that was exactly what they were going to have to do. I wasn't sure if this was just some cog in a greater scheme of Callum's, some detail that had to fall into place for the future he most desired, or if maybe he was doing this for me. Because I mattered. Because maybe I was worth it.

My chest tightened, and I could almost hear the sound of glass shattering as something inside me broke, but I couldn't risk letting anyone else see the breaking, so I kept my face carefully neutral, like someone who'd learned from the very best.

"I think we're done here," I said, daring the alphas, any single one of them, to tell me we weren't. "You can see yourselves to the door." For a moment, I thought Callum would throw his head back and roar with laughter, but he didn't. He just glanced up at the ceiling as one by one, I met the other alphas' gazes, and one by one, they turned away and filed out the door, their hatred for me and the way Callum had tied their hands palpable in the air. As I watched them go, I couldn't shake the feeling that someday they'd be back. Maybe not to this cabin. Maybe not anytime soon, but eventually, some or all of these alphas would decide that the prize was worth the gamble. They'd call Callum's bluff and take their chances. And when they did, things were going to get ugly.

Finally, I brought my face back to Callum's, and out of habit, my hand went to my waist, to the Mark that had once connected the two of us into something more. For a moment, I felt a pang for what we'd lost, but that longing was drowned out by a moment of prescience, one that told me that Callum knew as well as I did that this wasn't the end. Not between the two of us and not with the Senate. Someday, the other alphas would strike back.

And when they did, we'd be ready. *I'd* be ready.

For the first time in my life, Callum looked away from my gaze before I looked away from his, a slight, knowing smile playing at the corners of his lips. Then, without a word, he turned and followed the other alphas out the door, until the only ones left in the cabin were the ones whose minds and heartbeats I knew as well as my own. The ones whose strength and power pulled at me from all directions, with the familiar call of *alpha, alpha, alpha.*

Pack, pack, pack, I whispered back, my mind to theirs. *Let's run.*

CHAPTER TWENTY-NINE

"HEY, COULD I GET A REFILL ON THIS COFFEE?"

"That depends," Lake said, looking at the customer with dancing eyes before turning to shout toward the bar. "Maddy, you want me to shoot him?"

Maddy—who'd joined Lake as a waitress and proven that the only thing more terrifying than one of them was two—pretended to think it over for a moment and then shook her head. "If you shoot him, it'll take him longer to run far, far away. And besides, it might hurt your tip."

Lake turned back to the man in question—one of many Weres who'd ventured into the Wayfarer in the two months since it had become the center of a new territory. Montana and western North Dakota no longer belonged to the Stone River Pack. The Wayfarer and the land surrounding it for a good hundred miles on either side belonged to the newly minted Cedar Ridge Pack, courtesy of Callum.

Technically speaking, the new territory belonged to me.

There was a part of me—the human part—that still believed

it was all semantics, that I was an alpha in name only, because Weres couldn't understand the idea of a pack without one. But there was another part—the part of me that knew every second of every day where each and every one of my wolves was—that recognized that the title wasn't a meaningless one. It wasn't empty.

It was real.

But it was different, too, from the way things had been in Callum's pack. The wolves in Cedar Ridge and I were all connected, but until or unless we were threatened, I didn't control that connection, and I didn't use it to control anyone else. I hadn't spent my entire life referring to Callum as a patriarch only to turn into his female counterpart overnight. If there was a problem, I solved it. If they needed me, I was there, but in their human lives, the wolves in my pack could choose when to follow me and when not to, and most of the time, I didn't make an active attempt at leading. It wasn't like Lake was ever going to let me live under the delusion that I ran things. She bossed me around as much as she always had, and that wasn't even taking her dad or Keely or Ali into account.

None of the adults in our lives had been particularly pleased with our adventure to Alpine Creek. Our parents had arrived at the cabin just after the battle of wills with the Senate had ended—and needless to say, Lake and I hadn't fared quite as well against Ali and Mitch as we had against the entire werewolf establishment. I'd spent most of the summer grounded, and with the new school year fast approaching, Ali and Mitch had only backed off because, laissez-faire alpha or not, my mood tended to trickle down into the others, and a pack of stir-crazy juvenile wolves was nobody's friend.

"Want another root beer?" Keely asked me.

I shrugged. "Sure."

The man who'd futilely asked for more coffee turned to glare at me, but all I did was raise an eyebrow, and he looked very quickly away.

There were seventeen werewolves permanently in residence at the Wayfarer now—Lake, Mitch, Katie, Alex, Devon, and twelve of the kids we'd rescued from Alpine Creek. Some of the others—mostly teens—had chosen to make their way elsewhere. I hadn't objected. The two who'd been attacked most recently had gone home, with the understanding that the local pack would treat them like visiting dignitaries and not try to claim them or enforce any dominance of their own. For now. Two or three others, all eighteen years old (or close enough to it to convince Ali they didn't need constant supervision), were playing at being peripheral, though my pack-sense—*alpha-sense*—told me that none of them would stay gone for long.

You're quiet today.

The sound of Chase's voice in my head made my lips curve slowly upward. There were moments when my pack-sense was still, and for seconds, maybe minutes at a time, I could remember what it had been like when the two of us were the only people in my head.

The only people in the world.

I knew without asking that he was nearby. That if I snuck out my window late at night and tiptoed into the forest, I'd see him. I'd bring him clothes, and he'd shed his wolf skin, and under the blanket of darkness, he'd tell me everything he'd seen since he'd been gone.

Chase was my eyes and ears. Lake and Devon were my guard, the way Devon's parents were Callum's, but Chase was my emissary, the one who ran the perimeter of our territory and reported back.

The job suited him, and it suited Ali that he wasn't always here, that some days, there was space between us and she could pretend that since he hadn't Marked me and I hadn't Marked him, we were just two crazy kids with a crush.

You're always quiet, I replied to Chase's comment by turning it around on him. *I miss you.*

I felt the reply from his wolf, the kind that told me that sometimes, they thought they'd spent their whole lives missing me.

Dork.

Cynic, Chase retorted.

I wished that I could leave my root beer on the counter and run out to meet him, but being alpha meant that I didn't always get to do as I pleased. Sometimes, I had to do things just because they needed to be done, even if they terrified me.

Even if they made me feel like there was a possibility that the entire world might fall out from underneath me.

That was what I was doing in the restaurant today—besides watching Maddy and Lake torturing the clientele. The alpha of the Stone River Pack had requested a meeting with me.

I'd agreed.

Callum and I hadn't seen each other since he'd walked out of that cabin in the woods. He hadn't called me. He hadn't written. He hadn't made a single move to even talk to me until now.

Pack. Pack. Pack.

I took some relief in their presence, and I opened up my senses, reminding myself that I was doing this for them. That Callum was an ally, not my keeper. That I was an alpha, not his girl.

Sipping on my root beer, I swung my feet back and forth and found amusement in the way that Lake zeroed in on a target—human, most likely—to hustle at pool. A low hum in my pack-bond brought my eyes to look for Maddy, who had fallen into a quiet spell, the kind she still had every hour or two, and I reached out to her with my mind, reminding her that I was here. That we all were. And that she was herself.

Maddy, not Madison.

Ours, not Wilson's.

Healing, not broken.

She hadn't been able to go back to her family. Not after

being dead for ten years, not when she couldn't go more than a mile away from the rest of our pack without her wolf driving her back—to pack, to safety, to home.

"Bryn."

I turned toward Callum's voice, and something inside of me began to dissolve. Seeing him would always make me feel like a kid, and it would always remind me of the things that had brought me here. The things he'd done and the things he hadn't. Some days, I thought everything went back to Callum—

He'd saved me from the Rabid when I was four.

He'd Marked me.

He'd raised me.

He'd given me Ali, who loved me enough to take me away.

He'd trained me.

He'd pushed me.

He'd lied to me.

And ultimately, he'd let me discover the truth, because based on everything I'd learned about Callum's *knack*, he had to have known that I would.

"Let's walk," I said.

For a long time, Callum and I walked and said nothing. And then, finally, he spoke. "How are your grades?"

Somehow, I hadn't pictured that as being his opening.

I rolled my eyes. "It's summer. No school, ergo no grades. Ali's been homeschooling the youngest of the new Weres, though. They aren't quite elementary school—ready yet, so she's got her hands full." I paused. "Lake, Maddy, and I will be driving in to the closest high school starting in September. Chase and Devon, too." I was babbling, but I couldn't seem to help it.

"How is Ali?" Callum asked me.

I nodded. "She's good. She misses Casey, but I don't think she'll ever go back to him."

Casey had dropped by, with my permission, a few weeks after we'd gotten back from Alpine Creek. He'd come to see the twins and to talk to Ali. It killed me that I'd been the one to tear the two of them apart, but the simple truth was that Ali might eventually forgive him for the part he'd played in hurting me, but she'd never let him in again. Not when she knew that if push came to shove, pack loyalty would always run deeper than anything he felt toward her.

"He visits the twins sometimes," I said. "We're thinking of taking them to Ark Valley for Christmas. If the alpha of that region gives us permission."

Katie and Alex were nine months now, but they looked more like two-year-olds. They were gaining on Lily every day, much to her indignant dismay. Ali said the twins' growth would slow down by their first birthday, but that they'd always be a little ahead of the curve.

"Is this what you came here to talk about?" I asked. "Ali and the twins? My grades?"

"Education is important," Callum argued reflexively.

This wasn't what I'd expected for my first interaction with one of the other alphas as their equal. Callum had walked out that door the day my pack had killed Wilson, the same as the others alphas had, and he'd signed off on giving me part of his territory from afar. Somehow, I'd imagined our first face-to-face meeting being more ominous.

I'd imagined it hurting more.

"We miss you," Callum said. "And Devon."

Sora and Lance couldn't have been happy about the fact that Devon had left Ark Valley, but at the same time, I doubted they were surprised. Their oldest son had left his pack and fought his way to the top of another when he wasn't that much older than Devon was now.

With or without me, Dev would have left Ark Valley eventually. He was too strong and too independent to stay.

"I miss you, too," I told Callum. A month earlier, I wouldn't have been able to say the words. I wouldn't have even been able to think them, and I certainly wouldn't have meant them. I wondered if he knew that I wasn't talking about the pack. For most of my life, he'd been one of the most important people in it. He'd lied to me and he'd beaten me and he'd helped me and then left me alone to deal with the fallout, but he was still Callum. I still had his Mark carved into my body.

I always would.

Moving with fluid grace, Callum turned and pulled me into a hug. He didn't rub his cheek against mine, didn't Mark me as his or try to get me to submit. He just held me, and then he moved back and looked me in the eye.

I felt his wolf reaching out to me, calling to me through the power that bound me to others of his kind. At first, my instinct was to slam up my psychic shield, but a small sound escaped Callum's mouth, and I realized that he wasn't asking to be let into my head, or to control my bonds.

He was offering to let me into his.

Cautiously, I looked into his eyes, and I reached out to him, my heart speeding up as I did. Part of me recoiled, waiting to be slapped back, and throughout my territory, Cedar Ridge wolves stopped what they were doing and answered my distress.

I'm fine, I told them. *I'm going to be okay.*

And I would be. This was Callum. And even though a large part of me didn't trust him, there were also parts of me that always would.

So I let down my own walls, and I stared into his eyes, and Callum reached out and caught my mind, the way he'd caught my body when I'd launched myself at him as a child, putting me on his shoulders and spinning me around.

In those seconds that I was inside Callum's head, I saw the world through his eyes, and I realized that Mitch had vastly understated the power of Callum's prescience. It wasn't just a habit for knowing what was going to happen, an instinct. It was a web, an intricate web of possibilities, of dominoes that could fall, paths that might be taken, and the futures that might result from each.

Everything was connected. Every action had a consequence, and though it was very hard to get the drop on Callum, he wasn't all-knowing. His power was limited by physical proximity—of all the children Wilson had attacked, I'd been the only one close enough for him to see. And even when an event was close enough, when he could make out the threads crisscrossing the time line's web, he wasn't perfect. He couldn't control the future. He could only steer it—stay away from actions that led to dead ends; do things that he didn't want to do to save the people he cared about in the long run.

Slowly, I unraveled his interactions with me. He'd come to save me when I was four, because he'd known I'd need saving, but he hadn't gotten the vision in time to save my parents as well. And when he'd failed on that front, he'd seen horrible things in my future if he left me there, so he took me with him. And he'd known that the pack wouldn't accept me unless they had to, so he'd Marked me and forced their hands, and he'd seen that he couldn't give me to any of the other wolves or keep me himself without putting me at the center of a firestorm, so he'd chosen Ali and shown her what awaited me if she said no.

And then I flashed forward, and I saw myself from his perspective, the moment I'd heard those three little words from Chase's lips.

I got bit.

The possibilities in my future rearranged themselves, and Callum fought against them, trying to keep me safe. It was the reason he'd kept Chase away from me—down that path had been danger, and at the time, it had been the last thing that Callum had wanted for me. He'd always known that I'd be important someday, but he hadn't foreseen the way I'd come to be a part of him. He hadn't realized that he couldn't always be the one saving me.

And from the moment I'd met Chase, he'd known. He'd known what could happen, known a thousand ways it could have gone wrong. I'd asked permissions, and he'd laid down the conditions. He'd trained me—not for fear of what might happen during my meeting with Chase, but in preparation for what I would face afterward. He'd made me open my pack-bond so that I would connect to Chase, not to keep me from it.

And then came the hardest thing to see, the hardest decision he'd made. Telling me to obey the others.

But if he hadn't wanted to keep me from Chase, if he hadn't been trying to keep the Rabid a secret—why?

Because, his eyes seemed to whisper, *you had to leave.*

If he hadn't given me the order, I wouldn't have disobeyed it. If I hadn't disobeyed it, he couldn't have had Sora beat me, and Ali would never have taken me away. And if I'd never left Callum's territory, I wouldn't have had the time or the space or the room to grow up. I wouldn't have recruited Lake to our fight. I wouldn't have been forced to use the dreamscape to communicate with Chase. I wouldn't have found my way into the Rabid's head.

Changing one piece of the puzzle changed them all, and this was something that Callum had constructed very carefully.

I came back into my own body and sat down hard on the ground. I'd realized that Callum had probably planned for me to throw Shay's line about democracy back in his face, that he'd known or at least suspected that the Rabid's victims would claim me as their alpha, but I hadn't really let myself hope that I was anything more than a detail.

That to Callum, the big picture had always gone back, again and again, to *me*.

For months, years, maybe my entire life, Callum had been preparing me to save the children Wilson had Changed; he'd been pulling my strings and Chase's and everyone else's. And that moment—the one that had nearly destroyed me—when he'd ordered me beaten, he'd done it not to save face with the pack, but because he needed Ali to take me to Montana.

He'd done it for *me*.

"I'm not sorry for it, Bryn. I'd do it again. And I needed you to know that."

I got the feeling that he wasn't here looking for forgiveness, and he wasn't here just to let me know that even when I thought he'd left me, I'd been loved. He was warning me—because sometime, down the line, his knack for seeing and manipulating the future might involve me again. Depending on what he foresaw—for his pack, for me, and for mine—he might be left with some tough choices and he wouldn't promise to deal me in, not if keeping me in the dark pushed things in the direction he wanted them to go.

I nodded. "Consider it known," I said. "And for the record— everything I did? I'd do it again. And if it ever comes down to the safety of my pack versus the safety of yours…"

Callum smiled. "Consider it known."

There was something about the expression on his face that made me suspicious, made me wonder if it was starting already. If he knew something that I didn't.

"It's not going to come down to the safety of my pack versus the safety of yours, is it?" I asked. "At least not immediately. There'll be other threats. Outside threats. The other alphas, maybe. Or something worse." I paused. He said nothing, and I knew without asking that I couldn't push my way back into his head no matter how hard I tried.

"You're not going to tell me, are you?"

"The future's always changing, Bryn." That was it. That was all he gave me. I wanted to scream, but I didn't. He was an alpha. So was I. Things were different. I couldn't just bait him into giving me an answer.

I'd have to wait it out.

"You really are the most impossible man I've ever met," I told him. He flopped down beside me on the grass and brushed his grizzly cheek against mine. "And you are, without question, the most troublesome and irksome child I've ever had the displeasure of knowing."

Callum and I had been family once. We bore each other's Marks still. I savored this moment, because deep down, I knew that I wasn't a little girl anymore, that I wasn't his *anything* anymore, and that for as long as I was alpha of my pack and he was alpha of his, we would never just be Callum and Bryn again.

Mine.

Mine.

Mine.

I belonged to my own pack now, and they belonged to me—Devon and Lake and Chase, Maddy and Lily and the rest of the Resilients, most of whom weren't even into their teens. A random and rather twisted thought occurred to me, and I smiled.

"What are you smiling about, Bronwyn Alessia?"

I shrugged. "It's just that I was raised by wolves, and now in a twisted way, with all the kids around here, I'm raising them. Ironic, huh?"

Callum snorted. "Bryn, m'dear, if there's any justice in this world, they'll be nothing but trouble."

I groaned. Knowing my luck—and *theirs*—they probably would.

ACKNOWLEDGMENTS

Before this book had a title, I referred to it simply as "love book," because it was written for the sheer love of storytelling, and I owe an incredible debt to those who helped bring it into print. At the top of that list are my agent, Elizabeth Harding, who believed in this book from day one, and my editor, Regina Griffin, whose editorial input and passion for this project both challenged and thrilled me. I'm also thankful to the rest of my Egmont and Curtis Brown families— Mary Albi, Elizabeth Law, Alison Weiss, Nico Medina, Greg Ferguson, Rob Guzman, Doug Pocock, Holly Frederick, Dave Barbor, and Ginger Clark.

The single biggest blessing in my life as a writer has been the incredible and constant support of my writing friends, who really are my people (or, to put things in werewolf terminology, my pack). Melissa Marr, Ally Carter, and Sarah Cross keep me sane and make me smile, and I'm also grateful to Team Castle, for recharging my writerly batteries when I needed it most, and Bob, who's always there for a late-night email.

Finally, thanks go to my family and friends for putting

up with my total absorption into this project. Thanks to my mom, who's always been my first reader; my dad, for providing valuable weapons expertise for some of the later scenes; my brother, Justin, who taught me everything I know about overprotective alpha males (Just kidding! Kind of.); and my sister-in-law, Allison, who does an excellent job at curtailing aforementioned brother's protective instincts. I love you all!

There can only be one alpha.
Bryn's adventures continue in

"Quite simply, the most compelling YA werewolf series out there."
—Melissa Marr, *New York Times* Best-Selling author of *Wicked Lovely*

Trial by Fire

Jennifer Lynn Barnes

A RAISED BY WOLVES NOVEL

Available from Egmont USA in Summer 2011.

Turn the page for a sneak peek.

CHAPTER ONE

❧

"No more school, no more books, no more teachers' dirty looks..."

For a two-hundred-twenty-pound werewolf, Devon Macalister had a wicked falsetto. Leaning back in his chair with casual grace, he shot a mischievous look around our lunch table. "Everyone sing along!"

As the leader of our little group—not to mention the alpha of Devon's pack and his best friend since kindergarten—the responsibility for shutting down his boy-band tendencies fell to me. "It's Thanksgiving break, Dev, not summer vacation, and technically, it hasn't even started yet."

My words fell on deaf ears. The smile on Devon's face widened, making him look—to my eyes, at least—more puppy than wolf. To my left, Lake, whose history with Devon's flare for the dramatic stretched back almost as far as mine did, rolled her eyes, but her lips parted in a grin every bit as irrepressible and lupine as Devon's.

A wave of energy—pure, undiluted, and animalistic—

vibrated through my own body, and I closed my eyes for one second . . . two.

Three.

In control of the impulse to leap out of my chair and run for the woods, I glanced across the table at the last member of our little quartet. Maddy was sitting perfectly still, blinking her gray eyes owlishly, a soft smile on her lips. Images—of the night sky, of running—leapt from her mind to mine through our pack-bond, as natural as words falling off lips.

The impending full moon might have been giving the rest of our table werewolf ADD, but Maddy was perfectly Zen— much more relaxed than she normally would have been when all eyes were on the four of us.

Despite our continued efforts to blend in, the buzz of power in the air and the unspoken promise that within hours, my friends would shed their human skin were palpable. I recognized the feeling for what it was, but our very human—and easily fascinated—classmates had no idea. To them, the four of us were mysterious and magnetic and just a bit unreal— even me.

In the past nine months, my life had changed in more ways than I could count, but one of the most striking was the fact that at my new high school, I wasn't an outsider, ignored and avoided by humans who had no idea why people like Devon and Lake—and to a lesser extent me—felt *off*. Instead, the other students at Weston High had developed a strange fascination with us. They didn't approach. They didn't try to penetrate our tight-knit group, but they watched and they whispered, and whenever Devon—*Devon!*—met their eyes, the girls sighed and fluttered their eyelashes in some kind of human mating ritual that I still probably wouldn't have completely understood even if I'd grown up like a normal girl.

Given that I'd been raised as the only human child in the largest werewolf pack in North America, the batting of eyelashes was every bit as foreign to me as running through the woods, surrounded by bodies and warmth, and the feeling of *home* would have been to anyone else. Some days, I felt like I knew more about being a werewolf than I would ever know about being a teenage girl.

It was getting easier and easier to forget that I was human. *Soon. Soon. Soon.*

The bond that tied me to the rest of the pack vibrated with the inevitability of the coming moon, and even though I knew better than to encourage Devon, I couldn't help the way my own lips tilted up at the corners. The only things that stood between the four of us and Thanksgiving break were a couple of hours and a quiz on Shakespeare.

The only thing standing between us and delicious, feral freedom was the setting of the sun.

And the only thing that stood between me and Chase—*my* Chase—was a distance I could feel the boy in question closing mile by mile, heartbeat by heartbeat, second by second.

"Bronwyn, please, you're making me blush." Dev—who could read me like a book, with or without whatever I was projecting through the pack-bond—adopted a scandalized tone and brought a hand to his chest, like he was seconds away from demanding smelling salts and going faint, but I sensed his wolf stirring beneath the surface and knew that it was hard for Devon on a day like today to be reminded that I wasn't his to protect in the same way anymore.

That I was alpha.

That Chase and I were....whatever Chase and I were.

"Fine," I said, flicking a French fry in Devon's general direction. "Have it your way. No more school, no more books ..."

Dev made an attempt at harmonizing with me, but given my complete lack of vocal chops, it did not go well, and a horrified silence descended over our entire table.

After several seconds, Devon regarded the rest of us with mock solemnity. "We shall never speak of this moment again."

"In your dreams, Broadway boy." Shaking out her long blonde hair—a motion laden with excess adrenaline—Lake stood and stretched her mile-long legs. If the girls in school were all secretly pining for Devon, the boys were absolutely smitten with Lake. Clearly, they'd never met the business end of her shotgun or had their butts whipped at pool.

Soon. Soon. Soon.

Across the table, Maddy sighed and Devon bumped her shoulder with his, a comforting gesture meant to communicate that he understood. Soon, our entire pack would be gathered in the woods. Soon, the Weres would Shift and I would let their power flow through me, until I forgot I was human and the difference between four legs and two virtually disappeared.

Soon—but not soon enough.

"So," I said, my voice low and soothing, intent on keeping my pack-mates focused, however briefly, on the here and now. "*Hamlet.* What do I need to know?"

"New girl."

I balked at Lake's answer. "I was thinking more along the lines of Guildencrantz and Frankenstein."

"Rosencrantz and Guildenstern," Devon corrected absentmindedly as he followed Lake's gaze to the double archway at the front of the cafeteria. I turned to look, too, and the rest of the student body took their cue from us, until everyone was looking at the girl who stood there.

She was small—the word *tiny* wouldn't have been a misnomer—and her eyes seemed to take up a disproportionate amount of her face. Her skin was very pale, and she was dressed almost entirely in black, save for a pair of white leather gloves that covered her arms from the elbows down.

She looked like a porcelain doll, and she felt like a threat. Given that I could tell, even from a distance, that she wasn't a Were, I had no idea why something inside me insisted I track her every move.

"The natives are getting kind of restless," Devon commented

offhand. Weston wasn't a big school, and mid-semester trans-fers were practically unheard of, so White Leather Gloves was garnering more than her fair share of murmurs and stares.

Including mine.

"Mayhaps I should go play the white knight, divert the spotlight a little?"

Devon's suggestion was enough to make me switch my gaze from the new girl to him.

"No."

I wasn't sure who was more shocked by the sharpness with which that word exited my mouth—Devon or me. Our pack didn't *do* orders. Given the way I felt about people get-ting dictatorial with me, I wasn't prone to pulling rank on anyone else. Besides, Devon and I had spent so much time together growing up that even if he hadn't been my second-in-command, I still wouldn't have been able to force my will on him. The closest I could come to ordering him to do anything was threatening to decapitate him if he didn't stop singing *The Best of ABBA* at the top of his lungs, and even that was mostly futile.

With a lightly inquisitive noise, Devon caught my gaze and held it. "Something you'd like to share with the class there, Bryn?" he asked, arching one eyebrow to ridiculous heights while keeping the other perfectly in place.

I debated answering, but it was probably nothing—just that time of the month, with emotions running high and my heart beating with the power of the impending full moon. Still, I hadn't spent my entire life growing up around people capable of snapping my neck like a Popsicle stick without learning to pay attention when my instincts put me on high alert.

If my gut said someone was a threat, I had to at least consider the possibility that it was true—even if the *someone* in question was five foot nothing and human down to the tips of her leather-clad fingers.

Instead of mentioning any of this to Devon and opening that can of worms, I threw another French fry in his general direction, and the tension between us melted away as he reached for his plate and armed himself. "You know, of course," he said, pitching his voice low, "that this means war."

I couldn't help glancing back toward the archway and the new girl who'd been standing there a moment before, but she was already gone.

Pack. Pack. Pack.

Protect. Protect. Protect.

I let the feeling wash over me, absorbed it, and then relegated it to the back of my head, with the promise of *soon, soon, soon* and the desire to *run*. At the moment, I had more immediate concerns—like the fact that my retention of *Hamlet* definitely left something to be desired and the incoming French fry flying directly at my face.

That night, I was the first one to arrive at the clearing. We hadn't had a fresh snowfall since the second week in November, but this time of year, the layer of white on the ground never fully melted away, and I breathed in the smell of cedar and snow. I was wearing wool mittens and my second-heaviest winter coat, and for a moment, I closed my eyes and imagined, as I always did just before the Shift, what it would be like to shed my clothes, my skin, and my ability to think as a human.

There had been a time in my life when the last thing I wanted was the collective werewolf psyche taking up even a tiny corner of my brain, but a lot had changed since then.

Different pack.

Different forest.

Different me.

Without opening my eyes, my hands found their way to the bottom of my puffy jacket, and I pulled it upward, exposing the T-shirt I wore underneath. My fingers tugged at the end of the shirt, and my bare skin stung under the onslaught of winter-cold air.

Opening my eyes, I traced the pattern rising over the band of my jeans: three parallel marks, scars I would carry for the rest of my life. For most of my childhood, the Mark had been a visible symbol to the pack that had raised me that I was one of their own, that anyone who messed with me messed with the werewolf who'd dug his fingers into my flesh hard enough to leave scars.

Callum.

He was the alpha of alphas, the Were who'd saved my life when I was four years old and spent the next decade plus grooming me for a future I'd never even imagined. No matter how many months passed, every time my pack assembled, every time I lost myself and ran as one of them, I thought of the first time, of Callum and his wolves and knowing that for once in my life, I belonged.

Every time I heard the word *alpha* beckoning to me from my pack's minds, I thought of the man who'd once been mine—and then I thought of the other alphas, none of whom would have been particularly distraught if I went to sleep one night and never woke up.

Ah, werewolf politics. My favorite.

Bryn.

The moment I heard Chase's voice, soft and unassuming, in my mind, every other thought vanished. It was always this way with the two of us, and the anticipation of seeing him, touching him, taking in his scent was almost as powerful as the feeling that washed over my body the moment he emerged from the forest, clothed in shorts and a T-shirt that didn't quite fit.

Chase had been a werewolf for less than a year. Ironically, that made him seem far less human than Weres who'd been born that way or the members of our pack who'd been Changed as kids. The difference was visible in the way he moved, the tilt of his head. For as long as I'd known him, he'd been in flux, defined by the wolf inside as much as the boy he'd been before the attack.

Now, slowly, things I'd felt in his memories and dreams, quirks he'd shown only in flashes seemed to be fighting their way back to the surface. Each time he came home from patrolling our territory as my eyes and ears, I saw a little bit more of his human side.

Each time, he was a little more *Chase*.

"Hey, you." Chase smiled, more with one side of his mouth than the other.

"Hey," I echoed, a smile tugging at my own lips. "How's tricks?"

I took the fact that those words actually left my mouth as a sign that I'd been hanging around Devon for way, way too long, but Chase didn't so much as blink.

"Same old, same old." He was quiet, this boy I was getting to know piece by piece—thoughtful, observant, and restrained, even as the power in his stride betrayed the wolf inside. "How's school going?"

"Same old, same old."

"There's no such thing as 'same old, same old' with you," Chase said wryly. "You're *Bryn*."

Given my track record, he kind of had a point there, but I wasn't about to admit it out loud.

With that same half smile, he leaned toward me, hesitant, but inhumanly graceful. I answered the question in his eyes, reached for the back of his head, brought his lips down to mine.

Soon. Soon. Soon.

I could feel his heart beating, feel his mind and thoughts blending with my own as the two of us stood there, bathed in moonlight and feeling its effects like a drug to our systems.

Whoever Chase was, he was mine.

"Ahem."

I'd known before I kissed Chase that we'd be interrupted. There was no such thing as a secret in a wolf pack—let alone privacy. But I'd been foolishly optimistic and hoped that the interrupter would be Lake or Maddy or one of the younger kids.

Instead, as Chase and I pulled away from each other, we were confronted with the oldest member of our pack, a gruff, weatherworn man who didn't look a day over thirty-five. Based on the way his lips were twitching, I concluded that the man in question was torn between smiling and scowling.

"Hey, Mr. Mitchell," I said, hoping to push him toward the smiling end of the spectrum. A guarded look settled over Chase's eyes, but he echoed my greeting, and Lake's dad gave us a long, measuring stare in return.

"I suspect the earth would keep rotating round the sun even if the two of you called me Mitch."

In the time I'd been living on the Mitchells' land, Mitch and I had had this conversation more than once, but I wasn't really the type to give in once I dug my heels in about something.

"So noted, Mr. Mitchell."

The smile finally won out over his scowl, but it lasted only a second or two before Mitch eyed the space (or lack thereof) between my body and Chase's. "Last I heard, Ali was on her way here with the twins," he said, which I took as a not-so-subtle hint that Chase and I should give each other some breathing room. Chase must have interpreted it the same way, because he stepped back—away from me and away from Mitch, who delivered the rest of his update with a nod. "Lake and Maddy are rounding up the troops, and I believe Devon said something about making an entrance."

I was fairly certain that I was the only alpha in the history of the world to have a second-in-command who appreciated the impact of arriving fashionably late. Then again, I was also the only alpha with as many females in her pack as males and more toddlers and tweens than grown men.

Besides, it wasn't like the whole *human* thing was status quo.

"Bryn!" The unmistakable sound of a very small person bellowing ripped me from my thoughts, and I smiled. There was nothing quite like hearing my name yelled at the top of a three-year-old's lungs—unless it was having the aforementioned three-year-old barrel into me full blast and throw her arms around my legs like she was afraid that if she let go, I'd disappear off the face of the earth forever.

"Hello, Lily," I said wryly. The kid acted like she hadn't seen me in a lifetime or two, even though it had only been an hour, if that.

Moon! Happy! Fun!

With the older wolves, I had to go looking for thoughts, unless someone was using the pack-bond to actively send them my way, but with Lily, everything was right there on the surface, bubbling up the way only the strongest emotions did in adults.

Alpha-alpha-alpha! Bryn-Bryn-Bryn!

The two words—*alpha* and *Bryn*—blended together in her mind. As the youngest of the kids I'd saved from the werewolf equivalent of a psychopath, Lily was one of the only ones who couldn't remember the time before our pack, or the things that the Rabid had done to her, to all of them.

In Lily's mind, *Bryn* meant *alpha*, and *alpha* meant *Bryn*. It was as simple as that.

"Can we Change yet?" Lily asked. "Can we, can we, can we?"

Not yet, Lily, I answered silently, and she stilled, mesmerized by a power I'd never asked to hold over anyone.

"Lily, I told you to wait." The voice that issued that statement was aggrieved, and the look on its owner's face was one I recognized all too well from my own childhood.

Come to think of it, it was a look I recognized all too well from about a week ago, two tops.

"Hey, Ali," I said, glad that Chase and I had heeded Mitch's warning and put a little space between my body and his.

"Hey, baby," Ali replied, a twin on each hip. "Everyone's been fed, but I make no guarantees about their state of mind."

For most of my life, it had been just Ali and me, but she'd taken to managing an entire brood with the same efficiency with which she'd once transformed herself from a twenty-year-old college student into my protector within Callum's pack. Ali was human, but the words *force of nature* still applied, and I would infinitely rather have tangled with an irritated werewolf than Ali in mama bear mode.

"Now?" Lily asked, right on cue with Ali's disclaimer about the younger werewolves' state of mind. "Now-now-now?"

"Shhhh," I said, and Lily closed her mouth and laid her head against my knee.

"You know, Bryn," Ali said thoughtfully, "if Lily minded me half as well as she minds you, I wouldn't be considering renaming her Bryn Two."

"Ha-ha," I retorted. "Very funny."

Ali smiled. "I try." She looked toward Mitch, and without saying a word, he walked over and took Katie and Alex from her arms. Not even a year old, Ali's babies already looked more like toddlers, and in identical motions, their hands found their way almost immediately to Mitch's beard.

He smiled. "I've got them," he told Ali, and she nodded before kissing the twins and turning to walk back out of the woods. Ali never stayed to run with the pack.

As far as I knew, she never had.

Now, Bryn? Now?

Lily refrained from asking the question out loud, but I heard it through the pack-bond all the same, and this time, the answer—*soon, soon, soon*—seemed to come from outside my body, from instincts I couldn't have explained to the human world. Lily seemed to feel it, too, and a keening, whimpering sound built in the back of her throat. I ran a hand gently over her bright red hair and she began rocking back and forth on her feet. Within moments, the others had arrived, filling the clearing, and the effect was magnified a hundred times.

Our pack was small—twenty-two total, only eighteen there that night—but the air was electric, and as their thoughts swirled with my own, the connection between us became a living, breathing thing. I felt them, all of them: Lake and Maddy, Lily and the twins, Chase. From the youngest to the oldest, from those who thirsted for a hunt to those who wanted nothing more in life than to run …

They were *mine*.

Devon slid in beside me, and the moment I felt the brush of his arm against mine, I knew.

It was time.

In other packs, this was formal. There were petitions and ceremonies and marks carved into flesh, but here and now, I didn't have words, and they didn't need them.

Now. Now. Now.

I couldn't deny the Change any more than they could. The

treetops scattered moonlight across our faces, and I inclined my head. That was all it took.

At any other time of the month, the sounds of fabric tearing and bones crunching weren't pleasant ones, but under the full moon, the effect was like the beating of a drum.

Run. Run. Run.

All around me, they could taste it. They could feel it. Furred bodies pushed at each other to get closer to me, to touch me, to sniff me, to be with me, and the roar from their minds was overwhelming.

Alpha. Alpha. Alpha.

I forgot about Chase, about Devon, about each and every one of them as anything other than my brothers, my sisters, my people, my pack.

Mine.

This was what I'd been born for. This was all that I wanted and all that I was, and as one overwhelming, unstoppable, incredible force, we ran.